Between Then and Now

Hallow's End Book One

Patricia Prior

Cover art by Natalia (Getcovers.com)

Interior design and formatting by Lauren Kaye (Wonderporium Ink)

Editing by Lauren Kaye (Wonderporium Ink)

BETWEEN THEN AND *Now*

HALLOW'S END

BOOK ONE

Official Playlist

You can find the **Hallow's End: Between Then and Now** playlist on Spotify.

Noah Kahan - Stick Season

Taylor Swift - Back To December (Taylor's Version)

Dan + Shay - From the Ground Up

Taylor Swift - Daylight

Kacey Musgraves - Rainbow

Taylor Swift - Our Song

Lorde - Ribs

Darren Kiely - Can't Hold You

Taylor Swift - Enchanted (Taylor's Version)

Taylor Swift - Lover

Taylor Swift - Change (Taylor's Version)

Taylor Swift - Clean (Taylor's Version)

Taylor Swift - I Knew You Were Trouble (Taylor's Version)

Taylor Swift - Delicate

Taylor Swift - cardigan

Kacey Musgraves - Butterflies

Edward Sharpe & The Magnetic Zeros - Home

Alan Silvestri - Amas Veritas

Tame Impala - Feels Like We Only Go Backwards

Lisa Loeb - Stay (I Missed You)

Natalie Imbruglia - Torn

The Goo Goo Dolls - Iris

Adele - Water Under the Bridge

Lord Huron - The Night We Met

Colbie Caillat - Brighter Than The Sun

Fleetwood Mac - Dreams - 2004 Remaster

Kelly Clarkson - Breakaway

Bruno Mars - Count on Me

Taylor Swift - Everything Has Changed (feat. Ed Sheeran) (Taylor's Version)

Rihanna - Stay

The Cranberries - Dreams

Lord Huron - Ends of the Earth

The Lumineers - Slow It Down

Bon Iver - Skinny Love

Taylor Swift - The Tortured Poets Department

Florence + The Machine - Cosmic Love

Gotye - Eyes Wide Open

Sia - Breathe Me

The 1975 - Somebody Else

Gregory Alan Isakov - The Stable Song

OneRepublic - Good Life

The Lumineers - Ho Hey

Haley Reinhart - Can't Help Falling in Love

Taylor Swift - the lakes - bonus track

The Lumineers - Flowers in Your Hair

Calum Scott - Dancing On My Own

Taylor Swift - How Did It End?

Stevie Nicks - If You Ever Did Believe - 2023 Remaster

Taylor Swift - The Smallest Man Who Ever Lived

Taylor Swift - All Too Well (10 Minute Version) (Taylor's Version) (From The Vault)

Florence + The Machine - Never Let Me Go

Taylor Swift - my tears ricochet

To those who have ever felt lost, may you find the courage to carve out your own path, and the strength to embrace the journey ahead. This book is for the seekers, the dreamers, and the brave hearts who dare to create their own destiny

4 you enjoyed the book, please leave a review on GoodReads!

Patricia xx

Chapter 1

T HE ROAD TO HALLOW'S END was winding and narrow, each twist and turn flanked by towering trees dressed in vibrant autumn colours. Golden leaves fluttered down like confetti, carpeting the road in a mosaic of amber, crimson, and russet hues. As I drove closer to the town, apprehension and hope churned within me.

My hands tightened around the steering wheel, the leather cool and familiar under my fingertips. The small, old hatchback car—my pride and joy—rattled and hummed with each bump in the road. I had named her Betty, and she was a comforting companion through thick and thin. She wasn't much to look at, with her faded paint and occasional sputter, but she symbolized something far more valuable than luxury—my independence.

I bought Betty a year ago, at twenty-three, using money I had painstakingly saved from selling my art online and working as a waitress during college—pursuits I had to keep secret from my parents, who would have dismissed them as distractions beneath our status. They had offered me a state-of-the-art luxury car, but I wanted nothing to do with their money. Every dollar I saved was mine, and was a small but significant step toward the independence I craved. Betty, with her quirks and occasional rattles, became more than just a vehicle. She was a reliable companion through late-night drives, long diner shifts, and countless moments of reflection—a tangible symbol of the life I was building on my own terms.

A sudden ring jolted me back to the present. I glanced at the phone mounted on the dashboard, where Sebastian's name popped on the screen. I groaned. It had been three months since we broke up, yet his calls and texts hadn't stopped. They had slowed down, sure, but there was always the occasional message to remind me of the lingering threads of our past. With a sigh, I focused back on the road, ignoring his call. I wasn't ready to dive into that emotional quagmire, especially not while driving.

As I checked the GPS map for directions, I took a right turn onto a winding road, and the scenery shifted, revealing the stunning beauty of Massachusetts in autumn. The air was crisp and fresh, carrying the earthy scent of fallen leaves and the faint aroma of woodsmoke from distant chimneys.

The engine sputtered slightly as I glanced at the GPS one more time before the signal cut out completely. Only the rhythmic crunch of tires over fallen leaves, and the occasional creak of the suspension, filled the silence that followed. I sighed and muttered to myself.

"Welcome to the middle of nowhere, Vinnie."

The picturesque town of Hallow's End appeared before me as my car emerged from the dense forest, bathed in the gentle glow of the late afternoon. Cobblestone streets wound through clusters of quaint houses and shops, each one decorated with pumpkins and cornstalks, embracing the season's festive spirit.

As I drove through the town, I marvelled at how charming everything looked. The residential area was picture-perfect, with white picket fences surrounding well-kept lawns, vibrant flower beds, and cozy porches adorned with seasonal wreaths. It felt like I was stepping into a classic movie set. The kind of small town where everyone knew each other's names, and life moved at a slower, more deliberate pace. I couldn't believe I had lived so close to something this beautiful for so long—if you could call a two-and-a-half-hour drive close.

Eventually, I turned onto a narrow, dead-end street called Evergreen Way, which led to my new home—a rustic, ivy-covered cottage that seemed plucked from another era. Nestled at the lane's end, it was framed by towering pine trees, with rolling hills stretching out to the horizon beyond. The sight was both comforting and intimidating.

This was supposed to be my fresh start. My escape from the chaos of Cresden—and the memories of Sebastian Sterling. As I sat in my car outside the cottage, I couldn't shake the notion that I was an outsider in this tranquil, tight-knit community. Driving through the town, I had noticed a few townspeople glancing my way with mild curiosity, like they could instantly tell I was new here, their lives so intricately intertwined that a stranger's presence was an unusual occurrence.

I'd half-expected people to step out of their homes, waving and offering a warm welcome, as if in some heartwarming story where newcomers are embraced with open arms. But that moment never came. Instead, the people of Hallow's End continued their routines, subtly acknowledging my presence, but keeping a respectful distance. The picturesque streets and peaceful atmosphere were exactly what I had hoped for, yet now, sitting in my car, the silence felt more isolating than comforting. It was a stark contrast to the anonymity of Cresden, where blending in was easy. Here, in this perfect small town, people noticed every unfamiliar face, and every unfamiliar car stood out.

With a deep breath, I stepped out of the car and stretched my stiff limbs. The crisp autumn air filled my lungs, carrying with it the scents of pine, rain, and burning wood—a welcome change from the exhaust fumes and constant hum of the urban environment I was used to.

I approached the front porch, finding the key right where the owner had promised—in a small, rusted tin hidden under the welcome mat. I couldn't help but smile at the simplicity of it all. Only in a small neighborhood like this, would people consider it normal and safe to leave a key out in the open. In Cresden, the very idea would be laughable. Cresden was a city where everyone double-locked their doors, installed security systems, and looked suspiciously at strangers. There, the pace of life was fast, and trust was a rare commodity, guarded as closely as one's belongings.

This charming town was another world—one where the air was cleaner, the pace slower, and the sense of community stronger. The idea that someone could feel safe enough to leave a key under a mat spoke volumes about the trust and simplicity that permeated this place. It was a charming anachronism, a relic of a more innocent time that still lingered here, far removed from the cynicism and hustle of city life.

I unlocked the door, and the hinges creaked as I let it swing open, before heading straight back to the car and popping the trunk to unload the few boxes I had brought along. It wasn't much—just enough for a short stay. This trip had been a spontaneous decision, and I wasn't sure how long I'd remain here. I'd rented the cottage for just a couple of weeks, hoping to figure out my next steps during this brief escape.

I'd packed only the essentials: a few changes of clothes, my art supplies, and some personal mementos I couldn't bear to leave behind. It was a bare-bones setup, perfectly reflecting my uncertainty, and the transient nature of this decision. The minimal luggage contrasted sharply with the weight of the life I had left behind in Cresden, where I'd felt so entrenched and suffocated.

Carefully balancing the boxes, I made my way back to the front porch. Lanterns lined the stone pathway, their flickering lights promising warmth and welcome. As I reached the door, a gust of wind kicked up, sending a stack of art supplies tumbling from my arms and across the yard. Brushes, canvases, and sketchbooks scattered like fallen leaves.

"Great," I muttered, chasing after the runaway items, frustration bubbling up as I struggled to gather everything. My mind drifted back to the neatly organized studio I had left behind in Cresden. The spacious loft had been a haven of creativity and order, with its large windows letting in natural light, pristine white walls covered with my favorite pieces, and shelves meticulously organized with every brush, canvas, and tube of paint in its proper place. I remembered the comfort of my ergonomic chair, the smell of fresh coffee from the Starbucks downstairs wafting through the open window, and the soft hum of urban life that provided a constant, familiar backdrop to my work.

In Cresden, I had a sense of control, even amidst the chaos of my personal life. Here, in this unfamiliar and unpredictable place, everything was already seeming to slip through my fingers—both literally *and* figuratively.

A worn photograph slipped free from one of the sketchbooks and fluttered to the ground. I paused, staring at the picture of Sebastian and me from a few months into our relationship. We were on a crowded street in Cresden, the city lights twinkling like stars behind us.

I had taken the selfie, capturing us in a moment of pure joy. Sebastian's arm was wrapped around my shoulders, pulling me close. He held an ice cream cone in his other hand, and we both were laughing, our smiles wide and genuine. I had just turned twenty, and my gray eyes were still full of hope, a soft smile playing on my lips. Sebastian, three years older, looked down at me with a playful glint in his emerald eyes. A smudge of ice cream marked his chiselled jawline, his blonde hair messy from the windy day.

Looking at the photograph now, a pang of nostalgia struck me. We were so happy then, so full of life and dreams. But those carefree days felt like a lifetime ago, overshadowed by the reality of our breakup, and the weight of everything that had followed.

With a sigh, I tucked the photograph back into the sketchbook and stooped to gather the scattered art supplies. As I picked up the sketch pencils and pads, I thought back to how much had changed since that photo was taken. Sebastian had finished college a year into our relationship, and his carefree, fun-loving side gradually gave way to the pressures of long meetings and responsibilities. He started working for his father, putting his business degree to use.

I understood the need for him to take things more seriously, but I felt the distance grow between us. While I was still in college, enjoying the freedom and creativity it afforded, Sebastian became absorbed in his new job. He tried to make time for me, and our families being so closely connected helped. We still had weekends at home, and family dinners, but it wasn't the same. It had felt like he was slowly leaving behind the part of himself that I had fallen in love with—the spontaneous, joyful side.

As I carried the boxes to the door and set them down with a soft thud, I thought back to the occasional glimmers of his old self that would still emerge. Every now and then, that carefree, fun-loving Sebastian would resurface, surprising me with an impromptu date night, or a spontaneous road trip. Those fleeting moments reminded me of the man I had fallen for, and they kept me holding on.

Despite the changes, those brief glimpses of our past happiness made me believe we could rekindle what we once had. For years, I had clung to that hope, convincing myself that the man I loved was still there, just buried under the pressures of his new responsibilities. It was those moments, rare and precious, that made me stay, hoping they would become more frequent, and that we could find our way back to each other.

"Need a hand?" a bright voice interrupted my thoughts.

I looked up to see a woman with dark-blue hair and a whimsical smile standing at the gate. She looked to be about my age, perhaps a year or two older at most.

As she approached, her outfit caught my eye—a mix of sheer black lace and velvet that gave off a distinct Stevie Nicks vibe. Layers of fabric flowed around her, and a fringed shawl draped over her shoulders. Beneath it, a green dress, embroidered with intricate patterns of leaves and vines, shimmered in the sunlight.

"Yes, please," I replied, grateful for the distraction. She stepped forward, her movements graceful and fluid, and handed me a brush she had picked up

.

"I'm Ivy Hart," she said, her smile warm and inviting. "Welcome to Hallow's End."

"Thanks," I uttered, tucking the supplies in the box and returning her smile. "I'm Lavinia Carlisle, but everyone calls me Vinnie."

As she stood closer, I noticed more details. Ivy was about five-foot-three, with a curvy figure that perfectly captured a girl-next-door charm mixed with a touch of mysticism. The charm bracelets on her wrists chimed softly as she adjusted her shawl. There was something undeniably enchanting about her whimsical ensemble and her striking blue hair, making her seem like a modern-day fairy.

Ivy's blue eyes sparkled with curiosity. "I know who you are. Everyone does. We rarely have newcomers this early in autumn. Most people visit later in the year. There's been quite a buzz about you staying for so long. Most only come for a week or two." Her whimsical smile widened. "I run the bookshop, Enchanted Quill. Stop by if you need a good read, or some herbal tea."

The thought that everyone already knew about me sent a flutter of anxiety and curiosity through my stomach. It was strange to be the center of attention in a place I barely knew.

"That's . . . good to know," I remarked, trying to maintain a smile. "I'll definitely come by."

As Ivy chatted with me, she reached into a large, bohemian-style tote bag, adorned with embroidered flowers and tassels, that was slung over her shoulder. She pulled out a small bundle of herbs tied with a delicate ribbon and handed it to me. The fragrant mix of lavender, rosemary, and basil filled the air.

"For new beginnings," she said with a knowing smile.

I took the bundle, glancing at it curiously. Sensing my confusion, Ivy's smile widened, and she explained, "These are herbs from my garden. Rosemary for protection, lavender for good luck, and basil for prosperity and abundance. Hang it by your front door to welcome all these blessings into your home while you stay here."

As Ivy spoke, I thought back to my college days. While I had never been particularly interested in the *witchy* side of life, my college roommate Sandra was an enthusiastic believer in crystals and tarot cards. During a full moon, she used to place jars of water on the windowsill, claiming it was for making *moon water*, though I never quite understood what that meant. I had always found it odd, smiling politely at her explanations while secretly wondering if it actually did anything.

Now, standing in front of Ivy, I wondered if she did similar things. Her gift of the herb bundle, and her talk of blessings, had a charming sincerity to it, even if it *was* outside my usual realm of belief. Still, there was something comforting about the idea of welcoming positivity into my new space, even if it came in the form of herbs from a garden.

"Thanks," I said, with a glimmer of hope. Perhaps this place, and these people, were precisely what I needed to move forward.

As we finished gathering the scattered art supplies, Ivy began chatting about the town's upcoming Halloween festival. "It's a really big deal around here," she said, her eyes sparkling with excitement. "Everyone in the community gets involved. There are stalls, games, a costume parade, and a bonfire. We call it Spooktacular Hallow's Eve, and it's what attracts most of our visitors and tourists. The town can get pretty busy toward the end of October—it's the perfect way to experience the town's spirit!"

Her enthusiasm was infectious and, for the first time since arriving, I felt a flicker of excitement. "That sounds amazing," I said, genuinely intrigued. "I'd love to check it out."

"You definitely should," Ivy replied with a warm smile. "And we're always looking for volunteers to help with the setup. It's a great way to get to know everyone, and really feel like part of the community."

I nodded, feeling a sense of belonging start to take root. "I'd love to help out. Count me in."

Ivy's face lit up. "That's fantastic, Vinnie! We could always use an extra pair of hands. It's going to be so much fun!"

"Looking forward to it," I said, genuinely excited about the prospect of diving into the town's traditions and getting to know more of the locals.

Halloween was seven weeks away, and I realized it would be a perfect way to wrap up my stay at Hallow's End. By then, I hoped I would have a clearer idea of where to go next and what steps to take in my life.

After Ivy left, I carried the last box inside and set it down in the living room. The cottage was modest but cozy, with wooden beams on the ceiling adding a rustic charm. The warm and inviting space featured walls painted in a soft, creamy white, and a floor made of polished hardwood.

Clearly targeting tourists seeking a picturesque getaway, the layout was open, and thoughtfully designed. The living room flowed seamlessly into a small but fully equipped kitchen, complete with quaint, vintage-style appliances. A comfortable-looking sofa was positioned in front of a stone fireplace, perfect for curling up on chilly nights. A wooden coffee table sat in front of it, adorned with a few carefully selected magazines, and a vase of fresh flowers.

To the left, a set of French doors led to a small dining area, which featured a round table and four chairs, all made of sturdy oak. Light, gauzy curtains draped the windows, letting in plenty of natural light and brightening the space. On the right side of the living room, a narrow hallway led to the bedroom and bathroom. The bedroom was simple yet charming, with a large, plush bed covered in soft linens and decorative pillows. A small TV sat on a low dresser opposite the bed, providing a touch of modern convenience in the otherwise quaint setting.

I stood in the middle of the living room, surrounded by boxes, and took a deep breath. This was a temporary refuge, a place to pause and gather my thoughts away from the expectations and pressures of my old life. This cottage, with its perfect blend of comfort and quaintness, offered a peaceful escape where I could find some clarity and decide on my next steps. A quiet space to breathe, and figure out what I truly wanted for my future.

Yet, as I unpacked my things and tried to make the space my own, I couldn't shake the sensation that something was missing

Leaving Cresden hadn't been easy. The city's relentless pace, the constant pressure from my parents, and the suffocating way of a life I hadn't chosen for myself, had all become overwhelming. But leaving Sebastian had been hard. Yet, our relationship had been a mess, and I'd finally reached a point where I couldn't take it anymore. Even though I knew it was the right thing to do, the ache in my heart was still there, lingering and persistent.

Despite the bad stuff, there were moments of pure, undeniable passion and connection. His intense green eyes, the way he could evoke a sense of vitality and invincibility with just a look, and the dreams we had once shared—all of it haunted me. I missed the thrill he brought to my life, and the excitement that seemed to follow him wherever he went.

The cozy nook, with its soft natural light, seemed perfect for setting up a temporary art station. As I unpacked my art supplies, the familiar scent of the paints, and the feel of brushes in my hands, brought back memories of our time together. As I arranged my canvases and paint tubes, I thought back to one, particularly vivid night.

Sebastian, in a rare burst of spontaneity, had suggested something daring—naked modelling. He'd proposed the idea with a mischievous grin, and I couldn't resist the excitement it promised. We set up in my studio, the room alive with the scent of paint, and the soft glow of dimmed lights. As I sketched him, the air seemed charged with anticipation. His intense green eyes never left mine, and soon, he was behind me, his hands playfully smudging paint on my skin.

"Let me paint you," he whispered, reaching for a brush. We laughed as he gently traced patterns on my body, the cool sensation of paint contrasting with the warmth of his touch. It became a game of distraction. Every time I tried to concentrate on the sketch, he'd kiss my neck, or lightly run his fingers along my sides, making me giggle and squirm. Before long, we were both covered in paint and tangled together on the floor, lost in a messy, passionate embrace.

The memory was bittersweet.

Despite the superficial aspects of our relationship, there was a genuine love between us. I loved how he made me feel alive and invincible, a feeling I hadn't recaptured since. Those wild, carefree moments unveiled my hidden potential, allowing me to channel my creativity into something raw and beautiful. They were a reminder of the intense, unconventional love we shared, a love that was both exhilarating and fleeting.

Here, the calm was burdensome—almost stifling—enhancing the void left by Sebastian's absence. As I put the last sketchbook away, the same photograph that had slipped out earlier caught my eye, its corner sticking out from the pages. It was a snapshot of a past life I was trying to leave behind, and I pulled it out, glancing at the familiar image one last time. The ache of those memories was still there, but I needed to move forward. Determined to bury the past, and the lingering presence of Sebastian, I tucked the photograph into a drawer, out of sight and, *hopefully*, out of mind.

This marked a new beginning, and I was determined to make it work. I just hoped that, in the process of finding myself, I wouldn't lose sight of who I wanted to become.

Seeking further solace, I wandered into the kitchen and found a welcome basket the owner of the cottage had prepared. They had filled it with thoughtful items: a bottle of red wine, a loaf of freshly baked bread, a jar of homemade jam, and a selection of local cheeses. Tucked inside was a folded note. I opened it and read the warm message:

Welcome to Willow Cottage!

I hope you enjoy your stay, and that this place feels like a home away from home. If you need anything, don't hesitate to reach out. Just a quick note: the hot water in the shower does work, but it takes a minute or two to come through, so don't worry if it seems cold at first! Also, please remember to secure the trash and recycling bins outside—raccoons can be quite the little bandits around here!

P.S. I've asked Ivy to pop by and welcome you, as I'm visiting family at the moment. Hope to see you around our charming town soon!

Best, Margie.

Smiling at the personal touch, I poured myself a glass of wine and felt a bit more settled. The warmth of the fire, and the simple pleasures from the basket, eased the tension in my shoulders. Taking the glass, and a piece of bread and cheese, I settled onto the comfortable sofa, sinking into its plush cushions. The long drive had left me weary, both physically and emotionally, and it felt good to finally relax.

As I nibbled on the bread and cheese, I chuckled to myself, thinking about how this was such a typical girl-dinner—wine and snacks, the perfect end to a tiring day. It was a small indulgence, but one that felt right in this quiet, cozy setting.

The bundle of herbs Ivy had given me sat on the coffee table, their subtle fragrance filling the room. I made a mental note to hang them up tomorrow—perhaps they really would bring in some good luck. God knows, I could use a bit of that right now.

The sun was setting out the window, casting a warm, golden hue over the landscape. The sky was a canvas of vibrant oranges, pinks, and purples, each color blending into the next in a breathtaking display. And with that, I felt a small spark of hope. Maybe this place, with its quaint charm and quiet comfort, was exactly what I needed to find my way again.

Chapter 2

I WOKE UP IN MY NEW PLACE, the silence of Hallow's End pressing down like a heavy blanket, the oppressive quiet making me miss the familiar city buzz I once found irritating—honking cars, distant conversations, and comforting white noise. I threw off the covers and padded to the window, peeking out at the misty morning. The rising sun cast an amber glow over the rolling hills and dense forest.

After rummaging through my suitcase, I chose a stylish autumn ensemble: a fitted, cream-colored turtleneck sweater with statement sleeves, paired with sleek, high-waisted black jeans. I slipped on my favorite ankle boots—suede with a subtle heel—and wrapped a deep plum scarf around my neck for a pop of color. I brushed my coffee-brown hair into soft, effortless waves.

Craving coffee to start my day, I ventured into the town center. The ground was covered in pine needles and acorns, their earthy tones punctuated by the occasional burst of crimson berries, creating a textured canvas that heralded autumn's arrival.

Townspeople smiled and nodded as I passed, some offering cheerful greetings. Their warm expressions and easy-going nature were a stark contrast to the rush and grumpy indifference of city life. The air felt fresh and clean, carrying the crisp scent of pine needles, mixed with a faint hint of spiced apple from a nearby bakery. Worlds away from the usual city smog.

As I walked through town, I noticed how the locals dressed in comfortable, laid-back clothes. Cozy flannel shirts, jeans, and sturdy boots, that made them effortlessly blend in to their rustic surroundings. In contrast, the softness of my cashmere sweater felt too refined, and I tugged at the hem, while the sharp clicks of my heeled boots on the cobblestone streets echoed loudly, making me feel out of place.

I wondered if I should ask Ivy to take me shopping. We'd only met yesterday, but she was warm, and exuded an easy friendliness that made me feel like we'd get along. I've always connected quickly with people in my almost-desperation to seek out real, meaningful relationships. A new friendship could be just what I needed—something unconnected to my family, *or* Sebastian. The idea of forming genuine ties in a new place felt refreshing.

Hallow's End was nothing like Cresden. Here, people strolled leisurely down the sidewalks, pausing to chat with neighbors and shopkeepers. An elderly man sat on a bench, feeding birds, while a group of children played hopscotch nearby, their laughter echoing down the street. Every passerby seemed genuinely interested in the next, exchanging warm greetings and stopping for unhurried conversations. It was strange but refreshing.

In Cresden, the atmosphere was starkly different. The city buzzed with the constant rush of hurried footsteps and honking cars. People rarely made eye contact, let alone stopped to chat. Everyone was too busy with their own lives. Heads down, earbuds in, always hurrying from one place to the next.

I found the caffeine haven easily enough—Harvest Moon Coffee. The quaint brick building, similar to my cottage, had ivy draped over it, and a charming sign swinging above the door. Seasonal decorations—pumpkins of various sizes and twinkling fairy lights—dotted the small tables and chairs arranged on the sidewalk.

Inside, the rich aroma of freshly brewed cappuccino and warm pastries enveloped me. Shelves lined the walls, filled with intriguing books and lush potted plants, adding a touch of greenery and life to the space. Warm, earthy tones painted the walls, with one wall showcasing a vibrant mural depicting a whimsical forest scene. String lights hung overhead, casting a soft, cozy glow.

An assortment of inviting seating, from plush armchairs upholstered in rich colors, to rustic wooden benches with colorful cushions, beckoned visitors to sit and stay awhile. The soft hum of a jazz melody played in the background, blending with the soft murmur of conversations and the occasional clatter of dishes from the counter.

I approached the counter, where a friendly barista greeted me. She had her curly auburn hair pulled back into a loose ponytail, and a nametag reading MARLENE. "Good morning! What can I get for you today?" Her smile reached her bright green eyes.

"A large, iced pumpkin spice latte, please," I said, stifling a yawn.

Marlene chuckled as she began preparing the drink. "You must be Lavinia, right?"

I raised an eyebrow in surprise. "Just Vinnie. How did you know?"

"Between your outfit and that pumpkin spice latte, you're a dead give-away," Marlene said with a smile. "Most locals here skip the syrup in their coffee."

"I guess my city habits are showing," I chuckled. "Do you get a lot of tourists around here?" I asked, watching her write my name on the cup.

Marlene nodded. "We don't get that many visitors this early in September, but things will be buzzing during the week of Halloween. That's when the pumpkin spice and seasonal drink requests really start pouring in."

As I waited for my drink, I absorbed the inviting atmosphere. The café was lively with activity, with a steady stream of customers chatting and placing their orders. I watched as one man poured five packets of sugar into his coffee, making me wonder if he had a death wish, or just a serious sweet tooth.

Marlene called my name, pulling me back from my musings. She handed me my pumpkin spice latte, and I wrapped my hands around the cool takeaway cup, savoring the rich aroma that promised a perfect start to my day.

Distracted by the inviting scent of freshly brewed coffee, and lost in thoughts of how different everything was here, I turned to leave, and collided head-on with someone standing behind me. My coffee cup slipped from my hand, and time seemed to slow as the liquid arced through the air, splashing onto the person I'd bumped into.

"Oh my gosh, I'm so sorry!" I exclaimed, quickly grabbing napkins from the dispenser on the counter.

The poor guy was drenched, his white shirt soaked with the coffee.

He laughed, a deep sound that sent a pleasant shiver down my spine. His hazel eyes sparkled with amusement, and his warm smile lit up his face. "No harm done. I needed a wake-up call anyway. Plus, I've always hated this shirt."

As he looked down at his soaked shirt and dabbed at it with napkins, I couldn't help but notice how it clung to his lean, muscular frame. Accentuating his broad shoulders and defined chest. He was undeniably attractive, and I found myself staring, captivated by his sharp jawline and the way his slight stubble added to his rugged appeal. Realizing I was gawking, I quickly averted my gaze, a flush rising to my cheeks.

"I can't believe I just did that," I muttered, embarrassed. "I'm not usually this clumsy. Sorry about that. By the way I'm Lavinia Carlisle, but everyone calls me Vinnie."

I looked up, meeting his gaze, and my breath caught. His eyes were a warm brown, flecked with gold, giving them an amber glow. They were filled with curiosity and amusement, drawing me in. A soft, playful smile tugged at his lips as he took in my appearance, making the embarrassing situation feel unexpectedly charged with a spark of attraction.

As he smiled down at me, I realized just how tall he was—about six-foot-two, towering over my five-foot-five frame, even with my heels on. The height difference added to his magnetic presence, making me feel both intrigued, and a little flustered, by the chemistry between us.

"Nice to meet you, Vinnie. I'm Ethan Brown," he said with a warm smile as he stepped aside. He glanced at Marlene behind the counter and added, "Could you get Vinnie another drink? Put it on my tab, please."

His smooth, confident tone made my cheeks warm. I was surprised by his kindness, feeling both flattered and a little flustered by the gesture.

"Oh, you don't have to do that," I protested lightly. "I'm the one who spilled the coffee. I should be the one buying *you* a drink."

He chuckled, running a hand through his tousled hair. "Letting a pretty girl pay for her own coffee wouldn't be very gentlemanly of me," he teased, with a playful glint in his eye.

I felt my cheeks heat. Trying to keep my composure, I offered, "Well, at least let me pay for the dry cleaning? It's the least I can do."

He glanced down at his coffee-stained shirt and shrugged, his eyes never leaving mine. "No need, really. It's just a shirt," he said casually. Then, with a curious tilt of his head, he added, "So, are you new in town, or just passing through?"

"I'm visiting here for a few weeks, from Cresden," I explained, trying to match his easy-going tone. "I'm still getting used to the slower pace here, but it's a pleasant change from the city's chaos."

He nodded, his smile making my heart race. "Cresden, huh? This is quite a shift from city life. That's just next to Boston, right? I've never been, but I hear it's a busy place. Hallow's End is a change of pace if you're used to all that hustle and bustle. But it grows on you, after a while."

"It *is* a big change," I agreed. "I'm staying at Willow Cottage for a few weeks, trying to adjust. Ivy was actually the first person to welcome me, and she's been great. Everyone I've met so far has been really friendly. It's nice to see such a close-knit community."

Ethan chuckled. "Yeah, Ivy's basically our unofficial welcome committee. She loves meeting new people, and making sure everyone feels at home. She's the reason so many visitors end up coming back."

Just then, Marlene approached with a fresh cup for me, and handed Ethan a drink as well. "Your usual," she said with a playful grin. "Though I still don't get how anyone can drink two shots of espresso with no sugar or milk. You're a braver soul than me."

Ethan laughed. "What can I say? I like my coffee strong," he replied, taking the cup from her.

He surprised me by lingering instead of saying his goodbyes and continuing with his day. Ethan glanced back at me, a playful spark in his eyes. "So, has Ivy already tried to rope you into the Spooktacular Hallow's Eve festival, yet?"

I raised an eyebrow at him, intrigued. "How did you know? Is there an inside joke I'm missing?"

Ethan chuckled, his laugh lighting up his face. His smile revealed straight, white teeth. "It's practically a rite of passage around here. Ivy's super passionate about Halloween, and makes sure everyone in town gets involved. She's really persuasive, so if she's pitched it to you, I hope you agreed—especially if you're planning on sticking around for it."

I couldn't help but smile back. "Actually, Ivy didn't have to do much convincing. I volunteered to help out with the festival. Plus, I love Halloween, so it should be fun."

We stood in a comfortable silence, an undeniable spark humming between us—warm, exhilarating, and unexpected. His presence made the room feel cozier, and also made me acutely aware of every little detail around me: the cool feel of my coffee cup, the faint scent of his cologne, and how easily we fell into conversation.

I hadn't felt this kind of immediate chemistry in a long time—not since Sebastian—and it caught me off guard.

Ethan seemed to hesitate, his brow furrowing slightly as if he was searching for something else to keep the conversation going. Finally, he broke the silence with a question. "So, what brings you to Hallow's End?"

I hesitated. "I needed a fresh start. Life in the city was . . . complicated."

Ethan didn't press on, sensing my reluctance to elaborate. He simply nodded, offering a gentle smile that conveyed understanding. His respect for my boundaries made me feel relieved and oddly comforted, as if he was someone I could actually open up to, given time.

"Well, welcome to Hallow's End, Vinnie. If you ever need someone to show you around, or just want some company, I'd be more than happy to oblige." The thought of seeing him again was exciting, and I couldn't help but feel a flicker of anticipation.

"Thanks, Ethan. I appreciate that," I said. My heart fluttered a little at his kindness, noticing again how good he looked.

Despite the coffee stain on his white shirt, he wore it well, tucked into a pair of fitted brown trousers that complemented his lean build. A navy sweater was casually draped over a nearby chair, next to his briefcase. I wondered what he did for work but, before I could ask, he glanced at his watch, a flicker of urgency crossing his face.

"I've got to run, but I'd love to see you again. Maybe over a coffee that stays in the cup?"

I laughed. "That sounds great. I'd like that." As I said it, a swirl of emotions rushed through me. Part of me wondered if he really meant it, or if he was just being polite. Still, the prospect of seeing him again filled me with a hopeful anticipation.

As he took a step back, he glanced at my outfit and flashed another one of those disarming smiles. "By the way, I'm glad the coffee went on me and not your lovely sweater. It really suits you." His compliment caught me off guard, putting me at ease about something I'd been feeling insecure about earlier. "See you around, Vinnie."

As he walked away, I felt a fluttering in my stomach. My heart beat a little faster, and there was a lightness in my chest that felt new and exhilarating. There was something about him that made me feel alive again, stirring emotions I thought I had lost with Sebastian. As I watched him disappear into the crowd, a smile tugged at my lips.

With my heart still racing from the encounter, I headed to Enchanted Quill, Ivy's bookshop. The charm of the town extended to this particular spot, where large windows displayed beautiful books. Above the door, there was a sign featuring an ornate quill and inkpot, which invited readers inside.

The interior was even more captivating than I had imagined. As I pushed the door open, bells chimed faintly, announcing my presence. The sound mingled with soft murmurs and the occasional rustle of turning pages, and

I paused to take it all in. Tall bookshelves lined the walls, brimming with a meticulously curated selection of books, from bestsellers to rare finds. In the corners, inviting reading nooks beckoned, their armchairs bathed in warm light. The scattered plush cushions invited visitors to lose themselves in a story.

At the back of the shop, an enormous fireplace crackled gently, its warmth radiating through the room. It was easy to imagine this as a gathering place for community events, the flames casting a flickering glow on eager faces. I breathed in deeply, the air infused with the scent of old books mingling with the soothing aroma of Ivy's herbal teas.

Ivy looked up from behind the counter, her face lighting up when she saw me. "Vinnie! How was your first night?" she called out, her blue eyes sparkling with tenderness. She brushed a few strands of dark blue hair from her forehead, revealing a light dusting of freckles across her nose and cheeks. Her heart-shaped face and warm smile was youthful and inviting.

"It was . . . different," I admitted, laughing softly. "I'm still getting used to the quiet."

"Understandable," Ivy said with a smile as she carefully priced a stack of books. Her flowing purple dress, which hugged her curvy figure, swayed gently as she placed the stickers on the covers with precision. The soft light caught the collection of charm bracelets on her wrist, and a pendant that shimmered around her neck. "Big change from city life, huh?"

"Certainly," I remarked, taking in the whimsical, witchy décor. The shelves were artfully arranged with crystals, tarot cards, and other mystical trinkets. Dried herbs hung from the ceiling, filling the air with their earthy scent. Intricate tapestries adorned the walls, depicting moon phases and enchanted forests. "This place is amazing."

Ivy's gaze twinkled with delight. "Thank you. I've put a lot of love into it. It's my little sanctuary."

"What inspired all of this?" I asked. "It's so . . . unique."

Ivy leaned against the counter, her expression thoughtful. "I've always felt a strong attraction to the mystical and magical. There's something enchanting about the idea that there's more to this world than what meets the eye. Witchcraft, to me, is about connecting with nature, harnessing its energies, and finding balance." She paused, a fond smile crossing her face. "After finishing college two years ago, it just felt right to open this place. I've always followed my intuition, and this shop seemed like the perfect way to share that part of myself with others."

I raised an eyebrow, doubtful. "Do you really believe in all this . . . witchy stuff?"

Ivy's smile became even more whimsical. "Belief is a powerful thing, Vinnie. Sometimes, what we believe shapes our reality beyond our awareness. Besides, who's to say what's real and what's not? After all, we're all just stardust in the grand scheme of things."

I smiled at her cryptic response. Her dreamy demeanour was oddly comforting. "I guess that's one way to look at it."

"Exactly," Ivy replied. "Life is full of mysteries. Embracing them makes everything a touch more magical."

She turned to a shelf behind her and extracted a stunningly bound volume with intricate designs on the cover. "Speaking of mysteries, I think you might like this book."

I took the book, feeling its weight and the textured cover beneath my fingers. The cover of the book had gold and silver patterns embossed on it. As I flipped through the pages, I marvelled at the beautiful illustrations and inspiring quotes about creativity and self-discovery. "These illustrations are stunning," I remarked, my voice filled with genuine admiration. "Art is my passion. I could spend hours just getting lost in these pages."

Ivy's eyes lit up with interest. "Art, you say? That's wonderful. What kind of art do you do?"

"Mostly painting and sketching," I replied, feeling more at ease. "I had a small studio back home. It was my sanctuary, just like this shop is for you. A place where I could escape from everything and just create."

"I can understand that," Ivy nodded. "Art is a powerful form of expression. It's like casting a spell with colours and shapes. Have you thought about setting up your own gallery? It could be a wonderful way to share your passion with people instead of keeping all that beautiful expression locked away in a studio for no one to see and appreciate."

"Actually, I have," I admitted. "But I'm not sure where to start."

"Must be a coincidence," Ivy said, her eyes twinkling. "There's a small place for rent in town that would be perfect for an art gallery. I can show it to you on my lunch break. If you're interested?"

"That would be amazing," I said, experiencing a surge of excitement. "Thank you, Ivy."

"Anytime," she replied. "You're going to love it here, Vinnie. Trust me."

While Ivy attended to other customers, I found a seat by the window and savored my morning drink, taking in the charming view of the town. Old-fashioned buildings lined the streets of Hallow's End, each painted in warm, inviting colors. Strings of twinkling fairy lights crisscrossed above the cobblestone streets, adding a magical glow even in the daylight.

Parents walked hand-in-hand with children bundled up in cozy sweaters, their laughter echoing as they skipped along. An elderly couple strolled by, arm in arm, wearing matching knitted hats, their steps slow but content. It was idyllic, and so different from the impersonal atmosphere of metropolitan life.

Despite the beauty, and the palpable sense of community, I couldn't shake the feeling of being out of place in Hallow's End. I missed the familiarity of city life. A young couple passing by the window, laughing and sharing a playful moment, brought back memories of Sebastian and me. We used to have moments like that—spontaneous, joyful, and filled with laughter.

One evening stood out vividly in my mind, as if I were reliving it all over again.

It was late, and the city buzzed with its usual electric energy. Sebastian had insisted on a spontaneous adventure, his intense green eyes shining with excitement. We found ourselves at an upscale bar with a rooftop view, the city sprawled beneath us like a glittering tapestry.

"Let's play truth or dare," he suggested, his confident grin infectious.

The dares escalated quickly—from daring each other to flirt with strangers to Sebastian challenging me to dance provocatively on the bar top. The thrill of it all was intoxicating. When it was his turn, Sebastian leaned in close, his voice low and daring. "I dare you to sneak into the VIP section."

My heart raced at the challenge, a mix of nerves and exhilaration coursing through me. I nodded, a mischievous smile spreading across my lips. We managed to slip past the bouncer, our playful antics drawing amused glances and laughter from other patrons. Eventually, we were caught and kicked out, but it only added to the thrill of the night.

Afterward, we wandered to a quiet corner of a nearby park. The city's lights twinkled around us, casting a magical glow over the moment. We were still giddy from our escapade, and the adrenaline made every touch and glance more charged. Sebastian pulled me close, and our lips met in a heated kiss. The world around us seemed to disappear as we stumbled into a secluded area. His hands roamed over my body, his breath hot against my skin. Our laughter and soft moans mingled with the distant hum of the city, creating a private symphony of our own.

The intensity of our connection in moments like that was undeniable. The wild, unrestrained, and thrilling times with Sebastian made me feel alive and invincible. Those moments, filled with electric energy and unrestrained joy, made me believe we had something real and profound.

But then, the cracks started to show. Between the highs, there were lows that gnawed at me, like the nights I spent begging him on the phone to visit me at college after he'd been away on business trips for weeks. He always had excuses—too busy, too tired—only for me to later discover he had been out that night. When I confronted him, he insisted it was for work, and I wanted so badly to believe him. There were many more instances like that, but the good parts clouded my judgment, making it hard to see the truth through the haze of our intense connection.

Now, as I sat and observed the idyllic scene outside, a new flicker of excitement sparked within me. The idea of taking a risk and opening my own art gallery felt different from anything tied to Sebastian—it was a desire purely my own.

For the first time, I wondered if Hallow's End could be more than just a stop on my journey. Perhaps it could be my destination, a place where I could build a life that felt authentically mine.

Chapter 3

I VY'S CHEERFUL VOICE broke through my reverie as she slipped a knitted cardigan over her dress. "Vinnie! Are you ready to go see that gallery space?"

Startled, I looked up and smiled. "Oh, yes! Let's go."

Ivy led the way down Hallow's End's cobblestone streets, alive with Halloween spirit. Twinkling orange lights framed the quaint storefronts—Sweet Crumbs Bakery, Maple & Spice Grocery, and Timeless Toys—each decorated with carved pumpkins sporting mischievous grins.

Townspeople, some already dressed in Halloween costumes despite it only being the start of September, added to the festive atmosphere. Children darted between shops, their laughter mingling with the scent of cinnamon and cloves, whilst ghostly figures and cobwebs hung from lampposts. Curious about the early costumes, I asked Ivy, who laughed and explained, "We do love Halloween a lot here, but these costumes are actually for the play that the local theatre group is putting on for the festival."

As we strolled through the town, Ivy's enthusiasm was contagious. "You know, last year's costume contest winner was John—the guy who owns the bakery we just passed—and his little boy. They dressed up as Pennywise and Georgie. They even had matching balloons. It was both adorable and terrifying," she recalled with a chuckle.

I laughed. "I love that movie! I'm into anything horror, as long as it doesn't go overboard with gore."

Ivy grinned. "Same here. You'll definitely enjoy our haunted house. This year's theme is *Zombie Doomsday*. We have scare actors, but it's all in good fun—nothing too intense, since we usually keep it family-friendly."

"That sounds perfect," I said, eyes lighting up with excitement.

We continued our walk, and the town's festive decorations became more apparent. The lampposts were wrapped in twinkling orange lights, and the storefronts displayed painted windows and spooky props.

"The parade is a big draw, too," Ivy continued. "The local high school kids make these amazing themed floats. You never know what they'll come up with. Although, there was that one year they went all-out with a spider theme—absolute nightmare fuel. I still get chills thinking about it."

I cringed in sympathy. "Spiders? No, thank you! Although, I figured with your whole witchy vibe, you might have a pet tarantula or something," I joked.

Ivy burst out laughing. "Oh, gods, no! The only creature I have at home is a cat. I'm definitely not the spider-keeping type!"

As we walked, it became evident that all the shops were conveniently arranged around the town square, which was the hub and heart of Hallow's End. The central area swarmed with activity, serving as a focal point for both locals and visitors.

"Is this where most of the town's action happens?" I asked, observing the lively scene.

Ivy nodded. "Yes, we like to keep everything centralized. It just makes sense to have the buzz and business in one area. It keeps the rest of the town quieter."

"That makes sense," I agreed, glancing around. As we continued walking, a larger building caught my eye. It was an old, stately structure with a brick facade, large arched windows, and a clock tower perched on top. "What's that place?" I asked, pointing towards it.

Ivy followed my gaze. "Oh, that's the town hall. It's used for all sorts of things—parties, social events, anything that requires a bigger space. We also host local meetings there. Actually, there's one tonight if you want to see what it's all about."

I cringed slightly at the thought. "I'm not sure a town meeting is really my scene."

Ivy laughed, waving a hand dismissively. "It's not that formal. It's more like friends getting together and throwing around ideas. Plus, if you're seriously considering opening a gallery here, it's an excellent opportunity to show your face. The locals love getting involved with new businesses and supporting each other."

I considered her words. It made sense, but I still felt uncertain about committing to the idea of opening my own space here. "I'll think about it," I said, keeping my tone casual.

Ivy smiled. "Well, I hope you come. I could use an extra vote—or at least someone new to chat with when Danny starts his rant about his darn garden. He's convinced someone in town is stealing from it, and *I swear* he brings it up at every meeting. Poor guy doesn't seem to realize that being this close to the forest means it's basically a free-for-all for raccoons and other rodents. He really thinks there's a veggie bandit out there," she added with a laugh.

We both chuckled as we turned onto a quieter street, just past the town hall. Ivy gestured ahead. "The space for rent is just a little further up. It's not right in the thick of things, but still close enough to catch the foot traffic. A great spot for a potential gallery."

I nodded, intrigued. The idea of a slightly quieter location appealed to me—somewhere people could escape to and really take in the art.

"I think you'll love it," Ivy continued with a reassuring smile. "It's got great bones, and a lot of potential. You could really make it your own."

"I hope so," I replied, trying to shake off my doubts.

We walked a few more steps before Ivy stopped and turned to face a building. "Here we are," she said, gesturing towards it.

The structure was historic, with a stone façade that spoke of centuries gone by. Weathered wooden shutters framed large windows, allowing an abundance of natural light to flood the interior. The building exuded an air of elegance, with intricate stonework detailing the facade and a sturdy oak door that hinted at its rich history.

Peering through the large windows, I could see inside. The high ceilings and exposed wooden beams gave the space an airy, open feel, while the original hardwood floors added a touch of rustic charm. The walls were bare, eagerly waiting to be covered with vibrant paintings and detailed sketches. I could already envision it brimming with my artwork, drawing the townspeople in to share in my passion.

One wall could be dedicated to a rotating exhibit of local artists, offering a platform for hidden talents in the community. Comfortable seating areas with plush armchairs and small tables would invite visitors to linger and discuss the art over a cup of coffee or tea. A corner could be transformed into a mini studio space for hosting art classes and workshops, encouraging creativity and learning. Soft, ambient lighting would highlight each piece of art, creating an intimate and inviting atmosphere. My mind raced with possibilities.

"This spot is perfect," I said, my voice tinged with excitement. "I can see it all coming together."

Ivy grinned. "What would you call it?"

"The Cozy Canvas," I replied without hesitation. "Art has always been a refuge for me, a source of comfort and creativity. I want this gallery to be that for everyone who walks through the door."

As we admired the building, an elderly man with mesmerizing blue eyes and a genuine smile approached. His tweed jacket and flat cap gave him a scholarly air. He pulled out a set of keys, unlocked the door, and held it open for us.

"Did I hear the name 'The Cozy Canvas'?" he asked, his voice rich with approval. "That's a fantastic name."

I beamed. "Thank you."

As we stepped inside, the features of the building spoke of its storied past. Old wooden shelves lined one wall, hinting when the space might have served as a quaint shop or bookstore. A dusty counter stood at the back of the room, a relic from another era, adding to the charm and character of the place.

"Are you the owner?" I asked, casting a hopeful gaze around the room.

"Indeed, I'm Harold Thornton," he said, extending a hand with a warm smile. "This property has been in my family for generations. It used to house a medical practice many years ago, then an antiques shop and, most recently, it served as a library, which eventually moved to a larger location because of growing demand." He glanced around fondly. "Each incarnation has contributed its own unique charm to the community."

I shook his hand. "It's wonderful to meet you, Mr Thornton. What an incredible history this place has."

"Please, call me Harold," he said, his vibrant blue eyes crinkling at the corners. His grip was firm yet gentle, though I noticed a slight tremor in his aged hand.

"Alright, Harold. What made you decide to rent this place out again?" I asked, curious.

He sighed, a wistful expression crossing his face. "I'm getting older, and can't manage running a business anymore. This place needs a new energy. Something lively and creative, perhaps." He raised an eyebrow at me, and I couldn't help but smile back at him.

A sense of hope tugged at my heart. The idea of creating something meaningful in this space was tempting, the vision of the gallery already forming in my mind. But then, the reality hit me.

Settling down here would mean leaving behind the life I had known—the fast-paced energy of Cresden, the familiarity of city streets, and even the lingering memories of Sebastian. My parents were expecting me to return home soon. They thought this was just a brief holiday, a break before I started working for my father and set aside my dream of pursuing art. That was the plan. The pressures of my old life that I was supposed to return to.

My mind was torn in two—one part longing for the fresh start that Hallow's End promised, and the other clinging to the comfort of my old life, despite knowing it no longer fit who I wanted to become.

"I'll have to think about it," my voice faltered, betraying the conflict within me.

"Take your time," Harold said kindly. "I believe you'll make the right decision."

After leaving the gallery, Ivy suggested we grab lunch at a nearby café. We strolled to a lovely spot called The Sunflower Bistro, its wooden tables and a fireplace inviting us in. As we stepped inside, the scent of freshly baked bread and simmering soups wrapped around us. Sunflowers in vases brightened each table, adding a cheerful touch to the atmosphere.

A waitress behind the counter spotted Ivy and waved enthusiastically. "Hey, Ivy! Thanks again for that special tea blend you made for me. It worked wonders! Can you whip up some more when you have the time?" she called out loudly, drawing a few amused glances from other customers. She didn't seem fazed by the attention, grinning widely as she made her way over to the table where we had just sat down.

Ivy's face lit up. "Of course, Em! I'm glad it helped. I'll bring you a fresh batch tomorrow. The moon's energy is perfect for brewing something extra special tonight."

The waitress grinned and shook her head, clearly accustomed to Ivy's strange ways. "Thanks, Ivy. You're a lifesaver. And this must be Vinnie?"

Ivy turned to me with a friendly smile. "You got it. Vinnie's new in town, and might just be our next favorite artist."

The waitress extended a hand to me, her smile genuine. "Nice to finally meet you, Vinnie. I'm Emily. Welcome to The Sunflower Bistro!"

I shook her hand, awkwardly. "Thanks, Emily. It's nice to meet you, too."

We settled at our table, the soft gingham tablecloth smooth under my fingertips. After we glanced over the menu, Emily took our orders, and Ivy turned her attention back to me, her gaze brimming with curiosity.

"So, what brought you to Hallow's End?"

Spending the day with Ivy had been refreshing. There was a genuine sense of friendship forming between us, something I hadn't felt in a long time. Her kindness and easy-going nature made me feel like I could trust her and, despite the weight of my past, I felt the urge to open up to her.

"It's a long story," I began, gazing out the window at the colorful town square. A woman was trying to walk a golden retriever puppy, who seemed more interested in exploring everything around them. The puppy bounced around excitedly, tugging at the leash and nearly toppling over a small display of pumpkins. The owner struggled to keep up, laughing as she tried to gently steer the puppy away from further chaos.

The brief amusement from the scene outside faded as I turned back to Ivy. "I grew up in Cresden," I began, my tone serious. "My parents are both highly successful—my father runs a large corporation that acquires and restructures smaller firms, and my mother thrives in high society. She's always pushing me to *marry well*," I added, the words dripping with disdain. That was the last thing I wanted.

"My father expected me to take over the family business, Carlisle Enterprises, seeing it as my destiny, while my mother envisioned me navigating elite social circles. To them, art was a frivolous hobby with no money in it. It's ironic, considering our home was filled with expensive artworks that they didn't understand—they were just there to showcase their wealth."

Ivy's eyes widened as she recognized the name. "I've heard of Carlisle Enterprises. There was news recently about a successful takeover of some small businesses in a town not far from here—Brookside, I think. People around here have been talking, wondering if the same thing could happen in Hallow's End."

I winced at Ivy's mention of the takeover. "Yeah, that was all my father's doing," I admitted. "The idea is to *improve* smaller businesses. Streamline their operations, cut costs, and then either integrate them into larger corporate structures, or sell them off at a profit. It's all about maximizing efficiency and profit margins.

For small towns like Brookside, it can be a tough decision. Sometimes, these businesses are struggling to stay afloat, and a takeover can mean an influx of capital and resources that keeps them open. Plus, having a well-known corporate brand attach its name can attract more customers and tourism, making the shops more appealing. But, it often comes at the cost of losing the local flavor, and unique character, that made those businesses special in the first place."

Ivy raised an eyebrow playfully, though there was a subtle undertone of concern in her voice. "You seem to know a lot about how it all works. You're not here to scout and plan a takeover of our little town, are you?" she joked, but I could sense she was gauging my reaction.

I let out an uncomfortable chuckle. "No, definitely not," I assured her. "It's just that my father made me work for him and learn the ropes during my summer breaks in college. It was part of the deal he set if I wanted to pursue an art degree, which had nothing to do with the future he envisioned for me." I paused, reflecting on how complicated my feelings were. "I realize now, how lucky I was that he even funded my education. It was partly because I convinced him that I'd eventually join the business, even though I never really wanted to. I guess I've always felt torn between following my passion, and meeting my family's expectations."

Ivy nodded, her expression softening. "That sounds really complicated. It must be tough trying to balance what you want, with what your family expects. I can't imagine the pressure you're under."

"It's exhausting trying to keep everyone else happy, while still figuring out what *I* really want." I sighed, the weight of it all sinking in. "I've been saving up from part-time jobs during college, and I've even squirreled away some of the allowance my parents give me. I opened a separate bank account they don't know about, so they can't keep track of it."

Ivy raised an eyebrow, clearly surprised. "Would your parents really do that? Monitor your spendings?"

"Yeah, they would. It's not just about control—it's more about the family wealth. They've always been careful about where the money goes, and are very protective of it. They wanted to make sure I wasn't spending recklessly, or on things they didn't approve of. Even now, they like to keep tabs on everything, just to make sure I'm staying on the *right path*, as they see it."

Ivy looked thoughtful for a moment. "So, has all that made it hard for you to move out and do what you really want?"

I nodded, feeling a pang of disappointment. "Pretty much. Even with the savings I've got, it's not enough to really strike out on my own in Cresden. My parents have always been my safety net, and I guess I've been afraid to cut those ties completely. They've made it clear that, if I don't follow the path they've laid out, the financial support stops. And honestly, I don't have much experience in the real world outside of their influence. It's scary to think about going it alone, especially when they've controlled so much of my life up until now."

As the words spilled out, I suddenly realized how much I was sharing, and a wave of awkwardness hit me. I barely knew Ivy, and here I was, unloading my whole life story. I bit my lip, feeling a bit exposed. "I'm sorry," I said, glancing away. "I didn't mean to drop all of that on you. It's probably too much to share with someone I just met."

It felt good to let it out, though, and Ivy's quiet attentiveness made it easier than I expected. Despite the embarrassment, it was comforting to finally have someone who listened.

Ivy smiled warmly, her understanding evident. "It's okay. Everyone needs to let it out sometimes, and I'm glad you felt comfortable enough to share with me." She paused, as if considering her next words carefully. "I get that it's scary, but I believe everything happens for a reason. You're here in Hallow's End now, and maybe that's exactly what you need, to figure things out. The scariest paths often lead to the most beautiful destinations. Change is frightening, but it's the only way to grow. Sometimes, the things we fear most are the very things that lead us to where we're meant to be."

"Thanks, Ivy. I really appreciate you saying that. It's nice to feel like I've already got a friend here." I smiled, feeling a bit more at ease. For someone so whimsical and dreamy, she had an uncanny ability to say exactly what I needed to hear.

Just then, Emily arrived with our orders. She placed a steaming bowl of creamy tomato basil soup in front of Ivy, its rich aroma mingling with the scent of the freshly baked breadsticks on the side. In front of me, Emily placed a vibrant autumn salad, which featured a mix of crisp greens, roasted butternut squash, tangy feta cheese, and dried cranberries. Thin slices of ripe pear added a touch of sweetness, while a light balsamic vinaigrette tied everything together.

The arrival of the food provided a welcome break from the heavy conversation, allowing us to savor the simple pleasure of a good meal and, throughout lunch, Ivy and I chatted about the town, and the gallery space. Our conversation left me with much to consider. After we finished our meal, my mind continued to churn with thoughts of the gallery, and the possibilities it held. I wasn't sure what the future would bring, but for the first time in a long while, I felt a glimmer of hope.

Chapter 4

R AIN DRUMMED SOFTLY against the windows, filling the cottage with a soothing rhythm. After putting away groceries from a quick shopping trip to Maple & Spice Grocery—the quaint store I had noticed earlier in town—I felt a sense of settling in. Ivy had mentioned it was the best spot for all the essentials, unless I wanted to drive out of town for a bigger selection.

Tonight's town meeting lingered in my thoughts. Ivy had assured me it was a good way to connect with the locals and show interest in the community, but I still wasn't sure if I wanted to go. The idea of walking into a room full of strangers felt awkward. It was an opportunity to fit in, but the thought of being the outsider was daunting.

Just as I settled in, the shrill ring of my phone shattered the peace, and seeing MOM flash on the screen sent a wave of anxiety through me. Having already ignored a few of her calls, I knew avoidance couldn't last forever. Taking a deep breath, and bracing for the inevitable conversation, I answered.

Ignoring my greeting, her voice came through the line, tinged with irritation. "You arrived yesterday and haven't called yet. Why do I have to chase you down just to hear how you're doing?"

I winced at her tone. "Sorry, Mom. It's been a busy day getting settled in, and unpacking. I was going to call you tonight. Everything's fine, really."

My mother's exasperated sigh was audible. "Your father and I agreed to this little country escape, and are even paying for it. The least you could do is call, or at least *text* us, when you arrive. It only takes a moment." I bit my lip, knowing full well that, with my mother, it never just took a moment. A quick call could easily turn into a lengthy interrogation about every detail of my day.

She continued, her voice sharp with concern, "For all we knew, you could've been dead in some run-down town in the middle of nowhere!"

"Mom, you're being paranoid. I'm fine," I replied, trying to keep my voice calm. "This place is actually really nice, and I feel safer here than I did in Cresden. The biggest threat here is probably the raccoons raiding the trash bins."

There was a brief pause, followed by a gasp of disbelief. "Raccoons? Oh, Lavinia, that sounds dreadful! Why would you ever put yourself in such a situation? It's bad enough you're in the middle of nowhere, but dealing with wild animals is just . . . ugh." Her voice was laced with horror and disapproval.

I rolled my eyes. "Mom, it's not as dramatic as you're making it out to be. The raccoons aren't a big deal."

As I tried to reassure her, I heard faint voices in the background on her end of the line. A familiar greeting from the staff at Serenity Spa filtered through. "Welcome back, Mrs Carlisle. Your usual, I presume?" She always went to that place once a week, more for the socializing and gossip than actual relaxation.

My mother sighed, the impatience clear in her voice. "Give me a second, darling," she said, muffling the phone, but not quite enough to hide her conversation.

I could hear her addressing the staff, her tone clipped. "After so many years of coming here, you'd think they'd get it right by now. It's not that complicated." Her irritation made it clear that something had gone awry with her appointment.

Sensing an opportunity to end the call, I said, "I can tell you're busy, Mom. We can catch up another time."

But she wasn't having it. "Don't be ridiculous, Lavinia. We haven't even talked properly yet."

I hesitated, "Are phones even allowed inside a spa?"

She laughed dismissively. "Please, I pay them well enough. Those rules don't apply to me." Her tone exuded nonchalance and entitlement.

I cringed internally, uncomfortable with her attitude. I had never been like her in that regard, and moments like this reminded me just how different we were. But I knew better than to argue. It wouldn't change anything, and it would only lead to more tension.

As the conversation continued, my mother's voice took on a more eager tone. "When you come back, I was thinking we could go shopping. You need some new business attire for your first day at your father's company."

The thought of shopping with her made my stomach twist. She always criticized my choices, insisting on outfits that never felt like me. Spending that much time under her scrutiny was unbearable. I tried to deflect, keeping my voice as neutral as possible. "I have enough clothes as it is, Mom. We don't have to do that."

"Nonsense," she replied dismissively. In the background, I could hear the clatter of lockers, and the soft chatter of people in the changing room. She continued, oblivious to my discomfort. "I was also thinking we could turn your studio into an office. Wouldn't it be nice to have a proper workspace at home? That studio will be just a waste of space with how busy you'll be with work, and the social calendar I've planned."

Her words struck a nerve, and I couldn't suppress a groan. The studio was the one place where I could escape the expectations and pressures they placed on me. The thought of it being repurposed into a sterile office, just another extension of their control, filled me with frustration. Yet, as much as I wanted to argue, I knew it would be futile. The conversation was a painful reminder of the life they had laid out for me, one that left little room for my own dreams.

I tried to interject, but my mother was already on a roll, outlining plans for when I returned. Her voice became a distant hum as my thoughts drifted back to the gallery space I'd seen today. That place filled me with hope and excitement. The idea of moving here, and opening an art gallery, felt so right, but I knew my parents would never approve. Being away for a few weeks was one thing, telling them I wanted to move here *permanently* to start my own business would be a bloodbath.

As my mother continued, I caught a snippet about a Christmas gala she was planning, but I quickly tuned her out again. She enjoyed the sound of her own voice, often filling the silence with her plans and expectations, requiring little more than a passive listener. My thoughts drifted back to the gallery. I started to mentally calculate a rough estimate of the startup costs.

Could I really make it happen? I had some experience managing finances, and a basic understanding of running a business, thanks to my father. But the thought of doing it all on my own was daunting.

Yet, the more I thought about it, the more the idea took root. It was risky, but it was also an opportunity to finally follow my own path. The uncertainty was scary, but the potential for freedom and fulfilment was tantalizing. I mentally ran the numbers.

I had saved up around $15,000 from my part-time job as a waitress and selling a few art pieces over the past four years. Setting up the gallery would likely cost around $8,000 to $9,000, leaving me with just enough to cover basic living expenses for a couple of months.

It would be tight, but manageable if I was careful. I could find a part-time job to help with the costs, or focus more on selling my art. The thought of taking that leap was both exhilarating and terrifying, but I found myself seriously considering the possibility, even if it meant facing their inevitable disapproval.

As my mother droned on about the Christmas gala and her endless plans, my thoughts drifted until I suddenly caught the mention of Sebastian's name. My attention snapped back, confusion settling in. I interrupted her mid-sentence, "Wait, what did you just say?"

There was a brief pause, and I could almost feel her frustration through the phone. "I was saying," she repeated with a touch of annoyance, "you and Sebastian can go to the gala together. It would be nice to see you two there as a couple."

I felt a sharp pang of hurt, the wound still too fresh, and I let out a bitter, shaky laugh. "Mom, that's not happening. We broke up, and you know that. It's still so recent, and I can't believe you'd suggest something like that." My voice cracked slightly, hurt and frustration spilling over. "It's like you're pretending it never happened, and it's not fair."

My mother scoffed, her voice tinged with impatience. "Oh, Lavinia, don't be dramatic. It's not too late to fix things. How long has it been, really? A couple of weeks?"

I mumbled, correcting her softly, "Actually, it's been three months."

She dismissed my correction with an exasperated sigh. "Three months, three weeks—what's the difference? The breakup never made any sense to me. You two were perfect together. Sebastian is everything a girl could want, and you know he misses you. This isn't something you should throw away so easily. You need to call him and sort this out."

I felt a twinge of guilt, knowing she was right about one thing: Sebastian did miss me. He had made that abundantly clear through the constant stream of texts he sent, telling me how much he regretted everything. Eventually, I had to mute them. I couldn't bear to read them anymore. And then there were the *'I'm sorry'* flowers, the *'let's talk and sort it out'* chocolates, and the most absurd of all—a diamond necklace with a note saying, *'I love you.'* He was trying in the only way he knew how, by throwing gifts and sweet words at the problem.

But none of it could fix the four years of emotional highs and crushing lows. The rollercoaster of a relationship that had drained me. Sebastian's grand gestures felt hollow now, unable to bridge the gap that had grown between us. They were just band-aids on a wound that needed more than material apologies to heal.

My mother's voice took on a persuasive tone, relentless in her push for reconciliation. "Lavinia, you need to consider the bigger picture. Sebastian has been so involved with our family; he's practically part of it already. And now, with his recent promotion at Sterling Enterprises, you'll be seeing a lot of him at work, too."

The mention of his promotion hit me like an icy wave. I hadn't known about it, and the news filled me with a sudden sense of dread. The idea of returning to work and being forced to see him, especially after everything, was suffocating. My mother's words continued, but my mind was already spiralling at the thought of being in such close proximity to Sebastian, day in and day out. It was like a trap I hadn't even realized was being set around me.

She paused, as if to let that sink in, before continuing. "You know, Sterling Enterprises has just signed a major partnership agreement with Carlisle Enterprises. It's a strategic alliance that will have the two companies working closely on several projects. Your father has been planning this for years, ever since you and Sebastian started dating. The idea was always for the two of you to eventually get married, which would make the merger of our businesses seamless and beneficial for both families. It makes perfect sense, Lavinia. You two were meant to be together, both personally and professionally."

Her words weighed heavily on me, highlighting the long-established expectations. Sebastian had been working under his father, learning the ropes with the aim of one day taking over the family business. It was all part of a grand plan—two powerful families merging. not just in their personal lives, but with their similar business empires. In their eyes, my relationship with Sebastian wasn't just a love story, it was a strategic move. A way to solidify alliances and ensure mutual success.

Taking a deep breath, I tried to voice my feelings, though my voice was still timid. "What if I don't want any of that, Mom?"

She laughed. A light, dismissive sound. "Don't be ridiculous, darling. Of course, you do."

Her casual dismissal stung, a familiar pain that sparked anger deep within me. For years, my parents had dismissed my desires, and I had often let it slide for the sake of keeping the peace. But this time, something felt different. My mother continued, seemingly oblivious to my rising frustration.

"Sebastian's mother agrees with me. She thinks this breakup is just a silly phase. We all do. You're just going through something and, once you're back, everything will be fine again."

I clenched the phone tighter, trying to keep my voice steady. "Mom, Sebastian and I weren't working. We had different goals, and it wasn't fair to either of us. I need to figure things out on my own. This isn't just a break, it's a break*up*, and I need you to understand that."

She continued as if I hadn't spoken. "Sebastian is a great catch, Lavinia. At your age, I was already married and expecting you. Maybe your father and I have been too lenient, letting you pursue that art degree and giving you too much freedom. Perhaps that's why you're acting this way."

Her words felt like a slap, the blame on my choices and passions cutting deep. I gritted my teeth, trying to maintain my composure. "Mom, I—"

"Maybe I should talk to Sebastian's family. We're seeing them for dinner next week, and they might help you see reason. You're clearly not thinking straight. You can't just walk away from this."

The pressure in my chest built until it was unbearable. "Just stop!" I yelled, my voice echoing in the quiet cottage. The silence that followed was heavy, my mother's stunned reaction palpable even through the phone. There was a muffled sound as she likely covered the receiver, and I heard the click of a door closing. It was a familiar move, masking any sign of discord in front of others.

"Well," she finally said, her voice trembling slightly, "things must be worse than I thought. I've never heard you speak to me like this before."

"You weren't listening to me. You never do," I said, my voice strained with frustration and hurt. "It seems like you care more about appearances, and your social circle, than your own daughter."

"Darling—" my mother began, but I cut her off.

"No, let me finish. If you knew me at all, if we actually had a two-sided conversation, you would've seen how miserable I was with Sebastian. This past year was *hell*! You were too busy with your friends, or at those fancy dinners with Dad, to notice me coming home in tears because Sebastian stood me up again. At your galas, you were so obsessed with keeping up appearances that you missed the nasty comments from Sebastian's friends, the ones who made me feel like I didn't belong!"

I sighed, the anger easing into a weary sadness. "You knew I was seeing a therapist. You paid for it! But you never asked why. It was because of Sebastian, and partly because of you and Dad. I felt alone and depressed. I was so isolated, without friends of my own—just the same social circles as Sebastian. He didn't like the girls I met in college, and he always made me cancel plans with them. I was so lonely, and all I wanted was for you to notice, to be there for me, but you weren't."

The silence on the other end was deafening. Then, in a defensive tone, she said, "Well, how was I supposed to know? You should have told me. It's not my fault I didn't know."

The dismissal in her words stung, but I could hear a crack, a sliver of doubt. Still, it wasn't enough. I needed to end this before I broke down completely. "I have to go. There's a town meeting I need to attend."

"A town meeting?" she scoffed. "How quaint."

"Goodbye, Mom," I said, trying to wrap up the conversation, but she cut me off.

"Just think about what I said, Lavinia," she pressed, her voice softer but still insistent. "This doesn't have to be like this. We can fix everything when you come home."

A wave of exhaustion washed over me. "Sure, Mom."

"Call me again soon," she continued, her tone regaining its composed edge. "And maybe your father can join us. We need to have a serious discussion about your future."

The thought of a conversation with my father made my stomach churn. Our talks were always stiff, like a formal evaluation. "Okay," I mumbled, just wanting the call to end.

As I finally hung up, a heavy silence filled the room. Despite the tension and frustration from the conversation, a strange sense of relief washed over me. For the first time, I had stood up to my mother, expressing my true feelings rather than keeping them bottled up. Letting out all that frustration felt like a release and, for a moment, I felt lighter.

The idea of opening the gallery had been a mere fantasy, but after standing my ground, it felt more like a tangible possibility. I knew it wouldn't be easy, especially breaking the news to my parents, but the decision filled me with nervous excitement and determination. I had time to prepare for the inevitable confrontation, to find the right words and muster the courage. For now, the thought of pursuing something that was entirely my own was intoxicating.

The town meeting, which I'd originally used as a convenient excuse to escape the call, suddenly felt like a crucial next step. If I was serious about staying in Hallow's End and opening a gallery, I needed to immerse myself in the community. The meeting was an opportunity to connect with the people here, to understand the town better, and to plant the seeds of my new life.

I grabbed my coat and headed out the door. It was time to make my own choices and take control of my future, starting tonight.

Chapter 5

I T WASN'T HARD TO FIND the town hall, especially since Ivy had pointed it out earlier during our walk-through town. The building's sturdy stone façade was easy to spot in the evening light, its intricate carvings subtly highlighted. The tall arched windows, softly glowing from within, cast a warm and inviting light onto the cobblestone streets. As I approached, the elegant wrought iron details on the heavy oak door caught my eye, adding a timeless charm to the historic structure.

Inside, rows of neatly arranged wooden benches faced a small stage with a well-worn podium. The warm lighting accentuated the dark wooden beams overhead, enhancing the welcoming atmosphere. Framed photographs and memorabilia lined the walls, each telling a piece of the town's rich history.

There were sepia-toned portraits of the town's founding families, candid snapshots of community events like parades and fairs, and old newspaper clippings celebrating local milestones. One area displayed medals and ribbons from various town competitions, while another showcased vintage tools and artifacts, a nod to the town's early industries. These displays weren't just décor, they represented the shared stories and deep connections that made Hallow's End a tight-knit community.

I spotted Ivy near the front, her smile lighting up as soon as she saw me, and she waved me over, scooting to make room on the bench.

"I saved you a seat, just in case," she said with a knowing grin. "Had a feeling you might end up coming."

With a grateful smile, I slid onto the bench next to Ivy. "I decided last minute. I wasn't sure if I'd make it on time."

"Better late than never. You didn't miss anything, don't worry." Ivy chuckled softly and added, "Margaret isn't exactly known for her punctuality."

I was about to ask Ivy who Margaret was when a tall woman with striking silver hair and a commanding presence stepped up to the podium. She tapped the microphone, drawing everyone's attention. Curious, I leaned over to Ivy and whispered, "Who's that?"

Ivy leaned in, whispering back, "That's Margaret Hale. She's our mayor, and a superb one. She's very dedicated to the town and its people."

"Good evening, everyone. Thank you for coming," Margaret began, her voice strong and steady. "I'd like to start by welcoming Lavinia Carlisle, who is visiting our town for a few weeks. It's great to see her taking an interest in our community and attending a meeting, something we rarely see from visitors."

Caught off guard, I felt my cheeks flush as all eyes turned to me. The sudden attention was mortifying. Forcing a smile, I gave an awkward wave. Beside me, Ivy chuckled, amused by my discomfort.

"Welcome, Vinnie!" someone called from the back. I nodded awkwardly. The unexpected warmth of the reception made me feel more at ease, but I was sure my face was now a shade of red that matched the autumn leaves outside.

"Now, let's talk about the upcoming Spooktacular Hallow's Eve festival," Mayor Hale continued with enthusiasm. "This is a cherished tradition in Hallow's End, and we have some exciting plans this year."

Relief washed over me as the focus shifted away from me. It was a welcome distraction, and I found myself interested in hearing about the festival.

"The haunted trail is fully planned out in Ravenwood Park," Margaret announced, her excitement contagious. "We've decided on a new location for the pumpkin-carving contest this year, closer to the main square, for better accessibility. And if anyone would like to volunteer at the first-aid station, there's a sign-up sheet on the notice board at the back. We could use a few more hands to help out."

She continued with updates on various activities and events, each detail sparking a bit more excitement in the room. The atmosphere was light and filled with anticipation, making it clear just how much this festival meant to the town. Mayor Hale smiled, visibly satisfied with the response.

"And don't forget about the famous apple pie contest," she said with a twinkle in her eye. "It's one of the highlights of the festival, and we need some new participants this year to keep the tradition alive. Last year's winner, Carl, has held the title for three years running. It's about time someone steps up to give him a run for his money, so we can crown a new champion," she chuckled, glancing around the room, her tone light and encouraging. The audience responded with laughs and murmurs, clearly enjoying the friendly competition.

Ivy nudged me playfully. "You should enter the contest," she whispered with a grin. "I do every year, but I'm absolutely terrible at baking. Last year, my pie had a soggy middle, and a crust that was burned to a crisp—pretty much charcoal." She laughed, not the least bit embarrassed by the disaster.

I laughed along, shaking my head. "Trust me, if I entered, I'd probably set the kitchen on fire before I even got to the pie part. My baking skills are non-existent. The last time I tried to make cookies, I ended up with something resembling hockey pucks."

Ivy burst out laughing, her eyes sparkling with amusement. "Well, that makes two of us! Maybe we should team up and make a disaster pie together," she joked. "At least we'd win for the most . . . unique entry. It's all about having fun, right?"

I grinned, shaking my head. "Sounds like a plan. We could call it *The Pie That Shouldn't Be*. At least we'd give everyone a good laugh." The idea of participating, even as a joke, was surprisingly appealing. It felt good to share a moment of levity, and I appreciated Ivy's easy-going nature.

Yet, her suggestion stirred a memory of Sebastian, and suddenly, I was back in that cozy kitchen on a rainy afternoon.

Sebastian stood at the counter, sleeves rolled up, expertly rolling out dough. His dark blonde hair, slightly tousled, had a dusting of flour over it that highlighted the warm beige tone of his skin. With his sleeves pushed up, the muscles in his forearms flexed as he worked, showcasing the definition and strength that made him effortlessly attractive.

"We have to do this right," he insisted, a playful smile revealing a charming dimple. *"My grandmother's recipe is all about precision."* His focus and light-heartedness as he looked at me were captivating, drawing me in with his effortless charm.

The scent of apples and cinnamon filled the air, warm and inviting. I watched him with amusement and admiration as he moved gracefully around the kitchen. He handed me a bowl of peeled apples, already coated in sugar and spices. *"Your turn,"* he said, grinning. *"Just layer them in carefully."*

As I layered the apples into the pie crust, Sebastian hovered close, his presence comforting and electrifying. His tall, six-foot-four frame towered over my more delicate build, enveloping me in a heady mix of warmth and intensity. I could feel the heat of his body as he leaned in, pressing me gently against the counter. His nearness made it hard to focus, especially when he reached out to push a stray strand of my dark hair behind my ear. His lips brushed against the nape of my neck, sending a shiver down my spine, and causing me to momentarily forget about the pie altogether.

"Not bad," he murmured, stepping back to admire our work, a satisfied gleam in his eyes. The subtle brush of his kiss lingered on my skin, a sweet distraction that made my heart race. He had a way of making even the simplest moments feel charged and special, and I found myself getting lost in the sensation of his closeness.

As we finished layering the apples and prepared to put the pie in the oven, Sebastian playfully flicked a bit of flour at me. I gasped and retaliated, quickly escalating into a full-on flour fight. Laughter filled the kitchen as we tossed flour at each other, the room becoming a snowy chaos of white powder. Amid our playful banter, Sebastian suddenly pulled me close, his lips capturing mine in a passionate kiss. For a moment, the pie was forgotten, and all that existed was the heat between us.

The kiss was electrifying, a fusion of lingering joy and a hidden longing. His hands were firm on my waist, drawing me closer, while mine tangled in his flour-dusted hair. It was a spontaneous and unguarded moment, free from the usual complexities that often hung over us.

❋ ❀ ✻ ❋ ● ❀ ✿ ❧ ❀ ● ❀ ✿ ❋ ❀ ✿ ❧ ❦ ❋

Lost in the memory, I almost missed Ivy's curious gaze. "You okay, Vinnie?"

I shook off the lingering sadness and managed a smile. "Yeah, I'm okay."

Mayor Hale's words broke through my thoughts. "Remember, everyone, the Halloween festival is a joint effort. It's an opportunity for us to gather, celebrate our traditions, and create new memories. Let's make this year's festival one to remember."

As the meeting continued, various concerns and suggestions were discussed. "Next up for discussion, is the matter of our town's declining revenue," Mayor Hale stated, her expression becoming more solemn. "We need to find ways to boost it without compromising our values."

An older gentleman stood up, frustration evident in his voice. "We've all seen those leaflets from Carlisle Enterprises, promising to revitalize our town by opening a chain store. They claim it'll boost revenue and bring more business, but we can't let them come in and change what makes Hallow's End special. These constant mailings are becoming annoying, and we need to put a stop to it."

He paused, glancing around the room. "We know what they really want—pushing out our local shops, and replacing them with generic stores. Just look at Brookside. They swooped in with promises of development, and now all the unique, independent businesses are gone, replaced by chains. If we let them do the same here, we'll lose the charm and character that make our town unique. We need to stand up for our community and support our local businesses, not let some corporate giant homogenize our town."

As he spoke, a wave of discomfort washed over me. I shifted in my seat, avoiding eye contact, and hoping to blend into the background. My father's influence was clearly being felt here, and the mention of that made my stomach churn. *Does everyone read the news these days?* I thought, feeling exposed.

The man's description of the company's tactics—constant mailings and grand promises—sounded more like hounding. That wouldn't be surprising. My father's business style had always been about aggressive pursuit. *"Promise big, deliver bigger, and never take no for an answer."* It was practically the family motto, drilled into me from a young age. Hearing the impact of those methods on this community left me feeling conflicted. I knew how his strategies worked, but seeing the negative side of them in real life was unsettling.

Growing up, I had only seen the business side—how my father's tactics were designed to expand and dominate the market. But hearing these townspeople voice their concerns made me realize the impact on real lives and communities. It was jarring to witness firsthand how something that was just another business move for my father, could feel like a threat to the fabric of a town like Hallow's End.

Murmurs of agreement rippled through the room. A middle-aged woman with a worried expression added, "John's right. The chain store promises revenue, but at what cost?"

As I listened, a knot tightened in my stomach. I knew exactly how Carlisle Enterprises operated. My father's company specialized in acquiring undervalued properties and struggling businesses in small towns. They promised redevelopment and revitalization, using chain stores as anchors to draw in more foot traffic. It was a lucrative model—buy low, rebrand, and sell or lease at a significant profit.

But the reality was often far from the ideal they sold. The same homogenized stores that could be found anywhere pushed out unique local businesses, all in the name of maximizing profit, often at the expense of the community's character and spirit.

Mayor Hale raised her hands to calm the crowd. "I understand your concerns, Margie, truly. The town council has been aware of the situation, and has been in discussions about it. We haven't made any decisions regarding the free land and properties yet and, as I've advised before, no one is obligated to accept any deals they offer. Yes, the leaflets and constant calls to small businesses can be concerning, but I assure you that we're addressing it, and exploring other ways to improve revenue."

"Is that the same Margie who owns Willow Cottage?" I whispered to Ivy.

She nodded with a small smile. "Yeah, that's her. She just got back earlier today from visiting her family in Brookside. She's always been vocal in town matters."

A younger man, perhaps in his early thirties, chimed in, "What if we find alternative ways to boost our revenue? We could promote more local events, or create attractions that draw visitors, without compromising our town's identity."

Mayor Hale nodded thoughtfully. "That's a great idea, Scott. Council has been brainstorming similar approaches."

Ivy leaned in closer to me and whispered, "This discussion has been going on for weeks now, but we've made little progress. Everyone's worried about the town's future, but finding a solution is tough."

The weight of my family's legacy hung heavily over me, adding to my uncertainty about fitting in here. Seeing the genuine concern these people had for their town made me feel even more strongly about separating myself from Carlisle Enterprises. The idea of staying in Hallow's End, and making my own path became more appealing, especially now that I was getting to know the people, and experiencing the tight-knit, supportive nature of the community. It felt like a world away from the cold business strategies I grew up with, and the last thing I wanted was to be associated with disrupting such a close and caring town.

As the room quieted down, Ivy glanced at me, then stood up, her voice clear and confident. "Let's not forget," she began, "we have a thriving, dynamic community here. Supporting each other, and promoting local talents and businesses, is the heart of Hallow's End. If we focus on that, we can find solutions that protect what we love about this town without compromising its essence." She paused, her eyes scanning the room. "We've faced challenges before, and we've always come through stronger. Let's keep pushing forward together."

The space filled with a chorus of supportive murmurs and nods. Mayor Hale smiled at Ivy, appreciating her words. "Thank you, Ivy. It's voices like yours that remind us of the importance of unity and creativity. As always, we're committed to keeping our community informed and involved in the decision-making process."

She paused, looking around the room. "We want to hear from all of you. If you have ideas or concerns, please share them. We've set up a suggestion box at the entrance—feel free to drop in your thoughts anonymously, if you prefer. We also have forms available for more detailed feedback. Your input is invaluable, and together, we can find the best path forward for Hallow's End."

Mayor Hale moved on to the next item on the agenda, her tone more relaxed. "Now, let's discuss the upcoming charity bake sale. We're aiming to raise funds to renovate the town playground. We're still looking for volunteers to bake and help out on the day of the event."

A few hands shot up, and someone joked about Carl needing to bring his award-winning pie to the bake sale. This sparked a few laughs and light-hearted comments.

Next, a young woman with purple hair in the front row spoke up about organizing a community garden. "We've been talking about starting one for a while," she said. "It would be a great way to bring everyone together, and provide fresh produce for those in need."

As soon as she finished, a man stood up. "Speaking of gardens," he said, voice tinged with frustration, "the veggie thief struck again! I swear, I had five pumpkins yesterday, but when I was watering this morning, there were only four. And don't get me started on the carrots—gone without a trace!"

A collective groan mixed with chuckles rippled through the room. A few people rolled their eyes, murmuring, "Here he goes again," while others stifled laughter. Ivy leaned over to me, whispering with a wry smile, "Like clockwork."

I stifled a giggle, whispering back, "I thought you were exaggerating. Does he always think someone's out to get his garden?"

Ivy nodded, her eyes twinkling. "Every single meeting."

Mayor Hale, clearly accustomed to Danny's regular complaints, addressed him with a patient smile. "Thank you, Danny. We're aware of the ongoing issue, and we're looking into ways to help prevent these . . . incidents," she said, her tone a blend of sincerity and gentle amusement.

Danny sat back, still muttering about his disappearing pumpkins and pilfered carrots. "She says that every time."

Ivy leaned closer once more, her voice low and amused. "Poor Danny, he's convinced there's a vegetable conspiracy."

twisted closer, their voices low and intimate. Theo Vance had assumed they'd regarded each other

Chapter 6

A S THE MEETING CAME TO A CLOSE, the room filled with friendly chatter. People seemed in no hurry to leave, instead lingering to catch up with neighbors and discuss the evening's topics. It was clear this was as much a social event as it was a meeting, with everyone enjoying the chance to connect.

Not quite comfortable enough to join in the post-meeting conversations, and wary of any further mention of my father's business, I quietly slipped out. The cool night air greeted me, refreshing and crisp.

A sense of calm washed over me as I took in the scene: the stars twinkling brightly in the clear night sky, the occasional hoot of an owl echoing in the distance. It was a stark contrast to the city nights in Cresden, where the skyline was always lit up, masking the stars, and the constant hum of traffic replaced any chance of hearing nature.

"Hey, Vinnie," Ethan called out, his voice warm and inviting. I turned to see him strolling over, looking attractive in a flannel shirt that fit him just right. His sleeves were rolled up, showing off his toned forearms, and his dark jeans with sturdy boots gave him a rugged, approachable vibe.

"Hi, Ethan," I said, trying not to stare too much. He had a way of making casual look incredibly attractive.

"So, how did you find the meeting?" he asked, his eyes twinkling with curiosity.

I gave a small, uncertain laugh, trying to find the right words. "It was . . . intense," I finally said, then added with a grin, "But Danny's rant about the veggie thief was definitely entertaining."

Ethan chuckled, his laugh rich and contagious. "Yeah, Danny's a character. Most of us think the *thief* is just a bunch of raccoons with a taste for fresh veggies."

I giggled at the image. "Honestly, that sounds pretty plausible."

A sudden gust swept through the square, causing a speck of dirt to fly into my eye. I blinked and rubbed at it, wincing slightly.

"Hold still," Ethan said softly, stepping closer. He peered into my eye, a concerned expression crossing his face. "Looks like an eyelash," he murmured, his voice gentle. His fingers brushed my cheek, carefully coaxing the tiny eyelash away. His touch radiated a gentle heat, lingering a moment longer than necessary. The warmth of his breath mingled with the cool evening air, creating a charged silence between us. It felt like we were the only ones there, wrapped in an intimate bubble.

"Thanks," I whispered, meeting his gaze. His smile was gentle, but there was an unmistakable spark in his eyes that made my heart race. The concern in his eyes softened into something warmer, more magnetic. His lips curved into a slight, teasing smile as he leaned in just a fraction closer, the air between us thick with unspoken anticipation.

"No problem," he murmured, his voice low. Realizing how close he was, Ethan stepped back with a playful grin. "Didn't mean to invade your personal space," he joked, his tone light.

As he stepped back, I felt a sudden emptiness where his warmth had been, a chill creeping in to replace it. My heart, which had been racing, slowed, leaving a fluttery sensation in my chest. Even with the distance, I could still catch the scent of his cologne, a mix of woodsy notes and a fresh citrusy hint that lingered in the air. The moment was brief, but it left a lingering sense of excitement, and a surprising desire for more of that closeness.

Ethan cleared his throat, breaking the comfortable silence that had settled between us. "So, I've been hearing some rumors," he began with a playful grin. "Word around town is that you're thinking about opening an art gallery. News travels fast in Hallow's End."

I couldn't help but laugh at that. "I'm not surprised. Small towns and their grapevines, right? But I wouldn't say I'm opening anything just yet. I've just been looking around, seeing if it might be a possibility."

He nodded, his eyes gleaming with interest. "That's exciting. We don't have anything like that here, and honestly, it's something the town could really use. My students would love it—getting out of the classroom and seeing some real art. They could use a cultural day out."

His mention of students piqued my curiosity. "Wait, are you an art teacher?"

Ethan chuckled, shaking his head. "No, I don't have the eye or the patience for that. I can appreciate art, but teaching it? Let's just say I prefer *not* to inflict my terrible drawing skills on anyone." He grinned. "I teach English and literature. I love helping students dive into stories and discover the magic of words. That's where my passion lies—guiding them through new worlds and watching their faces light up when they connect with a book."

As he spoke, I found myself imagining him in a classroom, standing confidently at the front, his sleeves rolled up just enough to reveal his strong forearms. I could picture him gesturing animatedly as he explained a classic novel, his deep voice filling the room with excitement and passion. The thought of him captivating a room full of students with his charm and enthusiasm made him even more attractive, his arms moving gracefully as he wrote on the board, each stroke deliberate and sure. It was easy to see why his students would be drawn to his classes.

I smiled, pulled from my daydream. "That sounds really fulfilling, helping kids find their voices through literature." I paused, glancing around at the empty street before looking back at him. "Are your parents teachers, too?"

Ethan nodded, a fond smile spreading across his face. "Yeah, they both taught at Hallow's End Elementary before they retired." He hesitated, then continued with a chuckle, "We were all in one house for so long, including my little sister, Lily, who's six now. It was getting a bit crowded."

I tilted my head, intrigued. "Did you live with them the whole time?"

"Actually, I moved out of the family home when they retired early about two years ago. My mom wasn't thrilled about me leaving the nest, but at twenty-five, I was ready for my own space, especially with the new job. Though I still just live down the street, so I'm not too far." He grinned. "I guess I can't escape home that easily."

"That sounds really nice," I said, genuinely touched by the close-knit nature of his family. It was a stark contrast to my own experiences, and a part of me wished I had that kind of warm, uncomplicated relationship with my own parents. Ethan's life seemed filled with the happy, familial connections I craved. It made me wonder what it would be like to have that kind of support and closeness.

As we stood there, people finally began filtering out of the town hall, done with their socializing for the night. I smiled. "I guess the meeting is over now, huh?"

Ethan chuckled, glancing around as the last few people trickled out of the town hall. "Looks like the excitement's winding down," he said, shifting his weight slightly, his hands slipping into his pockets. There was a brief pause, and a hint of awkwardness in the air, as if he was searching for something to say to keep the conversation going.

"So . . . what kind of things do you paint?" he asked suddenly, his tone a bit hesitant, almost as if he'd blurted out the first question that came to mind.

I couldn't help but smile, noticing how he was clearly eager to stay and talk, even if it meant asking a random question. It was endearing, and it made me want to keep the conversation going, too

"I mostly paint bold and intense abstract pieces. Playing with colors and textures to evoke emotions is something I love. My work is all about capturing the essence of a moment, or a feeling, rather than something realistic. It's a way for me to express things that are hard to put into words."

"That sounds really cool. I'd love to see your work someday—though, fair warning, I might be terrible at understanding it. You might have to explain it to me like I'm five," he joked, his eyes sparkling with playful sincerity. His genuine warmth made me smile.

Ivy emerged from the town hall with Mayor Hale and Margie, all chatting enthusiastically and, as they drew closer, a wave of disappointment washed over me. I had enjoyed talking with Ethan far more than I expected, and I wasn't quite ready to say goodbye.

"By the way, I'm sorry again about the coffee this morning," I said, feeling a pang of guilt. "I hope I didn't make you late for work or anything."

Ethan chuckled, shaking his head. "No worries. The students thought it was hilarious, though. I had to hide the stain with my sweater all day. Gave them a good laugh, at least."

Out of the corner of my eye, I noticed Mayor Hale saying goodbye to Ivy and Margie. But Ivy lingered, not approaching me yet, giving me a bit of space and privacy with Ethan. Whether or not it was intentional, I appreciated it nonetheless. It felt nice to have a few more moments with him.

Ethan glanced over at Ivy and then back at me.

"I wanted to—" I began.

"Vinnie, I was thinking—" he said, our words overlapping. We both paused, then laughed.

Ethan's gaze softened, a playful intensity in his eyes. With a slight, almost bashful smile, he said, "You know, I really meant it this morning when I said I'd like to see you again."

I felt a blush rising to my cheeks. "I would like that."

Before he could say anything else, Ivy and Margie approached, popping our little bubble. Ivy's eyes twinkled with curiosity, and Margie gave us both a warm smile, as if she had been watching us all along.

"I see you two are getting along well," Ivy said, a mischievous glint in her gaze.

"We were just talking," I said, my voice slightly awkward, my gaze drifting to the floor as I struggled to meet Ivy's eyes.

"Oh, really?" she nudged me playfully.

Margie and Ivy exchanged knowing looks and grinned at each other. Ethan noticed and chuckled. "Well, I've got an early morning."

He paused, his gaze lingering on me for a moment as if considering his next words. He glanced at Ivy and Margie, then back at me. A slight hesitation flickered in his eyes, but then he simply smiled and said, "I'll see you soon, Vinnie."

The air between us felt charged, but Ivy smoothly broke the tension by turning to Margie with a warm smile. "Vinnie, I don't think you've officially met Margie, the owner of Willow Cottage."

Margie stepped forward, her wild red hair catching the light from the streetlamps. She looked to be in her mid-thirties, with kind eyes that shone with a gentle, motherly aura. She extended her hand to me. "It's great to meet you, Vinnie. I'm sorry I wasn't there to greet you when you arrived. Hope you have settled in okay?"

"It's been lovely, thank you." I shook her hand, grateful for the easy shift in conversation. "And no worries, Ivy's been wonderful, and made me feel right at home."

"I'm glad to hear that. Ivy's great at making everyone feel welcome. If you need anything, or have questions, just ask. We're all here to help." She chuckled. "Though, knowing Ivy, she's probably already told you everything you need to know."

Ivy grinned, crossing her arms playfully. "What can I say? I'm thorough."

Margie glanced at her watch and sighed. "I'd love to stay and chat more, but I've got to run. It's my kids' bedtime, and the babysitter has to get home soon." She smiled apologetically. "Mom duties never end, right?"

I nodded, returning her smile. "It was nice to meet you, Margie. I hope to see you around town."

"I'm sure you will," Margie replied with a warm laugh. "This place is small enough that it's hard to miss anyone. Have a great night, Vinnie, and enjoy your stay." With a quick wave, she turned and headed off.

Ivy turned to me. "Want some company on the walk back? The cottage isn't far from my place." I nodded, appreciating the offer.

After a few moments of comfortable silence, Ivy glanced over at me with a slight smile. "So . . . Ethan is nice, yes?" Her tone was casual, but there was a hint of teasing curiosity in her eyes.

I shrugged, a small smile playing on my lips. "I spilled coffee on him at the café this morning. It was a pretty embarrassing way to meet someone, but he was really nice about it."

Ivy nodded, her eyes glinting with playful interest. "He's one of the good ones around here. Solid guy. The kids at school love him, and he's always involved in community events." She paused, giving me a sideways glance. "And he's single, if you're wondering."

I laughed, feeling a bit of a blush creep up. "Noted. But honestly, it's just nice talking to someone who isn't . . . complicated, you know?"

We strolled past the darkened shops of the town square, the twinkling string lights casting a soft glow on the cobblestone streets. Even with the businesses closed, the town kept its charming allure, the lights giving everything a warm, magical feel.

Ivy grinned, nudging me playfully. "You know, Margie and I were talking, and we both thought Ethan seemed pretty interested in you. We didn't want to interrupt, but Margie was eager to meet you."

A blush crept up my cheeks, and I chuckled softly. "It's fine, really."

I thought about the nature of small-town gossip. It was different here—nothing like the catty and malicious rumors that spread in Cresden. This felt more innocent, a kind of harmless curiosity.

We moved through the residential area, where quaint houses lined the street, and I recognized the route as the one I drove through on my first day.

Feeling a bit awkward and unsure, I hesitated before blurting out, "Do you really think he was into me, or was he just being nice?"

Ivy gave me a reassuring smile. "Oh, definitely. Ethan's always polite, but he rarely lingers after town meetings, or shows much interest in the women around here. He's definitely nice, but this was different."

My heartbeat picked up, excitement and nervousness fluttering through me. "Really?"

Ivy leaned in, clearly enjoying the chance to share a bit of town gossip. "You remember Emily?" I nodded, trying to hide my curiosity. "She's been pining for Ethan for years. She's always been very . . . persistent, trying to flirt and catch his attention, but he's never asked her out. Despite all her efforts, it's always just been polite exchanges and nothing more."

Hearing this sparked a curiosity within me. Ethan's apparent disinterest in the women of Hallow's End only made his behavior with me stand out more. Was there really something there, or was I reading too much into it?

Ivy continued, "Ethan's always been a bit of a mystery in that way. The fact that he seemed genuinely interested in talking to you is . . . well, it's notable."

I couldn't help but smile. "Well, he did ask me for coffee."

Ivy's eyes lit up, and she squealed. "That's fantastic! I'm so excited for you."

I laughed, feeling embarrassed. "It's just coffee. We didn't make any actual plans, and he doesn't even have my number."

"Semantics," Ivy said with a dismissive wave of her hand. "Sometimes the most meaningful connections start with just a simple cup of coffee."

As we reached the turn for the cottage, Ivy stopped and smiled. "I live just a bit further down this street," she said, gesturing ahead. She pulled out her phone. "Here, give me your number, and I'll text you mine. We should plan something together soon."

I handed her my phone and, after exchanging numbers, we said our goodbyes. As I walked down the star-lit road towards the cottage, I felt a comforting sense of belonging. It was strange how, in just two days, Hallow's End already felt more like home than Cresden ever had. Maybe it was Ivy's warmth and openness, or perhaps the charm of small-town life itself. Either way, the simplicity and kindness here were a refreshing c hange.

Looking up at the twinkling stars, a rush of possibility washed over me. The idea of dating again made me a little nervous—was I ready? But there was something about being in Hallow's End that made me feel brave and free. I wanted to see Ethan again, and Ivy was right; it was just coffee, and that was a good place to start. Baby steps, I thought, smiling to myself.

Chapter 7

S UNLIGHT FILTERED THROUGH the windows of my cottage, illuminating the art supplies scattered across the floor—paint tubes, brushes, and sketchbooks forming a chaotic circle around me. Yesterday, after the phone call with my mother, I had been on a roll, brimming with confidence and ready to embrace my dreams. The idea of staying in Hallow's End felt not only possible, but right.

But today, I woke up feeling like my old self again. The confidence I'd felt yesterday seemed to have evaporated overnight, leaving me uncertain and questioning my choices all over again. Was I really brave enough to follow through with my dreams? To stay in this small town, away from everything I knew, and carve out a new life for myself?

I sat on the floor, gazing at the empty easel before me. Normally, painting was my escape, and the one thing that always made sense. It grounded me, gave me clarity. But now, as I stared at the untouched canvas, my mind felt as blank as its surface.

I tried to focus on the positive aspects of my new life. I thought about my blossoming friendship with Ivy, the potential art gallery that could be mine, and even the possibility of dating Ethan. It was a beautiful dream—a fresh start, a new chapter filled with creativity and genuine connections. But my thoughts kept drifting back to Cresden and, inevitably, to Sebastian. The small voice in my head was relentless, mocking me with doubts: *It's a nice dream, Vinnie, but it's just a dream. You won't make it a reality.*

I struggled to silence that voice, trying to remember the way Ethan's golden eyes had lit up when I talked about my art. He seemed genuinely interested in me and what I was passionate about. But then, my thoughts would circle back to Sebastian, and how he never really cared for my art. While Ethan's encouragement felt refreshing, it also highlighted the lack of support I'd experienced in my past relationship.

Even as I felt a flutter of excitement thinking about Ethan, there was still a heaviness in my chest from the unresolved feelings surrounding Sebastian. The memories of him were tangled up with the doubts that plagued me. No matter how much I wanted to move on, the wounds from my breakup were still raw. As much as I longed for a new beginning, I couldn't shake the feeling that the past was still holding me back.

The bright red paint dripped from the paintbrush I had picked up, splattering onto the white shirt I was wearing. It was Sebastian's shirt—one of the few remnants of our relationship I couldn't let go of. Even now, it still carried the faintest hint of his cologne, a bittersweet reminder of what we once had. The familiar scent was like a mocking echo, reminding me of the comfort and affection I used to find in his arms, now just a hollow memory.

I groaned and put the paintbrush down, closing my eyes. Normally, the smell of paint would spark a creative fire in me, a rush of inspiration. But today, the fumes, mingling with his lingering scent, felt overwhelming, like they were closing in on me. I opened my eyes, determined not to let these feelings of doubt and regret paralyze me. Art had always been my way to work through emotions too complex to voice.

Picking up the brush again, I dipped it back into the red paint and made a bold, harsh line across the canvas, but it didn't feel right. My thoughts drifted back to the city, where inspiration had always flowed effortlessly. The bustling streets, the ever-changing skyline, and the vibrant energy of Cresden all served as fuel for my creativity. The constant noise and movements were like a symphony that guided my brush. But here in Hallow's End, everything felt too quiet, too stagnant. The tranquillity I had longed for now seemed to stifle my imagination.

Feeling a surge of frustration, I ripped the canvas from the easel and tossed it aside. The usual bold strokes and bright colors just weren't speaking to me—they felt wrong, jarring. I picked up a fresh canvas, determined to try something new, and my eyes fell on a box of paints I hadn't touched in years. The soft pastel tubes sat in neat, untouched rows. They'd never appealed to me before but, today, they seemed to call out. The colors looked soothing, offering a gentle alternative to my usual intensity.

I picked up a fresh palette and squeezed out the pastel hues, watching as the soft pinks, blues, and greens pooled together. *This is right*, a quiet voice inside me whispered, and a small smile played on my lips as I picked up a clean brush and dipped it into the paint. I tried capturing Hallow's End's tranquil beauty—its charm and silent moments, so different from the chaos of my old life.

This fresh approach to my art felt like a way to leave Cresden behind, to forget about the noise and pressure that had suffocated me. But, despite

Hallow's End's charm and beauty, every time I tried to capture its essence on canvas, it didn't work. My attempts to translate the quaint town into art fell flat. The simplicity of this place seemed to drain the colors from my mind, leaving me with a palette of dull shades, and I couldn't understand why it wasn't coming together. The frustration built up inside me, gnawing at my confidence.

Frustrated by my failed attempts to paint from memory—something I'd always excelled at in college—I turned my attention to the scenery outside the cottage window, hoping it would help.

The towering pines swayed gently in the breeze, their deep green needles catching the light like tiny emeralds. Each tree had a unique shape, with branches reaching out like gnarled fingers. The forest floor was a mix of rich browns and muted golds, with fallen leaves scattered among the roots, creating a patchwork of textures.

Beyond the forest, the majestic mountains stood tall, their rugged peaks dusted with the first snow of the season. The snow glistened in the sunlight, a blend of icy whites and soft blues that contrasted beautifully with the darker, shadowed crevices. Mist capped the mountains, adding a dreamlike quality to the scene.

I swiped the brush across the canvas, determined on capturing it. But the stroke felt devoid of any feeling, flat and uninspired. Frustrated, I wiped it away and tried again, and again, each attempt more disheartening than the last. Every time I put brush to canvas, it felt flat, lifeless. The tranquillity of Hallow's End, which should have been a muse, instead felt like a shroud, muting the colours and energy that I longed to express. The creativity that used to flow effortlessly from my hands now felt foreign, wrong, like trying to play an instrument with someone else's hands.

My frustration grew with every failed attempt, the serene landscape taunting me with its unyielding calmness. It was as if my art was still anchored to the urban frenzy, and I didn't know how to tap into this new, tranquil landscape.

My mind began to wander back to Cresden and Sebastian. He was chaotic and unpredictable, and often the spark behind my most inspired works. His solution to everything was spontaneous nights out with friends, filled with drinking, laughter, and mischief. The thrill of those moments, the rush of being swept up in his energy, had often served as my muse. Since the breakup, I hadn't truly painted anything that felt alive. Admitting that, even to myself, was a fear I wasn't ready to face.

The notion ate away at me, a painful reminder that without him, my artistic endeavors might never be the same again. Our breakup had been a shock to Sebastian, a decision that had taken me weeks to muster the courage for. It wasn't just the chaotic nights out that had fuelled my art; it was also the instability and uncertainty of our relationship.

Sebastian was a master of mixed signals—one moment, he was all in, making grand gestures and declarations of love. The next, he was distant, and he thrived on spontaneity, which often left me feeling unsteady and unsure of where we stood.

Then there was the constant pressure to fit into his world. Sebastian thrived in the high-energy circles of Cresden's elite, always rubbing elbows with people who could never understand me or my passion for art. I often felt like an accessory, a background character in his larger-than-life story. Our lives revolved around his social calendar, leaving little room for my own interests and needs.

The final straw came one night when he drunkenly confessed that he saw my art as *just a silly hobby* he entertained in hopes I would eventually outgrow it. It was clear he envisioned me following in my mother's footsteps, hosting dinners and attending charity events, all while abandoning my passion for art.

The first few weeks after the breakup were the hardest. Sebastian had been so integrated into every part of my life that it felt like I couldn't escape him. Both of our families immediately sided with him, conveniently overlooking the real issues. They made endless excuses for his behavior, and *accidentally* orchestrated situations where we'd end up at the same events, all under the guise of giving him a chance to talk to me. It was stressful and exhausting. All I wanted was to mourn our relationship and begin healing, but I couldn't. Despite Cresden being a big city, it was suffocating, like there was nowhere to hide.

Sometimes, even I doubted my decision to break up. There were moments when I questioned if I had been too hasty, if perhaps I had exaggerated the issues. The good times we shared—the laughter, the spontaneous adventures, the way he could make everything seem exciting—those memories were hard to shake. They clouded my judgment, making me second-guess whether I had made the right choice.

On top of that, there was the looming shadow of my parents' expectations. I knew they were disappointed, seeing Sebastian as the perfect partner for their vision of my future. They wanted the seamless blending of two influential families and the stability that came with it. Letting them down added another layer of guilt, making me question if I had been selfish in pursuing what I wanted instead of what was expected.

As these thoughts raced through my mind, I found myself absentmindedly stroking a brush against the canvas, the bristles barely touching the surface. The paint was smeared in soft, meaningless lines, more an expression of my scattered thoughts than any actual attempt at creating art.

Hallow's End was supposed to be a refuge, a place where I could find clarity and maybe even a fresh start. Yet, here I was, still haunted by the past, my thoughts circling back to Cresden and the life I'd left behind.

My confidence wavered, chipped away by years of trying to meet every-one's expectations. I wondered if I could truly stand on my own, or if I had been fooling myself all along. The soft pastel colors on the canvas, painted in my usual bold, abstract style, felt strange and unfamiliar. The gentle hues, applied with my characteristic intense strokes, clashed in a way that mirrored my own mixed emotions. A sad laugh that turned into a sob escaped my lips. It was as if the painting itself was caught in the same uncertain, in-between stage I was in.

Tears brimmed in my eyes as I sat there, clutching the paintbrush. The weight of my insecurities, and the heartbreak I had tried to bury, threat-ened to overwhelm me, and I angrily ripped the canvas from the frame, throwing the brush across the room. My eyes landed on the small table by the window, where my phone lay.

The urge to call Sebastian gnawed at me, despite knowing it wouldn't solve anything. It was a pull, born out of a deep-seated need for comfort and familiarity. The breakup had left me feeling untethered, like a ship adrift without its anchor. Sebastian had been that anchor, my constant during uncertain times.

I thought back to my first year of college, to a particularly painful mem-ory.

It was a cold, gray evening during my first year of college, and the words of my professor stung like a fresh wound: "Your work lacks depth and feeling, Vinnie. While it is technically proficient, it lacks an emotional connection.

It's all too safe, too controlled. Art should evoke something in the viewer, and right now, your pieces just don't."

He had critiqued my latest series—geometric landscapes and meticulously detailed sceneries. I had poured hours into perfecting each line and color, but it still wasn't enough. His words cut deep, leaving me feeling exposed and inadequate.

Desperate and defeated, I called Sebastian. He picked up immediately, his voice warm and soothing. "Hey, what's wrong?"

The tears spilled over as I choked out that I needed to see him. Without hesitation, Sebastian told me to come over. His dorm was just a short walk away, and soon I was knocking on his door, my heart heavy with disappointment.

Sebastian opened the door and immediately pulled me into a comforting hug. "It's okay," he murmured, his hand stroking my back. "Come in."

I sank onto his bed, feeling the weight of the day's events. Between sobs, I explained how the professor had dismissed my work as lacking emotion and depth. Sebastian listened, his jaw tightening in anger. "What a jerk," he muttered, shaking his head. "He has no idea what he's talking about."

After a pause, Sebastian's expression shifted to one of mischievous defiance. "You know what? Maybe you should throw some paint at the canvas," he suggested, a hint of sarcasm in his voice. "Seems like that's all some modern art is these days. Just slap some colors on there and call it a masterpiece."

I looked up at him, a small, disbelieving smile forming despite my tears. "You mean just make a mess?"

He grinned, his eyes lighting up with a playful spark. "Yeah! Why not? Show that professor how wrong he is. Forget all the rules and just . . . go wild."

His words struck a chord, igniting a spark of rebellion in me. "That's actually . . . not a bad idea."

With a shared glance of conspiracy, we decided to sneak into the college art studio, the thrill of breaking the rules adding an exhilarating edge to the night. We found ourselves standing before a large blank canvas, the studio lights casting a soft glow around us. Sebastian grabbed a can of bright red paint and handed it to me. "Go on, show me what you've got."

For a moment, I hesitated. Then, with a surge of emotion, I dipped my hand into the paint and flung it at the canvas. The splash of color felt freeing, a defiant release of all the frustration and anger I had been bottling up. Sebastian joined in, mockingly smearing paint with exaggerated strokes, laughing as we both created a chaotic masterpiece.

We lost track of time, caught up in the rebellious joy of it all. Our clothes were splattered, our hands covered in paint, but we didn't care. We stepped back to admire our work—a wild, abstract explosion of colors and emotions. It was messy, imperfect, and absolutely liberating.

Later, as we lay on the studio floor, our bodies sticky with drying paint and the smell of turpentine in the air, we talked about everything and nothing. The exhilaration of the night still buzzed between us, a shared sense of rebellion and freedom. Eventually, we cleaned up, and snuck back to Sebastian's dorm, laughing softly to ourselves, careful not to wake his roommates.

In the dim light of his bathroom, we stepped into the shower together, the hot water washing away the paint and sweat. The steam enveloped us and, as the paint swirled down the drain, so did the last remnants of my fears and inhibitions. It was there, under the warm spray, that we made love—not for the first time, but it felt different. More intense and raw. It seemed like the paint washed away the last of the walls we had both put up. The vulnerability and passion of the moment was overwhelming, leaving us both breathless and deeply connected.

From that day on, my art changed. The structured, precise lines of my earlier works gave way to bold, chaotic strokes and vivid colors. I no longer feared the judgment of others or the potential mess of failure. Sebastian had helped me embrace the chaos, to express my emotions on the canvas without *restraint. My paintings became a true reflection of my inner world—wild, unpredictable, and deeply felt.*

As I sat in the cottage, lost in the vivid memories of that night, a sudden sharp sound brought me back to the present. The wind had picked up outside, causing a tree branch to tap persistently against the windowpane.

I was left with a bittersweet ache from the memory of that night. For a moment, all the reasons I had for leaving Sebastian seemed to blur, overwhelmed by the longing for the comfort and passion we once shared. It was as if all the bad stuff—the neglect, the dismissive comments about my art—faded away, leaving only the warmth of his encouragement and the thrill of our rebellious adventure. My hand instinctively reached for my phone on the table, the urge to hear his voice, to feel that connection again, almost overpowering.

We hadn't spoken since my mother's birthday a few weeks ago, and the conversation had been stiff and polite, tinged with the awkwardness of our unresolved breakup. Sebastian had made small talk, trying to find a way to connect, but I kept my responses short, not wanting to give him any false hope. It was clear he wanted to fix things, to go back to the way things were, but I couldn't pretend that everything was fine. The weight of our shared history, and the expectations from both our families, made every word feel like a minefield. I quickly excused myself, sneaking away from the party, not wanting to confront the reality of our broken relationship.

That night, I felt the overwhelming need to escape the pressure and confusion that had become my life in Cresden. I realized I needed to get away, to find a place where I could think and breathe without constant reminders of what others expected of me. That was how I decided on Hallow's End—a place where I could start fresh, away from the complications of my old life.

I scrolled to his name in my contacts, pausing as his picture appeared on the screen. It was a goofy selfie he had set as his contact photo when we first started dating—his attempt at making me laugh during one of our dates. My finger hovered over the call button. It was a dangerous temptation, a pull towards the familiar comfort and chaos he represented.

I never told Sebastian I was leaving, but I knew my mother had likely informed him. The day I was supposed to leave, a package arrived at my door—a gift from Sebastian. He always had a flair for grand gestures, and this was no exception. Inside was an expensive leather travel journal, embossed with my initials, and a set of high-quality sketching pencils. It was thoughtful, almost too perfect, like he was trying to cover all the bases. But it felt wrong, like a gift from a stranger who didn't truly understand what I needed. I left the journal behind, unopened, as if doing so would sever the lingering ties between us.

If only it were that easy.

His messages and calls were still muted on my phone, the notifications piling up like tiny ghosts haunting my screen. I never opened them, afraid of what I might find. His apologies, his pleas, his attempts to pull me back into his orbit. The allure of those unopened messages was a constant temptation, especially in moments of weakness, but blocking him felt like a step I wasn't ready to take. A final severance that was too daunting to confront. The fear of truly cutting him out of my life kept me tethered, even as I tried to move forward.

I wondered if he still thought about me, if he missed us as much as I sometimes missed the comfort of what we had. I imagined what it would be like to hear my name on his lips again, the familiar honey of his voice washing over me. The thought of his touch, the way he knew exactly how to make me feel needed, pulled at my heart.

But a new fear crept in—what if he had started to move on? I had ignored his calls and messages for weeks. What if, in my absence, he had given up on us? The idea that he might have found a way to move forward without me, despite his efforts to reconnect, made me hesitate. I knew it was selfish, to want him to still chase after me, to hope he might change and become the partner I needed. It made little sense, yet the thought lingered. My finger hovered over the call button, paralyzed by the possibility of both hope and heartbreak.

The idea of calling him felt too daunting, too final. Instead, I decided to text him, a safer, less intimidating step. I unmuted his notifications and my thumb hesitated over the screen as I opened our chat, skipping over the numerous unread messages he'd sent. My eyes caught on the last one, simple but full of weight.

> **Sebastian:** When you're ready to talk, I'll be here.

That message made my chest tighten. Despite everything, he was still waiting. Taking a deep breath, I started typing, the words coming slowly, hesitantly, as I tried to figure out what to say. How to bridge the gap between us.

Hey, Sebastian. It's Vinnie. I was just thinking about—I deleted it.

Sebastian, I miss—Delete.

I don't know why I'm writing this—Delete.

Nothing felt right, nothing captured the turmoil in my heart. My head knew better, reminding me that we were truly over, but my heart hadn't caught up yet. The pull was almost addictive, a craving for the comfort his voice once brought. Sniffling, I wiped my face roughly. In a moment of weakness, I surrendered to the impulse and pressed the call button.

The line rang once.

My heart pounded, and I wondered if he would even pick up.

Was he busy? Did he see my name and hesitate?

It rang twice.

I clenched the phone tightly, anxiety building with each passing second.

What would I even say if he answered?

It rang three times.

Panic set in.

Why am I doing this? Why was I calling him after all this time?

My finger hovered over the END CALL button, debating whether to hang up and pretend this never happened.

Then, the call went to voicemail. His voice, cheerful and familiar, brought me back to reality.

"Hey, it's Sebastian. Sorry I missed you. Leave a message, and I'll get back to you."

The beep echoed in the silence, and I dropped the call, the reality of my situation crashing down on me.

What was I doing?

This was stupid.

I let the phone slip from my hand, tears streaming down my face and soaking into the shirt. How could a single text leave me feeling so undone?

I sat there, the weight of my choice pressing down on me. A mistake born from a moment of weakness. This wasn't the way forward. It was a step back. A regression into a past I needed to let go of. My breaths came in shallow gasps. I wanted to move on, to build a new life here, but my heart was still tethered to a world that no longer existed.

Breaking up had seemed like the hard part, but the aftermath was proving even tougher. The reality of moving on was far more challenging than I had anticipated. Breakups sucked. They tore at the soul, leaving scars that didn't heal easily. I'd been avoiding my therapist, cancelling all sessions because I didn't want to deal with this pain. Suppressing it all had seemed easier at the time, but now it was boiling over, overwhelming me with a vengeance.

After what felt like hours, I finally took a deep, steadying breath, my chest aching from the sobs. This wasn't the end. It was a beginning—a painful, messy beginning, but a beginning nonetheless.

Chapter 8

T HE SOFT RUSTLE OF WIND outside my window stirred me awake, infusing a sense of calm into the morning. My small bedroom, with its rustic wooden furniture and quilted bedspread, radiated a warm, homey feel, and sunlight filtered through the lace curtains, casting gentle patterns on the walls. The once unfamiliar bed now felt like a comforting embrace, and the tranquillity of Hallow's End was slowly but surely soothing my city-tuned nerves.

At the start of the week, I'd felt overwhelmed by everything. Just arriving in Hallow's End had been a whirlwind and, after struggling to paint, I felt sad and homesick, missing the city's constant hum of energy. That day had left me feeling lost, and I spent the rest of the week letting myself cry and process all the emotions I'd been suppressing. It was a much-needed step forward.

I kept to myself during the week, needing the solitude to work through my thoughts. This was, after all, supposed to be a holiday. Ivy, ever kind and welcoming, texted me every few days to check in, and our conversations were light and easy, a gentle way to build the beginnings of a friendship. She didn't push, respecting my need for space, but her presence was a comforting reminder that I wasn't alone in this little town.

Throughout the week, I spent a lot of time painting, experimenting with new colors and strokes. It was different from my usual style, but the act itself was soothing, offering a semblance of normalcy. The paintings were strange and unfamiliar, but they represented a motion towards something new, something that felt necessary.

Last night, Ivy had come over with a tub of ice cream. We watched movies and laughed, our shared company easy and relaxed. It wasn't a deep conversation, but it was comforting to have someone there, sharing the space with me.

During this week, I also took practical steps toward figuring out my next move. I sorted through my finances, making a plan for the potential gallery. A list of next steps now sat on the kitchen counter, a tangible reminder of the future I could create. Yet, I still wasn't entirely sure I could go through with it. The fear of failure and the weight of my parents' expectations loomed large, but at least I felt somewhat prepared for when they inevitably called.

This week had been a time to breathe, to process, and to begin the slow work of moving forward. Now, on this fresh Monday morning, I was determined to make the most of it. It was time to get dressed and face the world outside.

I rummaged through my closet, searching for an outfit that would blend in with the town's vibe, while still flaunting my city style. Ivy had promised to take me shopping this week if I was up for it, and I was looking forward to it.

I pulled on dark skinny jeans, a soft cream sweater with lace details, and stylish ankle boots. As I looked in the mirror, I sighed. The outfit looked nice but felt a bit off, like I was trying too hard to fit in.

With a final glance in the mirror, I grabbed my bag, eager to explore the town's quirky, independent shops. I'd been thinking about them all week, curious to see what treasures they held. Ivy had mentioned she'd be at the Enchanted Quill, and suggested we grab lunch together during her break. I smiled at the thought, looking forward to catching up with her. It felt good to be excited about something again.

I grabbed my phone and keys, ready to head out, when my phone rang. I glanced at the screen and saw an unknown number. Curious, I answered.

"Hey, it's Ethan," came the familiar voice, slightly nervous but warm. "Hope you don't mind that I asked Ivy for your number. I didn't see you around town this week and, uh, just wanted to check in."

A smile crept onto my face, my heart fluttering. "Hi, Ethan. No worries. It's nice to hear from you."

He continued, speaking a bit too quickly, "Yeah, sorry I didn't reach out sooner. It's been kind of crazy. You know, work and stuff. And then, this weekend I was helping my dad with his garden shed. The thing's like, this old relic that's somehow still standing, but barely. We were fixing it up, and I'm pretty sure we spent more time laughing at how it's a miracle it hasn't fallen apart yet." Ethan laughed nervously. "Sorry, I'm going off on a tangent, aren't I? I'm usually not this nervous. I just didn't want you to think I was ignoring you after asking you out."

His rambling was endearing, and I couldn't help but chuckle. It was clear he was flustered, which only made him more charming. "It's cute, really," I reassured him, then immediately cringed, wondering if I was coming on too strong. Quickly, I cleared my throat and added, "I mean, it's fine. Life gets busy."

In the background, I could hear kids shouting, likely his students. "Anyway," he continued, clearly trying to focus, "I was wondering if you're free today for that coffee? I'm finishing around noon, and The Sunflower Bistro makes an amazing latte. No pressure, but I thought it could be nice."

I could practically hear him holding his breath, waiting for my response. "That sounds perfect," I said with a thrill of excitement. "Noon works for me."

"Awesome! Great! I'll see you then," he replied, relief and happiness evident in his voice. A bell rang in the background, and he hurriedly added. "I should get back to class now. The kids are . . . well, you know," he let out a small laugh.

"See you at twelve," I said.

As soon as I ended the call, anticipation surged through me. After a week of moping and wallowing in my emotions, something in me had shifted. I was tired of feeling sad and uncertain, of being weighed down by the past. Now, I wanted to be this new version of myself—confident, bold, and ready to take on whatever came my way.

Maybe it was the idea of a fresh start in a new town, or maybe it was the thrill of someone like Ethan showing interest in me. But it felt good, like a shot of adrenaline. I was ready to put myself out there and take risks, even if it was just for a simple coffee date. It felt liberating, like a chance to prove to myself that I could move on and start anew.

After spending the morning exploring the town, I found myself standing outside The Sunflower Bistro, a bag full of goodies from the local shops swinging at my side. I had picked up a handmade candle scented with lavender and sage from Wick & Whimsy, a delicate silver bracelet from

Trinkets & Treasures, and a jar of locally made honey from Sweet Haven Honey Shop.

Stepping into the bistro, warmth and the lively buzz of activity immediately enveloped me. Conversations mingled with the clinking of dishes, and the hiss of food sizzled in the open kitchen. Wooden tables and chairs contributed to the rustic charm, with the soft, buttery yellow walls surrounding it all.

Ethan sat at a corner table near the fireplace and, as I walked in, he looked up with a broad smile, genuine excitement lighting up his eyes. He wore a crisp white dress shirt under a knitted vest, the soft wool adding a casual touch to his otherwise polished look. The vest, which shouldn't have worked on anyone else, somehow looked hot on him, accentuating his athletic frame.

A wave of self-consciousness hit me as I made my way toward him. I pushed a strand of hair away from my face, then quickly tugged off my scarf, stuffing it into my bag. I thought maybe I'd look a bit more sophisticated without it. As I approached the table, I nervously played with the dainty gold necklace I wore—a habit that surfaced whenever I felt anxious.

Ethan's smile broadened as he looked up. "Hey, Vinnie," he greeted warmly, standing to pull me into a brief hug. His arms were strong and comforting around me, and he smelled of fresh wood and zesty citrus, mixed with a hint of fresh cotton. The combination was both energizing and soothing, making my heart flutter a little. "You look great," he added as he pulled back, his eyes bright with sincerity.

I felt a blush creep up my cheeks. "Thanks, Ethan. It's nice to see you." As he pulled out my chair, excitement fluttered in my chest at his thoughtful gesture. I smiled, settling into the chair and placing my bags on the seat next to me.

I glanced down at the menu, trying to steady my nerves. It had been so long since I'd been on a first date—if this even *was* a date—that I'd almost forgotten how jittery they could make me feel. The thought crossed my mind that Ethan hadn't explicitly called it a date, and now I was overthinking it.

As I tried to sort through my thoughts, a waitress approached, ready to take our orders. Before she could say a word, Emily appeared beside her, quickly interjecting. "I've got this table," she said, smiling down at Ethan with dreamy eyes.

"Hey, Ethan! How have you been?" Emily greeted him, completely ignoring me. I found it odd, especially since Emily had met me just the other day when Ivy and I were here. Maybe she didn't remember, or perhaps she was just caught up in seeing Ethan. Either way, her focus solely on him made me feel a little out of place. I tried not to let it bother me, telling myself it was easy to forget faces in a busy place like this.

"Hey, Em," Ethan replied, keeping his tone polite but neutral. He glanced briefly at me, perhaps sensing the awkwardness. "I've been good, thanks. Just busy with work and all."

Emily giggled, twirling a lock of her blonde hair around her finger as she leaned in closer. Her soft makeup accentuated her striking blue eyes, which she fluttered at Ethan. "Work, huh? Always keeping you busy," she purred, her voice taking on a more intimate tone. "We should catch up some time," she added, her eyes lingering on him with clear intent. The subtle shift in her demeanor was unmistakable—she was clearly trying to capture his attention, her smile warm and inviting, almost desperate.

Ethan kept his polite smile and glanced at me before replying, "Yeah, lots of lesson planning and grading lately." He brushed off Emily's suggestion to catch up so smoothly that it eased the tension for me a little, though the situation still felt awkward.

He then gestured towards me, shifting the conversation. "Hey, Em, have you met Vinnie yet?" Ethan's tone was friendly but had a subtle firmness, signalling his intent to include me in the conversation.

I cleared my throat, trying to break the awkwardness. "We've actually met before. I was here with Ivy the other day."

She turned to me, her smile turning noticeably strained. "Oh, right! I remember you," she said, dismissing me with a quick glance before re-focusing on Ethan. The dismissal stung, making the situation even more uncomfortable.

Ethan, sensing the tension, quickly tried to steer the conversation back on track. "I'll have a black—"

"Coffee with an extra shot of espresso and no sugar. I know," Emily cut him off with a sweet smile. She leaned her hip against the table, subtly blocking me out of the conversation, making me feel small and unimportant. Ethan's jaw tightened slightly, a flicker of annoyance crossing his face.

"And for you?" He turned to me with a gentle smile, trying to include me again.

"Pumpkin spice latte, please," I mumbled.

Emily barely glanced my way as she said, "We haven't received the seasonal syrups yet. Sorry."

I felt my face heat, doubting her words since I was sure I had seen the seasonal drinks listed on the chalkboard when I walked in. But I didn't want to make a fuss. "Then just a latte will be fine, thanks," I said quietly.

Ethan looked expectantly at Emily. "If you need anything else, just let me know," she said, her tone dripping with sweetness, and directed solely at him. She turned away, adding an exaggerated sway to her hips as she walked back to the counter. Her tight dark blue flare jeans, and the fitted black T-shirt with the bistro's logo, highlighted her tiny waist and curvy figure. It was hard not to notice how attractive she was, and I felt a pang of insecurity.

Ethan turned back to me, an apologetic look on his face. "I'm sorry about that. I'm not sure what's up with Em today. She's usually really friendly."

I gave him a small smile, trying to brush it off. "It's okay. I'm sure she's . . . nice."

An awkward silence settled between us as we both fumbled for what to say next. I glanced over at Emily, who was now busying herself at the coffee machine. Despite her focus on her work, I noticed her sneaking glances in our direction, her gaze flickering between Ethan and me. The whole situation felt uncomfortable, and I shifted in my seat, unsure of how to break the tension.

Ethan seemed to notice my fidgeting, and my fingers unconsciously playing with the necklace around my neck. His brow furrowed slightly, and he leaned forward, pulling his chair in a little closer. His movement brought him nearer, creating a sense of intimacy that felt different from the casual coffee shop setting.

He looked at me with a soft, focused gaze, his eyes warm and sincere. There was something in the way he looked at me that felt different from how he interacted with Emily earlier—like I was the only woman in the room.

"Hey," he said gently, his voice low. "I'm really glad you agreed to meet up. It's nice to get a chance to talk, just the two of us." His smile was genuine and, for a moment, the awkwardness melted away. It felt like he was genuinely interested in me, not just making polite conversation.

"So, how are you finding Hallow's End?" he asked.

"It's growing on me," I admitted with a small smile. "I've started to get used to the town, and I'm enjoying the beautiful scenery. It's a nice change from the concrete jungle of Cresden." I chuckled softly and added, "In Cresden, the closest thing to nature was the potted plants in office lobbies."

"I can't even imagine not being surrounded by nature. The tranquillity here is something I couldn't live without." He grinned, leaning back in his chair. "The constant noise of the city would probably drive me mad. I guess I'm just not cut out for the big city life."

I chuckled. "Trust me, it does drive you mad. But there are things I like about it, too. In a city like Cresden, with all the constant noise and so many people around, you're never really alone. There's always something happening, and there's a certain energy to it that can be pretty exciting."

Ethan smiled, a stray strand escaping his styled hair. With a smooth, practiced motion, he pushed it back, his forearm flexing subtly as he did. The brief glimpse of muscle caught my attention. There was something undeniably attractive about the effortless way he moved, like he was completely at ease in his own skin. It was hard not to be drawn in by it.

"That sounds like the city life has its perks. Must be quite the switch coming here." He leaned in, a playful glint in his eyes. "So, what made you trade all that excitement for the peace and quiet? Searching for a different kind of thrill?" His tone was teasing, but there was genuine curiosity in his gaze.

I hesitated. Part of me didn't want to burden him with my problems, but Ethan's genuine interest made me feel surprisingly comfortable.

"I needed a break from Cresden and everything that came with it," I began, sighing softly. "Honestly, I was hoping a change of scenery would help me get back into my art. But it's been tough. I've hit this huge creative block, and it feels like I'm just banging my head against a brick wall."

Ethan tilted his head, considering my words. "That sounds rough. It's funny how a new place can sometimes make things harder, instead of helping, right?"

"Exactly!" I exclaimed, feeling a bit of relief that he understood. "I thought the beauty of nature would get my creativity flowing, but it's just not happening." I paused, then added with a wry smile, "Maybe my muse prefers the sound of traffic, and the sight of skyscrapers."

Ethan chuckled. "I remember you saying your art is bold and full of emotions. Maybe your muse is having a tough time with the calm, muted vibes of Hallow's End. It's like trying to paint a storm in a place that's always sunny."

I laughed and shook my head. "For someone who claims not to know much about art, you sure seem to understand my creative struggles pretty well. Maybe you missed your calling as an art therapist," I teased.

He grinned and gave me a playful wink. "Well, if you need help finding some new inspiration, I'm your guy. Just say the word."

I felt a blush creeping in, but, before I could respond, Emily appeared, slamming down my latte on the table with an icy smile. A bit of the drink splashed out of the cup, and she shot me a faux-apologetic look. "Oops, sorry about that," she said, though her tone was anything but sincere.

She turned to Ethan, her expression softening into a sweet smile as she leaned in a bit too close, clearly showing off her cleavage as she placed his black coffee in front of him. "Here's your coffee, Ethan," she said in a sugary tone.

He seemed visibly uncomfortable as he glanced up at her. "Uh, thanks, Em," he replied, his voice polite but lacking enthusiasm.

Undeterred, Emily continued with a flirtatious smile, "Don't forget about trivia night on Saturday. You promised you'd think about joining my team this time. Maybe I can help break that losing streak of yours." She practically purred the last part, her tone dripping with insinuation.

I felt a wave of frustration building up inside me, annoyed at how Emily kept interrupting our time together. Her blatant attempts to draw Ethan's attention away were grating, and I could feel the tension simmering just below the surface.

Ethan seemed to catch on it. He flashed me a warm smile, one that made my annoyance melt away a little. "Vinnie, how about you join us for trivia night? I'd love to have you there. It could be a lot of fun, and I could definitely use the help. I haven't won a single one yet—I'm starting to think the trivia gods might have it out for me."

Emily's smile tightened as she crossed her arms over her chest. "Oh, actually, our team is already full," she said, feigning regret. "I wouldn't want Vinnie to feel left out."

Ethan didn't skip a beat. He flashed a reassuring grin in my direction. "No problem. We can always form our own team," he said confidently. "Right, Vinnie?"

Emily's eyes narrowed slightly as she turned to me, her tone dripping with fake sweetness. "Are you sure? Trivia night here might be a bit boring for someone used to the city's club scene on Saturdays."

I laughed, unfazed by her petty jab. "Honestly, that sounds like a dream compared to sweaty bodies and drunk people spilling drinks. I'd love to join you, Ethan."

He chuckled, clearly pleased. "I'm sure we can keep Vinnie entertained."

Emily's smile became a thin, forced line. "Great! I'll see you both there then," she said, her voice tight with irritation. She flipped her hair over her shoulder with a dramatic flair, then turned on her heel and walked away briskly, her usual bouncy steps noticeably absent.

Ethan turned to me with a shy, playful smile, nervously fidgeting with his coffee cup. "So, it looks like we have plans for Saturday," he started, his voice a little uncertain.

I smiled at Ethan's nervousness, finding it endearing. "It seems so," I said, taking a sip of my latte and meeting his eyes with a warm expression.

He continued, his voice a touch hesitant, "So, how about we make it a date? I mean, if you're up for it. It might not be as exciting as a night out in the city, but I think small-town trivia nights can be pretty fun."

The word *date* sent a flutter through my chest, making my pulse quicken. My palms were clammy, and I wiped them on my jeans. I had come here to embrace dating and be the new Vinnie, and now was the chance to do just that. There was something about Ethan that drew me in, and I felt eager to see where this could lead.

I grinned, feeling a spark of excitement. "It's a date," I said, my voice steady despite the butterflies in my stomach.

Ethan's face brightened, breaking into the most charming smile that reached his eyes. They twinkled with a genuine delight that sent a rush of warmth through me. He leaned forward, propping his elbow on the table, his bicep flexing slightly. There was a playful glint in his eyes as he continued, "Fair warning, though. Crazy Larry will probably be there."

I glanced away from Ethan's toned arms, feeling a slight blush rise to my cheeks. Meeting his warm, honey-colored eyes, I asked, "Who's that?"

"He's got a reputation for turning even the quietest nights into something wild. Last month, he brought in a karaoke machine and started a sing-off between trivia questions. It was . . . memorable, to say the least." He leaned in even closer, our hands nearly touching, separated only by the coffee cups. "In his youth, Larry swears he was in a rock band—at least, that's what he keeps telling us. Whether or not it's true, he definitely has the spirit for it." Ethan's fond smile made it clear that, despite Larry's antics, he was a beloved character in the town.

I laughed, shaking my head. "He sounds like fun. Although," I winced slightly, "I really hope it's not karaoke this time. That's my worst night-mare."

I could feel Ethan's curiosity, so I continued with a sheepish grin. "Back in college, my dorm mates somehow managed to drag me to this local karaoke bar. It was all fun and games at first, listening to everyone butcher classic songs. But then, they signed me up to sing *My Heart Will Go On*. Let's just say I didn't exactly channel my inner Celine Dion."

I grinned at the memory, though it still made me cringe. "Being the center of attention is one thing, but having everyone watch me while I'm bad at something? That's a nightmare. If Larry starts pulling out the karaoke machine, I'm definitely slipping out the back."

"Well, if it comes to that, I'll take one for the team and grab the mic myself," he joked. As we both reached for our coffee cups, our hands brushed against each other, and we both pulled back, a soft blush creeping up our cheeks.

With a playful grin, Ethan added, "But . . . if I *do* end up singing, promise to cheer me on. I might not be Celine Dion, but I can do a pretty entertaining *Bohemian Rhapsody*—all the different voices and notes included."

"Well, that's a performance I can't miss. I'll be there, front and center, to witness your Freddie Mercury impression," I teased. "Just don't expect any backup vocals from me. I'm strictly an audience member."

"So, tell me more about your college life," he said. "I'm guessing you studied art?" He raised an eyebrow playfully. "Was it all wild nights and art classes? Or was there more to it?"

I smiled, nodding. "Yeah, I studied fine arts, much to my parents' dismay. They wanted something more *practical*, but I loved it. It felt like the right place for me to explore and create."

I paused, thinking back to my college days. "There were definitely some wild times," I said with a laugh. "This one time, a few girls from my dorm and I crashed a sorority party. We'd heard they were throwing this huge *Anything But Clothes* party, and we just had to see it for ourselves. We made these ridiculous outfits out of trash bags and duct tape—super creative, right?"

Ethan laughed, clearly amused.

"We snuck in and, honestly, the party was everything you'd expect from a cliché college movie," I continued. "Red solo cups everywhere, people dancing on tables, and terrible pop music blasting. It was my first time cutting loose and getting drunk. I remember ending up in their backyard with a few of my friends, singing along to some throwback hits and attempting the worst dance moves imaginable. At one point, we even tried to build a human pyramid, but it collapsed after about two seconds."

I chuckled, shaking my head. "I think we avoided getting caught because everyone was too busy having their own fun to care about us. It was definitely one of those quintessential *first-time-getting-drunk-in-college* experiences. Messy, a little embarrassing, but a lot of fun."

Ethan chuckled at my story, shaking his head. "That sounds like a classic college experience," he said, grinning.

I leaned in, curious. "What about you? Any fun stories from your college days?"

Ethan nodded, still smiling. "I studied to be a teacher at the local college in Brookside, about a thirty-minute drive from here. I stayed at home to save money, so I missed out on the dorm life. But there was this one time when they had a big bonfire night, and I decided to go."

His eyes twinkled with amusement as he recalled the memory. "It was this huge event, with music, drinks, and way too many people crammed into one backyard. My friends convinced me to join them, and things got pretty wild. People were drinking like there was no tomorrow and, at one point, this girl who'd had way too much, threw up on me. Right in front of everyone."

He laughed, shaking his head. "It was like a record-scratch moment. Everyone around us stopped and stared, and then there was this mix of reactions—some people laughed, some cringed, and a few even cheered like it was some sort of party milestone."

Ethan grimaced at the memory. "It was mortifying. I ended up standing there, covered in puke, while my friends scrambled to find napkins. The entire scene was enough to put me off partying for a while. After that, I decided that wild college parties weren't my thing. The whole loud, chaotic vibe just isn't worth it when you can't even hold a decent conversation with anyone."

He paused, then added with a playful grin, "Besides, at twenty-seven, getting messily drunk isn't exactly a great look. Especially since I work at a school, and everyone knows everyone in this town. I'd hate to end up as the subject of small-town gossip because I couldn't handle my drinks."

I laughed, and shook my head in sympathy. "Yeah, that would definitely be a party-killer. I've had my fill of the party scene, too. Both in college, and in Cresden. These days, I'm not really into the wild nights anymore."

We continued to chat, the conversation flowing easily. At one point, our eyes locked, and the conversation naturally paused, leaving a charged silence hanging in the air. We leaned in slightly, as if drawn by an invisible force, the space between us narrowing. Ethan's gaze dropped to my lips, lingering there for a heartbeat too long, and the air seemed to thicken with anticipation, every breath we took amplifying the intensity of the moment.

My skin tingled, aware of every small movement, and the subtle tension building between us felt almost tangible.

Just as the moment seemed poised to escalate, Emily appeared beside our table, her blue eyes blazing with barely concealed irritation. She shot me a sharp glare, her expression hard and unfriendly.

"Sorry to interrupt," she said, her tone clipped. She looked directly at me, clearly annoyed, before turning her attention to Ethan. "Do you need anything else?"

Ethan blinked, leaning back in his seat, momentarily flustered. "No, we're good, thanks," he replied politely, though I could see a flicker of frustration cross his face.

Emily didn't miss a beat. "Well, if you change your mind, just let me know," she said curtly, her tone far from friendly. With that, she turned on her heel and walked away, her steps brisk and agitated.

Ethan's eyes warmed again, the moment lightening. "Should we grab the bill and head out?"

I nodded, still smiling. "Sounds good."

As we gathered our things, I couldn't help but feel a twinge of disappointment. The charged moment we'd shared was interrupted just as it seemed to be leading somewhere, and a part of me wanted to see where that tension would have taken us. But I shook off the feeling, reminding myself that we had a date set for Saturday.

Ethan, ever the gentleman, smoothly picked up the check before I could even glance at it. "This one's on me," he said with a charming smile, not giving me a chance to protest. His easy-going nature and thoughtfulness made my heart flutter a little. It was a small gesture, but it made me feel cared for, and it was another reason to look forward to our date.

Chapter 9

W E WALKED SIDE BY SIDE down the street, and I asked, "So, what about your parents?"

We were just off the town square, passing a line of quaint, family-owned eateries. Each place had its own charm—one with checkered tablecloths, another with rustic wooden signs. This little street was tucked away like a hidden gem, perfect for an intimate conversation.

Ethan's face brightened. "They're fantastic. My parents still live in the house where I grew up, just a few houses down from my place. I live in the residential area with all the other town folks, but my street leads to a dead-end road. There's a beautiful hiking trail there that goes right into the forest. It's great for getting a bit of peace and quiet, and I love that it's close to nature whilst still being part of the community."

I smiled, picturing the peaceful setting. "That sounds really nice. It must be great having your family nearby."

Ethan chuckled. "Yeah, even though I've moved out, I still see them all the time. My mom is always trying to teach me how to cook. She says every man should know his way around the kitchen. Last week, we tried making her famous lasagna together. It was a complete disaster—we ended up with sauce everywhere and flour all over me. But it was a lot of fun, and she couldn't stop laughing at the mess we made."

I laughed, easily picturing the scene. "And your dad?"

Ethan's eyes lit up with warmth as he reminisced, a soft glow reflecting the affection he held for those moments. "We have this tradition of watching old war movies together. Most Sunday nights, we pick a classic, and just sit back and enjoy. My dad loves to point out all the historical inaccuracies, which drives me crazy, but it's kind of our thing. He'll go on these rants about how they got the uniforms wrong, or how that particular battle never happened like that."

I chuckled. "Sounds like a good time. Your family seems really close."

"We are," Ethan said, his voice carrying a touch of pride. "I'm lucky to have them. They've always supported me, no matter what. I think that's why I love this town so much—it's filled with good memories."

As we continued walking, he gestured around us, sharing pieces of his past. "Over there," he pointed to a small park with a well-worn path, "is where I learned to ride my bike for the first time. I was so excited and, a few minutes later, I crashed right into that old oak tree." He chuckled. "I scraped my knee pretty bad, and my mom rushed over with a band-aid and a hug. I think I was more embarrassed than hurt."

Ethan continued, pointing to one of the colourful houses along the street. "And that house over there," he said with a nostalgic grin, "belongs to Eddie's parents. He's been my best friend since kindergarten. Every Saturday, I'd head over to his place, and we'd spend the whole day in his backyard. They had this epic treehouse, and it was our own little kingdom.

We used to pretend we were pirates, or secret agents on a mission. We even had a secret password to get in, though I can't for the life of me remember what it was now."

He chuckled, the memory clearly bringing him joy. "We spent entire summers up there, reading comics and trading baseball cards. It was our escape from the world. But last year, we had to tear it down because of termites. It was a real bummer. Felt like saying goodbye to an old friend."

I smiled, imagining the scene. "That must have been sad."

Ethan nodded, but there was a hint of amusement in his eyes. "Yeah, it was. But we made the best of it. Eddie even came back from Cedarville, where he's been living since he finished college. We had this whole farewell ceremony for the treehouse. We toasted with root beer, and shared stories about all the crazy stuff we did up there. It was kind of goofy, but it felt like the right way to say goodbye. We even joked about building a new one, but I think our days of climbing trees are behind us."

As Ethan finished recounting the story about the treehouse, we passed by a few locals. They greeted him warmly, waving and smiling as they went about their day, and it was clear he was well-liked in the community. Ethan responded with friendly nods and smiles, his demeanor relaxed and approachable.

Ahead of us, an older man struggled to bend down by his gate, trying to pick up a newspaper that had slipped from his grasp. "Excuse me for a second," Ethan said, stepping away. He quickly approached the man, stooping to grab the paper and handing it over with a kind smile. "Here you go, Arthur. Take it easy, alright? Don't go pushing yourself too hard."

Arthur smiled, grateful for the help. "Thanks, Ethan. You're a good kid."

Ethan smiled apologetically as he walked back. "Sorry about that," he said, glancing back at Arthur with a soft expression. "Arthur's been on his own for a while. He never had kids, and his wife passed away a few years ago. He's a good guy, and I like to help him out when I can. It's the least I can do."

I smiled back. "That's really thoughtful of you. It's nice to know someone cares, especially when you're alone. I'm sure Arthur appreciates having you around." I realized that Ethan wasn't just a *nice guy*—he was genuinely good-hearted, and that made him even more attractive.

We continued walking down the street, the cool afternoon air carrying a hint of pine from the nearby forest. As we reached a sideroad, Ethan gestured toward it. "That's where I live," he said with a smile, gesturing toward a cozy-looking cluster of houses. "Want me to walk you to your cottage? It's a nice day for a stroll, and I don't mind the extra walk."

"I'd like that," I replied, happy for the chance to extend our time together. The sun began to dip lower in the sky, casting a golden glow over the town. I couldn't help but appreciate how effortlessly easy it felt to be around him.

Ethan glanced over at me and smiled. "I've been rambling on about myself," he said with a playful tone. "I'd love to hear more about you. What's your family like?"

As he asked about my family, I hesitated. A part of me would rather listen to more stories about his perfect-sounding childhood than dive into my own complicated relationship with my parents. But I figured it was best to just get it over with.

I sighed, searching for the right words. "Well, my mom . . ." I began, letting out a small, humorless laugh. "She's always been focused on maintaining appearances. My childhood memories are filled with her dragging me to galas and charity events, and all these stuffy gatherings where I had to be on my best behavior. I wasn't even allowed to sit on the furniture in our house, because she didn't want it to look *lived in*. Everything had to be perfect, like a showroom."

I remembered how she would dress me up in designer clothes, carefully picking out my outfits and styling my hair. "She'd spend hours making sure I looked just right, like a little doll. It was all about the image. Smiling for the cameras, shaking hands with people I didn't know, and saying all the right things."

I glanced at Ethan, who was listening intently. Encouraged, I continued. "And then there's my dad. He was more like a ghost in our house when I was growing up. Always busy with work, constantly in meetings, or traveling for business. There were so many nights when he'd miss dinner because he was stuck at the office, and sometimes he'd be gone for weeks at a time."

I remembered sitting at the dinner table, the seat at the head always empty. The silence was deafening, with only the ticking of the antique clock filling the void. "It was like he had his own separate life, completely disconnected from us. I can't count the number of times I wished he would just come home and spend time with us, but it rarely happened."

As I continued, more memories surfaced. "My mom also kept our social calendar packed with events, lunches, and all sorts of plans. Looking back, I think she did it to keep herself busy and distracted. It was like she needed the constant activity to avoid noticing my dad's absence. We were always on the go, attending high-society gatherings and brunches with other families."

I recalled how those events had felt like obligations rather than enjoyable outings. "There was never any downtime. Even weekends were filled with something—a luncheon, a fundraiser, a tea party. It was her way of maintaining appearances and staying connected with the *right* people, I guess." Looking back, I wondered if all those social events were her way of coping with being alone so much. Maybe she filled her days to the brim to avoid the emptiness at home. It was a thought that hadn't occurred to me before, but now it seemed so obvious.

Ethan paused for a moment, as if considering his words carefully. "That must have been tough, feeling like everything was for show," he said gently.

I smiled, feeling a surprising warmth. It was nice to be listened to for once, without judgment.

We reached my cottage, the sunlight casting a glow on the flowers outside the windows. The vibrant mix of lavender and roses swayed gently in the breeze, their sweet scent drifting toward us.

I turned to Ethan, feeling awkward as I tried to figure out how to say goodbye. "Well, this is me," I said, offering a small smile. "Thanks for walking me back."

There was a moment of hesitation. *Should we hug? Just wave?* Nerves fluttered in my stomach, and I was unsure of what was appropriate. It was clear Ethan sensed it, too, as he hesitated for a split-second before smiling warmly.

"My pleasure," he said.

The moment seemed to stretch, neither of us quite ready to break the connection. We stood there, just looking at each other, and the air between us felt charged, the same electric tension from the bistro returning. My heartbeat quickened as his eyes flickered down to my lips for a moment before meeting my eyes again. His pupils seemed to dilate as he looked at me, and I noticed the slight parting of his lips. There was a tension in his expression—nervous, yet unwavering. He didn't pull away. Instead, he leaned in ever so slightly, as if drawn by an invisible force. The moment grew, each second feeling like an eternity as we stood there, so close, yet not quite touching.

Is he going to kiss me?

The thought sent a thrill through me, stirring a heat that spread through my body. But just as quickly, a flicker of doubt surfaced. *Maybe it's too soon.* Another part of me reminded me I was embracing the new Vinnie. The one who wasn't shy about wanting more, and wasn't afraid to take chances.

Feeling a surge of boldness, I asked, "Would you like to come in?"

The invitation hung in the air, and I could feel my pulse quicken with both nerves and excitement. The offer a step into something new.

Ethan's eyes widened slightly at my invitation, and I could see a flicker of surprise mixed with something else—something warmer. But then, he offered a soft, apologetic smile.

"I'd love to, but I actually need to pick up Lily from school," he said. There was a hint of regret in his eyes, and he seemed reluctant to step back, as if torn between wanting to stay, and his responsibilities.

Disappointment flooded me, along with a flicker of self-doubt. Maybe I was rushing things, trying too hard to put myself out there after the breakup. The last thing I wanted was to scare him off. But, before I could dwell too much on that thought, Ethan seemed to notice the slight shift in my mood, and he smiled at me, his expression reassuring.

"Maybe next time?" he said, his voice kind and sincere. The warmth in his tone made it clear that he wasn't rejecting me, just postponing. It was enough to ease my worries.

"Sure," I nodded, offering a small smile.

Ethan stepped closer and opened his arms. I smiled, grateful for the gesture, and moved in for a hug.

It was awkward at first—both of us unsure how much space to leave or how tightly to hold each other. But then, as I felt his arms wrap around me more securely, I let myself relax into his embrace. The warmth of his body seeped into mine, his chest firm against me, and there was something comforting about the way he held me, steady and gentle.

For a fleeting moment, I couldn't help but imagine what it would feel like to be pressed against him in a different, more intimate way. The thought sent a shiver down my spine, and I felt a blush creep up my neck. When Ethan let go, I already missed the warmth of his embrace.

He gave me a gentle smile. "I'll text you," he said, his voice soft and reassuring.

"Okay," I replied, smiling back, still feeling flustered. "Bye, Ethan."

"Bye, Vinnie," he said, giving me one last look before turning and walking away, leaving me stood there, watching him go.

Chapter 10

T HE EVENING ENVELOPED Hallow's End as I snuggled into my bed, surrounded by fluffy pillows and wrapped in my favorite blanket. The room's warmth was a welcome contrast to the crisp autumn air outside, as I held my phone to my ear, chatting with Ivy about my time with Ethan today.

"Did you guys hit it off?" her voice crackled with curiosity through the speaker.

I smiled, thinking back to our conversation and the lingering tension. "It was . . . different," I admitted. "Ethan is so genuine. There's no guessing with him. He's just open and honest, which is refreshing. I'm so used to having to read between the lines, and not knowing where I stand with someone, or feeling like an afterthought."

I paused, trying to find the right words. "But with Ethan, it's like I can just be myself, without second-guessing everything. It's kind of scary how easy it feels to be around him, but in a good way, you know?"

Ivy's voice was filled with encouragement. "Different can be good, you know. Sometimes it's exactly what you need."

I nodded, even though she couldn't see me. "Yeah, it's just . . . I've developed this attraction to him so quickly. It's kind of crazy, but I can't help it," I giggled, feeling giddy. "And, oh my gosh, Ivy, he's so good-looking! Those eyes, that smile! It's just unfair!" I gushed. "And don't even get me *started* on his muscles! When he hugged me, I could feel how solid he is—like, he's not just a pretty face, if you get what I'm saying!"

My cheeks warmed as I continued, unable to stop the flood of words. "There was definitely tension between us. You know, that electric, can't-look-away feeling? I really wanted to kiss him, but he had to go pick up Lily. It was so frustrating! I was left all . . . wound up," I admitted with a laugh, the memory still making my heart race. "But hey, there's always next time, right? I just can't get over how perfect he seems."

"Honestly, Vinnie, if it feels right, then go for it. Don't let some arbitrary timeline hold you back. Society always has these ideas about when women should do and feel things, but that's just nonsense. If you want to kiss him, or even take things further, that's perfectly okay. You shouldn't feel ashamed for wanting to explore something real and exciting, even if it seems quick."

She paused, then added with a hint of mischief, "Besides, from what you're telling me, it sounds like he's worth it. So, why not enjoy it? If the chemistry is there, and you both feel good about it, then just go with the flow."

I nodded, appreciating Ivy's encouragement. "You're right. I shouldn't overthink it if it feels right." I paused, then let out a small sigh. "But then there's Emily. She was all over Ethan today, like she was trying to stake her claim or something. It was so obvious, and honestly, it kind of threw me off. She seemed really interested in him, and I couldn't help but feel a little jealous."

Ivy sighed on the other end of the line. "Yeah, I've known Emily for years, and she's always been like that—very intense and straightforward. If she wants something, she'll go after it without hesitation."

She paused, as if choosing her words carefully. "Ethan's been on her radar for a while. I remember this Adopt a Pet event we had last summer. Emily and Ethan were both volunteering, and he was just being his usual friendly self. He helped her set up, and was super sweet the whole time, especially with the animals. There were these adorable puppies, and Ethan was in the middle of it all, smiling and holding them. Emily totally misread the situation, thinking he was interested in her, but too shy to make a move."

The thought of him with those adorable puppies was almost too much.

Ivy continued. "So, she's had her sights set on him ever since. But honestly, if he hasn't made a move by now, I don't think he's that interested. So, don't let her intimidate you."

"I can totally see how she would've gotten the wrong idea," I admitted, still half-distracted by the image of Ethan with adorable dogs. "But honestly, he made me feel comfortable when Emily tried to interfere. He handled it so smoothly, and even included me in the conversation when she was trying to sideline me. It was like he was letting me know that he wasn't interested in her that way."

I paused, feeling a bit more confident. "I guess I shouldn't worry too much about her. If Ethan's interested in me, then Emily's not an issue. And if he's not, then I'll know soon enough."

Ivy paused thoughtfully before responding. "You know, now that I think about it, I haven't really seen Ethan date anyone seriously. There were a few rumors about him dating someone during college, but they were never confirmed. He just likes to keep to himself. It seems like no girl in Hallow's End has captured his attention."

"What's the catch?" I mused aloud. "He seems so great."

Ivy chuckled softly. "Honestly, there might not be a catch. Maybe he's just waiting for the right person. Ethan doesn't seem like the type to play games or string someone along. He's genuine, and if he's not interested, he won't waste anyone's time. It's kind of refreshing, actually. He's just a great guy who knows what he wants, or at least knows what he doesn't want."

My phone buzzed with a text message, and I glanced at the screen as Ethan's name lit up.

> **Ethan:** Hey Vinnie, I had a great time today. Sorry I had to run off so quickly, but I promised Lily I'd pick her up, and I try not to break my promises. Can't wait to see you on Saturday.

A flutter of excitement swept through me. "He just texted me," I told Ivy. "He said he had a great time, and can't wait to see me on Saturday."

I glanced at the message again, looking between the lines for something a bit flirtier, something that matched the fire I felt between us earlier. Instead, it was just nice and sweet. It was a lovely text, but it lacked the spark I was secretly craving. But I kept those thoughts to myself, not wanting to read too much into it.

"That's great! You sound a little unsure, though. Are you interested in him beyond just the physical attraction?" Ivy asked, picking up on the hesitation in my voice.

I paused, thinking about it. "It's too early to say," I admitted. "He's great, and there's definitely something there. He makes my heart race, and he's attractive, and sweet. But . . . it's not the same as it was with my ex, Sebastian."

I found myself thinking back to the intense start with Sebastian. With him, I knew right away. We kissed the very first night we met, and it was like an inferno of passion—intense and consuming from the beginning. I nestled deeper into the comfort of the plush pillows, playing with the thread of my blanket, lost in thought. But with Ethan, it feels different—more like a warm ember. The attraction is there, but it doesn't have the same fiery intensity. It's a slower burn, and I'm not sure what to make of it yet.

"Exes can be tricky," Ivy said, her voice thoughtful. "Comparing Ethan to your past relationship might not be fair to either of you. I don't know what happened with Sebastian, but he's an ex for a reason. It sounds like something's still holding you back, and that's okay. But whenever you're ready to talk about it, I'm here to listen."

Ivy paused for a moment, and I could hear the faint whistling of a kettle in the background, followed by the soft rustling of her moving around. There was a soft clink as she set down a teacup and stirred it with a spoon, the gentle tinkling sound filling the brief silence.

She then continued, with a warm, encouraging tone. "Just . . . don't let your past hold you back from something new. You don't have to have everything figured out right now, but give this thing with Ethan a fair shot. Take a leap of faith, and see where it leads. You deserve to find something that makes you happy, without all the baggage."

"You're right. Thanks for listening, Ivy. I'm really glad to have someone like you here in Hallow's End," I said, a warm smile spreading across my face.

Ivy chuckled softly. "I wish you were staying here permanently. It would be nice to have you around more." Her words struck a chord, and I felt a pang of realization. I had been thinking about staying in Hallow's End a lot lately and I really needed to talk to my parents about my plans soon.

"Listen, I've got to go. My friend Amelia is coming over, and we're about to watch our favorite crime series, *Murder Chronicles*. It's kind of our Monday night tradition," Ivy said with a laugh. "You should join us sometime. I think you two would get on well."

A little chuckle escaped from me. "I'd love that! I've been obsessing over it, too, but I'm a few episodes behind."

I heard the doorbell ring in the background. "Looks like she's here. I'll text you to sort out details for our shopping trip on Wednesday."

"Sure, can't wait," I replied with a smile.

"Goodnight, Vinnie."

"Goodnight, Ivy," I echoed warmly.

As I ended the call, I reflected on my growing friendship with Ivy. In Cresden, friendships often felt shallow and transactional. In college, most of my relationships were based on nights out and drinking, with no real depth or lasting connection. It was all about socializing and keeping up appearances, but there was no genuine care or support. Plus, most of my time was spent with Sebastian, anyway.

But here in Hallow's End, people seemed to genuinely care, and welcomed me with open arms. Ivy's kindness, and thoughtful advice, was refreshing. For the first time in a long while, I felt truly understood and valued as a person. I hadn't realized how much I was craving genuine connections and a sense of community until I found it here.

I settled back into my pillows, mindlessly scrolling through Instagram for a distraction. My feed was the usual mix of vacation photos, artwork, and inspirational quotes. It was a soothing routine, something to help me wind down before bed.

My thumb paused on a photo that made my heart sink.

It was a group shot at The Velvet Lounge, an upscale bar I knew all too well from my life in Cresden. Mark, a guy I had once considered a friend, mostly because he was part of Sebastian's circle, had posted the photo. He and the rest of the group were all dressed to the nines, surrounded by dim lighting, chic decor, and elegant cocktails.

As I looked closer, I recognized a few of the girls who had once been friendly to my face, but turned on me after the breakup with Sebastian. Claire, who used to confide in me about her boy troubles. Vanessa, who always had a friendly smile—until she sided with Sebastian—and Jessica, the ringleader who seemed to thrive on stirring up drama. They had all taken his side after we broke up, spreading rumors, and calling me names behind my back.

Sebastian's friends, both the girls and the guys, had always viewed me with a certain condescension. They'd compliment my art, but their words felt hollow, as if they couldn't see it as more than a whimsical hobby. I remember overhearing some of the guys say things like, "Yeah, Vinnie's hot, and her parents are loaded, but she needs to let go of that art thing. It's cute for now, but does she really think she can keep that up after college?"

Despite our similar privileged backgrounds, they never truly accepted me or our relationship. Their support felt fake, their smiles insincere, and I always sensed the unspoken judgment in their eyes. They tolerated me because of Sebastian, not because they valued me as a person. They saw my passion for art as trivial, something they expected me to grow out of once *real life* began. It was a painful realization that, to them, I was just another accessory in Sebastian's life.

Seeing them all together at that bar, laughing and enjoying their night out, brought a pang of sadness and frustration. It was a reminder of the superficiality and toxicity I had left behind. Part of me felt a twinge of nostalgia for the good times—the glamorous nights out, the sense of being part of a glittering social scene. Despite their flaws, those moments held their allure. They offered a distraction from deeper insecurities, and gave me a sense of belonging, however superficial. Sometimes, I missed the ease of slipping into that role, of being part of something larger, even if it was shallow.

As I scrolled further, a pang hit me when I came across a photo of Sebastian at the same bar. In the picture, he sat front and center, charming as ever. He had artfully tousled his blonde hair, giving him that perfect blend of casual and put-together. A tailored black suit hugged his athletic frame just right, highlighting his broad shoulders and lean physique. His emerald eyes sparkled with laughter, and his face lit up with an easy, carefree smile. The entire scene captured him at his best—relaxed, confident, and undeniably attractive.

Perched on his lap was Jessica, her long, sleek blonde hair falling over her shoulders in soft waves. She leaned into Sebastian, her head slightly tilted, allowing her hair to frame her face perfectly. Her dress, barely there and tightly fitted, clung to her petite figure, showing off her slim, tanned legs. Jessica's manicured fingers traced lightly over Sebastian's chest, a gesture that spoke volumes of possessiveness and intimacy. Her bold red lips curved into a satisfied smile, showcasing her self-assuredness, and indicating her seamless fit into the glamorous world of Sebastian Sterling. The image was striking, capturing a moment of ease and confidence that made them appear as the perfect, polished couple.

Seeing them together brought a sudden rush of jealousy, and a pang of bitterness. Jessica had always had a thing for Sebastian, flirting with him even when we were together. She seemed perfect for him, and her family was wealthy and well-connected, part of the same elite circle Sebastian thrived in. She embodied the kind of woman who could effortlessly maintain his image, fitting seamlessly into the glamorous lifestyle he valued.

It stung to see him move on so easily while I was still struggling to find my footing, despite my best efforts. The future felt uncertain and daunting without the safety net of our relationship. When I was with Sebastian, everything had seemed planned out and secure. There was a clear path, even if it wasn't one I wanted. Now, the fear of the unknown loomed large, and I couldn't help but feel lost.

There were moments when I wondered if Sebastian was the best I would ever have, which was a thought that lingered despite knowing our relationship was unhealthy. He had a way of making me believe that no one else would ever support me the way he did, or love me as much. He would say things like, "No one will ever understand you like I do," or "I'm the only one who really gets your quirks." His words hinted that he was doing me a favor by being with me, that I was too complicated or *difficult* for anyone else to love. It was a twisted form of validation, making me doubt my worth, like he was the only person who could ever accept me.

Seeing him with Jessica brought all those insecurities rushing back. It made little sense, especially after his last text saying he still wanted to talk. Had that been just a fleeting thought, easily dismissed now that Jessica was in the picture? He hadn't reached out since that last message, and the realization stung. The last time I called, he didn't return it, or even text to see what I wanted. Had he really just moved on like that? Were the last four years we spent together not worth anything to him?

My mother's words echoed in my head—*Someone like Sebastian wouldn't stay single for long.* It was a cruel reminder that maybe everyone had expected this but me, and the heartbreak I thought I was finally moving past suddenly felt as raw as ever. Despite my efforts to embrace a new life, and chase my dreams in Hallow's End, doubts now crept in. Had I been too quick to leave everything behind? The breakup seemed so final, yet now, it felt like an open wound.

And then there was Ethan.

Had I jumped into something too quickly? Seeing Sebastian move on so easily, with someone like Jessica, made me doubt whether I was truly ready for anything new. Maybe I was rushing things, trying to fill a void that was still very much present. I wanted to be over Sebastian, to move forward and find something real, but clearly, I wasn't there yet.

A wave of emotions hit me as I considered sending a text. I thought back to my conversation with Ivy, where she encouraged me to give Ethan a chance. But seeing Sebastian with someone else stirred up a storm of conflicting feelings. The jealousy and loneliness bubbled up inside me, along with a desperate need for validation.

Part of me didn't want to see him happy without me. It was selfish and unfair, but there it was, that raw truth. Sending a text felt like a way to reclaim some of that lost connection, to remind him—and maybe myself—that I still mattered.

I picked up my phone, my fingers hovering over the keyboard. The urge to reach out was overwhelming. But what could I possibly say that wouldn't sound petty or desperate?

I typed out a text, my fingers moving almost on their own.

> **Vinnie:** Hey, I know I didn't respond to your last message. Sorry about that - I needed some space to sort things out. Just wanted to check in and see how you're doing.

I tried to justify the message to myself, thinking it made sense to keep things friendly, given how involved Sebastian had been in my life, and with my family. Maybe staying in touch could be normal. Mature, even. It felt like a reasonable way to bridge the distance, a way to feel connected to something familiar in the midst of so much uncertainty.

To my surprise, Sebastian responded almost immediately.

> **Sebastian:** Hey, V! Good to hear from you. I've been thinking about you. Miss our chats. How've you been?

His flirty and upbeat tone sent a confusing rush of emotions through me. I questioned whether I'd blown the photo with Jessica out of proportion. Maybe it was nothing—just a moment caught on camera, not a sign of something deeper. But then, I mentally stopped myself. I shouldn't care either way. If I wanted to stay friends, I should be happy for him, regardless of who he was with.

Yet, a part of me still missed him. Missed the easy way we used to talk, and the comfort of being together. It was a struggle to balance those feelings, knowing that moving on was the right thing to do, but still feeling the tug of our past. Falling into old habits, I replied without much hesitation.

> **Vinnie:** Took a trip to Hallow's End, but it's been nice. It's a good place to think things through. I've met some lovely people here, as well. How's everything going with you?

> **Sebastian:** Lovely people, huh? I can't say I like the sound of that. Miss you, though. My bed feels pretty empty without you. You should come back. Things aren't the same here without you around.

His words made me pause. The hint of jealousy in his message suggested he wasn't thrilled about me meeting new people, but it felt superficial; more about control than actual concern. It seemed like he missed the physical comfort and presence I provided, rather than missing me as a person. It was a sobering and painful realization, highlighting the gap between the connection I was craving, and what he seemed to want. I decided to steer the conversation away from his insinuations.

> **Vinnie:** Let's not go there, Seb. We should try to be friends, right? I saw your post with everyone at The Velvet Lounge. Are you still out now?

I glanced at the clock. It was just before midnight on a Monday, and it crossed my mind that the post might have been from the weekend. Then again, knowing Sebastian, the fact that he had work in the morning never stopped him from going out for drinks and partying. I hit send, trying to keep my tone neutral, while curiosity and a touch of old concern nagged at me.

I waited for a response, but it didn't come. Feeling restless, I got up and headed to the bathroom. As I stood there brushing my teeth, a specific memory of Sebastian flashed in my mind, clearer than the rest. It was one of those nights I couldn't forget, no matter how hard I tried.

Sebastian had stumbled back to his flat late, well past midnight. We had made plans for me to stay over and have dinner together, something simple and intimate—a rare break from our usual social whirlwind. But when he finally walked through the door, it was clear that things hadn't gone according to plan. His usually sharp green eyes were glazed over, and he reeked of whiskey. He had dishevelled clothes, messy hair, and a reckless, carefree grin that masked so much.

He had clearly been out with his friends, celebrating a big deal they had just signed. Instead of our night in, he'd let himself get swept away by the excitement, the lure of drinks and congratulations too tempting to resist. It was a familiar scenario, one that left me feeling both frustrated and sidelined. Whilst I'd been looking forward to our evening, he'd been caught up in the buzz of his success, leaving me waiting and worried.

"Sebastian," I had said, my voice full of concern. "Are you okay? You didn't answer your phone."

He waved me off, staggering slightly as he kicked off his shoes. "I'm fine, V. Just needed to blow off some steam," he slurred, attempting to appear nonchalant. But I could see the tension in his shoulders, the way he was avoiding my eyes.

I reached out, touching his arm gently. "You scared me. You can't just disappear like that."

He pulled me close, his grip firm but not comforting. "I'm here now, aren't I?" he murmured, leaning in, his breath hot against my neck. His words were dismissive, brushing off my worry as if it were nothing.

I wanted to talk, to understand what had driven him to this state, but he wasn't interested in discussing it. Instead, he kissed me hungrily, almost desperately. His hands were all over me, pulling me closer, and I felt the familiar conflict rise within me. I wanted to take care of him, to be there for him, but he wasn't letting me in. He was using the physical connection as a distraction, a way to avoid whatever was bothering him.

We ended up having sex, not because I particularly wanted to, but because I could tell it was what he needed at the moment. It was a way to soothe his frayed edges, to give him some semblance of comfort. As we lay together afterward, the room heavy with the scent of sweat and alcohol, he was already asleep, the stress lines on his face softened. I, on the other hand, stared at the ceiling, feeling the weight of unspoken words and unresolved issues.

It was a pattern that had played out more than once—me trying to care for him, to reach the parts of him that were always just out of reach, and him shutting me out, opting for the simplicity of physical closeness over the vulnerability of emotional intimacy. I sighed, the memory a bitter reminder of the emotional distance that had always existed between us, even in our most intimate moments.

Once I was settled back in bed, snuggled under the covers, my phone buzzed with a new message.

> **Sebastian:** Friends, huh? You know that's not us. There's too much history, too much between us, to just be friends. Who are we kidding? I miss you, Vinnie. I miss everything about us. It just feels wrong without you here.

His words carried the familiar tone of someone who'd had a few too many drinks. There was a raw honesty in his message, a mix of wistfulness and drunken vulnerability. It was clear he was grappling with our new reality, just as I was, but in his own way.

I stared at the message, my thumb hovering over the keyboard. Part of me wanted to respond, to keep the connection alive, even if it was just a sliver of what we once had. But another part of me knew better. It was late, and nothing good ever came from texting after midnight, especially when alcohol was involved. His message only confirmed what I had been trying to convince myself of all along—that we weren't ready to have these conversations. Not like this, not now.

It was tempting to fall back into familiar patterns, to let his words pull me back into the emotional whirlpool of our past. But I needed to focus on myself. Engaging with him now, in this state, would only muddy the waters further and make it harder for me to move on.

I sighed and put my phone down, deciding not to reply. As much as it hurt, it was the right choice. I turned off the light and told myself that sometimes, the best response is no response at all.

In the middle of the night, the sound of my phone ringing jolted me awake. I groggily reached for it, squinting at the screen to see Sebastian's name flashing. The clock read 3:33 A.M. Without much thought, I declined the call. A moment later, it rang again, and I declined once more, knowing that nothing productive would come from talking to him in this state.

A few seconds later, text notifications started flooding in, each more desperate than the last.

Sebastian: Why aren't u picking up?

Sebastian: Are u with someone else??

Sebastian: No one will love you like I did.

Sebastian: Sweetheart, pls answer the phone. I need u.

Sebastian: U always took care of me, better than anyone. No one else gets me like u do.

Sebastian: Remember all our plans, all our dreams?? Just come back. I can't do this without u.

Sebastian: It's not the same. I miss u so much. Please, Vinnie.

Sebastian: I don't know how to move on without u. I need u.

The erratic punctuation and typos, coupled with the emotional intensity, made it clear he was drunk and struggling. He swung between jealousy and desperation, trying to convince me to come back with a mix of guilt, longing, and nostalgic reminders of our past. It felt like he was grasping at straws, trying to rekindle something that had already burned out, yet his words tugged at my heart, stirring up emotions that I had been trying to set aside.

Part of me wanted to text back. Despite everything, I still cared and worried about him. Seeing the pain and desperation in his messages made it hard to ignore. He sounded so lost and hurt, and part of me wanted to soothe him, to tell him everything would be okay. But I knew that comforting him now would only blur the lines, and keep us both stuck in the past. This wasn't about him missing me as a person, it was about the comfort and familiarity we once shared, which wasn't healthy for either of us.

As much as it pained me, I had to let him go. For both of our sakes.

Regretting unmuting his number, I hovered my thumb over the block button, hesitating. It was a drastic step, and one that would add a layer of finality to our breakup. My phone rang again—Sebastian. The sound of the ringtone was a harsh reminder of the chaos we were both trying to escape. I declined the call, my resolve hardening.

With a deep breath, I mustered up all my courage and blocked his number. It felt like closing a door that had been left ajar for too long. As I did, a wave of emotion hit me, tears welling up in my eyes. It was painful, like a small piece of my heart breaking all over again, and I cried quietly, mourning not just for him, but for me, and for the relationship we had lost.

But, amidst the tears, there was also a sense of rightness. Blocking him was a necessary step toward healing. A way to protect myself and start moving on. It was a hard, but needed, goodbye.

Chapter 11

YESTERDAY HAD BEEN A whirlwind of creativity. Blocking Sebastian made me feel surprisingly light, as if a weight had been lifted off my shoulders, and the inspiration I had been desperately seeking finally took root. I spent the entire day in my little makeshift studio, surrounded by canvases and splashes of paint, and the wooden floors were speckled with color, remnants of past works blending with new bursts of bright hues. I experimented with different colors and styles, blending bold strokes with delicate lines, trying something new, and even revisiting some of my old techniques. The hours flew by, with the sun setting outside the window, leaving the room bathed in the soft glow of my desk lamp. As I poured my emotions onto the canvas, the act of painting became a cathartic release, each brushstroke a step toward healing.

I only paused for brief breaks, during which I sipped on tea and exchanged texts with Ivy, confirming our plans for a shopping trip. It felt good to have something to look forward to. A break from the emotional rollercoaster of the past few days.

Now it was Wednesday, and I stood outside a quaint little boutique called Pixie & Posh. The shopfront was whimsical, with its name painted in playful, curling script above the door. Large bay windows showcased an array of colorful dresses, vintage accessories, and quirky decorations that beckoned passersby with their charm. The window displays showcased mannequins dressed in layered, bohemian-style outfits, with chunky jewelry and stylish shoes accenting their look. Fairy lights twinkled around the edges of the windows, adding a magical touch.

The air was crisp, carrying the earthy scent of fallen leaves, and the now-familiar aroma of fresh brews from Harvest Moon Coffee. The sky above was a clear, soft blue, with golden sunlight breaking through the few clouds in the sky

I glanced in the direction of the coffee shop again. It would have been nice to stop by for a quick latte, but I didn't want to be late, or keep Ivy waiting. She had only her lunch break to shop with me, though she'd reassured me that one of the perks of owning her own shop was the flexibility to take as long as she wanted. Katie, who helped her around the store, was perfectly capable of handling things in her absence.

Ivy approached, carrying two cups of coffee, and the distinct scent of pumpkin spice wafted towards me. She wore a soft, oversized crochet sweater, balanced with a green floral-print mini skirt that moved gracefully with her steps. Delicate lace tights covered her legs, and she added an edgy contrast to the softness of her outfit with chunky black boots. Her dark blue hair sported two playful space buns, and she had a small crocheted bag slung over her shoulder.

I couldn't help but admire her style, wishing I could pull off something as unique and put-together. I glanced down at my outfit—a leather mini-skirt paired with a mustard jumper. It was cute and trendy, but it felt more like a safe choice than a true reflection of my personality.

Ivy beamed with excitement as she reached me, somehow managing to pull me into a quick hug while expertly balancing the two coffee cups. Her energy was contagious, and I smiled back at her as she passed over one of the cups.

"I thought you might need a little pumpkin spice pick-me-up. We've got a lot of shopping to do, and we'll need all the energy we can get!" she said, with a playful wink,

I accepted the warm cup gratefully, inhaling the comforting scent. "You're the best," I said, touched by her thoughtful gesture.

As we stepped into Pixie & Posh, the gentle chime of the bell announced our arrival, blending seamlessly with the soft indie music playing in the background. Vintage posters adorned the walls, their faded colors contrasting with the warm glow of lights above. The air in the room carried the soothing scent of lavender and vanilla, which mingled with the earthy tones of the wooden shelves and racks.

With its bohemian dresses, flowing fabrics, vintage-inspired pieces, and quirky accessories, the boutique was a treasure trove of eclectic finds, where every item had a story waiting to be discovered.

Behind the counter stood a young woman with oversized, round glasses perched on her nose, her pixie-cut hair a vibrant shade of purple that contrasted strikingly with her soft features. She wore a lace-trimmed cami that peeked out beneath an oversized flannel, its worn softness hanging loosely off her shoulders. High-waisted cargo pants hugged her hips, the fabric heavy and utilitarian, contrasting with the delicate lace. Scuffed Converse peeked out from beneath the wide legs of her pants, while silver rings gleamed on her fingers, each one unique, catching the light as she moved.

"Hey, Amelia!" Ivy exclaimed, placing her coffee cup on the counter.

Amelia's face lit up with a bright smile. "Ivy! It's great to see you!" she responded, her brown eyes twinkling behind her glasses. She turned her attention to me, her expression warm and welcoming. "And Vinnie! It's so good to finally meet you! I'm Amelia," she said with a bright smile. "Ivy's told me a lot about you, so I feel like I already know you." She laughed, giving Ivy a playful nudge.

"How are you liking it here so far?" Amelia asked, her tone warm and curious. "Settling in okay?"

I smiled, easily matching Amelia's warm energy. "It's been great so far! And it's nice to finally meet you, too. I hear you're also a big *Murder Chronicles* fan."

Amelia's eyes lit up with excitement. "Oh my God, yes! I'm *obsessed*! Did you see the last episode? That cliffhanger was insane! I'm *dying* to see what happens next!"

I laughed, nodding along. "Seriously, that last episode? I'm still reeling! Can you believe they just left it with Brandon standing over the body like that? I need to know what happens next!"

"Exactly!" Amelia grinned. "Anyways, feel free to browse around. We just got a new shipment in yesterday. Oh, and there's this dress in the new arrivals that made me think of you immediately," she said, glancing at Ivy.

"You know me too well. But today's about Vinnie," Ivy said, though she couldn't hide her excitement at the prospect of new clothes.

Amelia laughed, nodding towards the back of the store. "Take your time and enjoy. If you need anything, just holler."

We made our way over to the racks, where the new arrivals hung. Ivy and I rummaged through the clothing, pulling out pieces and holding them up against each other.

She found the dress Amelia had mentioned—a stunning deep plum velvet dress, with bell sleeves, and intricate gold embroidery along the neckline and cuffs—and held it up, admiring the rich fabric and detailed design. "This is beautiful," she breathed, a smile spreading across her face.

"Go try it on," I encouraged, eager to see how it looked on her.

She nodded, heading towards the dressing room. Meanwhile, I continued browsing, finding a few pieces that caught my eye. As I pulled out a deep green wrap dress with delicate embroidery, Ivy reappeared, wearing the velvet dress.

"You look amazing!" I said, admiring how effortlessly she pulled it off.

Ivy twirled in front of the mirror, the velvet fabric hugging her figure perfectly. "It's gorgeous, but we're here for you, remember?" she reminded me with a playful smile. "Let's find *you* something amazing."

Encouraged, I tried on the green wrap dress, feeling the soft fabric glide smoothly over my skin. I stepped out of the dressing room to show Ivy and Amelia, who both nodded in approval. But, as much as I liked it, it didn't feel like . . . me, and my face must have showed it.

Ivy and Amelia worked quickly, darting between racks and pulling out pieces for me to try. Ivy handed me a dark floral maxi dress with bell sleeves, her eyes sparkling with excitement. "This one's so romantic, you've got to try it!" she urged.

Amelia, not to be outdone, selected a velvet blazer and matching skirt, both in a dark blue. "This would look amazing with some chunky boots. It's got that edgy-but-chic vibe," she suggested, her warm caramel eyes gleaming with enthusiasm.

As they both fussed over me, gratitude warmed me. This was what shopping should be like—fun and supportive, with plenty of laughter and discovery. It was such a contrast to my experiences in Cresden, where friendships felt more like competitions. Back there, shopping trips were about keeping up appearances, with an underlying edge of jealousy and snarky comments disguised as compliments. It always felt like a subtle game of one-upmanship.

Here in Hallow's End, Ivy and Amelia weren't interested in comparing or judging. They were genuinely excited to help me find something I loved. It was refreshing, and made me realize how much I'd been missing out on real, genuine friendships.

While trying on a mustard-colored sweater dress with lace details, I asked, "So, how long have you two been friends?"

"We've lived in this town all our lives," Ivy began, her voice carrying a note of fond nostalgia, "but we only really bonded in college. We found out we both have a love for tarot cards and manifesting."

Amelia laughed, adding, "Yeah, we were both deep into our *witchy* phase, even back then, and it just stuck. We still do tarot readings for each other whenever we need some cosmic guidance."

I laughed along with them, stepping out of the dressing room to face them. "Does everyone in this town get into the witchy stuff?" I teased, adjusting the hem of the sweater dress.

Ivy grinned playfully. "Kind of," she admitted. "It's a *thing* here in Hallow's End. The town has this delicious, mystical folklore background, especially around Halloween. The locals say the veil between our world, and the other side, is thinner here. There are all these stories about people finding what they've lost—things that disappeared ages ago suddenly reappearing in the most unexpected places. It's like the town helps you find your way back to what you need, even if it's not always in the form you expected."

Amelia nodded, her eyes twinkling with amusement as she leaned in closer, lowering her voice as if sharing a secret. "And it's not just about objects. There are tales of people bumping into old friends they thought they'd never see again, or running into someone who becomes unexpectedly significant in their lives. Some folks even say they've rekindled old passions. Hobbies, dreams—even relationships they thought were long dead. It's as if the town has a way of bringing things full circle, offering second chances, or nudging people toward their true path."

Ivy chimed in, "And then there are the *really* odd things. Like the stories of couples who get together during the Halloween festival, claiming to feel an inexplicable pull, as if some unseen force was matchmaking. Or the mysterious coincidences—people finding exactly what they need, just when they need it, like the town knows what they truly desire.

Amelia grinned, "According to legend, the town was established on an ancient ley line that amplifies energy. Some people think that's why strange things happen here, especially around Halloween. It's like the town's spirit comes alive and gets a little mischievous."

I listened, both intrigued and sceptical. The idea that a town could have some kind of unseen power, influencing the lives of its residents, felt like a stretch. Still, there *was* something captivating about the stories, and they made me think about the small coincidences that had happened since I'd arrived—things that seemed almost too perfect to be just chance. Like meeting Ivy and Ethan on my first day in town. Or how here, the dream of opening a gallery felt more within reach than ever before. I tried to dismiss it as just local superstition, but part of me was intrigued, making me wonder if there was more to the stories than met the eye.

"So, basically, anything can happen here, and it wouldn't even be that surprising?"

Ivy laughed. "Exactly! It keeps life interesting, that's for sure. And who knows? Maybe you'll find a bit of magic here, too."

After the chat, I continued browsing, and ended up selecting a few new pieces, including a cozy knit sweater, a flowy floral skirt, and a pair of high-waisted jeans. Just as I was about to say I had enough for one day, Ivy and Amelia exchanged a conspiratorial glance that made me raise an eyebrow.

"Wait, there's one more thing you have to try on," Ivy insisted, a mischievous smile playing on her lips as she pulled out a garment bag from a nearby rack.

I laughed, shaking my head. "I think I've tried on enough for one day. You two are relentless."

"Trust us," Amelia chimed in, her grin widening. "This one is *perfect* for your date on Saturday."

Their excitement was contagious, building my own anticipation alongside it. Earlier, while rummaging through racks and trying on various outfits, I'd mentioned my upcoming date, and they'd both been thrilled, especially Amelia, who couldn't hide her surprise that Ethan was finally taking an interest in something beyond his books and his sister.

"Okay, okay," I relented with a grin. "You two are really selling this. Let's see what you've got."

I walked into the dressing room and unzipped the garment bag with curiosity. Inside was a beautiful red dress. Like everything else in the shop, it had a vintage flair, with its puffed sleeves and a sweetheart neckline, reminiscent of old Hollywood glamour. The fitted bodice featured delicate ruching that accentuated the waist, while the skirt flowed gracefully, ending just below the knee with a subtle slit that added a touch of allure.

I slipped into the dress, fastening the small, delicate buttons that ran down the front. The material felt cool against my skin, and I smiled at my reflection as I studied myself in the mirror. I completed the outfit with a pair of sleek black heeled boots I had found and instantly fallen in love with.

The added height made me feel more confident, and balanced the playful elegance of the dress with a modern flair. The extra inches were also a bonus, considering Ethan's height. As the thought of us possibly kissing crossed my mind, a warm blush crept up my cheeks. The idea of being closer to eye level with him, and not having to stand on tiptoe, sent a flutter of anticipation through me.

I took a deep breath and stepped out of the dressing room. Ivy gasped, her eyes widening with delight. "Oh, my gosh, Vinnie! You look stunning!" she exclaimed. Her excitement was infectious, and I felt a flush of pride and confidence.

Amelia's face lit up with a broad smile. "Absolutely perfect," she agreed. "This dress was made for you."

I twirled, watching the skirt flare out beautifully around me. The rich red color made me feel bold and daring and, as I admired the dress, Amelia reached into a glass display case, pulling out a delicate necklace with a red crystal pendant.

"This is carnelian," Amelia explained, holding the necklace up to the light. The crystal glinted with a deep, fiery hue, complementing the dress. "It's said to boost confidence, creativity, and enhance passion, desire, and love." She winked playfully. "Just what you need for your date."

She fastened the necklace around my neck, the cool stone resting against my skin, and I looked at myself in the mirror, feeling a surge of excitement. The outfit felt like a small celebration of my new life, a bold statement that I was ready to embrace new possibilities.

Ivy leaned in, her eyes sparkling with mischief. " Ethan won't know what hit him."

Amelia wrapped up the dress and necklace in delicate tissue paper, placing them carefully in a beautifully decorated bag with the other items I'd picked out.

"So, how about a girls' night on Friday? A sleepover at my place, complete with snacks, movies, and a little card-reading before your big date," Ivy suggested with a playful grin.

Amelia perked up at the idea. "I'd love to, but I've got a date myself," she said, smirking. "Matched with a new guy online. He seems interesting."

Ivy raised an eyebrow. "What happened to the guy you were talking to last week?"

Amelia rolled her eyes and laughed. "Mike? He was sweet, but *way* too boring. Besides, I'm not trying to settle down, right now. I'm just having lots of fun. And by *fun*, I mean sex." She adjusted her gold-framed glasses with a cheeky grin, and we laughed, her candidness refreshing and unapologetic.

"We'll miss you, Amelia," I said with a mock pout. "But I'll definitely be there, Ivy. A girls' night sounds perfect."

Amelia grinned and wiggled her brows. "Next time, for sure. And you better text me all the details about your date on Saturday!"

"I promise," I laughed.

Before we left, Amelia surprised me with a warm hug. It was unexpected, but comforting, and a gesture that solidified my sense of belonging in this charming town that was starting to feel a little more like home

Chapter 12

F RIDAY NIGHT ARRIVED, and I busied myself in my bedroom, packing a bag for the sleepover at Ivy's. The room was dimly lit by a bedside lamp, shining a light over the rustic wooden furniture and the quilted bedspread. I folded a pair of comfy pajamas, and a favorite oversized sweater, placing them neatly in my overnight bag with my other essentials.

My phone buzzed on the nightstand, and I picked it up, grinning as I read the latest text from Ethan. We'd been texting all day, ever since he messaged me in the morning to confirm our plans for tomorrow. It had been a fun, easy conversation, with him joking about the quiz night and what kind of absurd questions we might face. His texts had quickly become the highlight of my day, especially the ones he sent between his lessons. I found myself waiting for them more and more, each one bringing a smile to my face.

Ethan: If the trivia topics are art or literature, we're set. But let's pray they don't ask us about cooking — we might end up naming ingredients that don't exist! 😊

Vinnie: Seriously! My idea of cooking is a salad — no stove required. If they ask about soufflés or reductions, we're doomed! 😄

Ethan: Haha, exactly! But honestly, I'm just excited to see you. Tomorrow's going to be great.

His last message left me smiling. It was comforting to know that he was looking forward to it just as much as I was.

As I packed, I imagined him at work, leaning against a desk with that casual confidence of his, explaining something with his warm, honey-brown eyes focused intently. Maybe he'd loosened his tie by now, the top button of his shirt undone, revealing a glimpse of his collarbone. I wondered if he ever wore glasses—somehow, that thought only made the image hotter. The idea of him in teacher mode, effortlessly charming and sexy, sent a warm thrill through me.

My mind wandered, daydreaming about an after-hours scenario in an empty classroom. The thought of him leaning in close, our faces inches apart, as he murmured something in that deep, soothing voice . . . I blushed, imagining a hot make-out session, his hands in my hair, pulling me closer, our breaths mingling in the quiet of the room.

Shaking off the fantasy, I zipped up my bag and glanced at the snacks and wine I had picked up earlier from Maple and Spice. I'd chosen a bottle of red wine—with a cute label that promised hints of dark berries and chocolate—an assortment of cheeses, and some salted popcorn.

When I stepped out the door, the crispness of the autumn night greeted me. The sky was clear, stars beginning to twinkle in the fading light and, maybe it was the talk with Ivy and Amelia that lingered with me, but there really *was* a sense of magic in the air; a feeling that anything could happen.

I started the short walk to Ivy's place on Willow Lane, a quaint street just a few minutes from my cottage. As I turned onto the main road, I smiled at the festive decorations that lined the street. The front porches were a delightful array of carved pumpkins, glowing with flickering candles inside. Charming little scarecrows were seated on benches outside some houses, while others were decorated with strings of orange and purple lights. Some even had skeletons on their front porches and gardens.

Ivy's house was number thirteen on Willow Lane, a little brick haven that fit perfectly with the enchanting vibe of the street. The house's window shutters were painted a soft, welcoming pink, adding a touch of whimsy against the classic red brick. Ivy vines gracefully climbed up the walls, weaving in and out of the window frames, and the front garden was a vibrant mix of wildflowers and herbs, their colors still bright and lively in the late September air. Thriving potted plants were arranged artfully around the porch.

Bundles of dried herbs and small bells hung by the door, which was a warm, rustic red, and adorned with a wreath made of dried flowers and twigs. Soft, warm lights glowed from the windows.

The door swung open before I could knock, as if Ivy had sensed my presence, and she greeted me with a warm hug. Her beautiful silk pajamas shimmered softly in the light, the shirt bearing the playful slogan: HEX THE STRESS.

"Hey, Vinnie! Come in, make yourself comfortable," she said, pulling me inside.

The enchanting atmosphere of Ivy's cottage immediately enveloped me as soon as I stepped inside. Dim fairy lights and candles twinkled from every corner, casting a soft, kaleidoscopic glow, and the air was rich with the earthy scent of herbs and incense. Posters of herbs and plant anatomy adorned the walls, blending seamlessly with the shelves overflowing with crystals, figurines, and various mystical trinkets. It was a charmingly cluttered space, and utterly filled with Ivy's personality.

Plants of all shapes and sizes sat on every surface, their green leaves adding warmth and life to the room, and a black cat with piercing green eyes weaved between Ivy's legs, purring contentedly.

"And this, is Salem," Ivy introduced, scooping up the cat with a smile. "He's my little guardian."

Salem blinked lazily at me, his eyes narrowing as if assessing whether I was friend or foe. "Hey, Salem," I greeted, reaching out to scratch behind his ears. He responded with a soft purr, settling comfortably in Ivy's arms.

I took off my boots, and we made our way further into the house to the living room. Deep purples, rich greens, and warm earthy tones blended together, and the flickering light cast dancing shadows on the walls, enhancing the mystical ambiance.

Vintage and modern elements were blended in an eclectic mix, creating the living room itself. A plush couch covered in soft blankets and cushions beckoned me to relax. An array of snacks and a couple of wine glasses were set on the coffee table, alongside a bottle of red wine ready to be poured. A large, worn rug covered the wooden floor and, in one corner, a low wooden bookshelf displayed books on various mystical subjects. Atop it, more plants sat beside a few well-placed crystals.

"Make yourself at home," Ivy said, gesturing to the couch with a warm smile, and I sank into the plush cushions, the fabric soft against my skin.

"It seems we had the same idea," I laughed, reaching into my bag to pull out the snacks and wine I'd brought.

"You can never have too much wine," Ivy chuckled, grabbing a bottle opener. With a practiced twist, she popped the cork, and poured us each a generous glass. The deep red liquid glistened in the soft light as she handed me a glass, then took a sip of her own. "I thought we could have a classic horror movie marathon tonight. It's been ages since I watched some of these. We can have it on in the background while we chat."

"Yes! I love *Scream*! It's one of my all-time favorites!" I exclaimed, already feeling the nostalgic thrill. I took a sip of the wine, savoring its rich, fruity taste.

Ivy grinned mischievously. "*Scream*? I'm *obsessed* with Ghostface! There's something about that mask . . . it's creepy, but also kinda sexy, in a weird way. It just gives me chills!"

I was in the middle of another sip of wine when her comment caught me off guard, and I snorted some out of my nose, which only made us both burst into laughter. "Seriously? That mask? *That's* what does it for you?" I asked, wiping my face with a napkin, still chuckling.

"Hey, don't knock it till you try it!" Ivy teased, her eyes sparkling with mirth.

As the first movie played, we settled into a comfortable rhythm in front of the flickering screen, chatting and laughing about everything, from horror movie tropes, to our favorite scenes, the wine flowing free and easy.

Ivy leaned in with a playful glint in her eyes. "So, spill the tea—what's the deal with Ethan? Are you excited for your date tomorrow?"

"Yeah, I am," I admitted, a shy smile tugging at my lips. "We've been texting a lot and, honestly, it's been really nice. I mean, he's just . . . different. And not in a bad way," I said, biting my lip as I tried to put my thoughts into words. "He's genuine and kind, and I don't feel like I have to put on a front around him."

"And . . .?" Ivy prompted eagerly.

I blushed, the warmth of the wine spreading through my cheeks, and the tipsiness loosening my tongue. "Okay, fine!" I laughed, covering my face with my hands. "I've been thinking about him in *that* way, too," I admitted, giggling nervously.

Ivy squealed with excitement and grabbed a handful of popcorn. "Tell me more!"

"It's just . . . there's something about him being a teacher that's *so* hot," I confessed, feeling my cheeks heat. "I keep imagining him in his element, being all smart and confident, and it just drives me crazy. And then I wonder—would he be as soft and sweet in bed as he is in person, or is there a wilder side to him?" I admitted, laughing nervously. "I can't help but let my thoughts wander, especially since we've been texting all day. It's like, the more I get to know him, the more intrigued I am."

Ivy grabbed the bottle of wine and refilled our glasses. "You *are* allowed to think about that stuff! There's no shame in it, at all," she said with a playful grin. She leaned back, looking thoughtful. "But really, have you even ever *had* the chance to just . . . be wild? Like, let loose, and do whatever you want?"

I shook my head, frustration and nostalgia washing over me. "Not really. I'm so used to the physical part of a relationship being a big deal. With Sebastian, that was a huge part of what we had. And honestly, I miss that. It's been four months, and I'm definitely feeling a bit . . . frustrated." I laughed, but the sound came out more strained than amused, and I took a big gulp of wine, trying to drown out the lingering memories of Sebastian's touch.

"I totally get that," she said, her voice gentle. "It's understandable to miss that intimacy, and to feel frustrated. It's a natural part of being human, after all."

I nodded, feeling a little lighter having said it out loud. There was a moment of comfortable silence, filled with the soft sound of the movie playing in the background. Ivy looked at me, her eyes curious but kind. "What exactly happened with Sebastian? You haven't really talked about it."

I hesitated, the memories rushing back and weighing heavily on my heart. I sighed, taking another sip of wine to steady myself. "It's a long story," I began. "Sebastian was . . . complicated. He had this way of making me feel special, and then tearing me down, all in the same breath. It was like I was constantly trying to prove my worth to him, and when things were good, they were really good. But when they were bad . . ."

Ivy gave me a sympathetic look, then brightened. "You know, it's a full moon tonight," she said with a playful smile. "There's this old tradition in Hallow's End, where you write down everything you need to let go of, then burn the paper and scatter the ashes outside. They say the town's magic helps resolve it, sometimes in ways you don't expect. It's usually done on Hallow's Eve night, when the veil between worlds is thin, but hey, it's the intention that counts, right?"

She leaned in closer, her voice dropping to a whisper as if sharing a secret. "The idea, is that the act of burning your burdens transforms them, releasing their hold on you. And ashes scattered into the wind are carried by the town's ancient ley lines. The lines amplify intentions and, under the light of the full moon, the magic becomes even stronger. It's like a mystical cleanse, helping you move forward and embrace new possibilities."

The way she described it, added an enchanting, almost otherworldly, quality to the simple act of letting go. The notion of tapping into the unknown felt strangely fitting, like this was the perfect place to initiate a new beginning and relinquish the past. Ivy's blue eyes sparkled with excitement, and I could feel the allure of the ritual.

"That sounds . . . kind of perfect," I admitted. Even though I didn't truly believe in magic, the process made sense. The idea of physically writing down and burning my burdens felt like a tangible way to let go of them.

"So, why not give it a try? Let it all out, burn it, and see what the town's magic does? Who knows? Maybe it'll help you let go of Sebastian, and everything else that's been holding you back," Ivy said, her expression earnest. "You can tell me what happened while I gather the supplies."

As I began to recount my past with Sebastian, Ivy moved around the room. She picked up a stack of paper, a few candles, and a pen, setting them on the coffee table. Her actions were calm and deliberate, comforting me as I delved into the memories.

"I guess I should start from the day we met," I began, staring into my glass. The images came flooding back, sharp and vivid. "Sebastian and I first crossed paths at a charity gala my parents insisted I attend. It was a big deal for my father's business, and my mother made it clear that I needed to make the right impression."

In my mind, I was back in the grand ballroom of the Sterling estate. The marble floors gleamed under the warm glow of chandeliers, and guests moved gracefully, their conversations a soft murmur in the sophisticated air. It was a world of tailored suits and exquisite gowns, and I'd felt out of place amid the elegance and expectations.

"My mother has always been obsessed with appearances," I continued, the image of her clear in my mind. Victoria Carlisle—tall and impeccably elegant, with her perfectly styled blond hair, and piercing gray eyes—always carried herself with a refined grace. She had a knack for reading people and situations, always aiming to maintain the perfect image for our family.

"That night, she was focused on Sebastian Sterling," I added, remembering her calculating smile. "To her, he wasn't just a great match for me, he was also a valuable connection for my father's business. She saw him as the perfect addition to our family's carefully curated image."

I took a deep breath, recalling how Sebastian had approached me that night. He towered over me, a tall and commanding presence that made my heart race. His honey-blonde hair was perfectly styled, highlighting his sharp jawline and high cheekbones, and his green eyes were piercing, locking onto mine with a gaze that felt almost hypnotic, as if he could see straight through me. The tailored black suit he wore fit him impeccably, accentuating his broad shoulders and lean, muscular frame. And he smelled *intoxicatingly* good—a mix of musky cologne and woodsy undertones.

He was two years older, a fact I was keenly aware of, which only added to my nervousness in his presence. There was something about him that made me want to impress him, to be the perfect, poised young woman my mother had tried to mold me into. For the first time, I regretted not paying more attention in the etiquette classes she sent me to. There was an undeniable magnetism to him, something that pulled me in despite my initial desire to resist. Looking back, it was almost surreal how perfect he had seemed that night—like he was too good to be true. And now, I realize he was.

"Sebastian suggested we escape the crowd," I continued, a faint smile tugging at my lips. "He led me to the gallery wing, away from the noise and chaos. The moment felt intimate, like we were stepping into a world of our own. We talked about art, cooking, and life. It was refreshing. Sebastian made me laugh, and he had this way of making me feel *seen*, as if he appreciated me for who I was, not just for my last name, or the way I looked.

"He listened to me talk about my passion for painting, and my dreams of becoming an artist. For the first time, I felt like someone understood and supported that part of me. He didn't dismiss it as a frivolous hobby. Instead, he seemed to admire my dedication. It made me believe he could be someone who would stand by me, even against my parent's expectations."

I sighed, taking a sip of wine. "But now, looking back, I realize it was all part of his act. His interest in my art, in my dreams—it was just a way to draw me in, to make me feel special. It felt so real then but, as our relationship progressed, it became clear that it was all surface-level. He just knew how to say the right things to keep me hooked, to make me feel like I mattered to him. I thought he saw *me*, but he was only ever interested in what I could *offer*—my family's connections, the way I looked on his arm, and the way I made him feel important. I was just another piece in his carefully constructed life, and I didn't see it until it was too late."

Ivy poured more wine into my now-empty glass and I took a sip, the warmth settling in my chest. As Ivy lit a few more candles and placed them around the room, the atmosphere became intimate and almost sacred, and a faint scent of herbs and incense filled the air.

"I was so caught up in the excitement," I admitted, my voice tinged with regret. "Sebastian had this way of making me feel like I had to constantly earn his attention. He'd make me feel like the most special person in the world one moment, and then he'd flirt with other women right in front of me, keeping me on edge. It created this constant push-and-pull, where I felt like I had to prove myself to him, like I wasn't quite good enough without his approval."

Ivy's face scrunched in annoyance. "What a dick," she muttered, shaking her head. She quickly apologized, her expression softening with empathy. "Sorry, Vinnie. It's just . . . I can't believe he made you feel like that."

I smiled faintly, appreciating her support. "Yeah, it wasn't great. But at the time, I was too caught up to clearly see it.

"Please, continue," Ivy urged, her tone gentle. "I want to hear it all."

Encouraged by her understanding, I continued. "He'd say things like, 'You're lucky I understand you,' or, 'Not everyone could handle your quirks.' It was subtle, but it made me feel like I should be grateful he was willing to put up with me."

"That's so messed up," Ivy said, her voice tinged with frustration. "What an ass! He totally gaslighted you into thinking you were lucky to have him, instead of him being lucky to have *you*!"

I nodded, feeling the weight of her words, and the truth they held. "It was like he had this hold on me, making me feel constantly insecure and unsure of myself. He made me believe I needed to be perfect to keep him interested. And I was so wrapped up in the fantasy of our relationship—the idea that someone like him could love someone like me—that I ignored all the warning signs. I didn't want to face the truth that the person I thought loved me was just using me to boost his ego."

Ivy shook her head. "It makes me so angry to hear that he treated you like that. You deserved so much better, Vinnie. It's hard to see it when you're in the middle of it, but I'm glad you're realizing it now."

I took a deep breath, letting her words sink in. The realization was painful, but also liberating. For the first time, I felt like I could let go of the guilt and confusion that had plagued me for so long.

Ivy reached over to the coffee table, grabbing the pen and a piece of paper she'd laid out earlier, and handed them to me. "Okay, Vinnie, now's your chance," she said softly. "Write down what you need to let go of. Be honest with yourself."

I started to write, the words flowing out in a steady stream: *I want to resolve my feelings about Sebastian so I can finally move on.*

Ivy watched me closely, sensing the significance of the moment. "You ready?"

Lightness floated over me when I burned the paper. The simple act, combined with Ivy's support, feeling cathartic. Though it was symbolic, the gesture carried real emotional weight and, as the last wisps of smoke faded, I silently hoped that this would help me to finally move on.

Chapter 13

THE REST OF THE NIGHT flowed effortlessly. Ivy and I watched classic horror movies, each scene punctuated by her playful commentary. Her jokes about the cheesy special effects, and her dramatic reenactments of the most ridiculous moments, had me in stitches. She'd grab a pillow and mimic the over-the-top screams or pretend to wield an imaginary weapon with exaggerated bravado, making the entire experience feel like we were kids at a sleepover again.

When credits rolled on yet another slasher film, Ivy leaned back with a satisfied sigh, popping a handful of popcorn into her mouth. "You know, I can never get enough of these," she said, grinning. "No matter how bad they are, there's something comforting about them."

I laughed, the sound light and free. "I don't think I've laughed this much in ages."

"Well, I aim to please." Ivy grinned. "My love for horror movies comes from my parents, you know. They got me into them when I was way too young, but I loved spending time with them."

I laughed, imagining a young Ivy. "Where are your parents now?"

"They're philosophers," she said, a hint of pride in her voice. "Currently, they're on an epic trip around Asia, delving into various spiritual and philosophical traditions. Traveling has always been a regular occurrence for them. When I was younger, I used to stay with my grandma when they were away."

"That sounds amazing," I said. "What was it like, growing up with parents like that?"

Ivy chuckled. "It was definitely interesting. Our dinner conversations were always deep dives into the nature of existence, or the ethics of modern society. They encouraged me to explore all kinds of different beliefs and practices. That's where all the witchy stuff comes from. My grandma taught me a lot when I stayed with her as well."

"What's your grandma like?" I asked, leaning forward.

"She's the coolest," she said, her eyes lighting up. "My grandma's name is Eliza. She's this tiny woman with a ton of spunk. She used to run a small herb shop here, and got me into all the witchy and herbal stuff. Staying with her was always an adventure. In fact, the space for Enchanted Quill was a gift from her. She told me to make it my own, and that's exactly what I did."

"That's so sweet," I said, smiling at the thought. "Where is she staying now?"

"She's at Brookside Haven," Ivy replied. "It's a great place just outside of town, more of a retirement community than a nursing home. She's really thriving there. Making friends, hosting social nights, and even doing tarot readings. Oh, and she's met someone, too! A gentleman named George.

He's a retired professor, and they bond over their love for literature and philosophy."

"Have you met him?" I asked, curious.

"Yeah, I've met him a few times," Ivy said with a fond smile. "He's great. Tall, with a kind face and a gentle demeanor. He's got this old-world charm about him; always wearing tweed jackets, and reading glasses perched on the tip of his nose. It's really sweet to see them together."

"That sounds perfect for her," I said. "Why Brookside, though?"

"Well, it's bigger than Hallow's End," Ivy explained. "They've got the college, and new chain stores popping up. I have a feeling it'll keep growing as more people see the appeal of moving there for the slower pace of life, whilst still enjoying some city comforts. Plus, Brookside Haven has excellent facilities, and Grandma Eliza loves it there. And it's close enough that I get to visit her most weekends."

"That sounds ideal," I said, smiling. "It must have been hard not having your parents at home all the time," I commented, feeling pang of empathy.

Ivy shrugged with a warm smile. "No need to feel bad. My parents are great. They always make sure they're home for important dates like Christmases and birthdays. Plus, now that I'm older, I don't notice their absence as much."

"They've always encouraged me to be myself, and explore my interests. I wouldn't be the person I am today without them. But enough about my family. What about your parents? Though I think I might have a pretty good idea already."

I chuckled, shaking my head. "Yeah, they weren't much of . . . parents. More like showrunners, really. They treated me like a doll, dragging me to social events and showing me off. I hated it."

Ivy's expression softened with sympathy. "That sounds tough."

I shrugged, trying to brush it off. "It wasn't all bad. I had some amazing nannies who took care of me. They were supposed to be strict, and teach me how to behave but, behind closed doors, they were wonderful. When I was around five or six, I convinced myself that I was adopted, because I didn't relate to my parents at all. I even told one of my nannies that I thought they had picked me up from the hospital by mistake."

Ivy laughed. "That's adorable. So, what were the nannies like?"

"There was Maria, my favorite," I said, a fond smile spreading across my face. "She was supposed to be strict, but she had a heart of gold. When I was twelve, and I started showing more and more interest in art, Maria noticed. She took me to my first art gallery, and signed me up to art classes."

Ivy leaned in, fascinated. "It sounds like Maria really made a difference in your life."

"She did," I agreed, feeling a wave of nostalgia. "She made me realize it was okay to be different from my parents, to have my own interests and passions."

We settled into the sofa, our legs tucked comfortably under us as we sipped the last of the wine. Ivy glanced at the clock, then back at me with a smile. "It's a little late, but I don't mind staying up longer. We could watch some more movies if you're up for it?"

"Absolutely," I nodded eagerly.

Ivy sighed, her expression softening. "I've missed this. Amelia's been going out a lot recently, and our other friend, Daphne, moved away after high school. We keep in touch, but it's not the same."

"What about Emily?" I asked, a playful grin on my face.

Ivy laughed, shaking her head. "Imagine trying to have a deep conversation with a golden retriever puppy. Emily is like that. All energy, and no focus."

I burst out laughing.

"I mean, I love her enthusiasm," Ivy said, giggling, "but sometimes, you just need to sit down, have a glass of wine, and talk about life."

Speaking about Emily caused my thoughts to wander to Ethan, and the idea of texting him flitted through my mind. I laughed at myself for even considering it, but the desire to reach out was strong. In my tipsy state, rational thoughts had fled, leaving behind a fluttering excitement.

In high school, I'd found the boys immature, and lacking the spark I craved. College wasn't much different, until I met Sebastian early in my first year and was immediately addicted to him. Our relationship moved fast. Within the first month, we were official and exchanging 'I love you'. At the time, it felt right, even if it was intense. But now, with Ethan, I found myself savoring the uncertainty and anticipation.

Ivy waved a hand in front of my face. "Earth to Vinnie," she laughed. "I think we've had a bit too much to drink."

"Sorry, Ivy. I'm just so tempted to text Ethan, right now," I confessed, giggling. "But I'm pretty drunk, so it's probably a bad idea. Right?"

"Oh, do it! But knowing him, he's probably either asleep or buried in a book." She paused, her eyes twinkling mischievously. "Do you think he reads spicy books?"

I burst out laughing. "I have no idea! But now I'm curious."

"You should ask him. If he does, I have some great titles that will make his reading list a lot more interesting." Ivy leaned back, grinning. "Go on, text him. Just keep it light and fun."

I pulled out my phone, my heart racing with excitement. The wine had made me bold and I embraced it as I contemplated what to write.

> **Vinnie:** Hey Ethan! Just wanted to see how your night is going. Hope you're not burped under a mountain of books. If you are, I might have to come rescue you 😊

I squinted at the screen, feeling less confident about my spelling abilities. "Ivy, can you check this? I don't trust myself right now."

Ivy giggled, took the phone from me, barely glanced at the message, and hit send.

I groaned, reaching to check the text, and my eyes widened as I noticed the typo. "It says 'burped' instead of 'buried!' Ivy, I thought you checked it!"

"Whoops, my bad" Ivy said, laughing. "Maybe he'll find it endearing."

I noticed the read receipt on the message.

"Oh my god, he's read it," I said, my eyes widening further. I watched the screen anxiously as the three 'typing' dots appeared.

"I need to calm down," I said, dropping the phone on the couch. "Why am I freaking out this much?"

"Maybe because you've got it bad for him?" Ivy smirked, raising an eyebrow. "And I bet Ethan could definitely help you . . . unwind."

I blushed even deeper, the warmth spreading from my cheeks down my neck. "Stop, Ivy! You're making it worse!" I said between giggles, my stomach aching from laughing so hard.

Ivy wiped a tear from the corner of her eye, still chuckling as my phone buzzed on the table. Our laughter halted abruptly, and we both stared at it, the anticipation hanging thick in the air.

"Go on, read it!" Ivy urged, nudging me with her elbow.

> **Ethan:** Hey Vinnie! Not BURPED under books, but I wouldn't mind being rescued from this boring night. Your typo made me laugh. It was cute. 😊

My heart skipped a beat, a giddy smile spreading across my face as Ivy peeked over my shoulder and grinned. "Looks like he's into you, typo and all."

"What should I text back?" I asked, my mind racing.

Ivy, clearly enjoying her role as my tipsy advisor, put on a mock-serious face. "Lay it on thick, girl. This is the perfect night for some flirtatious fun!"

> **Vinnie:** Having a fun sleepover with Ivy! 🍾 😵 She's got me tipsy and feeling like I'm back at college.

I hesitated for a moment, then quickly typed out a second message and hit send.

> **Vinnie:** So, you think I'm cute? 😊

I showed Ivy the message and she burst into laughter. "That's perfect!"

Both our stomachs growled in unison, sending us into another fit of giggles, and Salem, who had been lounging nearby, flicked his tail and sauntered out of the room, done with our antics.

"Wine and snacks seemed like a great idea," I said, still chuckling. "But now I'm craving something more substantial. Like a greasy pizza."

Ivy nodded and stood, making her way to the kitchen. "Yes! There's this awesome pizza place called Cheesy Delights. Caleb works there late on weekends and always makes the best food. I'll grab the menu," she called over her shoulder.

My phone pinged again with a text from Ethan, and I glanced at it, my heart fluttering.

> **Ethan:** Girls' night sounds like a blast! Closest I've ever gotten to one of those is with Lily. She makes me braid her hair, and puts these ridiculous strawberry clips in mine. Last weekend she even told me about her 'boy drama.' At six years old! Can you believe that? 😊

I couldn't help but giggle, imagining Ethan with strawberry clips in his hair. When Ivy returned, she found me grinning at my phone.

"What's got you smiling like that?" she asked, jumping onto the sofa next to me.

"Listen to this," I said, reading Ethan's message to her.

She giggled, shaking her head. "That's adorable!"

Before I could reply, another message came through.

> **Ethan:** And for the record, I do think you're cute. In fact, I can't stop thinking about you. Can't wait to see you tomorrow. Well, today actually, since it's past midnight. 😊

> **Vinnie:** That's adorable! Lily sounds like a fun kid. Can't wait to hear more about her. So, what exactly have you been thinking about me? 😊

Ivy peeked over my shoulder and giggled. "Perfect! Now, let's decide on our pizza toppings. How about their Four Cheese Special, and a Classic Pepperoni?"

"With pineapple?" I suggested.

Ivy's eyes widened in horror. "Vinnie, that's blasphemy!"

I laughed, holding up my hands in defense, and Ivy shook her head as she held the phone to her ear.

"Hey Caleb, it's Ivy! Can we get a Four Cheese Special with extra cheese, and a Classic Pepperoni with . . . pineapple? Yeah, I know. I did tell Vinnie that." Ivy's smile widened to whatever he said back before. "Oh, and make it quick, we're starving!"

I couldn't hear Caleb's response, but Ivy's face turned a shade pinker, and she giggled. "Knock it off, Caleb. Just get us the pizzas, okay?"

Ivy hung up and plopped back down beside me. "He said it'll be about twenty minutes."

"Do you and he . . ." I wiggled my eyebrows suggestively.

Ivy laughed, a blush creeping up her cheeks. "No, no, it's not like that with Caleb. He's just a friend."

"Sure. You're blushing, though." I raised an eyebrow.

Ivy shrugged, still smiling. "He's a nice guy, but we are just not compatible. Anyway, pick out another movie while we wait for the food."

I took the remote, scrolling through the options but not finding anything that caught my eye. Ivy handed me a soda and grinned. "Actually, I have a better idea. How about a tarot reading?"

"Sure, why not?" I laughed, the idea sounding both absurd and intriguing.

As Ivy dashed off to her room to grab her tarot cards, I thought about how strange it was, that pieces of cardboard could supposedly tell you about your life. Despite finding it silly, I was still interested.

My phone buzzed with a new message from Ethan, pulling my attention away from my thoughts.

> **Ethan:** There's just something about you, Vinnie. I love how easy it is to talk to you. And, I gotta admit, I love your smile 😊

A warm flush spread through me, and I smiled at his words. I was about to type a response when another message from him popped up.

> **Ethan:** I'm heading to bed now. But maybe we could grab dinner or drinks before the quiz?

Without hesitation, I quickly typed back.

> **Vinnie:** Yes, dinner sounds great! 😊

Ivy ran back into the room, nearly tripping over the rug in her haste, catching herself on the arm of the sofa as she stumbled. "Whoops! I'm just so excited!" she exclaimed, breathless and grinning as she flopped down next to me.

I laughed. "Careful! We don't need any accidents tonight."

Ivy waved it off, her face glowing with enthusiasm. "Okay, let's do a three-card reading. Past, present, and future. But first, we need to cleanse the space," she declared, standing up dramatically.

I couldn't help but laugh as Ivy waved a bundle of sage around the room, her blue hair messy. "You look absolutely ridiculous," I teased, giggling.

She stuck out her tongue playfully. "Hey, this is serious business! We need to make sure we're in a good-vibe zone. Have you ever had your cards read before?"

"Nope, this is a first," I admitted, still chuckling at her.

"Well, let me give you a quick rundown. Tarot cards are like a mirror reflecting your subconscious. Each card has different meanings and, when you draw them in a spread, it's like a snapshot of your life."

"Got it," I said, leaning in, curious despite myself.

"Perfect! Now, let's do this," Ivy said, shuffling the deck with expert precision. She spread the cards out on the coffee table and selected three. With a dramatic flourish, she flipped over the first card.

"This is your past: The Tower," Ivy announced, trying to sound ominous but failing to keep a straight face. The card depicted a tower being struck by lightning, figures falling from its heights. "The Tower represents upheaval, sudden change, and things falling apart. Basically, a hot mess."

I stared at the card. "Well, that's . . . accurate," I said.

Ivy's eyes widened in surprise when she saw the second card. "Death," she said, sounding intrigued rather than worried. "This is definitely interesting. Don't worry," she quickly added, seeing my tensed expression. "It's not a bad card. In tarot, Death signifies transformation, endings, and new beginnings. It's about letting go of what no longer serves you to make space for something better. Something in your life will come to an end, but it's necessary for your growth. I'm curious to see what this one's all about."

I chewed on my lip, trying to make sense of the card, before shaking my head. I reminded myself that this was just some silly fun. "That's . . . intense," I finally said, pushing the thought away.

"And now, for your future," she said, flipping over the final card. "The Ten of Cups!" The card showed a family standing under a rainbow of cups. "This is one of the best cards you can get! It represents emotional fulfilment, happiness, and harmonious relationships. Your future is bright, Vinnie. You're on the path to finding true contentment and joy."

I burst into laughter. "Well, that's good to know! I'll take that."

"The cards don't lie. It looks like Hallow's End is exactly where you're meant to be." Ivy squeezed my hand, her eyes shining with excitement.

We both settled back onto the sofa, giggling. "What did you think of your first tarot reading?" Ivy said.

"I think it was fun," I said, laughing. "I'm not sure I believe in all of it, but it was interesting."

Ivy grinned. "That's the spirit! It's all about the journey, not the destination. And hey, it's fun to think about what might happen, right? And who knows? Maybe the cards have a bit of magic in them, after all." She sighed dramatically and added, "It's going to be so dull without you around once you go back to Cresden."

Caught up in the warmth and spontaneity of the moment, and wanting to cheer her up, I blurted out, "Actually, I've decided to stay."

Ivy let out a delighted squeal and jumped up on the sofa, causing me to spill a bit of soda. "Are you serious? That's amazing, Vinnie!"

"Yeah, I still have to tell my parents, and I'm worried about their reaction. But I've made up my mind."

Ivy plopped down beside me, taking my hand in hers. "Don't worry. No matter what, I'll be here to help you through it. Plus, you've got me and Amelia. And maybe even Ethan?"

The mention of Ethan made my heart flutter again. "I'm really excited to get to know Amelia better. I wish she came tonight. I've always wanted my own girl group, you know? And with Ethan, everything is still so new. I don't want to have any expectations. I just want to keep it fun and see what happens."

A knock at the door interrupted our moment. "Pizza time!" Ivy exclaimed, hopping up and rushing to answer the door. Swiftly, Ivy opened the door, grabbed the boxes from Caleb, and stepped outside, shutting the door behind her before I could get a look at him. I could hear Caleb's faint chuckle through the wood as they exchanged a few words before Ivy returned with a triumphant grin, balancing the pizza boxes in her arms.

"Dinner is served!" she declared, setting them down on the coffee table.

The smell of the pizza made my stomach growl, and we dug in, the combination of cheesy goodness and laughter making the night even better. We continued chatting about everything and nothing as we devoured the food and, eventually, we both settled back on the sofa, feeling full and content.

Ivy yawned and stretched. "I don't know about you, but I'm about ready to call it a night."

"Same here," I agreed, my eyelids growing heavy. "This has been one of the best nights I've had in a long time."

"Come on," Ivy said. "I'll show you to the guest room."

She led me down the hall, stopping in front of a door. "Here you go," she said, opening it for me. "Make yourself comfortable."

"Thanks, Ivy," I mumbled, feeling utterly exhausted. I stepped inside, too tired to even take in the details of the room. The bed looked incredibly inviting, and I didn't bother with the lights.

"Sleep tight, Vinnie."

"Goodnight," I said, already half-asleep. I barely had the energy to kick off my shoes before collapsing onto the bed and sinking into the soft mattress.

Chapter 14

I WOKE UP GROGGY, the remnants of sleep still clinging to me as I blinked against the soft morning light filtering through the curtains. My head felt a little heavy from the wine but, as I stretched out in the bed, the ache faded, replaced by a sense of comfort. I had been too tired the night before to notice much, but now I took in the room around me, appreciating the subtle charm that was distinctly Ivy.

The walls were a soft sage green, with framed pressed flowers and delicate botanical prints in frames, each one chosen with care. A macramé wall-hanging draped artfully over the headboard, adding a touch of bohemian flair. The bed I had sunk into the night before was a haven of comfort, piled high with mismatched pillows and a quilted comforter that felt like a warm embrace.

In one corner, an antique wooden dresser held an assortment of candles, crystals, and small potted plants, their leaves trailing over the edges in a gentle cascade. A worn but well-loved armchair sat beside it, draped with a knitted throw in rich, earthy tones. On the opposite side of the room, a small bookshelf was crammed with books. A thick, woven rug, in shades of deep burgundy and gold, covered the floor.

Ivy had clearly put thought into every detail, creating a space that felt like a sanctuary for her guests. Even the scent of lavender lingered in the air, a calming presence that eased the mild ache in my head from the wine the night before.

As I lay in bed, stretching out the last remnants of sleep, faint sounds drifted in from beyond the door from the kitchen. The soft clinking of dishes, the gentle hum of activity. My senses gradually sharpened, and I caught the sweet scent of something cooking; a warm, sugary aroma that hinted at pancakes, or maybe waffles? But more than anything, the rich, comforting smell of freshly brewed coffee wafted through the air, making my mouth water, and coaxing me fully awake.

I reluctantly pulled myself from the bed, the quilted comforter slipping off as I swung my legs over the side. I rummaged for some clean clothes in the small bag I'd brought with me, and my fingers brushed against the soft fabric of my favorite oversized sweater. I pulled it out, along with a pair of leggings.

After slipping into the fresh clothes, I ran a hand through my hair, attempting to tame the mess that sleeping had made of it, before padding toward the kitchen. The aroma of breakfast grew stronger with each step, and my stomach gave a small, hopeful growl.

When I reached the kitchen doorway, I paused, taking in the scene before me. Warm morning light bathed the kitchen, casting a golden glow over the space. Ivy moved about with a practiced ease, her dark blue hair piled into a messy bun that seemed to defy gravity. She wore a pair of whimsical, mismatched socks that peeked out from under the hem of her pajama pants.

The kitchen itself was a charming blend of rustic farmhouse vibes, and Ivy's eclectic tastes. The walls of the kitchen were painted a soft, creamy white, and open wooden shelves displayed an array of mismatched dishes, jars filled with spices, and potted herbs that added pops of green. The polished wood of the countertops hinted at years of use, showcasing their worn but well-loved appearance, and a large farmhouse sink sat beneath a window, its apron front catching the sunlight. Above it hung a curtain with a delicate lace trim, fluttering in the morning breeze from the open window.

Ivy was at the stove, flipping pancakes in a cast-iron skillet with a flick of her wrist. The smell of butter and syrup filled the air, mingling with the rich aroma of coffee that brewed in an old-fashioned percolator on the counter. A small chalkboard hung on the wall nearby, with a handwritten note that read TODAY'S SPECIAL: CHOCOLATE CHIP PANCAKES.

Ivy turned and caught sight of me, and a bright smile spread across her face, lighting up her already glowing features. "Good morning, sleepyhead!" she called out, her voice warm and cheerful. "I hope you're hungry. I made enough pancakes to feed an army!"

"Morning," I replied, stepping into the kitchen. "You're really spoiling me with this. I usually just grab a bowl of granola for breakfast, if I'm lucky."

Ivy grinned as she flipped another pancake. "Well, that's going to change whenever you stay here. I'm all about starting the day with a sugar rush. Consider it my personal mission to get you hooked on the good stuff before lunchtime."

I laughed, the thought of Ivy's pancake breakfasts becoming a regular thing warming my chest. "I think I could get used to that."

"Go ahead, grab some coffee and have a seat. Breakfast will be ready in just a minute." She pointed to a steaming mug waiting on the counter.

I took the cup gratefully, wrapping my hands around it as I inhaled the rich scent. The coffee was strong and smooth; the perfect way to start the day. Ivy brought a plate piled high with chocolate chip pancakes to the table, setting it down with a satisfied grin.

As soon as the sweet aroma filled the air, Salem came trotting into the room, his sleek black fur catching the morning light. With a quick leap, he hopped onto the chair next to me, his big, green eyes fixed on the pancakes with undeniable interest.

"Looks like someone else wants breakfast, too," I joked, nodding toward Salem, who was now staring at the stack like it was his own personal feast.

Ivy glanced over and laughed. "Salem, you know you can't have pancakes! You're already spoiled enough with your fancy cat food!"

He let out a small, indignant meow, as if protesting his unfair treatment, making both of us burst into laughter.

As I poured syrup over the pancakes, Ivy slid into the seat across from me, giving me a playful but earnest look. "So, are you really staying in Hallow's End like you said last night? Or was that just the wine talking?"

I picked up my fork, hesitating for a moment before nodding. "No, I'm really staying. I think it's time I rip the band-aid off and talk to my parents today. It's embarrassing that it's taken me this long to stand on my own, but I need to live my own life."

Ivy reached over, squeezing my hand. "Hey, it's not embarrassing at all. Everyone has their own timeline. What matters is that you're making the choice *now*. It's brave, Vinnie, and it's never too late to start living the life you want."

I gave her a grateful smile and took a bite of the pancake. It was deliciously sweet and comforting, just what I needed. "Thanks, Ivy. At least I'll have my date to look forward to after all that stress. And with me staying here, I can actually think about giving Ethan a real chance."

Ivy's eyes lit up with excitement as she took another bite of her pancake. "Well, now I'm even more excited! We have to plan something with Amelia. I'm determined to have our own girl group—or witches' coven, if you will."

I laughed at the idea, imagining the three of us as a quirky, magical trio. "That would be cool! And Amelia seemed so open and welcoming the other day, like she was ready to be my best friend from the moment we met."

Ivy grinned, nodding enthusiastically. "That's Amelia for you. She dives in headfirst, no hesitation. It's like she pulls everyone into her orbit without even trying. She has this incredible ability to make you feel like you belong in her world from the moment you meet. It's one of her best traits. But when it comes to her heart and committing? That's a whole different story."

She grimaced, then quickly shook it off with a bright smile. "Oh, and heads-up, she's super grouchy in the mornings, and her humor? Definitely on the sarcastic side. But, you've got to love her."

I chuckled. "It sounds like she's exactly the kind of person I need in my life right now. Someone who's not afraid to go all in and embrace whatever comes her way."

Ivy nodded, her smile softening into something more sincere. "Exactly. We all need friends like that—people who remind us to be brave and take chances, even if we don't always know where we'll land."

"Well, I'm in. Let's build that coven."

Just as Ivy was about to say something, a sudden rustle caught our attention, and we turned just in time to see Salem, quick as lightning, leap onto the table and snatch a pancake between his teeth.

"Salem!" Ivy exclaimed, jumping up from her chair. "You petty thief!"

Salem darted off the table, the pancake flapping absurdly from his mouth as he bolted across the room. Ivy, her loose pajama pants trailing behind her, took off in pursuit. "Get back here, you rascal! That's not for you!"

I doubled over with laughter, until finally, Ivy halted, hands on her hips, her face full of exasperation. "Well, it looks like Salem's decided he's joining us for breakfast," she said with a sigh, her lips twitching into a smile as she made her way back to the table. "You'll have to forgive my furry little menace."

Still laughing, I wiped a tear from my eye. "I think he just wanted to be part of the fun. And it's nice to know someone appreciates your cooking as much as I do."

Ivy shook her head, still grinning as she sat back down. "Well, he's certainly got great taste, I'll give him that."

Later that day, I sat at my kitchen table, my laptop open in front of me, its screen casting a pale glow in the otherwise silent room. The weight of what I was about to do felt like a stone lodged in my chest, but I knew I had to tell my parents about my decision to stay in Hallow's End and open my art gallery. The very thought filled me with dread. This wasn't just a phone call—it was a declaration of independence. A step towards the life I wanted, and one I knew they wouldn't approve of.

Taking a deep breath, I clicked on my mom's contact in my video call app, and the familiar ringing tone began to echo through the room. My hands trembled, and I had to clench them into fists to steady myself. Each ring felt like a countdown.

When the call connected, my mother's face appeared on the screen, perfectly composed as always. Her blonde hair was styled impeccably, and her gray eyes sparkled with a warmth that I knew would quickly transform into disappointment in approximately two minutes, after she heard what I had to say.

"Lavinia, darling! It's so good to see you. How are you?" she asked, her voice full of genuine affection that took me by surprise.

"Hi, Mom. I'm good. How are you guys?" I replied, forcing a smile, though my nerves were getting the better of me.

I glanced at the familiar setting behind them—the elegant living room of our family home in Cresden. The soft glow of the crystal chandelier illuminated the room, showcasing carefully arranged furniture, and the grand piano that my mother insisted on keeping polished, even though no one played it. They seemed to be in the middle of one of my mother's forced *family bonding* activities—perhaps a game of chess that she always insisted my father play with her to keep his mind sharp.

Before I could say more, my father's stern face filled the screen, his neatly trimmed dark brown hair now peppered with gray, and his piercing blue eyes locked onto mine with that all-too-familiar look of disapproval. He wore a tailored suit, as always.

"Lavinia, when are you going to stop this childish rebellion and come home?" My father's voice was sharp, cutting through the small talk with the precision of a blade. His brows furrowed, and he set his jaw in that stern, unyielding way that always made me feel like a child being scolded. My mother, sitting beside him on the pristine white sofa, shot him a look of thinly veiled irritation as she gently placed a manicured hand on his arm; a silent plea for restraint.

"Jonathan, please," she said, her tone a careful blend of frustration and concern. Her eyes softened as they turned back to me, though the tension in her posture betrayed her own anxiety. "Let's hear what Lavinia has to say."

My father's mouth tightened into a hard line, but he gave a curt nod as he leaned back, his arms crossing over his chest in a defensive posture. My mother's fingers lingered on his arm for a moment longer, a subtle attempt to soothe the situation, before she turned her full attention back to me, her gaze expectant but not unkind.

I tried to muster a smile, but it felt forced under the weight of my father's bored, angry expression. His eyes had already glazed over with impatience, and the stern set of his mouth made my heart sink further. "It's been a while. I just wanted to check in with you."

My mother leaned forward, her eyes showing a glimmer of interest despite the tension in the room. She tucked a stray lock of blonde hair behind her ear, a soft smile playing on her lips as she tried to bridge the gap. "How have you been, dear? How's life in that little town treating you?"

I hesitated, feeling the weight of the real reason for my call pressing down on me, but I couldn't bring myself to dive into it just yet. I was stalling, and I knew it. "It's been really good, actually," I began, trying to keep my tone light. "I've made new friends, and the whole town is buzzing with excitement for the upcoming Halloween festival. It's such a beautiful place."

"That sounds lovely, darling," my mother said, her voice softening as she tried to be supportive. "It's good that you're making friends."

I smiled, feeling a small wave of relief. "And there's this amazing coffee shop, Harvest Moon. Mom, you have to try their coffee someday—it's even better than the one in Cresden."

My mother's smile remained, though it was tinged with scepticism. "Better than Cresden's? That's hard to believe," she said. "But I'm glad you're enjoying your time there, darling." She paused, her expression softening, "It's good that you're making the most of your trip."

My mother's gentle tone was a lifeline in the storm of my father's harshness, and I couldn't help but feel a pang of guilt. I knew I'd hurt her after our last call, where I had snapped and unloaded all my frustrations, and the memory of that argument still weighed on me, making this moment even more difficult.

"Mom," I began, my voice softer, "I'm sorry I didn't call sooner. I know the last time we talked . . . it wasn't easy."

She offered a small, understanding smile. "It's alright, Vinnie. We both needed time to collect ourselves and think things through. I'm just happy you set up this video chat today. It means a lot to me."

Her words gave me a bit of comfort, and I nodded, though my nerves were still bubbling beneath the surface. "I appreciate that, Mom."

"You've always been strong-willed. It's one of the things I admire about you, even if it makes things difficult sometimes."

"Enough with the small talk, Lavinia," my father snapped, cutting through the moment with as much subtlety as a machete. His tone was sharp, and his impatience stung. "Get to the point. Why did you really call?"

I flinched at his words, my smile faltering as the pressure mounted. This was it—time to face the music.

"Fine. I wanted to let you both know that I've decided to open an art gallery here. I'm staying in Hallow's End for good." I blurted it all in one go, wanting to get it over with.

There was a moment of stunned silence, and my father's face turned a deep shade of red, his jaw clenched so tightly that I could see the muscles twitch. My mother's eyes widened in shock, her hand coming up to cover her mouth.

"You can't be serious," my father finally spat out, his voice shaking with barely contained fury. "An art gallery? In that nowhere town? How could you throw away your future like this?"

My mother quickly lowered her hand, trying to intervene, her voice softer, though trembling with anxiety. "Jonathan, let's just calm down for a moment." She turned to me, her tone pleading. "Lavinia, are you sure this is what you want? Have you thought this through?"

"Yes, Mom," I replied, my voice trembling but firm. "I've thought about it a lot. This is what I want."

My father's fury only grew, and he leaned closer to the camera, his eyes blazing with anger. "You're making a colossal mistake, Lavinia! I've already planned for you to work with me, to learn the business from the ground up. Do you have any idea the effort that's gone into this? The partnership agreement with Sterling Enterprises, the plan for you and Sebastian to work together—all of it was done with your future in mind. The idea was for you to eventually merge our companies, to build something bigger and better! And now, you're throwing it all away for some . . . childish *dream*?"

Tears pricked at the corners of my eyes, but I held them back. "I understand, Dad, but—"

"You understand nothing!" he bellowed, slamming his fist down on the desk, making the camera shake. "Do you think this *hobby* of yours will sustain you? You'll be on your own, Lavinia! No more financial support, no more connections! I give it a few months before you're crawling back, begging for help."

His words cut deep, each one like a lash, but I refused to back down. Before I could even begin to respond, he delivered the final blow.

"I should have had a son. Someone who wouldn't throw away their future on a whim. You've been nothing but a disappointment."

"Jonathan, stop!" my mother cried out, her hand reaching toward him as if she could physically pull him back. But it was too late. With one last glare, he stormed out, the screen shaking as the door slammed behind him.

My mother and I were left staring at each other, the silence between us heavy and suffocating. Her face was pale, her eyes wide with shock and sadness. She opened her mouth to speak, but no words came out, her expression full of helplessness and heartbreak.

I felt utterly drained, the reality of what had just happened settling in. The path I'd chosen had just become even more daunting, but I knew, deep down, that I couldn't turn back now.

"Lavinia, darling, you know your father only wants what's best for you," my mother whispered, her voice softened by concern. "He's just . . . disappointed. He doesn't understand why you're throwing everything away."

I swallowed hard, trying to keep my composure as frustration welled up inside me. "Mom, I'm not doing this to hurt you or Dad. I just need to follow my own path."

She sighed, her eyes searching mine, her concern etched deeply into her features. "I understand that, Vinnie, but you have to see where we're coming from. Your father and I both want you to be happy; to have a secure future. To us, that means being a part of the world we've built—a life of comfort, stability, and connections. Marrying well, engaging in the lifestyle, and running your father's company—that's what we envisioned for you."

Her words twisted like a knife in my heart, but I forced myself to stay calm, even as anger simmered beneath the surface. "Mom, that world you're describing, it's never been *me*. I appreciate everything you and Dad have done for me, but those dreams are yours, not mine. I can't just fit into that mold and pretend it's what I want."

My mother's expression softened, but worry still lingered in her eyes. "But darling, think about what you're giving up. We just want you to be safe and secure. We thought by now you'd understand that this isn't about stifling your dreams. It's about ensuring you have a future."

Anger washed over me. She didn't understand. "Mom, I get you want what's best for me, but this isn't just about safety, or security. It's about *control*, and I can't live like that anymore. I need to do this, for myself."

She hesitated. "How will you sustain it, Lavinia? Opening an art gallery isn't easy. What will you do for money?"

"I've saved up," I said, my voice trembling slightly. "I've been putting money aside for a long time, and I'm confident I can make this work. Mom. I've given this a lot of thought. I'm not just jumping into it without a plan."

Her brow furrowed as she considered my words. "But Vinnie, this is such a big decision. What if it doesn't work out? You're giving up so much security. Are you sure you're ready for that?"

The desperation in her voice tugged at my heart, but I knew I had to stand firm. "I know it's a risk, Mom. But I need to take it. I've made up my mind. This is what I need to do."

My mother's face tightened, but her tone remained soft, almost coaxing, as if trying to soothe a stubborn child. "Sebastian has been asking about you, you know," she said, her voice dripping with concern. "He's worried, and talks about you all the time. Wondering how you're doing. If you come home, I'm sure I can talk to your father. We can make this all right again. You and Sebastian could pick up where you left off."

Her words were like a siren's song, painting a picture of a life that was easy, familiar, and safe. A life where I didn't have to fight so hard for everything.

"Think about it, Lavinia," she continued, her voice growing warmer. "Sebastian could take over the business, and you could focus on your art without the burden of running a gallery. We could host charity events and galas, showcasing your work, and you'd have the stability and support of your family. It's the best of both worlds. And don't forget, you and Sebastian were so close to marriage. A perfect life, with children one day. It's all within reach. A good compromise."

"Mom, I appreciate what you're trying to do. I really do. But I need to do this on my own terms. Yes, Sebastian reached out, but only when he was drunk and feeling sorry for himself. If he really missed me, he would have made more of an effort. Something real, not just the scraps he's willing to give when it suits him."

My mother's expression hardened. "Lavinia, Sebastian has responsibilities, a business to run. You know how demanding that world is. He can't just drop everything to chase after you."

A pang of bitterness rose up. "Sure, he can't drop everything for me, but he doesn't seem too busy to go out with his friends. I saw a picture the other night of him with Jessica Maddox. Looked like they were pretty cozy. Maybe *she's* the one keeping him busy now," I muttered, my voice thick with sarcasm. "I'm done being the afterthought in Sebastian's life. I want something *real*! Someone who's all in, not just halfway there when it's convenient!"

"Lavinia," my mother began, a touch of reprimand in her tone, "that's not fair. I'm sure there's an explanation."

I sighed in familiar frustration. Once again, my mother was glossing over the real issue with Sebastian, focusing on appearances, rather than the truth of how things had been between us. "Mom, it's not just about her. It's about how Sebastian and I were, how he made me feel—like I was only worth his time when he didn't have something better to do. I can't live like that anymore."

My mother sighed softly, her expression one of gentle insistence as she tried to find the right words. "Lavinia, I know Sebastian wasn't perfect, but he loved you in his own way. He's a good man. If you gave him another chance, I'm sure he'd try harder. He's always been so lovely, so *caring*, when he talks about you. People make mistakes, but that doesn't mean they can't change."

Hearing her defend Sebastian yet again made my stomach churn. It was like she couldn't see past the polished surface he presented to the world. Or maybe she didn't want to. The Sebastian my parents adored wasn't the same man I had spent so many years with, the one who had repeatedly taken me for granted.

"Mom, stop," I interrupted, the frustration bubbling over. "Please, just *stop* with Sebastian! I need to move on, and it would help if you and Dad—and Sebastian's parents—would just *let me*! I know you all mean well, but you're making it harder for both of us."

Before she could respond, I blurted out, "Actually, I'm seeing someone new." As soon as the words left my mouth, I realized how much I had overstated the situation. *Seeing someone* didn't exactly describe whatever it was that I had going on with Ethan. We'd been flirting, and there was definitely physical attraction, but we hadn't even gone on a proper date yet.

"Seeing someone already?" My mom's eyes widened in surprise. "Lavinia, that seems awfully quick. Why the rush?"

"Quick?" A wry laugh escaped me as I shook my head. "You didn't think it was quick when I jumped into things with Sebastian. In fact, you practically pushed me into it."

My mother opened her mouth to respond, but her words faltered. I could see her trying to process this new information, trying to reconcile her own insistence on my relationship with Sebastian with my sudden declaration of something new.

My mother sighed, her shoulders sagging as the fight seemed to drain out of her. "I just want you to be happy, darling. This is all happening so fast."

"I know, Mom," I said, my voice softening. "But for once, I need to do things my way. Please, just trust me on this."

There was a long pause as the weight of our conversation settled in. Finally, she nodded, though I could see the worry still etched in her features. "Alright, Lavinia. I'll try."

As we ended the call, I felt a sense of liberation, but also the heavy reality of what it meant now, to truly stand on my own.

Chapter 15

I STOOD OUTSIDE La Rosa Italiana, nervously smoothing out the red fabric of my dress. I tucked a strand of hair behind my ear, the sleek waves Amelia had expertly styled brushing against my cheek. The soft night breeze played with the hem of my dress, which ended just below my knees, and the high slit revealed a teasing glimpse of my legs. I wrapped my arms around myself, trying to steady the flurry of emotions that had been swirling since this afternoon's tense video call with my parents.

A few hours ago, I'd sent Ivy a panicked text. It had been so long since I'd gone on a first date, and I was suddenly overwhelmed. I was only half-serious when I'd texted: *I don't even have time to get ready! Help!* But, within minutes, Ivy and Amelia were at my door, ready to save the day. They had stayed with me until the last minute, fussing over the details, and making sure everything was perfect, before sending me off with hugs.

Now, as I stood outside the restaurant, I could hear their voices in my head, offering encouragement, and boosting my confidence as I paced outside, my heels clicking softly on the cobblestones. The empty street offered me a small mercy. No one was around to witness my nerves getting the best of me.

"You've been on dates before," I muttered to myself, taking a deep breath to steady the flurry of emotions that had taken over. "It's supposed to be fun. It's just dinner. Just getting to know someone new."

But, for some reason, tonight felt different. Maybe it was because Ethan was the first person in a long time who made me feel genuinely excited. Or maybe it was because, for the first time since Sebastian, I was letting my guard down.

I glanced up at the old clocktower, its hands pointing to six o'clock. Ethan was probably inside already, maybe wondering where I was. The confidence I'd felt earlier when we exchanged flirty texts seemed to have evaporated, leaving behind a bundle of nerves.

"It's just a date, Vinnie," I whispered again, trying to push away the doubts. Finally, I stopped pacing and took in the mouthwatering scent of garlic, tomatoes, and fresh bread drifting from the restaurant. The aromas stirred my appetite, and reminded me of why I was here. "Just dinner," I murmured, closing my eyes for a second and letting the warmth of the Italian cuisine wrap around me.

I could do this.

I *wanted* to do this.

Squaring my shoulders, I pushed open the door to the restaurant, and the warmth hit me first, a welcome contrast to the cool evening air, easing some of the tension in my chest. The place had a charm that made me feel like I'd stumbled upon a secret corner of Italy, with shelves of dusty wine bottles and vintage Italian posters lining the walls. Olive branches, intertwined with fairy lights, hung from the ceiling, casting a romantic glow. The tables were dark wood, each with a flickering candle that bathed the room in a golden light. Couples leaned in close at their tables, speaking in low voices, their laughter mingling with the soft strains of Italian music that played in the background.

I scanned the room, my heart thudding in my chest until my eyes finally landed on Ethan, who was seated at a small corner table, and the sight of him caught my breath. He looked effortlessly handsome in a crisp white shirt, layered with a dark sweater that clung to his broad shoulders. His brown hair was tousled, as if he'd been nervously running his fingers through it, and he kept adjusting his collar, and rolling and unrolling his sweater sleeves.

Seeing him there, a little fidgety and out of sorts, softened something inside me. It was comforting, in a way, to know that I wasn't the only one feeling nervous, and I watched him glance around the room, his fingers drumming lightly on the table, as if he couldn't quite sit still.

Then, as if he could sense my gaze on him, his eyes found mine, and the rest of the world seemed to blur at the edges as he broke into the most adorable, bashful smile. It wasn't the confident grin I was used to. It was sweeter, more vulnerable, as if he was just as eager for this to go well as I was.

That smile did something to me. It felt like a quiet promise, and suddenly, all my lingering nerves melted away as I smiled back, my lips curving into something genuine, something that came from deep within.

I reached the table and Ethan stood up, his smile widening as he stepped closer, his gaze never leaving mine. There was a palpable tension between us, the kind that made my skin tingle and my pulse race. It was the good kind—the kind that spoke of possibilities and new beginnings.

"Hey," he said, his voice soft and filled with warmth. There was a slight tremor in his tone; a hint of nerves that made my heart skip a beat.

"Hey," I replied, my voice barely above a whisper but, in that single word, I hoped he could hear the excitement.

Ethan stepped around the table with a nervous energy, pulling out my chair with an easy smile that softened the moment as his eyes swept over me in appreciation.

"You look amazing, Vinnie," he said. "I'm almost regretting not dressing up more."

"Thanks, Ethan," I replied, feeling a blush creep up my cheeks as I sat down, smoothing my dress out of habit. "Seriously, you look really good."

As he returned to his seat, an older-looking waitress approached, her smile broadening as she recognized Ethan. She had auburn hair pulled back into a ponytail; her uniform relaxed—black slacks, a fitted white shirt, and the restaurant's logo embroidered on the pocket. The name tag read LAURA, and her friendly demeanor felt instantly welcoming.

"Hey, Ethan! Finally out on a date, huh?" she teased, a playful smirk on her face as she glanced between us. Ethan blushed, running a hand through his hair with a sheepish grin.

"Yeah, I guess so," he admitted, glancing at me.

"Well, it's about time," Laura turned her attention to me, her smile warm. "You're in good company. Can I start you two off with something to drink? First date specials are my favorite to pour."

I smiled back. "I'll have a glass of the house red, thanks."

"Make that two," Ethan added, still looking a little flustered.

"Coming right up," Laura said with a wink before heading off, leaving us to exchange a look that was both amused and a little relieved.

Ethan leaned in, still smiling, but with a hint of embarrassment lingering. "Sorry about Laura. She's been friends with my mom forever, so I'm pretty sure I'll get the third degree about this later."

I laughed, the tension between us easing. "Oh, so this date comes with a follow-up interview? No pressure then."

"Exactly," he said, chuckling. "I'll probably get grilled about every detail. It's like having a whole town full of nosy aunts."

I grinned. "Well, I'll make sure to give you a glowing review. Five stars. Would recommend."

Ethan's smile widened, his eyes twinkling with amusement. "I'll do my best to earn those stars, then."

His light-heartedness was contagious, and I could feel the awkwardness fading, replaced by an excitement for the evening ahead. The night was young, and it already felt like we were off to a great start. We eased into light conversation about the town and exchanged stories about some of the quirky locals. The conversation flowed easily; his easy-going nature making it hard not to feel relaxed.

"So, what's next for you?" Ethan asked. "I mean, are you planning to stick around Hallow's End for a while?"

I smiled, feeling a spark of excitement. "Actually, I'm opening an art gallery here. I just emailed the owner about the lease, and it's all in motion now."

Ethan's eyebrows shot up in surprise, his mouth forming a wide grin. "No way! That's amazing, Vinnie! Where's the building?"

"It's that old space on Maple Street," I replied, the excitement in my voice unmistakable.

Ethan leaned back in his chair, nodding in recognition. "Maple Street? I know that place. You must be renting from Harold. He's a lovely man, always chatting up everyone at the farmer's market. That's a fantastic spot."

"Yeah, he's been really helpful so far," I said, my excitement bubbling up again. "Opening a gallery is a huge deal and, honestly, it's a bit overwhelming. There's so much to consider—like renovating the space to fit the vision I have in mind. I need to start with a fresh coat of paint. I'll probably go for something neutral that makes the artwork stand out. Then there's the lighting. Gallery lighting is *key*, and I need to figure out the best way to highlight the pieces without washing them out, or casting weird shadows. I'll also have to install track lights, or maybe even custom fixtures. And *then* there's the layout—making sure there's enough space for people to move around comfortably, whilst still creating a flow that guides them through the exhibits."

Ethan listened intently, and it spurred me on. "I've got to consider the kind of art I want to showcase, too. Initially, I plan to start with a mix of my own work to get things moving, but my ultimate aim is to showcase local artists and give them a platform. There's also the business side: setting up a proper website, social media marketing, maybe even collaborating with local influencers to spread the word. And *then* there's all the permits and insurance I need to sort out."

As I spoke, the words tumbled out faster. I shared my ideas for different exhibits, the vibe I wanted the gallery to have, and even the little details like the type of music I imagined playing softly in the background. I barely noticed how animated I'd become, my hands gesturing as I painted a picture of the future in my mind. But then, I caught myself, and a flush of embarrassment crept up my neck. "I'm sorry," I said, ducking my head slightly. "I'm rambling. I just get so excited about it."

I winced, suddenly worried that I might've overwhelmed him with too much information. What if he found all that boring? The thought made me nervous, and I braced myself for a polite smile or a change of subject. Instead, Ethan reached across the table, gently touching my hand.

"Don't be sorry, Vinnie," he said, his voice warm and reassuring. "I think it's adorable how you light up when you talk about it. Your passion is . . . infectious. It's rare to see someone so excited about something they love."

I looked up at him, meeting his gaze, and my heart skipped a beat. Sincerity filled his eyes, and there wasn't a trace of disinterest or boredom. Instead, he seemed captivated by what I had to say.

"Thanks," I whispered, a soft smile curving my lips. "It means a lot that you care."

"Of course I care," Ethan said, his thumb lightly brushing over my hand. "I want to know everything about you, Vinnie. And I'm here to listen."

"I'm hoping this gallery can become something special," I continued, my voice more confident now. "Not just for me, but for the entire community. I want it to be a place where people feel inspired, where they can connect with art in a meaningful way."

Ethan nodded, his smile broadening. "I can already see it. You're going to make it something amazing, Vinnie. I have no doubt about that."

The sincerity in his voice sent a rush through me. It was one thing to have a dream, but to have someone else believe in it, too—it made the dream feel more real, more achievable.

"Thanks," I said again, squeezing his hand. "You have no idea how much that means to me."

Before either of us could say more, Laura appeared, with a warm smile and a bottle of wine in hand. "Time for a top-up," she said, topping off our glasses with a smooth, red wine that caught the candlelight. "And here we go—dinner's served." With a practiced ease, she set our plates down in front of us.

The smell of the food hit me first, rich and mouthwatering. My fettuccine Alfredo looked like pure comfort on a plate, the creamy sauce clinging to the perfectly cooked pasta, with a generous dusting of fresh Parmesan melting into the top. Across from me, Ethan's lasagna was a masterpiece of layers—simmering tomato sauce, bubbling cheese, and seasoned meat that begged to be savored.

"This looks amazing," I said, already twirling some of the pasta around my fork.

"Definitely worth the wait," he agreed, taking a bite and letting out a contented sigh.

As we started eating, I realized I'd been doing most of the talking and smiled sheepishly at Ethan. "Sorry, I've been hogging the conversation. How's your week been?"

He chuckled, leaning back in his chair. "No need to apologize. I've enjoyed hearing about your plans. My week's been the usual—wrangling a bunch of teenagers and trying to convince them that literature is more exciting than their phones."

I grinned, amused by the image. "Sounds like quite the challenge. What's it like, trying to keep their attention?"

"Well, let's just say it involves a lot of creative tactics. Last week, I promised my class a movie day if they could get through *Macbeth* without any complaints. And it worked! Mostly because they thought they'd get to watch something like *The Lion King*. But nope, we watched the 1971 version of *Macbeth*, and they were not amused," he said, his eyes twinkling with mischief.

I burst out laughing. "Oh, you're evil! But that's kind of brilliant."

He grinned, clearly enjoying my reaction. "You've got to keep them on their toes. And hey, by the end, they were grudgingly admitting that it wasn't as bad as they thought. Victory for Shakespeare."

I took a sip of wine, still smiling. "I'm sure you make those classes way more interesting than you give yourself credit for."

Ethan shrugged modestly. "I do what I can. But honestly, the best part of my week is spending time with Lily. She's been on this wild kick lately where every day she's something new—last weekend, she was a detective solving the mystery of who ate the last cookie. Spoiler: It was me, but I played along."

"Did she crack the case?" I asked, grinning at the thought of little Lily playing detective.

"Oh, absolutely," he said, laughing. "She interrogated me, set up a cookie sting operation, and even tried to get me to confess by threatening to call in reinforcements—her stuffed bear, Mr Fluffles."

I smiled. "She sounds like a handful, in the best way."

"She is," Ethan agreed, his eyes softening as he talked about her. "She's convinced she's going to be a famous singer or a detective—or maybe she'll pull a Hannah Montana and do both. You know, get the best of both worlds."

I laughed, easily imagining a pint-sized Lily switching between solving mysteries and belting out songs on stage. "That's pretty ambitious."

Ethan chuckled. "Yeah, she's got it all planned out. I'll just be the older brother tagging along, trying to keep up with her adventures."

"Lily sounds like so much fun," I said, charmed by the way he spoke about his sister.

"She really is," he said, a small, thoughtful smile playing on his lips. There was a brief pause, and I could see him weighing something in his mind before he looked up at me, shyness in his eyes. "Maybe I could introduce you to her sometime, if you'd like? She could use another girl in her life. Plus, it might save me—and my hair—from being experimented on daily," he added with a playful grin.

I smiled back, touched by the offer. "I'd love that," I replied softly, the warmth in my chest growing at the thought of meeting someone so important to him.

Ethan's smile widened. "Great! Just a warning—she'll probably make you her new favorite person," he joked, but the sincerity in his tone made the moment feel even more special.

As we continued to chat, Laura returned to clear our plates, a mischievous glint in her eye as she set down a single plate, with a beautifully presented tiramisu upon it, and placed two spoons beside it.

"On the house," she said with a wink. "Thought you two might enjoy sharing."

Ethan gave me a playful look. "Guess we're splitting dessert, then. Hope you don't mind?"

I grinned, picking up a spoon. "Not at all. As long as you're okay with me stealing more than my fair share. Tiramisu happens to be my absolute favorite."

"Mine, too," he admitted. "And I'm not above fighting for the last bite."

We both laughed as we dug in, the first bite melting on my tongue with the perfect balance of creamy mascarpone and rich, espresso-soaked ladyfingers. The dessert was light yet indulgent, and sharing it felt unexpectedly intimate.

As we enjoyed the tiramisu, our conversation drifted into playful banter. We swapped stories about our most embarrassing moments—Ethan's involved leading his students into a restricted area of a museum during a class trip, and mine being about the time I tripped and spilled coffee all over a new piece of artwork I'd just completed.

Ethan laughed, his eyes crinkling at the corners. "I'd pay good money to see that," he teased. "Did the artwork survive?"

"Barely," I replied, grinning at the memory. "But hey, if you remember, you also survived my coffee-spilling skills. Maybe I'm just adding character to everything I touch."

He chuckled, nodding in agreement. "So, I'm a walking masterpiece now? I'll take it."

As Ethan took the last bite of tiramisu, I found myself captivated by the way he savored it, his eyes closing for a brief moment as he enjoyed the rich, creamy flavor. There was something oddly sensual about the way his lips lingered on the spoon, and I couldn't help but stare, a surprising heat rising in me.

When his eyes opened and met mine, I glanced away, my heart racing, mortified to be caught staring. I tried to focus on anything else—the flickering candle on the table, the soft hum of conversations around us—but I could still feel his gaze on me.

"You, uh . . . you've got a little something," Ethan murmured, leaning in closer. Before I could react, his thumb gently brushed against my lower lip, wiping away a tiny smudge of chocolate.

The unexpected touch sent a jolt through me, leaving me breathless, and I froze, my skin tingling where he had touched me, the gesture far more intimate than I had anticipated.

Ethan seemed to realize it, too, because he pulled back quickly, his face flushing. "Sorry about that," he said, looking sheepish. "It's just a habit. Lily always ends up with chocolate on her face, and I guess I didn't think."

I tried to laugh it off, though my voice came out shakier than I intended. "No problem. Thanks." The air between us felt charged with tension lingering from the brief touch and, for a moment, neither of us said anything.

Ethan cleared his throat, shifting the mood back to something lighter. "So . . . quiz night?"

"Yeah, let's do it," I replied, trying to match his tone and ignore the fluttering in my chest. "Just don't blame me if we lose."

Ethan laughed, easing some of the tension between us. "Don't worry, I'm on a losing streak, anyway. Maybe you'll be my good luck charm and turn things around."

I couldn't help but smile at that. "No pressure, right?"

"None at all," he grinned, his eyes twinkling with mischief.

Chapter 16

E THAN OPENED THE DOOR to The Sunflower Bistro, his hand resting lightly on the small of my back as I stepped inside. As we entered, the lively hum of the bistro hit me, the room buzzing with energy. The soft lighting bathed the space in a warm glow, casting long shadows over the rustic tables and mismatched chairs, the lights twinkling overhead.

The scent of freshly baked bread and savory dishes wafted through the air, mingling with the sound of laughter and clinking glasses. Colorful banners and streamers adorned the ceiling, and a large chalkboard near the entrance proudly proclaimed: QUIZ NIGHT EXTRAVAGANZA! in bold, playful letters. Each table sported a handwritten sign with quirky team names like SMARTY PINTS and QUIZZY MCQUIZFACE. The space was vibrant and alive, with question-mark-shaped balloons bobbing overhead.

We made our way through the crowd, and a few people waved at Ethan, their faces lighting up as he greeted them with a nod and an easy smile, effortlessly charming everyone around him. I admired the way he fit into his world so seamlessly.

Near the bar, a familiar voice called out, pulling us from our thoughts. "Ethan, my boy!" It was Mayor Margaret Hale, her grin wide and welcoming as she spotted us. "Still hoping to break that losing streak tonight?"

Ethan chuckled, shaking his head in mock defeat. "Oh, you just wait. I've got a secret weapon this time," he teased, giving me a playful nudge that sent a jolt of warmth through me.

Mayor Hale's eyes twinkled with amusement as she looked at me. "Ah, Vinnie! So *you're* the ace up his sleeve, huh? Good luck, you'll need it!" She winked, her good-natured ribbing drawing laughter from the nearby tables.

I laughed along, the energy of the bistro wrapping around me like a welcoming embrace. "I'll do my best," I promised.

The bistro was packed, the warm air buzzing with energy, and Ethan tugged off his sweater as we made our way through the crowd. My breath caught as the hem of his shirt rode up slightly, revealing a glimpse of toned, tanned skin just above his belt. It was a fleeting sight, but it sent a thrill through me, making my cheeks flush. As he adjusted his shirt, his fingers brushed against the exposed skin; a simple gesture that felt intimate amidst the lively crowd.

Ethan's hand returned to the small of my back, steady and reassuring. The touch was simple, but I found myself leaning into it, savoring the connection that was building between us. He guided me toward a table near the front, where the bistro had set up a small stage for the quizmaster, and my eyes were drawn to the way his shirt stretched across his broad back, highlighting the lean muscles beneath.

There was something undeniably sexy about the way he moved with such effortless confidence, his long strides hinting at a strength that made my pulse quicken. The room was alive with chatter and laughter, but my focus kept drifting back to him. I noticed the way his jawline, strong and defined, tightened slightly as he scanned the room, always aware of his surroundings. The combination of that sharp jaw and his slightly tousled hair sent a shiver down my spine, and I couldn't think of anything other than how incredibly irresistible he looked tonight.

After we settled into our seats, Ethan turned to me, his eyes warm. "Can I get you a drink?" he asked, his voice low and inviting.

I nodded, still a little breathless from the buzz of the evening. "A glass of wine would be nice."

Ethan caught the eye of a passing waitress, signalling her over with an easy smile. "Two glasses of your house red, please."

Just as the waitress brought our drinks, a flash of blonde hair made its way through the crowd, weaving purposefully between tables, and my heart sank as Emily approached, her eyes locked on Ethan with a determined glint. She dressed to impress, wearing a tight, low-cut top that accentuated her curves, and a short skirt that showed off her long legs. Her blonde hair cascaded down in perfect waves, catching the light with every step.

Emily squeezed through the last cluster of people, her gaze never wavering from Ethan, and my stomach twisted with unease. The last time we'd interacted, Emily had made it abundantly clear she didn't think much of me, and the memory still stung. Now, seeing her zero in on Ethan, I couldn't help but feel a surge of irritation. We were having a great time, and the last thing I wanted was for her to intrude on our night.

"Hey, Ethan!" Emily greeted, her voice overly cheerful, almost saccharine. She flashed a bright smile, but there was a calculated edge to it, and her eyes darted briefly to me before she turned her full attention back to him. "Great to see you here," she added, leaning in a bit too close, batting her eyelashes in a way that made my skin crawl.

She didn't wait for an invitation, instead continuing with a faux-casual tone that masked her intent. "Mind if I join you two for a bit? My friends ditched me, and I don't have a team for the quiz." The way she said it made it clear she wasn't actually asking.

How convenient.

I tried to catch Ethan's eye, silently pleading with him to turn her down, but my heart sank when he glanced at me, a flicker of apology in his eyes.

"Sure, Em," he said, though there was a slight hesitation in his voice. "You can join us."

I forced a smile, doing my best to hide my frustration. "The more, the merrier," I said, though the words felt tight and unnatural on my tongue.

As Emily settled in beside Ethan, my emotions twisted in a complicated knot. I knew Ethan was just being kind. It was in his nature to be considerate, and I liked that about him. But, as she slid her chair closer to his, I couldn't shake the feeling of being pushed to the side like an afterthought. It was the same way Sebastian used to make me feel—like I was there, but not really seen, and it left a bitter taste in my mouth.

I reached for my glass of wine, taking a longer sip than necessary, trying to drown out the unwelcome comparison. This was different. Ethan was nothing like Sebastian, and I knew that. I needed to stop letting old wounds cloud my judgment. But even so, the sting of it lingered, an uncomfortable reminder of how easily those old insecurities could resurface.

I forced myself to breathe, to focus on the warmth in Ethan's gaze when he looked at me, the way he'd made me feel special all evening. He wasn't dismissing me. This was just a minor hiccup, nothing more. I needed to let it go, to trust that this night was still ours, no matter who else tried to join in.

As Emily chatted away, her laughter occasionally ringing out a bit too loud, I stared down at my nearly empty wine glass, swirling the remaining liquid as my mind wandered back to old memories.

Suddenly, I felt the warmth of Ethan's hand covering mine, his touch bringing me back to the present. His thumb brushed lightly against my skin, and I looked up to find him watching me, concern softening his features.

"You okay?" he asked, his voice gentle, meant only for me, despite the lively atmosphere around us.

The way he looked at me—his eyes full of genuine care—made the tension in my chest ease. It was like he could see right through the facade I was trying to maintain, right to the heart of my worries. The frustration I'd felt moments ago began to melt away under the steady reassurance of his gaze.

I managed a small smile. "Yeah, I'm fine," I whispered, giving his hand a grateful squeeze in return. "Thanks."

He didn't let go, his hand resting on mine, grounding me in the moment. The noise of the bistro, the presence of Emily—it all faded into the background as I focused on the warmth of his touch.

The simple act sent a flutter of nerves through me. Was this just a kind gesture, or did it mean something more? The thought made my pulse quicken, and suddenly I became hyper-aware of everything—how our hands fit together, how his thumb lightly traced a soothing pattern on my skin, and how, despite the noise around us, this felt like the most intimate moment of the night.

I caught myself wondering if my hand was too clammy; a sudden rush of self-consciousness making me want to pull away. But Ethan didn't let go.

If anything, his grip seemed to tighten in a wordless reassurance that told me he was right there with me.

Emily's eyes flicked to our joined hands, and a flicker of irritation flashed across her face before she quickly masked it with a too-bright smile. "Ethan," she said, her tone sweet but with a subtle edge, "would you mind grabbing us a couple of drinks? It's so crowded tonight, and I can't seem to catch any of the waitresses." She gestured to the almost empty glass in front of me, a calculated move that forced Ethan's hand.

He hesitated, his thumb still gently brushing over my knuckles. I could feel his reluctance in the way his fingers lingered against mine, but after a moment, he nodded. "Sure," he said, giving my hand one last squeeze before letting go, his touch leaving behind a ghost of warmth that I immediately missed.

"I'll be right back," he promised. Then, with a final glance over his shoulder, he disappeared into the crowd.

The moment Ethan turned his back, Emily's smile faded into something sharper, more calculating. She leaned in closer, her perfectly manicured red nails tapping lightly on the table, her voice dropping to a lower, more private tone. "You know, Ethan and I go way back. He's a really great guy. Always so considerate. He's helped me out more times than I can count, especially when I needed someone to lean on."

Her words dripped with a possessiveness that made my stomach twist, and I could feel the old, familiar anxiety creeping in. The kind that reminded me too much of the girls back in Cresden. Those girls who mastered the art of the sharp smile and subtle insult, who could cut you down whilst pretending to be your best friend. The way Emily's glossy blonde hair framed her face, styled to look effortlessly chic, and the way she leaned in, just close enough to invade my personal space, felt like she was trying to assert some unspoken dominance.

"I'm sure he has," I replied, doing my best to keep my voice even, though my heart raced. I wasn't about to let her see how much she was getting to me. "Ethan's been nothing but kind and thoughtful since I met him."

Emily's blue eyes narrowed, the corners of her mouth lifting into a smug smile. "Oh, I'm sure. He's always been the type to help those who need it. But, just so you know, we have a lot of history together. It's hard to find someone who knows him as well as I do."

As she spoke, she adjusted the strap of her low-cut top, a subtle yet pointed reminder of her confidence in her own appeal. She was beautiful, no doubt about it. Blond hair, flawless skin, and a figure she wasn't shy about flaunting. But it wasn't her looks that made my chest tighten. It was the way she spoke, as if she was laying claim to Ethan, reminding me she had been in his life long before I showed up.

A flicker of doubt tried to take root, but I pushed it down, reminding myself of what Ivy had told me—Emily had an obsession with Ethan. One that was unreciprocated. Ethan had chosen to spend tonight with *me*, not her. That had to mean something.

I straightened in my seat. "I'm sure your history means a lot to you, Emily," I said, my voice steady despite the knot in my chest. "But tonight, Ethan and I are on a date, and I'd really like for us to enjoy it."

Her smile froze for a split second, eyes flashing with surprise. "A date?" she repeated, as if the word itself was foreign. Her tone was sharp, but she quickly smoothed it over with a forced laugh. "That's . . . unexpected. Ethan doesn't usually go on dates."

The way she said it, like she was pointing out some kind of anomaly, sent a chill through me. But I didn't flinch. "Well, I guess there's a first time for everything," I replied, keeping my voice light even though my heart was pounding.

Just as the tension between us thickened, I caught sight of Ethan weaving through the crowd, two drinks in hand, and that same kind smile on his face. When he reached our table, his eyes immediately found mine. "Here you go, Vinnie," he said softly, handing me my drink with a warmth that made my heart flutter. For a moment, his gaze lingered on me, as if he could sense something was off.

"Oh, thanks, Ethan," Emily chimed in as he handed her drink over, but his attention barely flickered her way before he settled back beside me, his knee brushing against mine under the table. The touch was subtle, but it was enough to anchor me in the moment.

Ethan turned to Emily, his smile easy and relaxed. "Oh, by the way, Em," he began, almost casually, "Larry's team is missing a member tonight. Since your friends didn't show up, I offered your help. He's pretty excited to have you join them."

Emily's face fell, the forced cheerfulness slipping for just a moment before she caught herself. Her attention was drawn to the bar, where a group of middle-aged men dressed in old-school rocker clothes were gathered, laughing and chatting loudly. One of them—Larry, I assumed—was already waving her over enthusiastically. The sight of Emily—with her meticulously styled hair and perfectly coordinated outfit—joining that rowdy group, was almost too much, and I bit down on the inside of my cheek to keep from laughing.

"Oh, that's . . .great," Emily said, her smile strained as she tried to hide her reluctance. She hesitated, clearly torn between making a graceful exit and staying put. But, with Larry still waving her over, she had little choice.

"Have fun," Ethan added, turning back to our table, already picking up the pen to write our team name on the paper provided. His focus was entirely on us again, leaving Emily no room to argue.

As she gathered her things and stood to leave, she leaned in close to me, her voice barely above a whisper. "This isn't over," she murmured, her tone icy as she shot me a sharp look before walking away.

I watched as she made her way to the bar, where the group welcomed her with open arms, thrilled to have her join them. The sight of her trying to keep up with their jokes had me fighting back my grin.

Ethan looked up from the paper, a playful glint in his eyes. "I've already got a name for us," he said, his knee brushing against mine again. "How about Artful Dodgers? A nod to your creative genius, and my dodging skills with Emily?"

"I love it," I said, grinning. "Wait, is that the same Crazy Larry over there that you warned me about? The one who brought the karaoke machine last time?"

Ethan grinned, nodding. "Yep, that's him. But this time, he said he's planning to bust out his old-school breakdancing moves. Something about reliving his glory days."

The quiz master, a tall man with a shock of gray hair and a jovial demeanor, stepped up to the small stage and tapped the microphone to get everyone's attention. "Good evening, everyone! Welcome to quiz night! I'm Paul, your quizmaster for the evening. I hope you're all ready to put those brains to work and have some fun. Let's get started with the first round."

The room buzzed with excitement as the teams settled in, everyone eager to prove their trivia prowess. Ethan and I exchanged a glance, the air between us crackling with anticipation.

Paul continued, "Alright, round one: general knowledge. Let's see how sharp you all are tonight."

The first few questions were relatively straightforward—geography, famous historical figures, a bit of pop culture. Ethan leaned in close, his voice warm and low as he offered answers, and the closeness of his presence made the hairs on my arms stand up. Every so often, our heads would tilt toward each other, our shoulders brushing; a warm, easy intimacy between us.

"Are you sure about that one?" I asked, my voice barely above a whisper as I caught the subtle scent of his cologne. It was a warm, musky fragrance, that was quickly becoming one of my favorite smells.

"Pretty sure," Ethan replied with a confident grin.

As the quiz moved to round two—music and movies—I felt a little more in my element, and it was fun watching Ethan's eyes light up when I knew an answer that he didn't. The questions ranged from classic films, to chart-topping hits, and we found our groove, working seamlessly together. When a question came up about a famous painting in a movie, I couldn't help but grin as I scribbled down the answer.

"You're a secret weapon," he said, leaning in even closer, his voice filled with admiration. "I knew I picked the right partner."

The compliment made my cheeks flush, and I ducked my head, trying to focus on the question at hand. "Well, you're pretty good yourself," I replied, glancing at him from under my lashes. Our faces were so close that I could feel the warmth of his breath against my skin.

As we continued, the air between us buzzed with unspoken tension, each correct answer feeling like a small, shared victory. We exchanged subtle, lingering glances, and every time he smiled at me, my heart skipped a beat.

Round three was a little trickier—science and nature. Ethan took the lead, confidently answering most of the questions, and I contributed where I could, but it was clear this was more his forte.

Yet, even as he tackled the questions, Ethan never let go of the easy rapport we'd built. Every now and then, he'd glance at me with a playful glint in his eye, sharing little inside jokes only we understood. His laughter was infectious, and the way he leaned in close to whisper a witty comment, or share an answer, made me excited.

By the time we reached the final round—Hallow's End trivia—I could feel the energy between us peak. The questions were all about local history and lore, and I marvelled at how much Ethan knew about the town's quirky past. His enthusiasm was contagious, drawing me in, and making me want to know more about this place that had quickly started to feel like home.

When Paul announced the end of the quiz, a collective sigh of relief rippled through the bistro, mingling with the hum of conversation and the clinking of glasses. "We'll tally up the scores and announce the winners in just a few minutes. Great job, everyone!"

I leaned back in my chair, letting out a breath. "That was intense," I said, glancing at Ethan with a grin.

He nodded, wiping an imaginary bead of sweat from his brow. "No kidding. I didn't expect trivia to get my heart racing like that."

Nearby, Larry had gathered a small crowd around him as he demonstrated dance moves from back in the day, but I barely registered the scene because Ethan had shifted closer, his shoulder brushing against mine. The warmth of his presence was almost overwhelming, and his laughter sent little shivers down my spine.

As Larry tried to demonstrate a particularly ambitious move, Ethan leaned in, his breath warm against my ear as he chuckled. "I think Larry's about to pull something."

His words barely registered. My whole attention was on Ethan. How close he was. How the space between us had shrunk to just a few inches. I didn't want the night to end; relishing in the easy connection we had built, and the nerves I'd felt before our date seemed like a distant memory, replaced by an excitement that bubbled up inside me. I couldn't wait to tell Ivy and Amelia how well it was going, how much fun I was having, and how glad I was that I'd pushed through the initial anxiety.

Ethan turned to me, his smile softening, his eyes catching mine. We were so close I could feel the gentle rise and fall of his breath. He licked his lips, a simple gesture that felt loaded with meaning, and I was acutely aware of the faint scent of wine on my breath. A wave of self-consciousness washed over me. What if I had food in my teeth? Or my lipstick had smudged? The possibility of a kiss hung in the air, but all I could think about was how unprepared I felt for it.

I found myself breaking eye contact, mumbling something about needing a quick bathroom break, and I slipped away, my heart pounding in my chest as I navigated through the crowded bistro.

In the bathroom, I took a moment to catch my breath, splashing cool water on my face. As I patted my cheeks dry, I pulled out my phone, opening a few unread messages. One was from Ivy, and the other from Amelia, in a newly formed group chat titled COVEN. Smiling, I opened the chat.

Ivy: How's it going, Vinnie? Are you having fun? 😊

Amelia: Any juicy gossip yet? 😏

Vinnie: It's going really well! But I totally chickened out when I thought he might kiss me 😅

Almost instantly, Amelia replied.

Amelia: Girl, just go for it! I bet he's a great kisser 😚

I chuckled, feeling a little more confident as I touched up my lipstick and fluffed my hair. A small surge of excitement thrummed through me as I exited the bathroom, making my way back to Ethan. As I approached our table, his eyes immediately lit up, and I felt that familiar warmth spread through me. With a deep breath, I decided that tonight, I wouldn't let my nerves get the better of me again.

Paul returned to the stage after tallying up the scores, the bistro buzzing with anticipation. Ethan and I exchanged a glance, both of us trying to play it cool. We had done pretty well, I thought, but I didn't want to get my hopes up too much.

"And the winners of tonight's Quiz Night Extravaganza," Paul announced, drawing out the suspense, "are none other than . . . the Artful Dodgers!"

I barely had time to process what he'd said before I jumped up from my seat, the thrill of victory coursing through me. Without thinking, I threw my arms around Ethan's neck, laughing with pure joy. He responded immediately, wrapping his arms around my waist and lifting me off the ground in a playful spin that made my heart soar.

My laughter filled the room, blending with the cheers and applause from the other tables, and the moment felt electric. When Ethan finally set me back down, I was still grinning ear to ear, breathless from the excitement.

Mayor Hale approached us with a broad smile, her eyes twinkling with a hint of something more. "Congratulations, you two! You make a fantastic team."

Blushing, I reluctantly let go of Ethan, but he kept one arm around my waist, his touch grounding me in the moment, and he looked at me with a soft, admiring gaze that made my heart skip a beat. "Thank you, but Vinnie here is the real star."

She chuckled. "Go on, collect your prize. You've earned it."

Ethan and I made our way to the front, where Paul handed us a bottle of wine, and a gift certificate for dinner. Ethan took the bottle and turned to me, a grin spreading across his face. "A little something to remember our first date by."

I smiled, feeling a warm glow inside and, after saying goodnight to everyone at the bistro, Ethan offered to walk me home.

The town of Hallow's End was quiet at this hour, the streets bathed in the soft glow of streetlights, casting long, gentle shadows across the cobblestone. The air was cool, carrying the scent of rain that hinted at the possibility of an impending downpour.

We walked side by side, our steps falling into sync. Every now and then, our shoulders brushed, sending tiny sparks of electricity through me, and I found myself hyperaware of every small movement. His hand occasionally grazed mine, the warmth of his skin a subtle but unmistakable invitation, and I could smell the cedarwood and citrus notes of his cologne mingling with the cool night air. It was an intoxicating scent that seemed to wrap around me, grounding me in the moment.

Our conversation had naturally paused, leaving us in a comfortable silence that hung heavy with unspoken words. There was a new kind of tension between us now, a magnetic pull that grew stronger with each step we took closer to my house. I could feel his gaze lingering on me, and each time I glanced up at him, my heart raced a little faster. There was a warmth in his eyes, and a softness that made me wonder if he was thinking about our first kiss as much as I was.

When we reached my door, the conversation tapered off, and we stood there for a moment, facing each other, the quiet of the night pressing in around us. Ethan took a small step closer, his hand reaching out to brush a stray strand of hair from my face. His fingers were gentle as they lingered on my cheek, sending a shiver down my spine. The air between us was charged with the electric promise of a kiss, and the world narrowed down to just the two of us, standing on the brink of something new and thrilling.

He leaned in slowly, his breath mingling with mine, his lips just a whisper away from touching, and my heart pounded in my chest, every nerve in my body alive with anticipation. Just as our lips were about to meet, a sudden crack of thunder tore through the sky, making both of us jump. Lightning flashed, illuminating the night for a brief, blinding moment before the sky opened up, and rain began to pour down in heavy, relentless sheets.

We both pulled apart, laughing as the sudden downpour broke the spell. Ethan wiped raindrops from his face, grinning as he shook his head. "I guess the universe has other plans."

"I'd better get inside," I replied, my words tinged with regret.

"Yeah," he agreed, though he looked just as disappointed as I felt. "I'll text you."

He leaned in and, instead of the moment we both had been on the verge of sharing, he placed a gentle, lingering kiss on my cheek, his lips warm against my rain-chilled skin.

"Goodnight, Vinnie," he whispered, his voice soft and full of promise.

"Goodnight, Ethan," I replied, watching him jog off into the rain, his figure becoming a silhouette against the stormy night.

I hurried inside, my heart still racing as I closed the door behind me. As I dried off and changed into my pajamas, my mind replayed the events of the night, the almost-kiss, and the way his hand had felt in mine. Just as I settled into bed, my phone buzzed on the nightstand.

> **Ethan:** Had an amazing time tonight, even with the storm trying to crash our date. So, how about we don't let the rain win, and plan date number two? 😊

My heart skipped a beat at the thought of seeing him again, and I quickly typed out a response, my fingers still trembling from the lingering excitement.

> **Vinnie:** Sounds like a plan. Let's just hope the weather's on our side this time 😳

> **Ethan:** I'm optimistic. But if it does rain, maybe we can plan something indoors? I usually spend weekends with Lily, and she's been asking to watch her favorite movies again. We could ask her to join us, if you're up for it. But fair warning—she'll probably think it's another girls' night, and bring all her hair accessories 😄

> **Vinnie:** That sounds adorable. I'm definitely up for it — just let me know what to bring!

> **Ethan:** Just bring yourself. Lily will handle the rest, trust me. Looking forward to it already 😊

I set my phone down and curled up into bed, still smiling with warm happiness as I snuggled under the covers to sleep.

Chapter 17

THE NEXT WEEK PASSED by in a blur of activity and excitement as I dove headfirst into getting the gallery ready. After signing the lease and picking up the keys from Harold, who had been beaming with excitement, I knew there was no turning back. The space was mine, and with it came all the responsibilities of turning my dream into a reality.

Mornings began early, often with a quick coffee before I headed over to the gallery. The first task on my list was sorting out the layout—a job that took up more time than I'd anticipated. I spent hours walking through the empty space, trying to envision where each piece of furniture would go, how the lighting would hit the walls just right, and where I could create little nooks for people to sit and enjoy the art. I even sketched out a rough floor plan, marking where the main exhibits would be, and where I could set up a small corner for workshops or private viewings.

By midweek, the supplies I'd ordered arrived, and boxes of paint, brushes, and rollers stacked up in the corner, waiting for the transformation to begin. Amelia, being the thrifting queen she was, had somehow managed to find the most incredible pieces of furniture—vintage chairs, quirky tables, and even a few statement light fixtures that were just begging to be hung. She seemed to know all the right people and places, making phone calls and pulling favors to get everything at a fraction of the cost.

Amelia and Ivy were a constant presence, offering their help wherever they could. Ivy, with her endless energy and can-do attitude, was always up for a task, whether it was helping to sort out the insurance paperwork, or brainstorming ideas for the grand opening. Most evenings, after a long day of planning and organizing, the three of us would collapse onto the floor of the gallery, surrounded by takeout boxes, chatting and laughing about everything from the day's mishaps, to Ivy's latest tarot card pulls.

As we lounged on the floor one night, I finally told them about my almost-kiss with Ethan, and Ivy nearly choked on her drink as Amelia's eyes widened with excitement, both of them eager for all the details.

"So let me get this straight," Ivy said, grinning from ear to ear. "You two were about to kiss, and then the universe literally rained on your parade?"

"Yep, thunder and all," I replied, laughing despite myself.

Amelia shook her head. "That's classic Hallow's End timing. Weird things always seem to happen when emotions run high."

Ivy nodded, her eyes sparkling with mischief. "Hallow's End has a way of making things more . . . interesting. It's like the town has its own agenda, and sometimes, it just likes to have a little fun at our expense. But don't worry, you'll get that kiss. And when you do, it's going to be epic."

"I hope so," I said. "But seriously, it's just my luck. First proper date in ages, and the weather decides to throw in some dramatic flair."

"Next time, just kiss him before the rain starts," Ivy suggested with a wink. "Problem solved."

Amelia smirked, leaning back. "Or maybe it was Hallow's End's way of building the suspense. There's always a little magic in the air, especially when it comes to matters of the heart."

The town *did* have a certain charm to it, a sense that anything could happen, especially when you least expected it. "Well, if that's the case, I'm definitely sticking around to see what happens next."

"You'd better," Ivy said, raising her glass in a mock toast. "Hallow's End isn't done with you yet, Vinnie. Not by a long shot."

Despite the challenges of the week, everything was starting to come together. I even sorted out the permits and insurance, which had been looming over my head like a dark cloud. It wasn't the most exciting part of opening a gallery, but it was necessary, and I felt a sense of accomplishment when it was done. The budget was tight—tighter than I'd hoped—but I reminded myself that this was all part of the process. Start-ups were never easy, but I was confident that every penny spent would be worth it once the gallery doors opened.

On Friday, as we were packing up for the day, Ivy turned to me with a thoughtful expression. "You know, Vinnie, if you need a place to stay once your lease is up, you're more than welcome to stay with me. I've got the spare bedroom, and it would save you the hassle of trying to find something else right away."

I hesitated, not wanting to impose. "I appreciate that, Ivy, but I can't just stay with you for free. I'll pay rent, or at least contribute to the bills."

Ivy waved her hand dismissively. "Don't even worry about it. You can thank me by helping around the house. Besides, I know what it's like to start a business from the ground up. I just want to see you succeed."

Her offer warmed my heart, and I realized how lucky I was to have found such supportive friends so quickly in Hallow's End.

As the working week drew to a close, I was exhausted, but the thought of seeing Ethan excited me. Throughout the week, his texts became the highlight of my day, each one more charming than the last. He had an effortless way of making me smile, keeping our texts light and fun, but always with that undercurrent of chemistry that had sparked between us on our first date.

One morning, just as I was heading out to the gallery, my phone buzzed with a message from him.

> **Ethan:** Guess who had to step in for a last-minute sex-ed class today because the counselor called in sick? The notes she left me were . . . not exactly detailed 😊

I laughed out loud, picturing Ethan trying to keep a straight face while dealing with a room full of hormonal teenagers who probably found the whole thing hilarious.

> **Vinnie:** That sounds like a nightmare. How did it go? 😄

> **Ethan:** Well . . . the class now thinks I'm an expert on awkward pauses. They wouldn't stop laughing, especially when I tried to explain . . . well, everything. I'm pretty sure I'll be known as Mr. Banana for the rest of the year.

> **Vinnie:** Please tell me they didn't actually draw you as one 😅

> **Ethan:** Oh, they did. Right on the whiteboard. I'm considering switching careers.

Vinnie: I think it's adorable. At least you gave them a day to remember.

Ethan: Adorable? That's one way to put it. I'm just hoping they don't start making T-shirts 😄

Vinnie: If they do, I'm definitely getting one 😊

Ethan: I'm sticking to Shakespeare from now on. Much safer territory.

Vinnie: Well, if you ever need a guest speaker for your next sex-ed class, I'm happy to help out 😊

Ethan: Careful, I might take you up on that 😏

Another day, while I was knee-deep in paperwork and permits, I got a text that had me grinning from ear to ear.

Ethan: One of my students asked me today why I've been smiling like an idiot all week. They're convinced I'm hiding something 😊

Vinnie: You should've told them you just discovered a new love for grading essays 😊

Later, as I settled in for the evening, another text from him popped up.

Ethan: Or I could've said I've been thinking about a certain someone who's been on my mind nonstop 😊

Vinnie: Must be someone pretty special to have that effect on you 😊

> **Ethan:** She's definitely got my attention. And by the way, when you start working on the inside of the gallery, I'm serious about helping. I can be your personal handyman for the day. I'm a pretty handy guy to have around 😊 🔧

I couldn't stop the grin that spread across my face, my mind wandering to all the possibilities that offer could entail. The thought of Ethan being my *personal handyman* led to more than a few daydreams—some more steamy than others.

> **Vinnie:** I might just take you up on it 😊

> **Ethan:** I'm counting on it 😊

The chemistry between us was undeniable, even over text. His messages were a perfect blend of sweet and teasing, each one pulling me in a little more, making me look forward to the weekend. Every time my phone buzzed, a little thrill shot through me, wondering what he'd say next, and how he'd make me laugh or blush this time.

Saturday rolled around again, and the cool morning air nipped at my cheeks as I sat in the back garden, cradling a steaming cup of coffee between my hands. October had arrived with a crispness that breathed new life into everything around me. Wrapped snugly in a fluffy blanket, I inhaled the earthy scent of fallen leaves, a deep sense of contentment as warm as the blanket.

Today I was meeting Lily, and the mere thought of it brought a smile to my lips as I took another sip of my coffee, letting the warmth spread through me. Excitement bubbled up inside me, mingling with a healthy dose of nerves. It was clear how much Lily meant to Ethan, and the desire to make a good impression was almost overwhelming.

It was hard to believe I'd only known Ethan for three weeks. In Cresden, three weeks might have been nothing more than a casual acquaintance or a handful of text messages exchanged. But here in Hallow's End, time seemed to move differently—slower in some ways, yet more meaningful in others. Somehow, everything felt more personal, more intimate, as if the town itself was weaving connections faster and deeper than I ever thought possible. Each moment carried more weight, and every interaction seemed to carve out a space in your life. Maybe it was the charm of Hallow's End, or maybe it was just the way Ethan and I clicked from the very first conversation. Whatever it was, it made these last few weeks feel like months. Hallow's End had a way of making things move at its own pace, and I was beginning to realize that sometimes, it was okay to let it sweep you along.

Finishing my coffee, I stood up and stretched, letting the blanket slide off my shoulders. The crispness of the morning air followed me inside as I started getting ready for the evening ahead. I glanced at the small tote bag I'd packed earlier in the week, filled with snacks I'd picked out just for tonight: Lily's favorite candies, some popcorn, and a couple of fun face masks I thought we could do together.

Deciding that a walk might help calm my nerves, I slipped on my jacket and headed out the door. The afternoon sun peeked through a few scattered clouds, and the town was bathed in a special kind of light, like it belonged in a painting, with each detail being brought to life with a touch of magic.

I smiled as I walked, thinking about how much this town had inspired me since I'd arrived. Now, in every spare moment, I'd found myself painting, the strokes on my canvas becoming softer and gentler with each passing day. There was something about this town that had transformed the way I saw the world. Its beauty was elusive, yet tangible; a blend of light and shadow that I was determined to capture. Each brushstroke felt like a step closer to that goal, like I was slowly uncovering the town's secrets and immortalizing them in my art.

But no matter how close I felt, there was always more to discover. This town had a way of revealing itself in layers, and I had a feeling I was on the brink of something special. That I could *almost* capture its true essence.

As I rounded the gentle curve at the end of Sycamore Lane, Ethan's house came into view, and the rustic charm of the place immediately wrapped around me, drawing me in with its warm, weathered exterior. The wood and stone blended seamlessly, as if the house had grown naturally from the earth itself, and ivy crept up one side, its green tendrils adding a touch of wildness that made the home feel alive, like it was part of the landscape rather than just sitting on it.

I slowed my pace, taking in the scene. The front porch, with its pair of well-worn rocking chairs, seemed to beckon me closer. I could almost hear the soft creak of the chairs swaying in a gentle breeze, see the flicker of candlelight as evening fell, and feel the warmth of a shared blanket on a cool night. Potted plants dotted the porch, their leaves dancing in the afternoon light, adding bursts of color and life to the space.

The front windows were open, and I could hear the soft strains of music drifting out—a gentle melody that matched the serenity of the afternoon. The house wasn't grand or ostentatious, but it had a warmth and authenticity that suited Ethan—unpretentious, grounded, and full of charm.

I reached the door and knocked lightly, the sound echoing through the stillness of the day. A moment later, the door swung open, and there stood Ethan—grinning, and dressed in a bright green dinosaur onesie. His eyes twinkled with mischief as he leaned against the doorframe, arms crossed.

"Hi," he said, his tone as casual as if he were wearing jeans and a T-shirt instead of a tail.

The sight of him standing there looking so good, even in a ridiculous dinosaur costume, made me laugh, the last of my nerves melting away. The onesie, soft and snug, clung to his lean frame, and the green fabric brought out the rich hazel of his eyes. His brown hair was delightfully messy, as if he'd just rolled out of bed, adding to the playful charm that radiated from him.

"Clearly, I didn't get the memo about dressing up," I teased, my mind already imagining what he looked like under that soft fabric.

Ethan's grin widened as he stepped aside to let me in and, as he did, our arms brushed ever so slightly, sending a small jolt of electricity through me. There was an unspoken tension in that brief touch, a spark that lingered even as he moved away. "Don't worry, I've got a matching one for you. Lily and I always coordinate—though hers is a unicorn, so you're welcome to switch teams if you want."

I laughed again, unable to resist the warmth of his playful banter. "Unicorns? Now that sounds way cooler. I'm definitely down to match with Lily," I said grinning, trying to ignore the way my pulse had quickened from that tiny spark.

His smile widened even further. "I knew you'd say that. Lily's going to be thrilled."

As I stepped inside, Ethan pulled me into a quick, casual hug. His arm wrapped around my waist, and his hand rested low on my back, sending a surge of warmth pooling in my stomach. Even through the soft fabric of the onesie, I could feel the solid strength of his body, and the gentle flex of his muscles as he held me close for just a heartbeat longer than necessary. His scent enveloped me—clean cotton mixed with a hint of lemon, and a deeper, earthy note of musk. It was intoxicating, wrapping around me like a comforting embrace.

I followed Ethan further in the house, the entryway opening into a modest living room that felt instantly welcoming. Shelves lined the walls, filled with books that had spines of various colors and genres. Each book was worn and well-loved. A large, overstuffed couch sat in the middle of the room, draped with a soft, plaid throw blanket. There was a coffee table in front of the couch, cluttered with a few scattered papers, a half-empty mug, and a stack of books—one of them open, a page marked with a folded corner.

"Make yourself at home," Ethan said, gesturing toward the couch. "Sorry for the mess."

I smiled. The house was clean but comfortably so, with just enough clutter to feel inviting rather than sterile. The wooden floors creaked softly underfoot, adding to the sense of history and character that seemed to seep from every corner. A large bay window let in streams of golden afternoon light, illuminating a reading nook complete with a worn armchair and a small side table, both perfectly positioned to catch the light.

"You call this a mess?" I teased, looking around. "This place is amazing. It feels like . . . you."

Ethan chuckled, rubbing the back of his neck. "Yeah, it's not much, but it's home. And hey, if you ever want to borrow a book, you're welcome to anything on those shelves. They're my pride and joy."

I glanced at the shelves, my fingers itching to explore the titles more closely. "I might take you up on that. But first, I'm going to need a tour. Show me where you keep all the other onesies."

Ethan's eyes sparkled with amusement as he turned and led the way further into the house. "Follow me, but fair warning—I've got an entire wardrobe full of them. You might want to brace yourself."

While moving through the house, I admired the simple, thoughtful details that made the space feel so uniquely his. A few framed photos dotted the walls—pictures of Ethan with friends, some of him hiking in the woods, and one of him and Lily, both grinning widely, with their faces covered in what looked like cake frosting. The kitchen was small but functional, with a well-worn wooden table in the center, surrounded by mismatched chairs that only added to the charm.

As we reached the end of the tour, Ethan stopped in front of a door at the back of the house. "And this," he said, opening the door, "is where the magic happens."

Inside was a small but comfortable office, with yet another wall of bookshelves, a large desk cluttered with papers, and a corkboard covered in notes and photos. A single window looked out onto the forest behind the house, the trees standing tall and silent, their leaves rustling in the breeze.

"Let me guess," I said, smiling, "this is where you plan all your lessons and grade all those essays?"

Ethan nodded, his expression softening as he looked around the room. "Yeah, it's my little sanctuary. It's nothing fancy, but it's where I can focus. Plus, it's got the best view in the house."

"It's beautiful," I said softly, turning to meet his gaze. "Everything about this place is."

Ethan's smile was warm as he looked at me. "I'm glad you think so."

He hadn't included his bedroom in the tour, and the thought made me smile inwardly. He hadn't wanted to make me uncomfortable, or give the wrong impression. But a small, curious part of me itched to know what his bedroom looked like, to see what secrets it might hold.

He cleared his throat, a playful glint in his eyes. "Lily should be here in about an hour. Want to help me build a fort in the living room? It's always a bit of a project, but it's totally worth it when she sees it. Her face lights up every time."

A smile tugged at my lips, but I hesitated for a moment. "I've never built a fort before. My parents were pretty strict, and they thought stuff like that was too childish, so it wasn't something we ever did."

His eyes widened in surprise, and then his expression shifted to one of determination. "Well, that just makes this even better. We're going to make this the most epic fort ever—one you'll never forget. It's long overdue."

I laughed, a rush of warmth filling me at the idea. "You're really committed to this, huh?"

"Absolutely," he said with a grin. "Everyone deserves at least one awesome fort-building experience in their life. And don't worry, I'm a seasoned pro. By the time we're done, you'll be a fort-building master. Who knows, you might even start a new hobby."

"Fort-building as a hobby?" I teased. "Sounds like a pretty serious commitment."

"Trust me," Ethan said with a wink, "it's worth it. Now, let's get to work. We've got a lot of fun to make up for."

With that, he led the way to the living room, his enthusiasm infectious as he began gathering blankets, cushions, and chairs. We started by rearranging the furniture, dragging chairs and couches into the perfect positions to support our masterpiece. The air between us buzzed with a playful energy, our movements synchronized as if we'd done this a hundred times before. When our gazes would meet, the corners of my lips twitched with the urge to smile.

"So," I teased, draping a blanket over a chair, "how does one become a master fort-builder? Any special tricks I should know about?"

Ethan chuckled. "Well, it's all about structural integrity, obviously. You want to make sure your roof isn't going to cave in at the first sign of trouble."

"Ah, right," I replied with mock seriousness, nodding as I spread another blanket across the chairs. "And I assume there's a secret fort-building society that you've been inducted into? With handshakes and everything?"

He laughed, shaking his head. "Not quite. But maybe after tonight, I'll nominate you for membership. You've got some serious potential."

We joked back and forth as we worked, the conversation flowing easily, punctuated by bursts of laughter that echoed through the living room. The playful energy between us made every moment light and effortless, as if we were two kids rediscovering the joy of something as simple as building a fort.

At one point, I was crawling under a makeshift canopy of chairs to secure a particularly stubborn blanket when the entire structure wobbled dangerously. I let out a small gasp, bracing myself as it threatened to collapse. But, before I could react, Ethan was there, his hands quickly steadying the chairs and holding it all together.

"You okay under there?" he asked, his voice laced with concern, but his eyes were dancing with amusement.

I looked up at him, a breathless laugh escaping my lips. "Yeah, thanks to you. That was close."

He grinned, his gaze locking onto mine as he crouched down beside me, still holding the chairs steady. The space between us suddenly felt incredibly small, the air thick with a tension that was anything but innocent, and my heart raced.

For a moment, neither of us moved. Ethan's fingers brushed against mine as he handed me the blanket to secure, the touch sending a spark straight through me. The heat of his body was just inches away, and the magnetic pull between us became almost impossible to ignore. His eyes held mine, a flicker of something in them that made my pulse quicken and my breath hitch.

"Thanks," I whispered, my voice betraying the flutter of nerves in my chest.

"Anytime," he replied, his voice low and full of something unspoken. The corners of his mouth lifted into a smile, but there was a new depth to it, something that hinted at more than just playful banter.

As I secured the blanket, my fingers trembling slightly, Ethan didn't move away. Instead, he stayed close, his presence grounding me even as it set my senses on high alert. When I finally emerged from under the fort, he was still there, his gaze lingering on me.

I took his hand, savoring the strength in his grip as he pulled me up, but neither of us let go. There was a brief pause, and a shared glance that held more weight than words, before we both released the tension with a light laugh and got back to work. But the sparks that had flickered between us remained, adding a new layer of excitement to every touch and every shared glance.

"Alright, how does this look?" I asked, stepping back to admire our handiwork. The fort was a charmingly haphazard collection of blankets draped over furniture, cushions scattered around for comfort, and a few twinkling string lights that Ethan had pulled out of a closet. It was cozy and inviting.

"It's perfect," Ethan said, nodding in approval as he surveyed the scene. His voice was warm with satisfaction, but there was a softness in his gaze that made my heart skip a beat. "Lily's going to love it. You've got a real talent for this."

I laughed, a sense of accomplishment swelling within me. "I think it's a team effort. Plus, I had a great teacher," I added, shooting him a playful look.

Ethan's grin widened, a mischievous glint sparking in his eyes. "Flattery will get you everywhere," he teased, his voice dipping low as he stepped closer, the space between us shrinking by the second.

"We make a pretty good team, don't we?"

"We do," I agreed, but my voice was quieter now, distracted by the way he suddenly was inching toward me, his playful grin still firmly in place. His gaze locked onto mine.

"You know," he said, stepping closer again. "I think we could start a business. Custom forts for all occasions. Birthdays, holidays, you name it."

I tried to laugh, but it came out more like a breathless sigh as he continued to close the distance between us. "I can see the ads now: Vinnie and Ethan's Fort Emporium—Where Imagination Meets Structural Integrity."

He chuckled, the sound low and intimate, as he took another deliberate step toward me. "I think we'd have a lot of customers."

Before I knew it, I found myself backed against the wall, my breath hitching as I realized just how close he was. The playful banter between us was quickly becoming an afterthought, replaced by the undeniable pull that drew us closer, inch by inch.

His eyes darkened with intent as they stayed locked onto mine, the teasing light still there, but now layered with something deeper. My heart pounded in my chest as he stepped in even closer, his body nearly pressing against mine, his hands lifting to rest against the wall on either side of my head, caging me in.

The air between us crackled with tension, every nerve in my body screaming with anticipation. Ethan's gaze flicked down to my lips, and I could feel the intensity of his stare as if it were a physical touch. My breath caught in my throat, the space between us charged with an almost unbearable heat.

Ethan leaned in, his face just inches from mine, his breath warm against my skin as his eyes searched mine, silently asking the question that hung heavily in the air.

Was this what I wanted?

The answer felt so obvious, and I hoped it was written all over my face.

Ethan's lips hovered just above mine and my heart raced, my skin burning with the need to close that final, excruciating distance. I wanted him to kiss me more than I'd wanted anything in a long time.

Just as our lips were about to meet, a sudden knock on the door shattered the moment and we both froze, the sound jolting us back to reality like a splash of cold water. Ethan let out a frustrated groan, his forehead dropping to rest against mine for just a second, his breath mingling with mine in a moment of shared regret.

"What timing," he muttered, his voice full of frustration and resignation, the moment between us slipping away as reality intruded.

"Seems like we're not catching a break," I whispered.

Ethan finally pulled back, his hand dragging through his hair with a rueful smile. "Yeah, seems like it."

I felt a blush creeping up my neck as I straightened, trying to shake off the lingering heat between us. Another knock sounded, more insistent this time, and Ethan shot me a look—one that promised we'd pick up right where we left off. As he turned to answer the door, I watched him go, my heart still racing.

Chapter 18

A LOUD BANG ECHOED through the house as the front door flew open and, before Ethan could react, Lily came barrelling in, her honey-blonde hair flying behind her like a wild mane. She was a blur of energy and excitement; a small, unicorn onesie-clad tornado racing through the hallway. Ethan barely sidestepped as she dashed past him, leaving a trail of discarded items—her backpack, a jacket, a pair of shoes—scattered on the floor.

"Lily! Slow down!" Ethan called after her, laughing.

But Lily was already halfway to the living room, her brown eyes wide with anticipation. The sound of a woman's voice drifted in from the open door, light and amused. "Lily, don't forget your manners! And have fun, sweetheart!" she called out, used to her daughter's uncontainable enthusiasm.

Lily skidded to a halt just outside the living room, her breath catching as she took in the sight before her. She stood frozen for a moment, eyes growing even wider as she absorbed every detail of the fort Ethan and I had built.

"Whoa . . ." she breathed, her voice filled with awe. "This is *amazing*!"

Then, her gaze shifted and, for the first time, she noticed me standing there, just a few feet away. The excitement in her eyes dimmed slightly, replaced by a curious, almost cautious look. My heart skipped a beat, a wave of nerves washing over me as I wondered what she might think.

Before I could even begin to worry, Lily tilted her head and, with all the directness of a six-year-old, asked, "Who are you?" Her voice was full of curiosity and challenge, as if she was sizing me up.

I opened my mouth to respond, but her gaze had already dropped to the jeans and T-shirt I was wearing, and her brow furrowed in confusion. "And why aren't you dressed up? This is a fort. You have to dress up," she declared, crossing her arms as if I'd just broken the most important rule of all.

I couldn't help but laugh at Lily's candidness. "You're right, I didn't get a chance to change yet," I admitted with a grin, glancing at Ethan. "But I do have a onesie—your brother made sure I wouldn't miss out."

"Oh! So you're Vinnie!" she exclaimed, her tone playful. "Ethan's been talking about you a lot! He said you're really pretty and that you make him laugh all the time."

My cheeks heated as I shot a quick look at Ethan, who suddenly looked like he wanted to disappear into the floor. "Lily!" he groaned, rubbing the back of his neck with an awkward smile.

"What?" Lily said, feigning innocence, though the twinkle in her eyes betrayed her. "It's true! He talks about you all the time."

I bit my lip, trying to suppress a smile as I turned to Ethan. "Really? All the time, huh?"

His embarrassment quickly shifted into something softer as he met my gaze. "Well, I might have mentioned you once or twice."

Lily giggled, clearly pleased with the impact of her revelation. "See? I knew it!"

Ethan, still recovering from his sister's bold honesty, stepped closer and rested a hand on Lily's shoulder. "Lily, this is Vinnie. She helped me build the fort today. What do you think?"

Her eyes widened with admiration as she looked up at me. "You helped? That's so cool! This is, like, the *best* fort ever!" she declared, her face glowing with excitement.

"Thanks," I said, bashful under her enthusiastic praise. "But I couldn't have done it without your big brother."

"You guys did great!" she exclaimed, before diving headfirst into the fort, her excitement bubbling over as she explored every corner.

Ethan and I watched as her little hands eagerly inspected the pillows and blankets we'd so carefully arranged. She grabbed her bag and started unpacking her treasures: coloring books, a stuffed unicorn, and a small flashlight that she flicked on and off with glee. The fort was quickly transforming into her personal playground, and her happiness was infectious. I glanced over at Ethan, catching the soft, shy smile that had settled on his face as he watched his sister.

"So . . . you talk about me a lot, huh?" I asked.

Ethan groaned, giving me a look that was part embarrassed, part amused. "I guess she couldn't wait to spill that, could she?" he sighed, his eyes meeting mine. "Yeah, I might have mentioned you a few times to my mom, and Lily must have overheard."

"A few? Or a lot?" I interjected with a grin.

"A lot," he admitted, rubbing the back of his neck again. "What can I say? You've been on my mind."

I smiled at his vulnerability. "Well, I'm flattered," I said.

Ethan shot me a grateful look, but then, as if remembering something, his expression turned a little more serious. "Actually, speaking of talking . . . my mom has been asking about you. A lot." He laughed, the embarrassment still lingering. "Apparently, Laura told her all about our date, and now she's convinced we're a thing."

I laughed at his awkward confession. "She sounds lovely," I said, my tone light. "And very . . . interested."

"Oh, she is," Ethan replied with a grin, rolling his eyes in a way that showed both affection and mild exasperation. "She's just excited for me, you know? But it can be a bit much sometimes."

I raised an eyebrow playfully. "And you didn't introduce us because?"

Ethan's smile turned bashful again, and he shifted on his feet. "Well, after what Lily said, I figured you might need a little break from hearing about how much I talk about you." He joked, but then his expression softened. "But really, I didn't want to overwhelm you. I know how my mom can be, and I didn't want you to feel like you were getting the third degree. Plus, she'd probably linger and ask you a million questions about . . . us. And I wasn't sure if you were ready for that, or if you even *wanted* to meet her yet." His words started tumbling out in a bit of a ramble, his nerves showing through, and he laughed at himself, shaking his head. "Sorry, I'm making this sound way more complicated than it is."

I laughed, touched by how much thought he'd put into it. "It's fine, Ethan. Really. Maybe next time?"

Ethan's eyes softened, and he smiled, relieved. "Yeah," he said, his voice gentle and a little more confident. "Next time."

Just as the moment settled between us, Lily's voice rang out from inside the fort. "Ethan, I'm hungry!"

She poked her head out, her big brown eyes expectantly fixed on her brother. Just like that, the intensity of our moment was shattered, replaced by the everyday reality of a six-year-old's priorities.

Ethan sighed dramatically, though his smile gave him away. "Well, can't keep the princess waiting, can we?" He shot me a quick glance that made my heart flutter, before turning his attention fully to Lily. "What are you in the mood for, Lil?"

Her eyes sparkled as she thought about it, and then she grinned. "Pizza! And ice cream!"

He laughed, glancing back at me with a look that clearly said: *This is my life.* "Pizza and ice cream it is."

Ethan ordered the food with the ease of a man who had clearly done this many times before, rattling off their usual order while Lily hovered nearby, practically vibrating with excitement. As soon as he hung up, she turned her big brown eyes on me with a determined expression.

"Okay, Vinnie," she said, hands on her hips like a tiny drill sergeant. "You have to change into your onesie now. No one is allowed in the fort unless they're properly dressed. It's the rule."

I laughed, charmed by her seriousness. "Well, I wouldn't want to break the rules," I teased, glancing at Ethan, who was watching the exchange with an amused grin.

Ethan pointed down the hallway. "Bathroom's right over there. Your onesie's on the counter."

With a mock salute to Lily, I headed off to change. When I emerged a few minutes later in a fluffy pink unicorn onesie that matched hers, a delighted squeal greeted me. "You look awesome, Vinnie!"

She took my hand and practically dragged me back into the living room, where Ethan had already started setting up the fort for movie night. She declared the fort her *castle*, and announced that no one could enter unless they were prepared to follow the royal rules—which, as it turned out, included having a spa night. Ethan tried to protest, but one look at Lily's determined face, and he was laughing and shaking his head, resigned to his fate.

Before long, we were all nestled in, surrounded by a mountain of pillows and blankets, and *Hocus Pocus* flickered on the small TV, casting a soft glow over the room. The scent of popcorn mingled with the sweet smell of face masks, as Lily convinced Ethan to join us in the spa portion of the evening.

"You know, this is not what I had in mind for tonight," he joked, his voice muffled slightly by the green mask slathered across his face. His hair was a mess of half-done braids and tiny clips, all thanks to Lily, who was currently sitting in his lap, concentrating fiercely on adding more decorations.

"Are you kidding?" I teased, adjusting my own face mask. "You're the one who said this fort was the best one yet. And besides, it's not every day you get to be pampered like this."

Lily giggled, her hands busy tying a bright pink ribbon into Ethan's hair. "Yeah, Ethan! You're supposed to be having fun. This is a girls' night! So stop complaining and let me finish."

"You're doing a great job, Lil," I said, encouraging her as she added another clip. "I think he could use more glitter, though. Really make him sparkle."

"Good idea!" she agreed enthusiastically, reaching for the glitter gel. Ethan shot me a playful glare.

"You're not helping, you know," he said, his tone mock-serious. "You're supposed to be on my side."

I grinned, shrugging innocently. "Sorry, but I'm team Lily on this one."

"See? Vinnie knows what's up." She beamed at me, pleased.

Ethan sighed dramatically, but couldn't hide his smile. "Well, I guess I'm outnumbered."

Lily paused in her work, tilting her head. "You should always join us for girls' night, Vinnie. It's way more fun with you here."

The sincerity in her voice caught me off guard. "I'd love that," I said softly, touched by her invitation.

Ethan laughed, shaking his head. "You two are going to gang up on me, aren't you?"

"Totally!" Lily insisted, sticking out her tongue before her expression turned determined. "Now, Ethan, you have to braid Vinnie's hair while I finish yours. It's only fair."

He looked at me with a raised eyebrow, trying to hide his amusement. "Orders from the queen," he teased as he shifted slightly closer. His fingers hovered near my hair, a silent question in his eyes.

"Is it okay if I . . .?" he asked, his voice suddenly softer, more tentative.

I nodded, my heart picking up pace. "Yeah, it's fine," I whispered, reaching up to undo my ponytail. My fingers brushed against his as I let my brown hair fall loose, and the contact sent a jolt of warmth through me.

Ethan hesitated, his gaze meeting mine, searching for any sign of discomfort. When he found none, he let his fingers thread through my hair, his touch impossibly tender. My breath caught as he separated the strands, his movements careful and deliberate, as if he were handling something fragile.

"Your hair's so soft," he murmured, almost as if he were talking to himself. His fingers brushed against the nape of my neck, sending a shiver down my spine that I couldn't hide.

"You're actually not bad at this," I said, trying to keep my voice light despite the electric charge that seemed to buzz between us.

"Honestly? I have no idea what I'm doing," he admitted with a laugh, though his fingers continued to work through my hair, his touch growing more confident. "But Lily's taught me a thing or two."

Lily, who was still perched in his lap and diligently working on his hair, nodded sagely. "He's okay," she said, trying to downplay her praise. "But I'm the expert. I'll have to fix it later."

Her cheeky grin broke the tension just enough to make us both laugh. Yet, when Ethan's eyes met mine, the warmth in his gaze made my pulse race.

As he continued to braid my hair, Lily kept up a steady stream of instructions, bossing him around with the authority of a seasoned stylist. "No, Ethan, you have to braid it tighter or it'll fall out!"

Ethan shot her a playful look, rolling his eyes dramatically. "Yes, ma'am," he said, his tone full of affection. "How's this?"

Lily leaned over to inspect his work, her brow furrowed in concentration. "Hmm . . . better, but you missed a piece." She pointed, and Ethan dutifully adjusted his grip, his fingers brushing against my scalp.

Ethan's expression softened as he finished the braid, his fingers lingering in my hair for a moment longer than necessary. He looked at me, his eyes holding something deeper.

"I'd like it if you joined us more often, as well," he whispered, his voice sincere, almost vulnerable. "Lily's right—it's more fun with you here."

His words, simple as they were, made my heart skip a beat. There was something intimate about the way he said it, as if he were letting me into a part of his life that he didn't share with just anyone.

"I'd like that, too," I replied, my voice just as soft. I could feel the weight of his gaze, and the warmth of his fingers still tangled in my hair, and I knew that something had shifted between us—something that couldn't be easily ignored.

Before the moment could grow too intense, Lily's voice broke through, her stomach growling audibly. "Ethan, I'm hungry!"

We both burst into laughter, the tension easing as reality rushed back in. Ethan shook his head, gently tugging at one of Lily's braids. "Alright, alright, food's on the way, Princess. Just a few more minutes."

Sure enough, a knock on the door sounded a few minutes later, and Lily was up like a shot, racing to the door. "Pizza!" she squealed, her excitement contagious.

Ethan got up with a grin, following her to the door as I tidied up a bit, making room. When they returned, Lily was carrying a box of pizza almost as big as she was, her face lit up with glee.

"Careful there," Ethan chuckled, taking the box from her and setting it down on the blanket-covered floor. "We don't want any pizza casualties."

She giggled, plopping down and grabbing a slice. "This is the best night ever!" she declared, her voice muffled by a mouthful of pizza.

We all dug in, the fort filled with the sounds of contented eating and the occasional laughs. Before long, Lily had a new idea.

"Ethan, can we watch *Halloweentown* next?" she asked, her eyes wide with excitement as she turned to me. "It's my favorite movie ever! Do you think Halloweentown is a real place, Vinnie?"

"I think it's as real as you want it to be," I said, leaning in conspiratorially. "But remember, it's a secret town, hidden away where only the people who believe in magic can find it."

Her eyes sparkled with delight at the idea, as Ethan chimed in. "You know, Hallow's End is pretty close to Halloweentown," he joked, winking at me.

Lily shook her head, clearly not buying it. "No way! We don't have magic, or monsters, or ghosts."

Ethan leaned back, a thoughtful look on his face. "Are you sure about that? Hallow's End has its own kind of magic. Haven't you ever noticed how things get a little strange around Halloween? Like how sometimes the lights flicker on their own, or how the fog rolls in just a little too thick?"

"You mean like real magic? Like in the stories?" Lily's eyes widened, her pizza forgotten as she stared at Ethan, completely captivated.

"Something like that," he said, lowering his voice as if sharing a secret. "Around Halloween, the magic in the air around here gets stronger. Strange things start to happen—things that can't be explained. Some people think it's just the town's way of reminding us that there's more to the world than what we can see."

Lily gasped, her imagination clearly running wild with the idea. "That's so cool"

We continued that way, sharing stories and pizza in the fort, a relaxed ease settling over us beneath the twinkling fairy lights. But, as the night wore on, the inevitable end began to creep in.

"Ethan," Lily said, her voice tinged with a hint of sadness, "can we have a sleepover? I don't want tonight to end."

He sighed softly, smiling down at her. "I know, Lil, but Mom's already on her way to pick you up. But don't worry—we can have a proper sleepover next time, okay?"

Lily's face lit up again as she turned to me with a cheeky grin. "Vinnie, you have to come to the sleepover, too! We can braid Ethan's hair again and make him wear a face mask!"

"I wouldn't miss it for anything." I laughed, touched by how much she wanted me to be a part of their world.

Ethan chuckled, shaking his head as he ruffled Lily's hair. "You two are going to be trouble together, I can tell."

Lily stuck her tongue out at him, giggling. "You love it!"

Ethan grinned, glancing over at me with a softness in his eyes that made my heart flutter. "Yeah," he said quietly, his voice full of warmth. "I really do."

The night was winding down, the fort dismantled, and the remnants of the pizza feast neatly tidied away, yet the air still hummed with the magic of the evening, and I could feel the warmth of the memories we'd created lingering in the room like the soft glow of the string lights.

A sudden knock at the door broke the comfortable silence, and Lily's eyes lit up. She hopped up from where she'd been sitting, giving both me and Ethan big hugs before bouncing toward the door. "Next time, right, Vinnie?" she asked, her voice filled with hope and excitement.

"Absolutely," I promised, returning her hug with a warm squeeze.

Lily's grin was pure joy as she turned to Ethan, her eyes gleaming with mischief. "And next time, you have to let me put even more glitter in your hair. And some more bows, too."

Ethan, who still hadn't had a chance to remove any of Lily's handiwork, looked comical, with his usually tousled hair now a chaotic mix of glitter, pink bows, and tiny clips, the glitter catching the light every time he moved, shimmering like a halo of sparkles around his head. A particularly enormous pink bow perched right on top, almost like a crown, while the rest of the ribbons were scattered haphazardly throughout his hair, adding to the absurdly charming look.

"I'm still finding glitter everywhere, Lil," he teased, his voice filled with mock exasperation. "I think I'll be sparkling for days."

Lily giggled, clearly proud of her work. "You look pretty, Ethan. Like a fairy prince!"

At that, I couldn't hold back my laughter, my gaze moving from Lily's beaming face to Ethan's glitter-covered hair. "She's not wrong," I said, trying to keep a straight face. "You *do* look like a fairy prince. A very sparkly one."

Ethan rolled his eyes, but there was a fondness in his expression as he looked at both of us. "I guess if it makes you two happy, I'll keep the look for a while longer," he conceded, though he couldn't hide the small smile tugging at the corners of his mouth.

Lily clapped her hands in delight. "Yay! Next time, I'll make sure you're even prettier."

"I can hardly wait," Ethan groaned, ruffling her hair. "You're lucky you're cute, kid."

"I know!" she chirped, sticking her tongue out at him before running off to grab her things. She returned with her backpack and jacket just as Ethan opened the door.

Standing there was Ethan's mom, her smile warm and welcoming. She had the same kind eyes as Ethan, with a few strands of gray threading through her brown hair, which was pulled back into a loose bun. She wore a knitted jumper, jeans, and a big coat that seemed to swallow her small frame, but there was an undeniable strength and kindness in her demeanor.

"Hi, sweetheart," she greeted Lily, crouching down to give her a big hug. Lily squeezed her mom tightly before pulling back with a grin.

"Mom, guess what! Vinnie's coming to our next sleepover!" she announced, bouncing on her toes.

Ethan's mom's gaze shifted to me, her eyes sparkling with curiosity. "So, this is the famous Vinnie I've been hearing so much about." She straightened up, offering me a warm smile. "I have to say, Ethan mentioned you were pretty, but you're *gorgeous*. I can see why he's been crushing on you."

Heat rushed to my cheeks, and I shot a quick glance at Ethan, who looked thoroughly embarrassed, his ears tinged with red. "Mom . . ." he groaned, clearly mortified.

"What? I'm just telling the truth!" She reached out to give Ethan a playful nudge before turning back to me. "By the way, I'm Caroline. It's lovely to finally meet you, Vinnie. I have to say, I'm not sure why Ethan's been hiding you. I had to hear about you from Laura, of all people."

Ethan immediately groaned, rubbing the back of his neck. "Mom, I wasn't hiding her. I was just trying to avoid situations like *this*," he muttered, embarrassed.

Caroline waved him off, her smile growing. "Oh, nonsense. You just need to come out of your shell a bit. There's nothing embarrassing about liking someone and being open about it." She turned back to me with a wink. "He's always been shy about these things."

"You're not helping, Mom," Ethan sighed, shaking his head, but unable to hide the small, embarrassed smile tugging at his lips.

Lily, ever the bundle of energy, nodded enthusiastically. "Yeah! He says you're really cool, but he gets all shy and blushes whenever we talk about you!" she said with a mischievous grin, enjoying her brother's embarrassment. "It's so funny, his face turns all red like a tomato!"

Ethan's face flushed even deeper as Lily's teasing hit home. "Alright, alright, time to get you two home," he said. "It's getting late, and I'm sure Lily is tired."

Caroline, however, wasn't about to let him off that easily. She stopped, turning back to me with a warm smile. "Before we go, Vinnie, you should stop by for dinner one night. We'd love to have you over."

Ethan shot his mother a look of mock desperation. "Mom, maybe we should let Vinnie breathe before bombarding her with invites."

"Oh, hush, Ethan. It's not overwhelming to invite someone for a nice meal." Caroline waved him off with a playful grin. "Vinnie, consider this an official invitation. I make a lasagna that's been known to change lives."

Lily jumped in, her excitement renewed. "Yes! Please come, Vinnie! It'll be so much fun!"

Touched by their genuine warmth, I smiled. "I'd love to. Thank you so much for the invitation."

Caroline's face lit up. "Fantastic! We'll sort out the details soon. Now, let's get this little monkey to bed." She ruffled Lily's hair affectionately.

Lily giggled, giving both Ethan and me tight hugs again. "Goodnight, Vinnie! See you soon!"

"Goodnight," I replied, hugging her back.

Lily gave one last enthusiastic wave before bouncing out the door, her unicorn onesie trailing behind her like a cape. Caroline followed, casting a final warm smile in my direction. Ethan walked them to the end of the driveway, where they lingered for a moment, exchanging a few quiet words that I couldn't hear. Caroline glanced back at me once more, her expression filled with approval, before she and Lily turned and made their way down the street toward their home.

Ethan stood there for a moment, watching them go, then turned back to me, a sheepish look on his face as he walked back up the steps. "Sorry about that," he said. "My family can be a bit . . . much. You really don't have to come for dinner if you're not up for it. I know they can be overwhelming."

I laughed, stepping closer to him, the cool night air brushing against my skin. "Ethan, don't apologize. Your family is wonderful. And it's sweet how much they care about you."

His shoulders relaxed as he looked at me, his eyes searching mine. "You really don't mind? I just don't want you to feel pressured."

"Not at all. I'm looking forward to it." I shook my head, a smile tugging at my lips.

Ethan's expression softened and he stepped closer. "I'm glad to hear that."

We stood there for a moment, the night settling around us, the air charged with a gentle, unspoken tension. The street was quiet, save for the distant hum of crickets, and the glow from the streetlights cast soft shadows across Ethan's face. He had pulled out all the hair clips and bows the minute Lily was gone but I could still see the lingering glitter in his hair.

"Thank you for tonight," he said, his voice low and sincere. "I really enjoyed it."

"Me too," I replied, my voice just as soft.

He smiled, the kind of smile that reached his eyes and made my heart flutter. "I'm really glad you're here, Vinnie."

"I'm glad, too," I whispered, the space between us shrinking until I could feel the warmth of his breath on my skin.

Ethan's smile lingered, his eyes locked on mine, and the air between us shifted, growing warmer, more charged. My heart began to race, each beat echoing in the quiet of the night as the space between us shrank further. His gaze flickered down to my lips, then back up to my eyes, as if silently asking for permission.

I didn't hesitate. Without a word, I closed the remaining distance between us, my breath hitching as his soft lips brushed against mine. It was a tentative kiss at first, gentle and unhurried, as though we were both savoring the moment we'd been dancing around for so long.

Ethan's hand came up to cradle my cheek, his thumb brushing lightly against my skin, and the tenderness in his touch melted away any lingering nerves. I leaned into him, deepening the kiss as my hands instinctively rested against his chest. His heart was pounding beneath my fingertips, matching the rhythm of my own.

The kiss was sweet, but there was a slow-burning intensity beneath it, a chemistry that had been building between us from the start. His lips were warm and soft, moving with a quiet confidence that sent warmth flooding through me. Ethan's other hand slipped around my waist, pulling me closer, until there was nothing between us but the steady thrum of our hearts.

When we pulled back, it was only because we needed to breathe, our foreheads resting against each other as we caught our breath. His eyes were half-lidded, his expression soft and content, and a smile tugged at the corners of his mouth.

"That was worth the wait," he murmured, his voice husky.

"Definitely worth the wait," I agreed, my voice barely above a whisper.

Ethan's thumb gently traced the outline of my jaw, his eyes drinking me in as if committing every detail to memory. "I've wanted to do that for so long," he admitted, his breath still mingling with mine.

"Me too," I whispered back.

He pressed a gentle kiss to my forehead, his lips lingering there for a heartbeat before he pulled back just enough to look at me again. "This feels . . . right," he said, almost as if he was as surprised as I was by how easily everything had fallen into place.

"It does," I agreed, my hand still resting on his chest, feeling the steady beat of his heart beneath my palm.

The warmth of his gaze, and the way his eyes softened as he looked at me, ignited something deeper inside me. A need—a *hunger*—that had been building for what felt like forever. Without thinking, I leaned in again, capturing his lips in another kiss, this one more urgent, more desperate than the last. The sweetness of our first kiss melted into something more intense, more primal, as I pressed myself closer to him, needing to feel the heat of his body against mine.

Ethan responded, his hands sliding down to my waist, pulling me flush against him as the kiss deepened. I could feel the tension in his body, the way he was holding back, but that only fuelled the fire burning inside me. I wanted more—more of him, and more of this connection that was quickly spiralling out of control.

With a moan, I urged him backward, guiding him through the door and into the living room. My hands roamed over his chest, feeling the strength of his muscles beneath the ridiculous onesie, and I couldn't help the grin that tugged at my lips. The contrast between the innocence of our surroundings, and the passion sparking between us, only made me want him more.

Ethan stumbled back onto the sofa, his eyes widening in surprise as I straddled his lap, my thighs bracketing his hips. I could feel how hard he was beneath me, and a thrill shot through my body as I leaned down to kiss him again, more hungrily this time. My teeth grazed his bottom lip, drawing a low groan from his throat that sent a shiver of pleasure down my spine.

I reached for the zipper of his onesie, my fingers trembling with anticipation as I began to pull it down. But just as I was about to expose the warm skin beneath, Ethan's hands caught mine, stilling my movements.

"Vinnie, wait," he murmured, his voice thick with desire. His eyes met mine, and I saw the conflict there—the longing, but also the restraint. "Slow down. There's no rush."

I froze, the heat in my body clashing with the coolness of his words. "But . . . I want to," I whispered, my voice wavering slightly. I leaned in closer, trying to close the distance again, but Ethan gently held me back.

He shook his head, his eyes filled with a resignation that sent a pang of uncertainty through me. "We don't have to do this now, Vinnie. Let's take our time."

His words hit me like a bucket of cold water, dousing the flames of passion that had been burning so brightly. I pulled back, suddenly feeling insecure, like I'd misread everything. Maybe I'd come on too strong. Maybe he didn't want me the way I wanted him. The hurt must have shown in my eyes, because Ethan's expression softened immediately.

"Hey," he said gently, reaching up to cup my cheek. "It's not that I don't want you. Trust me, I do. That kiss was ... *incredible*. But I want us to take this slower. I want to get to know you, *really* know you, without rushing into something we're not ready for."

I bit my lip, the sting of tears welling up—more from embarrassment than anything else. "But what if ..." I whispered, my voice small. "What if you lose interest?"

Ethan's eyes filled with something tender that made my heart ache in a different way. He shook his head slowly, his thumb brushing over my cheek. "Vinnie, I don't know who hurt you, or made you believe that you're not worth waiting for. But to me, you're special. Really special. And I want this to be right, not rushed."

His words wrapped around me like a comforting blanket, but the insecurity still lingered, gnawing at the edges of my mind. "I'm just ... not used to this," I admitted, my voice barely above a whisper.

"Vinnie, we don't need to rush this," he said softly, his voice steady. "We've got time to figure things out, to enjoy getting to know each other. I'm not going anywhere, okay?"

I looked at him, the sincerity in his eyes making my breath catch. This was all so different. It was gentler; more patient than anything I'd experienced before. And it scared me.

"Okay," I whispered, letting his words settle over me. This wasn't about pushing forward too fast. It was about allowing things to unfold naturally, at their own pace. And, for the first time in a long while, that felt like something I could embrace.

"Come on," he said gently, standing up and offering me his hand. "Let me walk you home."

I took his hand, letting him pull me to my feet. The room felt different now—more intimate, but in a way that was comforting, rather than urgent. We laughed as we slipped out of our ridiculous onesies, trading them for something more fitting for the cool night air. Once dressed, we left the living room behind and stepped outside.

When we reached my door, Ethan turned to me, his eyes still holding that same gentle warmth. Without hesitation, he leaned in, his lips meeting mine in a kiss that was tender and unhurried.

When he pulled back, his eyes lingered on mine, a soft smile tugging at his lips. "Goodnight, Vinnie," he murmured, his voice full of affection.

"Goodnight, Ethan," I replied, my own smile mirroring his as the warmth of his kiss still lingered on my lips. He waited until I was safely inside, then gave me a final wave before heading back down the path.

Once inside, I leaned back against the door, my mind still buzzing with everything that had happened tonight. Feeling the need to share, I pulled out my phone and dialled into our group chat. It didn't take long for Amelia and Ivy to answer, their voices full of curiosity.

"Tell us everything!" Ivy demanded, her excitement practically crackling through the phone.

"Did you kiss him?" Amelia asked, her voice eager and teasing.

I laughed, the sound lighter than I'd expected. "Yeah, we kissed," I admitted. "It was really sweet. But then things got a little intense, and he . . . he wanted to slow down."

"Slow down?" Amelia repeated, her voice curious but not judgmental. "Like, in a 'let's-take-it-slow-and-build-this-up' kind of way, or more like 'I'm too nervous to go further'?"

"Yeah," I said, searching for the right words. "He said we didn't need to rush anything. That we've got time to figure things out."

There was a brief pause before Ivy chimed in, her voice brimming with enthusiasm. "Vinnie, that's actually really sweet! He's not just in it for the physical stuff. He's showing you that he wants to really get to know you."

"Exactly," Amelia added, her tone supportive but still playful. "And honestly, when the time is right, it'll happen. But it sounds like he's taking you seriously, and that's a big deal."

I smiled, a sense of reassurance settling over me. "You're right. It just felt . . . different, you know?"

"Different is good," Ivy said, practically cheering.

Amelia chimed in, her voice full of playful encouragement. "Exactly! And look, when it happens, just make sure you enjoy every second. But until then, it's kind of hot that he's holding back, right?"

I couldn't help but laugh again. "Yeah, it is."

We chatted for a little longer, their excitement and encouragement making me feel even better. By the time we hung up, I was feeling more at peace, and the insecurities I'd been grappling with earlier began to fade away into the autumn night.

Chapter 19

THE NEW WEEK ARRIVED with a renewed sense of purpose, and I threw myself into transforming the gallery into the beautiful space I'd always envisioned. Each day was a step closer to making my dream a reality, and the blank walls and empty rooms took shape under my direction.

Ethan, true to his word, was there to help me every step of the way. He showed up at the gallery most evenings after work, rolling up his sleeves and diving into the work with a determination that I found both comforting, and *ridiculously* attractive. He handled the heavy lifting, installed the lights, and assembled the furniture, with an effortless strength that made my heart race every time I glimpsed his muscles flexing under his shirt.

Watching him work was a guilty pleasure, one I indulged in far more often than I should have. There was something about the way he moved—so focused, so capable. And when we stole kisses between painting walls and rearranging furniture, those moments were electric. Some kisses were quick and playful, but others lingered, simmering with a heat that left me breathless and wanting more.

Amelia and Ivy pitched in when they could, their enthusiasm infectious as they helped with decorating. But they were also careful to give Ethan and me space, especially in the evenings.

Those late nights in the gallery quickly became my favorite part of the day. After hours of work, we'd collapse onto the floor, or the makeshift couch, and we'd talk for hours, the conversation flowing easily as we got to know each other on a deeper level. I found myself opening up to Ethan in ways I hadn't expected, sharing bits of my past, my fears, and my dreams. And he was wonderful—patient, kind, and genuinely interested in every- thing I had to say.

The tension between us was still there, simmering just beneath the sur- face, but I found myself savoring it. The slow build-up made every touch, and every glance, feel even more meaningful.

Yet, there was a part of me that ached with a different kind of longing. As the week wore on, I couldn't help but wish I could share this part of my life with my mom. I wanted to call her up, to tell her about the gallery, about Ethan, about how everything was finally coming together. But every time the thought crossed my mind, the memory of our last conversation—the sharp words and the unresolved pain—quickly chased it away. The years of emotional distance between us felt too vast to bridge right now, so I left that wound untouched.

Friday arrived faster than I expected, the week a blur of activity and stolen moments. By the time evening rolled around, the gallery was looking like the space I'd always dreamed of—warm, inviting, and full of character. The lights were installed, the furniture was arranged just right, and the walls were freshly painted.

All that was left to do now was set up the social media accounts for the gallery, and hang the artwork next week. It felt surreal to be so close to the finish line, knowing that soon, people would fill this space, admiring the art.

The exhaustion was starting to catch up with me, though and, after tidying up the last few things, I decided to call it a night. As much as I wanted to keep pushing forward, my body was begging for rest, and I knew I'd need my energy for the final stretch.

I left the gallery feeling a deep sense of satisfaction, knowing that we'd accomplished so much in such a short time, and the cool night air felt refreshing as I made my way home, the quiet of the town soothing my tired mind. By the time I climbed into bed, it was just before 9 P.M.

I nestled into my pillows, my body sinking into the comfort of the mattress as I let out a long, contented sigh. Despite the exhaustion, there was a sense of peace settling over me—a feeling of accomplishment, of things falling into place. I was about to drift off when my phone buzzed on the nightstand.

> **Ethan:** Hey, I've got a surprise for you, if you're free tomorrow.

A smile tugged at my lips as I read the message, my heart doing a little flip at the thought of seeing him again.

> **Vinnie:** A surprise, huh? What is it? ☺

There was a pause, and then his reply came through, making me laugh.

> **Ethan:** It wouldn't be a surprise if I told you, now would it?

I rolled onto my back, staring up at the ceiling as I imagined what he could possibly have planned. The anticipation was enough to make my already tired mind race with possibilities.

> **Vinnie:** How am I supposed to sleep now with all this excitement? 😳

His reply was almost immediate, and I could practically hear the playful tone in his voice as I read his message.

> **Ethan:** You'll just have to wait and see 😊
> Sweet dreams, Vinnie. I'll swing by tomorrow morning.

I set my phone down, my eyes growing heavy as I settled deeper into the blankets. Despite the lingering curiosity about what he had in store for me, the exhaustion won out, and I soon drifted off to sleep with a smile on my face.

I woke up earlier than expected, the soft light of dawn filtering through my curtains. The room remained cloaked in a gentle hush, as the world outside had not yet fully awakened. I stretched beneath the covers, feeling the pleasant ache in my muscles from the week's hard work. Despite the exhaustion of the previous night, my mind was surprisingly alert, humming with a quiet energy that I couldn't ignore.

I glanced at the clock on my nightstand—7 A.M. The thought of Ethan's surprise tugged at the corners of my mind, but he hadn't said what time he'd be over. The house was silent, the perfect atmosphere for creativity and, as I lay there, inspiration started to take root, growing and spreading until I couldn't resist it any longer.

With a newfound sense of purpose, I threw off the covers and padded to the kitchen to make myself a cup of coffee. The rich, comforting aroma filled the air as I brewed a fresh pot, and I savored the warmth of the mug in my hands as I made my way to the living room.

I set my cup down on the table, the steam curling into the air as I began gathering my paints and brushes, a familiar excitement bubbling up inside me.

I hadn't planned on painting today, but something inside me had shifted, urging me to create. Maybe it was the culmination of the week's work, or maybe it was the anticipation of seeing Ethan later. Whatever it was, I needed to put it on canvas.

Sitting cross-legged on the floor, I arranged my paints around me, the colors calling to me in a way that felt almost instinctual. I didn't have a clear picture in my mind of what I wanted to paint, but that didn't matter. Today, I wanted to let go of structure and just let my emotions guide me. I reached for a brush, dipping it into a soft shade of blue.

As the brush moved across the canvas, I let myself get lost in the rhythm of the strokes, the colors blending and flowing together. Blues melted into greens, which softened into blush pinks and warm, earthy tones. The shapes and lines weren't precise. They were fluid, almost ethereal, like the emotions I'd been holding inside for weeks were finally spilling out in a language that only the canvas could understand.

Time slipped away as I painted, the morning turning into mid-morning without me noticing. The coffee in my mug had long since cooled, but I didn't care. I was lost in the act of creation, my heart and hands working together to bring this piece to life.

When I finally leaned back to look at what I'd done, I felt a swell of satisfaction. The painting was different from my usual work, but it was a *good* different. It felt right. It felt like me—like *us*. The abstract shapes and soft hues spoke of a connection that was still unfolding, still finding its form, but that was undeniably *there*.

I was just admiring the finished piece when I heard a soft knock at the door. My heart skipped a beat, excitement flaring as I realized it must be Ethan. I glanced at the clock that read 11 A.M, and I quickly wiped my hands on a rag but, as I stood up, a sudden wave of nerves washed over me. I looked down at myself. I was still in my messy paint-stained outfit, and my hair was pulled into a loose, haphazard bun, with stray tendrils falling around my face.

With a deep breath, I made my way to the door and opened it. I was greeted by the sight of Ethan standing on the porch, and my breath caught at how effortlessly handsome he looked. He was wearing a soft, plaid flannel shirt, unbuttoned, and worn like a jacket over a crisp white T-shirt that hugged his chest just right. The flannel's sleeves were casually rolled up, revealing his strong forearms, and the shirt hung loosely. His well-worn jeans fit him perfectly, sitting low on his hips, and a pair of sturdy boots completed the look, giving him that rugged edge that made my pulse quicken.

There was a playful glint in his hazel eyes, and I noticed he was holding something behind his back, but I was too distracted by how good he looked to focus on what it might be.

"Good morning," he said, his voice warm and inviting. His gaze swept over me, taking in my paint-splattered outfit and the smudge on my face, but instead of looking put off, his smile only widened. "Hope I'm not too early?"

"Not at all," I replied, feeling a little flustered. In my attempt to remove the paint from my cheek, I ended up smearing it even more. "Sorry about the mess. I was painting."

Ethan chuckled, his eyes twinkling with affection as he stepped closer. "Here, let me help," he said gently, leaning in. He reached up with his thumb, brushing it lightly across my cheek to wipe away the smudge.

"There," he murmured, his voice low as he pulled back, but not before our eyes met. "All better. And for the record, you look adorable with a little paint on you."

My nerves eased at his words, but I couldn't help but feel a little flustered. "Come in," I said, stepping aside to let him enter. "Just, um, give me a minute to change."

As Ethan walked past me, he revealed what he had been hiding behind his back—a charming bouquet of rustic, seasonal fall flowers. The arrangement was a perfect mix of deep oranges, warm yellows, and soft browns, with sprigs of wheat and dried grasses woven in. It was simple yet beautiful, the kind of bouquet that looked like it had been gathered from a sunlit meadow.

"These are for you," he said, his voice soft as he handed them to me. There was a touch of shyness in his smile, as if he wasn't sure how I'd react.

I took the flowers, my heart melting at the thoughtful gesture. "They're beautiful, Ethan," I murmured, a smile tugging at my lips.

"They made me think of you," he shrugged, his gaze meeting mine with that familiar warmth that always made me feel at ease.

A flutter of warmth spread through me at his words. "Thank you. This is really sweet."

He smiled, his eyes lighting up as he watched me. "Worth it, just to see that smile on your face."

Blushing, I hugged the bouquet to my chest, feeling my heart skip a beat. "I'll just put these in water and change real quick," I said, trying to calm the sudden rush of emotions. I gestured for him to make himself comfortable in the living room.

He walked past me, his presence filling my small space in a way that felt both new and completely natural. I watched him as he took in my personal sanctuary, filled with canvases, brushes, and the little things that made it mine. There was a quiet reverence in the way he moved, as if he understood how much this place had come to mean to me.

Seeing Ethan in my space felt right, but it also made me feel exposed, like he was stepping into a part of me I'd kept hidden from the world. I waited for any sign of judgment, but all I saw was curiosity.

I dashed to my bedroom to change, heart racing with excitement and a twinge of anxiety. What if clothes were scattered on the floor? Or dirty dishes in the sink? The thought of Ethan seeing any mess hurried me. As I pulled on fresh jeans and a soft sweater, I tried to push the worries aside. Still, I couldn't help but wonder what he'd think of my space. I heard his footsteps in the living room, and hoped he wouldn't stumble upon anything embarrassing.

When I returned, I found him standing in front of one of my paintings. It was the last piece I had done in Cresden, just before Sebastian and I broke up. The painting was bold, full of vivid colors and abstract forms, a chaotic mix that mirrored the turbulence of my relationship with him. I had planned to take it to the gallery next week along with my other works, but I hadn't gotten around to wrapping it yet, so it remained in the living room—a reminder of a chapter I was ready to close.

Ethan turned as I approached, his eyes filled with genuine appreciation. "This is beautiful, Vinnie. There's so much emotion in it."

I smiled, a mix of pride and vulnerability washing over me. This piece held so much of my past, so many raw emotions. "Thank you. What do you really think of it, though? How does it make you feel?" I asked, hoping for an honest reaction. His opinion mattered to me, and I wondered if he could see beyond the bold colors and abstract forms, to the feelings that had inspired it.

He glanced back at the painting, brow furrowing in thought. "It feels . . . intense. Like there's a lot going on beneath the surface. The colors almost seem to be in conflict, but they're also creating something striking and powerful." He chuckled softly, adding, "I'm no art critic."

I laughed, appreciating his effort. "Not bad, Ethan. Not bad at all. Honestly, I've never created art for critics, anyway. I create it for everyone. For anyone who sees it and feels something, whatever that might be."

He smiled, visibly relieved, and turned to face me fully, leaning against the wall in a relaxed, attentive stance. "Tell me the meaning behind it. What were you feeling when you painted this?" His eyes were earnest.

I took a deep breath. This was a poignant moment—letting Ethan in on a part of my past that I hadn't thought about in a while. But my history with Sebastian was part of who I was, and sharing it with Ethan felt like the right step.

"This piece is about conflict and passion. The bold, clashing colors represent the intense emotions I was feeling at the time. The red symbolizes anger and love, the blue represents sadness and longing, and the yellow is for moments of hope and happiness. It's an abstract depiction of the push and pull of my relationship with my ex, Sebastian. Everything was so vibrant and chaotic, but there were moments of beauty within the turmoil."

Ethan listened intently, his eyes never leaving mine. "I can see that now. It's incredible how you've captured so much emotion in a single piece."

A quiet pause hung between us, and then he asked. "Was he the reason you left Cresden? Your ex, I mean?"

"Yeah, he was part of it," I replied, my voice calm as I met Ethan's gaze. "Sebastian and I were together for a while, but it got to a point where we were both holding each other back. Things ended, and I knew I needed a fresh start. That's what brought me to Hallow's End."

Ethan nodded, his expression filled with understanding and patience. "It sounds like you made the right choice," he said softly. "You deserve to be somewhere that inspires you, with people who make you happy."

I felt a wave of gratitude for his gentle reassurance, his willingness to listen without judgment. "Thank you, Ethan," I said, my voice just as soft. "It means a lot that you're here, and that you get it."

He reached out, giving my hand a reassuring squeeze. "I'm here, Vinnie, and I'm glad you trusted me with that."

Ethan's eyes softened, and without a word, he stepped closer, his hand gently cupping my cheek. The warmth in his gaze made my heart flutter as he leaned in, pressing a soft, tender kiss to my lips. It was the kind of kiss that spoke volumes, without needing words. A connection that felt as natural as breathing.

When we pulled back, he smiled, his thumb brushing lightly across my cheek. "Shall we go?" he asked.

I laughed softly, the lingering warmth of the kiss making it impossible not to smile. "You're still not going to tell me where we're going, are you?"

Ethan's grin widened, and he shook his head, his eyes twinkling with playful mischief. "Not a chance," he teased.

I sighed dramatically, but the excitement bubbling inside me was impossible to hide. "Fine," I said, giving him a mock pout. "But you better not keep me in suspense for too long."

He chuckled, taking my hand in his as he led me toward the door. "I promise, it'll be worth the wait."

Chapter 20

E THAN'S OLD PICKUP TRUCK, with once-bright paint that was now a charmingly rustic patina, stood proudly parked outside my cottage. The softly dented bumper, and the faint scent of pine and motor oil that lingered in the cab, only added to its character. It was a vehicle that had clearly seen many miles, and every little scratch and dent seemed to have its own story to tell.

With a gentlemanly ease, Ethan opened the passenger door and offered his hand, helping me up into the high seat. The touch of his hand sent a small thrill through me, the warmth of his fingers lingering even after I settled into the worn but comfortable seat. Anticipation bubbled within me as he closed the door gently, his smile unwavering as he walked around to the driver's side.

He slid in beside me, turning the key, and the truck rumbled to life with a comforting, familiar growl. Suddenly, country music blared from the speakers, filling the cab with twangy guitars and heartfelt lyrics. I jumped at the volume, and Ethan's cheeks reddened as he fumbled to lower it.

"Sorry about that," he said with an embarrassed smile, his fingers still on the volume knob. "Didn't mean to startle you."

I laughed, the sound mingling with the fading music. "No worries. What kind of music do you usually listen to?"

He shrugged, still a little sheepish, but with a boyish charm that made my heart skip a beat. "I guess you could say I'm a country guy at heart," he admitted. "But I listen to a bit of everything, really. What about you?"

"I'm into country music, too," I replied, smiling. "And folk, depending on my mood. But if I'm being honest . . . I'm a Swiftie."

Ethan's eyes lit up with amusement, and he reached into the console between us, pulling out the AUX cord and handing it to me. "In that case, I'm handing over the reins," he said with a grin. "Play whatever you want."

I took the cord, a playful smile tugging at my lips as I plugged in my phone. "You might regret saying that," I teased, scrolling through my playlists.

He leaned back in his seat, his eyes never leaving mine, the corners of his mouth twitching up in that familiar, irresistible way. "I'm up for the challenge," he murmured, his voice low and warm.

"You know, at this rate, I'll be an old man by the time you pick a song," he teased, his lips curving into a grin.

I laughed as I scrolled, pretending to be overly dramatic about my selection. "Hey, you can't rush perfection," I shot back, giving him a mock-serious look. "I'm crafting the perfect playlist for this drive. You'll thank me later."

He chuckled, shaking his head in amusement as he shifted the truck into gear and pulled away from the curb. "Well, I'm counting on it."

Just as we settled into the rhythm of the road, the familiar chords of Taylor Swift's *Our Song* filled the truck and, to my surprise, Ethan started singing along without a hint of hesitation. His voice, unexpectedly warm and steady, carried the tune effortlessly as he tapped the steering wheel in time with the beat, glancing over at me with a playful grin as he exaggerated the lyrics.

I laughed, the sound bubbling up from somewhere deep inside. The way Ethan belted out the song, completely unbothered and full of confidence, was infectious. It wasn't long before I joined in, our voices harmonizing through the chorus as I matched his energy, laughing.

He glanced at me, eyes sparkling with mischief and delight. It was silly and fun, and yet it felt like one of those little moments you know will stay with you for a long time—something simple, but so full of life.

As the song faded into the next, I turned the volume down and looked at him, eyebrows raised in playful disbelief. "You know the lyrics?"

He chuckled, nodding. "Yeah, Lily's a big fan. She listens to Taylor Swift all the time, so I've picked up a few songs."

"That's adorable," I said, feeling a flutter in my chest. "I can't believe I didn't know she was a Swiftie. I like her even more now!"

Ethan's eyes twinkled with amusement as he glanced over at me. "Stick around, Vinnie. There's plenty more for you to find out."

"We should totally have a Taylor-Swift-themed night with Lily. We could dress up, sing all her songs, maybe even make some friendship bracelets. How fun would that be?" My words tumbled out in a rambling stream of enthusiasm, the idea taking shape in my mind even as I spoke.

Ethan laughed, the sound rich and full of warmth. "Lily would absolutely love that. You might just make her year with that idea."

I beamed at the thought, already imagining the three of us belting out lyrics together. "We could even bake cookies shaped like hearts or stars, and do a whole karaoke thing. Go all out." He glanced over at me again, his expression softening as he took in my excitement.

"You're something else, Vinnie," he said, his voice gentle. "I can see why Lily likes you so much." A blush crept up my neck, but I couldn't help the smile that spread across my face.

As we drove on, the country roads stretched out before us, framed by the bright autumn hues of the season. Golden leaves drifted lazily from the trees, carried by the gentle breeze, and the crisp air filled the truck with the earthy scent of fall. The music provided a comfortable backdrop, a slow country song playing softly in the background.

Ethan's hand rested casually on the steering wheel, his fingers tapping in time with the rhythm. The gentle sway of the truck as it navigated the winding roads, combined with the mellow music, created an atmosphere of peaceful contentment.

The scenery passed by in a blur of color and light, but I barely noticed, too absorbed in the comfortable silence that had settled between us. It wasn't the kind of silence that felt awkward or empty. It was the kind that was filled with the quiet understanding that comes from simply being in the moment together.

I glanced at Ethan, taking in the way the light played off his features, casting soft shadows across his face. There was something so steady about him, so grounded, that it made me feel safe in a way I hadn't expected.

Ethan looked over at me, a question in his eyes, before resting his hand lightly on my leg. The simple touch sent a spark of electricity shooting through me; my heart skipping a beat. I offered him a small, reassuring smile, though inside, my nerves were buzzing with a heady mix of excitement and desire.

As his hand stayed on my leg, warmth spread through me, intensifying with each passing second. Seeing this side of him—relaxed, playful, and so naturally at ease—was incredibly endearing. This was the happiness I'd been searching for and, with Ethan, it came so effortlessly.

Noticing my gaze lingering on him, he turned to me with a gentle smile. "You okay?" he asked, his voice soft.

I nodded, my smile widening as I met his eyes. "Yeah, I'm good. Just . . . happy."

His smile deepened, and he gave my thigh a gentle squeeze, sending a wave of heat straight to my core. As we continued down the winding country roads, the scenery outside became even more picturesque, but I found it hard to focus on anything other than the way his fingers began to slowly graze higher, rubbing gentle circles into my thigh.

The warmth of his touch radiated through me, making my breath quicken and my skin flush with a longing that was hard to ignore. Each subtle movement of his fingers sent a thrill through my body, heightening the anticipation with every slow, deliberate stroke. I couldn't help but curse the jeans I'd thrown on earlier—what I wouldn't give to be wearing a dress or a skirt, something that would let me feel his touch directly on my skin instead of through this maddening barrier.

I bit my lip, trying to suppress the shiver that ran through me as his fingers inched just a little higher. The tension between us was thick, and charged with an unspoken desire that simmered just below the surface. My mind raced with thoughts of what might happen if he moved his hand just a little further, if he pressed just a little harder—he'd know exactly how much I wanted him.

Just as the tension reached its peak, the truck rounded a bend, and the shimmering surface of a lake came into view. The sudden change in scenery jolted us both out of the moment, and Ethan's hand stilled on my thigh.

He glanced at me with a knowing smile, as if he could sense the shift in the air; the electric current that still buzzed between us. I took a deep breath, trying to steady the pounding of my heart as I turned my gaze out the window, the serene beauty of the lake offering a brief respite from the intensity. Yet, even as the cool autumn air drifted in through the open windows, the heat between us remained, waiting for the right moment to ignite once again.

Ethan's hand lingered on my thigh, his fingers brushing against me one last time before he reluctantly pulled away. He turned off the engine and looked at me, his eyes filled with desire.

"We're here," he said softly, his voice carrying a note of regret, as if he hated letting go just as much as I did.

Ethan quickly rounded the truck, opening my door and extending his hand to help me down with a steady, comforting touch. We both took a deep breath, savoring the crisp, clean air and the peaceful surroundings, allowing the tension to settle into something more comfortable, more grounding.

The lake before us was breathtakingly beautiful, the calm waters reflecting the bright colors of the surrounding trees, each one aflame with the brilliant hues of autumn. A small wooden dock jutted into the lake—the perfect vantage point for taking in the tranquil scene. A few ducks floated lazily on the surface, their gentle movements adding to the serenity. The place seemed like it had been lifted straight out of a painting, and I felt a surge of inspiration.

Ethan's hand found mine again, his fingers intertwining with mine in a way that felt so natural. So right. "I thought you might like this place," he said gently. "It's one of my favorite spots to come and think."

"Why this place? What makes it special?" I looked at him, curious.

He turned his gaze out over the lake, a soft smile playing on his lips as he considered his answer. "It's quiet and secluded. Whenever life gets too chaotic, I come here to clear my head. There's something about the stillness of the water, the way the light dances on the surface . . . it reminds me to slow down. To appreciate the little things."

I squeezed his hand. "It's perfect," I said, my voice filled with sincerity.

Ethan's smile deepened, his eyes soft as they met mine. "I've never taken anyone here before," he admitted, a hint of vulnerability in his tone. "It's kind of my secret spot. A local gem that not many people know about. I wanted to share it with you because I thought you'd appreciate it."

His words touched something deep within me. "Thank you, Ethan," I replied, my voice full of emotion. "It really is beautiful."

As Ethan pointed to an old wooden bench on the dock, a wave of nostalgia seemed to wash over him. "Those benches have been here for as long as I can remember. My dad and I used to come here when I was a kid. We'd sit and talk for hours. Sometimes fishing, sometimes just enjoying the silence."

His words hung in the air, rich with the warmth of cherished memories, and a pang of envy tugged at my heart—an unexpected ache that reminded me of how different my childhood had been.

"That sounds wonderful," I said, my voice soft, though a flicker of sadness touched my words. I could see why this place meant so much to him, why it was woven into the fabric of his life.

But, as I listened to him speak about the closeness he'd shared with his father, I couldn't help but compare it to my own experiences. There were no places like this with my father. No secret spots where we'd spent time together. No warm memories of long talks or shared silences. My father had been distant and cold, always driven by business and work. He rarely took time off and, when he did, it wasn't to spend it with me or my mother. He was a man of schedules and goals, someone who saw time as a commodity, not something to be shared or savored.

The realization stirred a mix of emotions within me. Regret, sadness, and perhaps a touch of resentment. I quickly pushed those feelings aside, not wanting them to taint the moment with Ethan. This place was special to him, and I wanted to honor that, even if it reminded me of what I'd never had.

"I can see why this place means so much to you," I said.

Ethan looked at me, his eyes searching mine as if he could sense the undercurrent of emotions I was trying to hide. "It's where I come to sort through things. I guess I wanted to bring you here because . . . well, you're becoming important to me, Vinnie. And I wanted to share something meaningful."

His words made my heart race and, as I looked into his eyes, the vulnerability of the moment washed over me. The intensity in his gaze made my cheeks flush and my stomach flutter. "Ethan, you have no idea how much this means to me. Sharing this place, your special place . . ."

In that moment, I realized something important—Ethan didn't need to know every detail of my past to understand me. He just needed to be here, with me, in this moment. And that was more than enough. That thought warmed me as we reached the dock, and he helped me onto the bench. As we sat down, the silence enveloped us and, for a moment, we simply absorbed the beauty around us.

Ethan's hand tightened around mine, his thumb brushing lightly over my skin, sending a cascade of shivers down my spine. The simple touch ignited a spark between us, and I felt heat rising, the air around us thickening with unspoken emotions. His gaze locked onto mine, so intense it made it hard to breathe.

"I'm really glad you're here," he whispered, leaning in closer. The space between us diminished, his breath warm against my face, and the world seemed to fade away, leaving just the two of us suspended in a moment charged with an undeniable pull.

I swallowed hard, my heart pounding in my chest. "Me too, Ethan. I'm really glad I'm here." His eyes flicked to my lips, and I saw the longing in his gaze, a reflection of the desire swirling within me.

My heart raced, each beat echoing the yearning that seemed to swell and expand, filling the space between us. I could see the same mixture of hesitation and desire in his eyes, as if he was weighing the moment, deciding whether to give in, or to hold back. His warm hand in mine, his thumb tracing gentle patterns on my skin, made my whole body tingle with anticipation.

Slowly, I leaned in. The cool breeze brushed against my flushed cheeks, but all I could focus on was Ethan—his steady breath, the subtle rise and fall of his chest, and the way his eyes softened as he looked at me. The air was thick with promise; a delicate thread ready to weave into something profound and beautiful.

Ethan hesitated, his gaze returning to mine, full of emotion. "Vinnie, I . . ."

Before he could finish, a sudden rustling in the nearby bushes startled us both, shattering the moment. We turned in unison to see a family of ducks waddling out from the underbrush, heading toward the water. The sight was so unexpected that we both burst into laughter, the tension easing as the ducks made their way to the lake.

"Guess we're not the only ones who enjoy this place," Ethan said, his smile warm and full of amusement.

I chuckled, disappointment washing over me. "Looks like it."

Ethan squeezed my hand, a silent promise that our moment wasn't over. "You know," he said with a teasing glint in his eye, "at this point, it seems like imperfect timing is our thing. Maybe we should just expect it."

"Maybe it's just the universe's way of keeping us on our toes," I laughed, trying to brush off the lingering tension, though part of me couldn't help but wish we hadn't been interrupted.

Ethan smiled at that, his eyes filled with affection. "Well, I'm not giving up that easily. Come on, let's walk around a bit more."

We strolled along the shore, the gravel crunching softly beneath our feet, and I came to the sudden realization that I was falling for Ethan a little more with each step. The way he effortlessly blended humor with sincerity, the warmth in his touch, and the way he made me feel seen and valued—it was all becoming more than I'd expected, more than I'd dared to hope for.

And though the moment had been interrupted, I wondered what he'd been about to say before the ducks startled us. The way his voice had softened, the intensity in his eyes—it was as though he was on the verge of something important, something that could change everything. The thought lingered in my mind, making me both curious and anxious, as I tried to piece it together.

We approached a small wooden rowboat tied to the dock and Ethan's eyes lit up with excitement. "How about a quick boat ride? It's pretty peaceful out there."

I hesitated, eyeing the boat sceptically. Though charming, it looked old and worn, with weathered wood and chipped paint. The thought of venturing out onto the water in such a rickety vessel made me uneasy. "Are you sure it's safe? That boat looks like it's about to fall apart."

Ethan chuckled, his eyes twinkling with amusement. "I promise, it's sturdier than it looks. This was my dad's boat, and he and I used to take it out all the time. I'll keep you safe, I swear." His reassuring smile melted away my apprehension, and I nodded, despite my initial reluctance.

"Alright, if you say so," I agreed.

"Trust me," he winked.

Ethan untied the rowboat from the dock, the old rope creaking as it loosened, and he stepped in first, holding out his hand to help me aboard. The boat rocked gently beneath our weight as I carefully stepped in, trying not to think about the small gaps between the wooden planks. Once we were both settled, Ethan took the oars in hand and began rowing us out onto the calm waters. The lake's surface was like glass, reflecting the beautiful colors of the sun. I leaned back, soaking in the beauty of the moment, and the warmth of Ethan's presence.

"I think this might be my new favorite place," I said softly, trailing my fingers in the cool water, the sensation both grounding and calming.

"I'm glad you like it," Ethan replied, his voice full of happiness.

A sudden urge to capture the beauty of the moment struck me, and I stood up to get a better view. "Let me see if I can get a good shot from here," I said, reaching for my phone.

"Careful," Ethan warned, his voice laced with caution. But it was too late.

In my eagerness, I misjudged the boat's balance. As I stood to take the photo, the boat tipped precariously, and I flailed my arms, trying to steady myself. "Whoa!" Ethan shouted, reaching out to catch me but, before either of us could react, the boat wobbled violently, and we both plunged into the lake with a loud splash.

The cold water shocked my system, sending a jolt through me as I surfaced with a gasp, spluttering and laughing. I glanced around, thankful that we hadn't drifted too far from the shore, and even more grateful that modern phones were waterproof.

Ethan emerged next to me, his hair plastered to his forehead, and an expression of disbelief mixed with amusement on his face. "Well, that's one way to enjoy the lake," he chuckled, wiping water from his eyes.

I couldn't stop laughing, my sides aching from both the plunge and the sheer absurdity of the situation. "You were supposed to keep me safe!" I teased, splashing water at him.

Ethan laughed, his grin infectious. "I tried! You're the one who tipped us over!" He swam closer, his warm hand finding mine in the cool water. "Come on, let's get you out of the water before you freeze."

As we splashed around, Ethan, ever the quick thinker, grabbed the boat's edge and guided it back to the dock, securing it with one hand.

With the boat now safely anchored, Ethan turned his attention to me, his touch steady and comforting as he helped me out of the water, his hands firm around my waist as he lifted me onto the dock. Despite the chill in the air, and the water dripping from our clothes, his presence made everything warmer.

Once we were both safely out of the water, Ethan gave the boat one last tug to make sure it was securely tied, leaving it ready for another day. Then, with a smile, he turned back to me.

"Thanks," I said, still laughing as I sat on the dock, water dripping from my clothes. "This definitely wasn't what I expected."

Ethan climbed out after me, settling beside me on the dock, water dripping from his clothes. He flashed me a playful smile, his eyes glinting with amusement. "You know, Vinnie, I'm starting to think you might be a bit accident-prone," he teased, his voice light but laced with affection.

I laughed, the sound blending with the soft lapping of the water against the dock. "Maybe I am," I admitted, unable to stop the grin spreading across my face. "But I like to think it keeps things interesting."

He chuckled, his gaze softening as he reached out to brush a wet strand of hair from my face, his fingers lingering just a moment longer than necessary. "Well, I can't argue with that," he murmured, his voice dipping into something more tender. "And honestly, I wouldn't have it any other way."

I glanced over at Ethan, an idea sparking in my mind. "Race you to the truck!" I called, a mischievous grin spreading across my face as I took off, my feet slipping on the uneven ground.

Ethan laughed, the sound full of surprise and delight. "You're on!" he shouted, sprinting after me. We stumbled and laughed our way back to the truck, our soaked clothes clinging to us as the cold air seeped into our bones.

By the time we reached the truck, we were both breathless and still giggling, and utterly drenched from head to toe. Ethan unlocked the door and pulled it open, and I climbed inside, grateful for the shelter from the biting wind. As he joined me, he rummaged around in the back seat and pulled out a small duffel bag, tossing it onto the seat.

"I keep some spare clothes in here," he explained, pulling out a dry T-shirt, a flannel shirt, and a pair of shorts. "I like to go hiking and camping, so I'm always prepared for getting a little wet or dirty."

He handed the clothes to me. "Here, these might be a bit big, but at least they're dry."

I took them, noting that they smelled like him—clean, with that familiar hint of his cologne that I found both comforting and intoxicating. I suddenly felt self-conscious, the reality of our situation hitting me. As much as I wanted Ethan, I realized I didn't want our first time seeing each other naked to be under these circumstances—rushed and out of necessity. I wanted it to be on our own terms, something we both chose and savored.

"Could you turn around for a moment?" I asked, my voice softer now.

Ethan smiled, his eyes twinkling with understanding. "Of course," he said, turning his back to give me some privacy.

As I quickly changed, I made the decision to shed my wet bra and panties, not wanting to soak the dry clothes. The oversized fabric of his T-shirt fell to just above my knees, and his scent wrapped around me, like he was holding me when we weren't even touching.

"Okay, all set," I said, putting on the flannel shirt like a jacket.

Ethan turned back, his smile widening when he saw me in his clothes. "You look adorable," he said softly. The heater whirred to life, filling the cab with toasty air that chased away the chill.

A blush crept up my cheeks, and a flutter in my stomach made me feel shy and giddy all at once. "Thanks," I replied, managing a small smile. "I might have to steal this shirt from you."

Ethan's smile turned into a playful grin, his eyes glinting with mischief. "You can have all my shirts if it means seeing you in them," he teased. "But just a warning, I might need to steal them back every now and then."

"I think we can work something out," I replied, my voice matching his playful tone, though there was an undeniable heat simmering beneath the surface.

As I settled into the seat, I watched Ethan pull out another dry shirt for himself. He hesitated for a moment, and I could feel the tension between us thickening. Without a word, he reached for the hem of his wet shirt and, in one fluid motion, pulled it over his head. The sight that greeted me made my breath catch in my throat.

His tanned chest and broad shoulders glistened with droplets of water that clung to his skin. I had only glimpsed hints of his physique before, through the way his clothes fit, or the way he moved. But seeing him like this, stripped down and unguarded, was something entirely different. He was more muscular than I'd imagined, his torso defined and strong, and every line of his body was a testament to the quiet strength he carried. The real thing was far better than I'd ever imagined, and I found myself unable to look away.

Ethan must have noticed the way my eyes lingered on him, because a slow, teasing smile spread across his face. "You're staring, Vinnie," he said, his voice low and full of amusement.

I blushed. Part of me wanted to look away, to preserve some semblance of composure, but the other part—the part that was captivated by the sight of him—couldn't quite manage it. "Sorry," I murmured, finally managing to tear my gaze from his chest. "I just . . ."

Ethan chuckled as he prepared to pull on his dry shirt. "You've got a little drool on your face, there."

I blinked, my hand instinctively flying to my mouth. "I do not!"

He grinned, as I let my gaze linger on him for just a moment longer. It was impossible not to notice how comfortable and confident he had become around me, especially over the past week. Ever since that kiss in the living room, something had shifted between us. Ethan seemed to be embracing the change, growing more at ease, while I found myself feeling the opposite—more shy, more vulnerable, like I was slowly unravelling in his presence.

As if sensing my thoughts, he paused. Looking at me with a soft, affectionate smile that made my heart skip a beat. He didn't say anything, but the warmth in his gaze was enough to calm the nerves fluttering in my stomach.

With a quick, teasing wink, he finally pulled on his dry shirt, the fabric sliding over his still-damp skin. "There, all covered up. Happy?" he joked, his tone light, though there was a hint of something deeper in his eyes.

"Maybe, and just so you know," I said, trying to sound casual but failing to hide the smile on my face, "I wasn't drooling."

"Sure you weren't," he teased, his voice low and playful as he settled into the driver's seat. "But if you were, I'd take it as a compliment."

Ethan gathered up our wet clothes and tossed them onto the back seat, the fabric landing with a soft thud on the leather. The interior of the truck was warm now, the heater doing its job, but the heat I felt had more to do with the way Ethan's eyes lingered on me as he settled back into the driver's seat.

A soft patter of rain began to fall, growing steadily until it drummed against the roof with a soothing rhythm, the world outside quickly disappearing behind the fogging windows. The rain created an intimate cocoon, and the rhythmic sound of the droplets matched the quickening pace of my heart, each beat echoing the longing I felt growing inside me.

Ethan's gaze dropped to my lips, the tension between us thickening. He reached out, brushing a stray lock of damp hair away from my face, his fingers lingering on my cheek, and the simple touch sent a shiver down my spine, igniting a fire in me.

"Vinnie," he murmured, his voice low and husky.

Before I could respond, Ethan leaned in, closing the distance between us. His lips met mine in a kiss that was soft at first, and tentative, as though he was testing the waters. But it didn't stay that way for long. He deepened the kiss, his hand sliding to the back of my neck to pull me closer, while his other hand traced a slow, deliberate path down my side, resting just above my hip.

A surge of heat rushed through me, settling low in my belly. The thin fabric of his shirt and shorts clung to my skin, and I was acutely aware of how exposed I was, of how little there was between us. The sensation of his body pressed against mine, and the warmth of his hand on my hip, sent a jolt of desire through me, making me even more aware of how much I wanted him.

Ethan's confidence surprised me; the way he seemed to savor every moment, as if he were testing how far we could go this time. His lips moved with a purpose, and when he nipped at my lower lip, a small gasp escaped me, which only seemed to encourage him. His mouth trailed down to my neck, and he nipped at the sensitive skin there, drawing a shiver from deep within me.

The intensity of his touch, the way his hands roamed my back and waist, set my skin on fire. I could feel the heat of his arousal pressing against me, and it only fuelled the desire that was building inside me. I wanted more—more of his touch, more of his kiss, more of *him*.

I shifted until I was straddling his lap, feeling the full length of him against me. Ethan's hands gripped my waist, pulling me closer but, as his fingers slid under my shirt to rest on the bare skin of my back, he suddenly paused. His touch hesitated for just a fraction of a second, as if he'd only just realized there was nothing but skin beneath the thin fabric.

He pulled back, his eyes searching mine. "Vinnie," he breathed, his voice rough around the edges.

My cheeks flushed. The heat between us was undeniable, and his eyes darkened as his hands, now more deliberate, traced the contours of my back. "Are you naked under this?" he asked, his voice dropping low, the surprise in his tone edged with something deeper—something hungry.

I bit my lip, nodding slightly. "It was all wet," I whispered.

His hands moved over my back with renewed purpose, his touch more confident, more aware of the vulnerable state I was in.

The sensation was almost overwhelming, the way his hands explored my back, the way his lips found mine again, this time with a hunger that matched my own. I pressed against him, feeling the heat of his body through the thin layers that still separated us, and the raw intensity made my breath come in quick, heated gasps.

Ethan's fingers tangled in my hair, pulling me even closer as the kiss intensified. He was confident, in control, but there was a gentleness to his touch that made me feel safe and cherished, even as the kiss became more demanding. The way he held me, and the way his hands moved over my body, made me feel like I was the only thing that mattered to him.

Just as the tension between us reached its peak, my back bumped against the steering wheel, and the horn let out a loud, jarring honk. The sound shattered the intensity of the moment, pulling us back to reality, and we broke apart, both of us laughing breathlessly. My cheeks were flushed, and my body still hummed with the aftermath of our kiss. Ethan's eyes were locked on mine, the warmth and desire evident in them.

"Guess that's our cue to slow down," he said, his voice low and teasing, though there was no mistaking the heat still simmering between us.

"Maybe," I replied, my voice soft and a little shaky from the adrenaline coursing through me.

He leaned in, brushing his lips against mine but, when he pulled back, there was regret in his eyes. "I'm sorry," he murmured, his voice rougher than usual. "I didn't mean to push things too far. We said we wouldn't rush."

I let out a breathless laugh, shaking my head. "Don't apologize. I'm glad you did." I smirked. "Honestly, I just wish that stupid horn hadn't interrupted us."

He chuckled, the sound low and warm, but his gaze remained heated. "You have no idea how much I want you, Vinnie," he said, his voice dropping to a husky tone that sent shivers down my spine. "But our first time isn't going to be in this truck." My breath caught at the intensity in his voice. There was no mistaking the sincerity behind his words.

His eyes locked on mine. "The things I want to do to you . . . I want to take my time. To explore every part of you. You deserve more than a quick moment."

"You're right," I admitted softly, my voice almost a whisper. "But, for the record, I want more, too."

"Then we'll make sure it's worth the wait," he said, his thumb brushing against my cheek.

The tension between us didn't fade. It only deepened, becoming something more meaningful, more powerful. As we drove in comfortable silence, the rain continued to patter against the windows, and the world outside became a blur of lights and shadows.

When we pulled up to my house, Ethan turned to me. "I had a great time today, Vinnie," he said, his voice filled with warmth. "Even with the unexpected swim."

"Me, too," I replied. "Thank you for sharing that place with me."

He leaned in again, pressing a lingering kiss to my lips that felt both sweet and full of promise. "I'll text you later," he murmured.

"Okay," I said, a smile tugging at my lips as I watched him drive away into the pouring rain.

That night, as I settled into bed, and the events of the day replayed in my mind, my phone buzzed, and my heart did a little flip when I saw Ethan's name light up the screen.

Ethan: Seeing you in my shirt tonight . . . Let's just say I'm having a hard time thinking about anything else. I might need to lend you my clothes more often 😊

Vinnie: Careful, I might just raid your closet next time 😊 But only if you promise not to get distracted by the view

> **Ethan:** No promises there. The way you looked at me in the truck . . . it took all my self-control not to lose it right then and there.

I bit my lip, remembering the intensity of that moment—the feel of his hands on me, the way our bodies pressed together. My fingers hovered over the keyboard, a thrill of excitement rushing through me.

> **Ethan:** Just the kiss? Because I've been thinking about how you felt in my lap, how close we were. How badly I wanted to keep going.

> **Vinnie:** You really know how to get a girl's heart racing. If it wasn't for that damn horn!

> **Ethan:** Next time, we'll make sure there are no interruptions. Because when I finally get to touch you the way I want, I'm not stopping until you're completely satisfied.

His words sent a bolt of heat straight through me, my whole body reacting to the intensity of his promise. My breath hitched, and I felt a deep, insistent ache settle low in my belly. The thought of Ethan's hands on me, his body pressed against mine, the way he had been so hard and eager—it all came rushing back, making my skin tingle with anticipation.

> **Vinnie:** You have no idea what you're doing to me right now. If you keep talking like that, I'm not sure I'll be able to wait until next time.

> **Ethan:** Good. Because I want you just as bad. And when we finally get there, Vinnie, it's going to be worth every second of this wait. I'll make sure of it.

His reply was like a match to gasoline, igniting a fire inside me that left me breathless, the hunger for him overwhelming. Every word he typed seemed to stoke that fire, making me crave him in a way that was almost unbearable. The anticipation was driving me wild, and I couldn't help but imagine what it would be like when we finally gave in to the desire that had been building between us.

> **Vinnie:** You'd better be ready then, because I'm not planning on holding back.

> **Ethan:** I wouldn't want you to. The thought of seeing you completely undone, wild and free, with my name on your lips . . . it's driving me crazy. I can't wait to see what you're like when you let go.

I could almost hear the low, husky tone of his voice in his words. It was a promise, a tease, and a challenge, all wrapped into one, and it made me burn for him even more.

> **Vinnie:** That sounds like a plan I can get behind. But you'd better be prepared, because I'm not going to make it easy for you to stop next time.

> **Ethan:** Vinnie, I'm counting on it 😊 Sweet dreams. I'll be thinking about you in that shirt — and the fact that you had nothing underneath.

His last message came through with a simple winking emoji, and I laughed as I settled back into my pillows. Sleep didn't come easily that night, not with the thought of what was to come lingering in my mind.

Chapter 21

I COULDN'T SHAKE ETHAN from my mind all weekend. His texts were a constant tease, each one more suggestive than the last, building the tension between us until it felt like a tightly wound string ready to snap. My body craved him with a need that left me restless, and no matter how much I tried to focus on other things, my thoughts kept drifting back to him—his touch, his lips, the way he looked at me like he wanted to devour me.

I threw myself into preparing the gallery, hoping the work would be enough to distract me. I spent hours painting, sorting through pieces, and arranging the space just right, tiring myself out enough that I could at least sleep at night. But even in my dreams, I couldn't escape him. I'd wake up breathless, covered in sweat, the ache between my thighs a constant reminder of just how badly I wanted him. It was as if every part of me was attuned to him, and the anticipation was driving me wild.

Halloween was fast approaching, and the town was buzzing with excitement, as preparations for the Spooktacular Hallow's Eve kicked into high gear. Pumpkins, flickering lanterns, and cobwebs that hung like eerie curtains from every streetlight and storefront decorated the streets of Hallow's End.

Even though the big event was still a week away, the town square was already a hive of activity. The local volunteers were busy setting up the haunted house, a centerpiece that drew visitors from miles around every year. Transformed into a spine-chilling maze of horrors, the old, abandoned mansion had animatronic ghosts, skeletons, and hidden surprises waiting to spook the bravest souls.

In the square itself, a large stage was being constructed for the live performances scheduled throughout the Spooktacular weekend—everything from local bands playing eerie tunes, to storytelling sessions where kids and adults alike would gather to hear ghostly tales. Vendors were setting up stalls, preparing to sell hand-carved pumpkins, homemade pies, candles, and Halloween-themed crafts. It was a true celebration of the season, with every detail meticulously planned to create a magical atmosphere, and the energy in the air was contagious.

With the town gearing up for the event of the year, I'd decided to open The Cozy Canvas a week before the big weekend. The timing felt right, as tourists were already trickling into town, eager to soak up the Halloween spirit. I hoped that, by opening early, I could start building a reputation ahead of the main event.

As I hung the last of the paintings on the gallery walls, I felt a deep sense of gratitude for Ivy's help. She had stepped in to manage the social media accounts, understanding how much was on my plate with the grand opening just days away. Ivy had been a lifeline, posting daily updates and countdowns that were both fun and engaging. Her content was a perfect blend of behind-the-scenes glimpses of the gallery coming together, playful shots of our progress, and even a few videos of Ethan and me working side by side. Those moments, sweeter than I'd expected, captured our budding relationship in a way that felt both tender and genuine.

Ivy had truly gone above and beyond, not just with the social media, but by setting up a GoFundMe page for the gallery, and organizing a raffle to help cover the costs of launching some lessons and workshops. The raffle prizes included private art sessions with me, and a beautifully curated giveaway basket filled with local business gems. The response from the community had been overwhelming, and it was touching to see how everyone rallied around The Cozy Canvas.

I knew Ivy's help with social media was temporary, just until the gallery found its rhythm and everything settled into a routine. After the opening, I'd take over running the accounts and handling the day-to-day operations. But for now, Ivy's support allowed me to focus on what mattered most: bringing my vision to life. Everything was coming together more beautifully than I could have hoped and, as the final touches were added to the gallery, I felt a swell of pride and anticipation for what was to come.

At the last town meeting, the community's support for the gallery had been more than I could have imagined. People offered to help in any way they could, from donating supplies, to volunteering their time. It was a heartwarming reminder that Hallow's End was a place where people truly cared about one another, where your neighbors became your friends, and where everyone looked out for each other. Experiencing that firsthand made me feel like I was finally part of something special—something I'd never had before.

Amidst all this, I received a text that caught me off guard. It was from my mom. She'd seen the social media posts, including one of Ethan and me together, and her message was surprisingly supportive. It was a timid text, but it was clear she was trying. She even mentioned that Ethan seemed *handsome*, which, coming from her, was a big step. It was a small gesture, but it meant a lot to me, like a bridge was being slowly built between us.

Before I knew it, Friday had rolled around again. The gallery was nearly ready, and Ivy and Amelia were there to help me with the final touches. We hung garlands of autumn leaves, arranged displays, and made sure everything was perfect for the opening. But, no matter how busy I was, my thoughts kept drifting back to Ethan, and I couldn't stop thinking about seeing him tonight. I was a bundle of nerves and anticipation, eager for what the evening might bring.

As the day came to an end, and the last of the decorations were in place, I locked up the gallery with a sense of accomplishment. My thoughts were already on Ethan as I made my way to his place, the cool evening air nipping at my skin as I hurried along the familiar path. The excitement whispering inside me only grew as I approached his place.

When Ethan opened the door, his warm smile instantly put me at ease, and the smell of something delicious wafted out from behind him, making my stomach rumble in anticipation. He looked relaxed, dressed in a simple dark Henley that hugged his chest just right, paired with worn jeans that clung to his lean hips.

"Hey," he greeted, stepping forward and pulling me in for a kiss. His lips lingered on mine for a moment, sending a rush of warmth through my veins, and the simple gesture had me feeling giddy, a smile already spreading across my face as I stepped inside.

We reached the living room, and I was immediately struck by the romantic setting. The soft, amber glow of candlelight danced across the walls, casting flickering shadows that seemed to sway in rhythm with the gentle crackling of the fireplace.

A small wooden table, that usually was in his kitchen, now stood at the heart of the room and, in its center, was a bouquet of fresh roses, the scent of the blossoms mingling with the subtle fragrance of the candles.

Everywhere I looked, there was evidence of Ethan's thoughtfulness. A bottle of red wine stood uncorked on the table, with two glasses set beside it, catching the light and gleaming like jewels.

"This is beautiful," I said, my voice barely above a whisper as I took it all in. My heart swelled with appreciation for the effort he'd put into tonight, and I looked back at him, my curiosity piqued. "I'm dying to know what you're cooking."

Ethan's eyes sparkled with a playful glint as he led me further into the room. "Well, I did warn you—I'm not much of a cook. But I make a decent spaghetti Bolognese and, tonight, that's what's on the menu."

I laughed, feeling the tension of the day begin to melt away. "That sounds perfect."

We settled at the table and, Ethan watched me as I took my first bite. The pasta was cooked to perfection, the sauce rich and flavorful, and the entire dish was clearly made with care and attention.

"This is really good," I said, savoring the taste. "You weren't kidding when you said you were good at this."

Ethan's smile widened, a blend of pride and relief in his expression. "Glad you think so. It's one of the few things I know how to make without burning down the kitchen. Though, I did have to call my mom for a refresher to make sure I got it just right."

I chuckled, warmth spreading through me at the thought of him wanting everything to be perfect. "Well, you've definitely mastered it. Tell your mom she's taught you well."

"I wanted tonight to be special for you," he said, his voice tender. "I know the gallery has been stressing you out, and I just wanted you to relax. Let someone else take care of you for a change."

His words wrapped around my heart. "Thank you, Ethan. This means more to me than you know."

He reached across the table, taking my hand in his, the warmth of his touch grounding me. "You've been working so hard, Vinnie. You deserve to enjoy this moment. The gallery is going to be amazing, and you've done everything you can to make it perfect."

"I hope so. It feels like everything is finally coming together, but I can't help but feel a little anxious." I nodded, feeling nerves flutter in my stomach.

Ethan's expression grew more serious, though there was still a hint of humor in his eyes. "There's something I should warn you about. My dad's coming to the opening tomorrow."

I looked at him in surprise. "Your dad?"

He nodded, a sheepish grin tugging at his lips. "Yeah, my mom hasn't stopped talking about you, and Lily's been talking nonstop about that Taylor Swift sleepover idea ever since you mentioned it to her. My mom's just thrilled to see both of her kids so happy, and now my dad's curious to meet the woman who's got all of us wrapped around her finger."

"I'd love to meet him," I said through the butterflies stirring in my stomach.

"Trust me," he said with a reassuring smile, squeezing my hand gently. "He's going to love you. And hey, if you can handle Lily's energy, you've already won him over."

Chapter 22

DINNER HAD BEEN A SUCCESS and, as we began to clear the table, I reached for the plates, but Ethan gently caught my wrist, a mischievous grin spreading across his face.

"Oh no, you don't," he teased. "Tonight, you're supposed to relax, remember? Let me take care of it."

I rolled my eyes, laughing softly. "I appreciate the gesture, but I'm not about to let you do all the work."

Ethan raised an eyebrow, enjoying the playful banter. "I had a whole plan, you know—wine, a good meal, and absolutely no work for you. But, if you insist . . ." He handed me a dish towel, our fingers brushing.

"I like doing this with you. It's nice." I said, smiling as I dried the dishes

"*Nice*, huh?" he echoed, his voice teasing as he handed me a plate. "That's not quite what I was going for, but I'll take it."

I laughed, nudging him with my hip. "Fine, it's more than nice. It's . . . comfortable. Like we're just . . . doing life together. It feels good."

Ethan's grin turned wicked as he leaned in closer. "But you know," he murmured, his voice dropping to a playful tone, "if you really want to help, I can think of a few things that are a lot more fun than dishes."

I raised an eyebrow, a teasing smile playing on my lips. "Oh really? Like what?"

Instead of answering, he took the dish towel from my hand, tossing it aside with a casual flick as he backed me against the sink, his hands sliding to my waist. The heat of his body pressed against mine, and I could feel his breath on my neck as he leaned in, lips brushing against my ear.

"Like this," he whispered before leaning in to capture my lips with a tenderness that took me by surprise. The kiss was gentle, almost reverent, his lips moving softly against mine, igniting a warmth that spread through my chest. I responded just as gently, my fingers curling into his shirt, pulling him closer as a sweet, comforting connection blossomed between us. When he finally pulled back, Ethan's eyes were dark with desire, a devilish glint shimmering as he leaned in.

A breathless laugh escaped me, my chest rising and falling rapidly. "You're not exactly relaxing me here, Ethan."

He smirked, his lips hovering just inches from mine. "Good," he breathed, the word dripping with intent. "Because relaxing isn't what I had in mind."

Without warning, his mouth claimed mine in a kiss that was more demanding. His hands slid down my sides, fingers digging into my hips as he pressed me firmly against the counter. The cool surface contrasted with the warmth of his body, igniting a fire deep within me.

I responded eagerly, my fingers threading through his hair, pulling him closer, desperate to erase any space between us. Every brush of his tongue, every nip of his teeth, sent electric currents coursing through me. But, even as the kiss deepened, there was a care in the way he touched me—a softness that told me this was more than just lust for him.

He pulled back slightly, his lips trailing down my jawline to the sensitive spot just below my ear. His hot breath against my skin made me gasp, knees weakening as he continued his assault, but his touch remained gentle.

"You've been driving me crazy," he whispered, his voice thick with long-ing. "Every time I see you, all I can think about is how much I want you."

I let out a soft moan, the confession fanning the flames of my own desire. "Ethan," I breathed, hardly recognizing my own voice.

He chuckled softly, the sound vibrating against my neck. His hands roamed upward, fingers lightly brushing the hem of my shirt, but never quite crossing the boundary. It was maddening, the way he teased, building me up only to hold back.

Swallowing hard, I mustered the courage to voice the truth. "I want you," I whispered, the admission hanging heavy between us.

A growl rumbled deep in his chest, his eyes flashing with renewed inten-sity, but there was still a gentleness in his touch as he cupped my face. "Say it again," he asked softly, his thumb brushing tenderly over my cheek.

"I want you," I repeated, louder this time, confidence growing.

In an instant, his lips were on mine once more, the kiss searing and pos-sessive, but filled with an underlying sweetness that made my knees weak. His hands slid beneath my thighs, lifting me effortlessly. Instinctively, I wrapped my legs around his waist, the new position pressing us even closer together.

As Ethan carried me from the kitchen to the living room, the tension between us coiled tighter with each step. His strong arms held me close, and the feel of his body, firm and powerful against mine, sent shivers down my spine. The anticipation was almost too much to bear. Every second that passed heightened my need; my longing for him.

When he reached the couch, he settled down with me straddling his lap, and I could feel his arousal pressing against me, hot and insistent, even through the fabric of our clothes. It made me gasp, a flood of heat pooling low in my belly. Ethan's hands were everywhere, exploring my body with a hunger that matched my own. He started by sliding his hands under my shirt, his fingertips grazing my bare skin.

His touch was electric, each stroke of his fingers igniting a trail of fire across my skin. I was achingly aware of how little separated us, how the dress I wore offered only the thinnest barrier between his hands and my bare skin. Beneath it, I had chosen to wear my nicest lacy underwear, a decision I now felt grateful for. The soft fabric brushed against my skin, adding to the sensuality of the moment, making every touch from Ethan even more tantalizing.

My breath caught as his hands moved higher, brushing against the curve of my breasts, his touch light and teasing. My pulse quickened, the anticipation building to an unbearable peak.

Ethan leaned in, his lips finding mine in a kiss that was tender and demanding. His tongue teased the seam of my lips, seeking entrance, and when I parted them, he deepened the kiss, his mouth hot and insistent against mine. His hands continued their exploration, fingers tracing the line of my spine, then moving down to cup my ass, pulling me closer until I was pressed tight against him. The friction between the lace and his firm touch sent a jolt of pleasure through me, making me moan softly into his mouth.

He pulled back slightly, his eyes dark with hunger as he looked at me. "God, Vinnie. You have no idea how much I've wanted this. Wanted *you*."

I responded by grinding my hips against him, desperate for more contact, more of him. His hands tightened on my hips, guiding me as I moved, the friction between us building a delicious pressure that made my head spin. But, just when I thought he would give in, he slowed, his hands sliding back up my body, tracing the curve of my waist, the swell of my breasts, teasing me, making me ache for more.

He kissed me again, his lips moving from my mouth to my jaw, then down to my neck, sucking and nipping at the sensitive skin there. I tilted my head back, giving him better access, my fingers tangling in his hair as I tried to pull him closer, to urge him on. But Ethan was in control, his pace slow and deliberate, driving me to the edge without ever letting me fall.

"You're killing me," I gasped, my voice trembling with a mixture of frustration and need. "Ethan, please . . . I *need* you."

He chuckled, the sound low and rough against my skin as he nipped at my collarbone. "Patience, Vinnie," he murmured, his breath hot against my ear. "I want to savor every inch of you."

But patience was the last thing on my mind. The need between my thighs had become a dull ache, the anticipation almost painful. "Ethan . . ." I pleaded, my voice a desperate whisper. "*Please.*"

His hands moved lower, sliding beneath the dress I wore, his fingers tracing the smooth skin of my stomach before moving up to cup my breast. His touch was both gentle and possessive, his thumb brushing over my nipple in a way that made me gasp. The sensation was exquisite, and a jolt of pleasure shot straight through me, making my hips buck against him. He groaned softly, his control slipping as he began to knead the soft flesh. His fingers rolling my nipple between them through the lacy fabric of my bra, sending waves of pleasure coursing through me.

Without breaking eye contact, he slowly lifted the dress over my head, tossing it aside, and the cool air hit my skin, making it tingle in contrast to the heat radiating between us. His eyes darkened as they roamed over my body, taking in the sight of the lace that clung to my curves.

"You're so beautiful," he whispered, his voice thick with emotion as he leaned back to fully admire me. His gaze was full of desire, but there was something else there, too—something deeper, more tender. "Every inch of you, Vinnie. I want to take my time with you."

With that, he gently lifted me off his lap, laying me down on the couch. I watched him through half-lidded eyes, my breath coming in quick, shallow gasps as he knelt between my legs, his hands sliding up my thighs, parting them. The anticipation was almost too much to bear, as he pulled down the black lace that barely covered me. When he finally touched me, his fingers brushing over the wetness pooling between my thighs, I couldn't hold back the moan that escaped my lips.

Ethan looked up at me, his hazel eyes connecting with mine. "I want to make you feel good," he murmured, his fingers moving with agonizing slowness, tracing circles around my clit. His touch was light and teasing, just enough to drive me wild with need. "I want to see you come undone for me, Vinnie."

My body trembled with anticipation as his fingers danced around the most sensitive part of me, building the tension with each gentle stroke. He wasn't in any hurry, savoring every moment as he watched me squirm beneath him, drawing out my pleasure until I was teetering on the brink of madness. Every touch, every subtle movement of his fingers, sent ripples of heat through me, tightening the coil of desire deep within.

"Ethan . . . *please*," I gasped, my voice laced with desperation as I arched into his touch, my body craving more, needing him to take me further.

He leaned down, capturing my lips in a kiss that was slow and sensual, filled with unspoken promises. As our tongues tangled, his fingers slipped inside me, and I gasped at the delicious intrusion. The sensation was overwhelming; the way he filled me, stretching me in just the right way. But he didn't rush. His movements were measured and deliberate, his fingers curling inside me with a precision that made me see stars. Each stroke was a gentle nudge toward the edge, and I felt myself unravelling with every slow, purposeful thrust.

His lips never left mine, swallowing my moans as he brought me closer and closer to release. The pressure inside me was mounting, each wave of pleasure pushing me higher, and when his thumb brushed over my clit with just the right amount of pressure, I shattered. The orgasm tore through me, my body convulsing around his fingers as I cried out his name, the sound muffled against his lips.

"Ethan!" I gasped, my voice a breathless moan as I clung to him, riding the intense waves of pleasure that surged through me. My entire body trembled, every nerve ending alight with the aftershocks of my release.

He didn't stop, his fingers still gently stroking me as I came down from the high, coaxing every last bit of pleasure from my trembling body. When I finally stilled, breathless and spent, he pulled back just enough to look into my eyes, a satisfied smile playing on his lips.

"You're incredible, Vinnie," he whispered, his voice thick with emotion as he brushed a stray strand of hair from my face. "I've imagined you saying my name like that, but hearing it—*feeling* it—it's even better than I could've ever dreamed."

But I wasn't done. The hunger inside me still burned. A deep, aching need that only he could satisfy. I shifted beneath him, pulling him closer, my voice breathless as I whispered, "I need more, Ethan. I need you inside me."

He hesitated, his eyes searching mine as if to make sure, the last bit of control hanging by a thread. "Vinnie . . ." he started, but the plea in my eyes, the raw need, broke through his resolve.

"Please," I begged, my hands gripping his shoulders, urging him closer. "I want you. I need you."

Something inside him snapped and, with a groan that was full of both desire and surrender, he captured my lips in a searing kiss, the last of his control slipping away as he pulled back to shed his clothes completely. I watched as his shirt joined my dress on the floor, revealing the broad expanse of his chest, the muscles beneath his skin rippling with each movement. His pants followed, and I couldn't help but reach out, my fingers exploring the hard lines of his body, tracing the path of his muscles, feeling the heat of his skin beneath my touch.

"Are you sure?" he asked, his voice husky, full of restraint as he hovered above me. "Should I go and grab a condom?"

I shook my head, the decision clear in my mind. "I'm on birth control," I whispered, my voice steady despite the storm of emotions inside me. "And I trust you, Ethan. I don't want anything between us."

The weight of those words seemed to hit him hard and, for a moment, he just looked at me, his expression full of emotion. Then, with a soft kiss pressed to my lips, he positioned himself at my entrance.

He entered me slowly and deliberately, like he was savoring every moment, and the sensation of him filling me made me gasp. But it wasn't enough. Not for me. Not after everything that had led up to this moment. I clung to him, my nails digging into his shoulders as pleasure rippled through me. But even as I urged him on, he kept his movements slow, controlled, drawing out the pleasure until I was begging for more.

"Ethan," I whimpered, my voice trembling with desperation as I nipped at his neck, feeling the heat of his skin against my lips. "I need more. I need you deeper. Please . . ."

The words spilled out of me, raw and unrestrained, each one a desperate plea driven by the overwhelming need building inside me. His breath hitched against my ear, a shudder running through his body.

"*Please,*" I gasped, my voice thick with longing. "Don't hold back." I begged, my body arching into him. My nails dug into his back, holding him to me like I never wanted to let go. I could feel him trembling with the effort to maintain control, but the moment I clenched my legs around him, pulling him even deeper, a guttural groan escaped his lips. The sound was raw, filled with desire, and I could tell his last shred of restraint was slipping away.

"Fuck, Vinnie," he rasped, his voice rough and thick with emotion. The way I clung to him, the way I pleaded for more, it pushed him to the edge. He loved hearing it—loved knowing just how much I wanted him, how desperate I was for him to lose himself in me.

I felt the shift in him, the way his body tightened, his muscles tensing as he finally let go of the control he'd been clinging to. He drove into me with a new intensity, his thrusts harder, deeper, each one sending a jolt of pleasure through me that left me breathless and wanting more.

"Yes, Ethan, just like that . . . don't stop," I begged, my voice breaking as I pressed my hips up to meet him, urging him on. The feeling of him moving inside me, the way he filled me completely, was intoxicating, and I could feel myself unravelling under his touch.

His hands gripped my hips tightly, holding me in place as he pounded into me, each thrust driving us both closer to the edge. The rhythm was relentless, the pleasure building and building until it was almost too much to bear.

"Vinnie, you feel so good," he groaned, his voice thick with pleasure.

His words, and the sound of my name on his lips, sent a thrill through me, and I cried out, my body tightening around him as the tension inside me reached its breaking point. Heat pooling low in my belly, the pleasure spiralling higher and higher with each thrust until finally, with a desperate cry, I shattered again beneath him, my orgasm tearing through me like a wave.

Ethan followed me over the edge, his release crashing through him as he buried himself deep inside me, his body trembling with the force of it. We clung to each other, our bodies locked together as the aftershocks rippled through us, leaving us both breathless and utterly spent.

Ethan collapsed against me, his breath ragged, his heart pounding in sync with mine. "You're undoing me, Vinnie," he murmured, his voice thick with emotion. "You're going to be the death of me."

I laughed softly, but the sound turned into a moan as the movement made us both aware that he was still inside me. "It was perfect," I whispered.

He pulled back slightly, his eyes softening as he looked down at me with a tender smile before leaning down and pressing a gentle kiss to my lips. "I'm not done with you yet."

His words made my heart swell. In the warm afterglow, wrapped in his embrace, a deep contentment settle over me. This wasn't just about the physical connection. There was something more here, something that went beyond the heat of the moment. As I looked into his eyes, a thought crept in. Almost too soon, too unexpected.

I might be falling in love with him.

The realization made my breath catch, but I kept it tucked away, not wanting to rush into something so profound while still caught up in the moment's bliss. Yet, the feeling that being with Ethan felt right—like this was where I was meant to be—lingered, warm and reassuring.

I smiled up at him, my fingers tracing the line of his jaw as I whispered, "I'm not done with you, either."

After a moment of shared smiles and lingering touches, Ethan gently scooped me up, carrying me to the bedroom. The atmosphere had shifted—still charged with desire, but softened by something deeper, more intimate. He laid me down on the bed with a tenderness, his gaze never leaving mine.

This time, there was no rush. We took our time, exploring each other with a newfound curiosity and reverence. His hands traced every curve of my body, his touch feather-light, as if memorizing every detail. I responded in kind, letting my fingers glide over his skin. Our lips met in a kiss that was both soft and deep, filled with all the emotions we couldn't—*wouldn't*—yet put into words. His hands cradled my face as he kissed me, his thumbs brushing over my cheeks, grounding me in the moment.

Ethan took his time as he entered me, moving with deliberate care, each thrust slow and measured. The pleasure built gradually, a slow burn that spread through my body, making every nerve come alive. We moved together in perfect sync, the world outside the bedroom fading away as we lost ourselves in each other. It wasn't just about physical pleasure. It was about being *seen*, being known—and knowing him in return.

When we finally reached the edge together, it was with a sense of completion, of having shared something profound. We held each other close, our breaths mingling as we came down from the high, the intimacy lingering in the air like a sweet memory.

Ethan kissed my forehead and whispered, "Let's get cleaned up." His voice was soft, and full of affection. He led me to the bathroom, where we stepped into the shower together. The warm water cascaded over us, washing away the remnants of our passion, but not the connection we'd just deepened.

I moved with deliberate care, my hands exploring every inch of Ethan's skin as the steam wrapped around us. My fingers traced the contours of his muscles, feeling the strength beneath his skin. His breath hitched as I continued my exploration, the tension in his body evident as he leaned back against the shower wall. His eyes were dark with want, but there was something else there too—a flicker of hesitation, as if he wasn't sure he should let me continue.

"Vinnie . . ." he murmured, his voice rough with emotion. "You don't have to do this. Tonight was supposed to be about you."

I met his gaze, my heart swelling with affection for this man who was always thinking of me, even in a moment like this. "I want to," I whispered, my voice steady despite the flutter of excitement in my chest. The simple declaration seemed to break something inside him, his control slipping as a groan escaped his lips. The desire in his eyes deepened, and he nodded, the last of his resistance crumbling.

I wrapped my hand around him, feeling the length of him against my palm, and stroked him slowly, matching the rhythm of the water as it streamed down over us. His head fell back against the wall, his eyes fluttering shut as he gave himself over to the sensations.

With each slow, deliberate movement, I watched as his control unravelled. His breath grew ragged, his muscles tensing beneath my touch, and the intensity of his reaction, the way his body responded to me, only fuelled my desire to give him everything.

I leaned in, capturing his lips in a kiss that was deep and unhurried, our mouths moving together in perfect sync. His hands gripped my hips, his fingers digging into my skin as if he needed something to anchor himself to. The feel of him trembling beneath my touch, the raw need in his kiss, sent a thrill through me that made my breath catch.

As I worked him closer to the edge, Ethan's moans muffled against my lips, each sound sending a jolt of pleasure through me. The tension in his body wound tighter and tighter, the pressure building with every stroke of my hand, every kiss we shared.

Finally, with a shuddering breath, he came undone in my arms, his release mingling with the water as his entire body trembled with the force of it. Just before the intensity overwhelmed him, he murmured, "Vinnie .. . you're everything." The words slipped out, heavy with meaning, but not quite crossing the line.

His head dropped to rest against my shoulder, his breath warm against my neck as he clung to me, his heart racing against mine. I held him close, feeling the unspoken depth in his words.

When his breathing slowed, Ethan pulled back, his eyes finding mine with a look that was both tender and full of wonder. "You're amazing," he whispered.

A soft smile curved my lips as I reached up to brush a strand of wet hair from his forehead. "So are you," I replied, my voice equally soft, the words carrying a depth of emotion that I couldn't quite put into words.

We stood there for a moment longer before Ethan leaned down to press a gentle kiss to my forehead. "Let's get out of here before we turn into prunes," he said with a soft chuckle, the warmth of his smile lighting up his eyes.

I laughed, nodding as I reached for a towel, my heart full and content as I realized that what we had just shared was more than just a moment of passion. It was a connection, and a strengthening of a bond that was growing stronger with each passing day

Chapter 23

I WOKE UP TO THE WARM weight of Ethan's arms wrapped around me, his chest rising and falling in a steady rhythm against my back. A soft smile spread across my lips as I basked in the feeling of his body curled around mine, his breath soft against the nape of my neck. For a moment, I just lay there, letting the contentment of the moment sink in. The softness of the sheets, the heat of his skin against mine, and the lingering scent of him on the pillow—all of it felt like a perfect dream I didn't want to wake up from.

Carefully, I turned in his arms, wanting to steal a glance at his face while he slept. His dark lashes rested against his cheeks, his lips slightly parted in that peaceful, unguarded way that only sleep can bring. My heart fluttered at the sight of him, looking so boyish and serene, worlds away from the confident, sometimes teasing man I was getting to know. Seeing him like this made my chest tighten in a way that was both terrifying and exhilarating.

My phone buzzed on the nightstand, jolting me out of my thoughts, and I reached over, trying not to disturb Ethan as I grabbed it, hoping it was just a random notification. The sight of multiple texts flooding the screen made my heart drop.

"Oh, no," I breathed, dread pooling in my stomach as I quickly scrolled through the messages—all them from Ivy and Amelia. Then I glanced at the time and realized I had overslept, and the gallery's opening was just an hour away.

I bolted upright, the sheet slipping off as panic surged through me. "I overslept!" I muttered, my voice thick with anxiety. My mind was racing—how could I be so careless? What if things weren't ready?

Ethan stirred beside me, his arms instinctively reaching out before his eyes blinked open. "What's going on?" he asked, his voice gravelly with sleep as he rubbed a hand over his face.

"I was supposed to be at the gallery ages ago," I blurted out, running my hands through my tangled hair. "I haven't even made it home to change, and the gallery—" I stopped short, looking around for my clothes.

Ethan sat up, instantly alert, his gaze focused on me. "Hey, hey, it's okay," he said, his voice calm and reassuring as he swung his legs over the side of the bed, already reaching for his jeans. "We'll figure this out. You've got time. We'll get you ready and you'll be there in no time. I'm here to help with anything you need."

"But I need to get home, change, and somehow get everything set up," I replied, pulling on my dress. "Ivy and Amelia have been trying to reach me, and I just . . ." My voice caught as the weight of the day pressed down on me.

Ethan crossed the room in just a few strides, his presence a solid, comforting force. He reached out, his hands warm as they settled on my shoulders, his thumbs gently rubbing the tension there. "Vinnie," he said softly, making me pause and look up at him. "You look beautiful no matter what. Seriously. But I get it. Go home, get ready, and I'll meet you at the gallery in thirty minutes. We'll tackle whatever needs to be done together, okay?"

The sincerity in his eyes made the frantic pace of my heart slow a little, and I nodded, swallowing back the tightness in my throat. "Thank you," I whispered, my voice thick with gratitude. The way he was so steady, so calm in the face of my panic, made me want to cling to him a little longer.

He leaned in, pressing a lingering kiss to my lips that was full of reassurance and promise. "You're going to be amazing today," he whispered against my lips. "Now go get ready. I'll be right behind you."

By the time I arrived at the gallery, the nervous energy coursing through me had settled into a steady pulse of excitement. The Cozy Canvas was about to open its doors for the first time. I'd handed Ethan the keys before I left his place, trusting him to get things started while I rushed home to get change and, as I approached the entrance, I could already see signs of the final preparations underway. Ethan, Amelia, and Ivy were busy setting up drinks and snacks, their movements coordinated like a well-rehearsed dance.

The gallery looked stunning; the culmination of weeks of hard work, late nights, and attention to detail. Ivy had outdone herself with the decor, her artistic eye adding touches that transformed the space into something truly special. I'd lined the walls with my paintings, carefully choosing and arranging each piece to tell a story—a story of my journey, from Cresden to Hallow's End, and everything in between.

As I took in the sight before me, my eyes were drawn to the first section of the gallery. The bold, bright abstract pieces that lined the walls told of my time in Cresden. The colors clashed and swirled in a chaotic dance, reflecting the intensity and turbulence of my relationship with Sebastian. Each painting seemed to capture a different moment and a different emotion—passion, confusion, anger, and heartbreak. The final piece in that section, the one I had painted right before everything fell apart, stood out. It was a vibrant explosion of color, raw and unfiltered, a visual representation of everything I'd gone through.

From there, the paintings transitioned to a mix of abstract art and pastels, a testament to my uncertainty when I first moved to Hallow's End. The colors softened, the forms became less chaotic, but there was still a sense of searching, of trying to find my place. These pieces spoke of moments of doubt, of quiet reflection, as I slowly found my feet in this new town.

And then, as the gallery curved around, the newer pieces came into view. Soft pastels, gentle lines, and detailed brushstrokes captured the essence of Hallow's End, and the people and places that had come to mean so much to me. Each painting was a love letter to the town and its people, and a celebration of the life I was building here.

I stood in the center of the gallery, my eyes tracing the path of my paintings, each one a chapter of my life laid bare for the world to see. And now, looking back, I realized how every twist and turn had led me to this moment.

Ethan must have noticed my stillness because, before I knew it, he was by my side, his arm sliding around my waist. "You okay?" he asked, his voice soft and full of concern. His presence was steadying.

I nodded, turning to him, my heart swelling with gratitude. "I . . . I just can't believe it's real," I whispered, my voice thick with emotion. "Thank you, Ethan. For everything."

He smiled, that familiar warmth in his eyes. "You've done something amazing here, Vinnie. I'm just happy I could be a part of it." His hand cupped my cheek and I leaned in, pressing a soft, lingering kiss to his lips.

When we pulled back, I could see the pride in his eyes, and it made my heart flutter. "Let's make today unforgettable," he murmured, his forehead resting against mine for a brief moment before he straightened up.

I nodded, a little more of the tension easing out of my shoulders. Together, we walked toward the back of the gallery where Ivy and Amelia were putting the final touches on the snack table. Ivy was adjusting a display of cupcakes, her brows furrowed in concentration, while Amelia arranged a selection of finger foods with a critical eye.

"There she is," Ivy said with a grin as she noticed me, her eyes sparkling with excitement. She set down the last cupcake and came over to give me a quick hug. "Everything's ready to go! How are you feeling?"

"Excited. Nervous," I admitted, walking over to join them. "But mostly excited. The place looks incredible. You've all done an amazing job."

Amelia straightened up, brushing a strand of her purple hair behind her ear. "We just wanted everything to be perfect for your big day. People are going to love it, Vinnie."

My eyes welled up as I looked at them, these women who had become so close to me in such a short time. "I couldn't have done this without you," I said, my voice shaking slightly as I tried to keep my emotions in check.

"Ivy, your meticulous checklists and planning were a lifesaver. I would've been lost without them."

"Oh, stop," Ivy waved a hand dismissively, but I could see the tears shining in her eyes as well. "You would've done just fine on your own. We just added a little extra sparkle."

Amelia nudged us both with a smirk. "Yeah, Ivy and her checklists. I swear, she had a list for everything—probably even one for how to cry gracefully."

Ivy rolled her eyes, laughing through her tears. "Hey, someone had to keep us all in line!"

"Suck it up, you two," Amelia added, her voice softer than usual as she blinked a little harder. "Don't go ruining your makeup before the doors even open."

I pulled them both into a hug, the three of us standing there, holding on to each other as the reality of what we'd accomplished settled in. "Thank you," I whispered again.

After we pulled apart, Ivy flipped the switch to illuminate the artwork, and the lights cast a warm, golden glow across the room. Just as everything seemed perfect, the lights flickered, once, twice, before steadying again.

Ethan laughed, breaking the momentary tension. "It's an old building," he said with a shrug, his tone light. "Probably just the wiring."

I managed a smile, though something about the flicker left me with an odd feeling. Still, I shook it off and gave the room one last glance. The largest painting from Cresden, the one that held so much of my pain and confusion, was slightly crooked, so I hurried over to adjust it, carefully straightening the frame until it hung perfectly in line with the others.

With everything in place, I took a deep breath and turned to the door as my nerves returned in full force. Ethan's hand slid into mine, and I looked up to see his reassuring smile. It was enough to give me the courage I needed.

"Ready?" he asked, his voice steady and calm.

I nodded, squeezing his hand. "Ready."

And with that, I reached for the door, my heart pounding in my chest as I opened the gallery to the world for the first time. People began to trickle in, their faces a blur of smiles and curious expressions, and I greeted each guest with a warm welcome, but my mind was spinning, barely able to process the fact that this was really happening. The Cozy Canvas, my dream, was now a reality, and it was buzzing with life.

Everywhere I looked, there were familiar faces but, in the whirlwind of emotions, they all seemed to blend together. My heart pounded in my chest, excitement and nerves making it hard to focus as I caught glimpses of people admiring the artwork, their murmured compliments a comforting backdrop to the chaotic thoughts racing through my head.

"Welcome, everyone!" Ivy's voice cut through the din, her tone cheerful and commanding. I turned to see her standing near the entrance, effortlessly taking charge of the crowd. She had set up a beautiful wooden donation box at the front of the room, decorated with hand-painted flowers and a sign that read, SUPPORT THE COZY CANVAS. Beside it, a small table was arranged with raffle tickets, and a variety of enticing prizes, on display.

"We have some wonderful raffle prizes up for grabs, including a private art lesson with Vinnie, a gift basket from Sweet Crumbs Bakery, and a weekend stay at the charming Hallow's End Inn. Tickets are just five dollars each, and all proceeds go directly to supporting The Cozy Canvas." Ivy continued, her smile radiant as she gestured toward the table.

Her presence was magnetic, drawing people in with her infectious enthusiasm. Guests eagerly approached the table, purchasing raffle tickets and making donations, their excitement adding to the lively atmosphere.

Ivy greeted each person with a genuine smile, engaging them in conversation and thanking them for their support.

Her outfit was as striking as her personality—a black lace maxi skirt that flowed gracefully with each step, paired with a soft, dark gray cropped top. Over it, she had draped a fringed, floral-embroidered kimono, adding a touch of bohemian elegance that perfectly matched the vibe of the gallery. Her dark lipstick and statement floral earrings added bold accents, whilst intricately designed platform wedges completed the ensemble.

As the gallery filled with more guests, I found myself momentarily overwhelmed by the sheer volume of people. The sound of laughter and chatter filled the air, mingling with the soft music playing in the background, and I tried to focus on the interactions, on the smiles and words of encouragement, but it was all so much, so fast.

Just as I felt myself beginning to spiral, a familiar melody cut through the noise, catching me off guard. The gentle strains of Taylor Swift's *Back to December* filled the gallery, the song's bittersweet lyrics tugging at memories I'd long tried to bury. It was a song I had played on repeat in the days following my breakup with Sebastian, each note a painful reminder of the past. Hearing it now, in this space that I had built as part of my new beginning, felt strangely out of place. I was certain I hadn't included it on the playlist for today.

The music transported me back to those lonely nights, when the weight of heartbreak felt like too much to bear. The memory of Sebastian's face, of the love that had once been so strong, flickered in my mind, but it was a distant, fading image, and one that no longer held the power it once did. I stood there, frozen, feeling the past creeping into a day that was meant to be about my future.

As if sensing the shift in my mood, Ethan appeared at my side. His warm presence brought me back to the present, his steadying hand resting gently on the small of my back. "You're doing great," he whispered, his voice a soothing balm to my frazzled nerves.

His touch anchored me, grounding me in the moment. The comforting warmth of his hand against my back, the quiet confidence in his words, made it easier to push the lingering ghosts of the past aside

"Thank you," I murmured, giving him a small smile as I tried to shake off the unease the song had stirred in me. "But I'm sure that song wasn't on the playlist. I have no idea how it ended up here."

Ethan shrugged, offering a reassuring smile. "Maybe it slipped in by accident. You are a big Swiftie, after all," he winked, his light-hearted comment breaking through the tension.

I let out a small laugh, his words easing the tightness in my chest. "Yeah, maybe you're right. It's probably nothing."

With a deep breath, I pushed the thought aside. This was my moment, and I wasn't going to let a random song choice take away from that. Ethan's hand remained steady on my back, a comforting presence that helped me refocus on the celebration unfolding around us.

"I didn't expect so many people," I admitted, glancing around the crowded room.

"Everyone's here to support you," he said, his voice full of warmth. "And they're all impressed by what you've created."

I nodded, trying to let his words sink in, but a small pang of sadness tugged at me. Amidst the sea of faces, one was noticeably absent—my mom. I had sent her an invitation, hoping she might surprise me by showing up, but there was no sign of her. The thought left a hollow feeling in my chest, a reminder of the distance that still lingered between us.

I pushed the feeling aside, not wanting to dampen the joy of the moment. This gallery was my dream come to life, and I needed to focus on that. Still, the absence of my mom weighed on me like a bittersweet note in an otherwise perfect day.

I began to move through the gallery, engaging with the guests, my earlier nerves easing as I immersed myself in the lively atmosphere. I caught sight of Amelia, her round golden glasses catching the light as she animatedly chatted with a guy I didn't recognize. Her purple pixie cut was perfectly styled, and she looked effortlessly cool in a burgundy slip dress, layered with a worn leather jacket and chunky black boots. Stacks of silver rings adorned her fingers, and layered necklaces glinted under the gallery lights.

As I walked past, Amelia caught my eye and waved me over with a grin. "Hey, Vinnie, this is Brodie," she said, nudging the guy playfully. "We went to high school together." Brodie smiled, looking every bit as laid-back as Amelia, and gave me a nod as she turned back to their conversation. Before I could say more, she winked at me, clearly in her element, and I kept moving, amused by the unexpected reunion.

As I continued to mingle, Ivy, always the social butterfly, navigated the crowd with ease, her phone seemingly an extension of her hand as she captured every moment. I watched her snap photos of guests admiring the artwork, the carefully arranged tables, and the raffle prizes. At one point, she turned her camera toward Ethan and me, capturing a candid moment where we were both laughing. The joy on our faces, the easy connection between us, felt like the perfect snapshot of everything this day represented.

While I was lost in conversation with a group of guests, someone gently placed their hand on my shoulder. Turning around, I found myself face-to-face with Ethan's parents, who had quietly entered the gallery.

"Vinnie, there you are!" Caroline's voice was full of affection as she pulled me into a hug, surprising me with her familiarity, but comforting all the same.

I returned the hug, feeling the genuine warmth of her embrace. "Caroline, it's so good to see you. I'm so glad you could make it."

"Are you kidding? We wouldn't miss this for the world," she said as she stepped back, a fond smile on her face.

Ethan, who had been just a few steps away, came over and stood beside his dad, a hint of pride in his eyes as he introduced us. "Vinnie, this is my dad, Robert."

Robert extended his hand, his grip firm but gentle as he shook mine. "It's a pleasure to finally meet you, Vinnie. We've heard a lot about you," he said, his voice deep and steady, much like Ethan's.

"The pleasure is mine. Thank you both for coming," I said, feeling a bit overwhelmed by their warm reception.

Ethan's smile grew as he looked between his parents and me. "We've all been looking forward to this," he added, his hand finding the small of my back in a reassuring gesture.

Caroline's eyes sparkled with pride as she glanced around the bustling gallery. "And from the looks of it, the gallery is a huge success," she said, her voice full of admiration.

"Thank you," I replied, feeling a little more at ease. "It's been a whirlwind, but I'm so happy with how everything's turned out."

I glanced around the room, suddenly realizing someone was missing. "Where's Lily?"

Caroline chuckled, nodding toward a corner of the gallery where Lily was darting from painting to painting, her face alight with excitement. "She's been running around looking at everything. I think she's decided she wants to be an artist like you."

As if on cue, Lily spotted me from across the room and came barrelling toward me, her small arms wrapping around my legs in an enthusiastic hug. She'd styled her blonde hair in two adorable space buns, each one slightly askew, adding to her charm. Her outfit consisted of a wild combination of colors and patterns that only a six-year-old could pull off—striped leggings, a tutu skirt, and a T-shirt emblazoned with a glittery unicorn.

I laughed, squeezing her back. "I thought you wanted to be a detective or a famous singer?"

Lily tilted her head up at me, her eyes sparkling with mischief. "I can do it all! I'll solve mysteries during the day, sing at night, and paint on weekends!"

I chuckled at her determination. "A triple threat, huh? I like it. But don't forget, we'll need to make some space in your schedule for our art lessons."

She grinned up at me. "Deal! But only if you promise to paint with me and let me use all the glitter."

"Glitter?" I pretended to wince. "You drive a hard bargain. But for you, I think we can make that work."

Lily's eyes lit up, and she squeezed my legs even tighter before dashing off to explore more of the gallery. Caroline and Robert watched her with fond smiles, and Ethan slipped his hand into mine, giving it a gentle squeeze.

Caroline then turned to me, a hint of excitement in her eyes. "By the way, Vinnie, we're having a family bonfire next Wednesday. Some of our family is visiting for Halloween, and we'd love for you to join us. It would mean a lot to us—and to Ethan."

I looked up at Ethan, who was watching me with a hopeful expression, as if he was unsure how I'd respond. The idea of spending more time with his family felt right, like the next step in whatever we were building together.

"I'd love to," I said, smiling warmly. "Thank you for inviting me."

Caroline and Robert beamed, happy with my response. As they moved on to mingle with other guests, Ethan turned to me. Without a word, he leaned in and pressed a soft kiss to my lips, a tender moment that conveyed all the relief and happiness he felt. The gentle brush of his lips against mine made my heart flutter.

As the gallery continued to fill with people, I found myself chatting with a couple of tourists who were drawn to one of the newer pieces—a painting I had created after that memorable day when Ethan took me to the lake. The piece was softer, yet still full of emotion, with hues of blues and greens that reflected the serenity and connection I'd felt in that moment. I realized how much that painting symbolized my journey—not just as an artist, but as a person finding her way, healing, and opening up to new possibilities. It wasn't just about the lake, it was about the peace I had found in Hallow's End.

Out of the corner of my eye, I saw Robert and Ethan standing together, deep in conversation. Every now and then, they glanced my way, and I couldn't help but wonder what they were talking about. The way Robert looked at his son, then at me, with a proud smile, made my heart skip a beat, and I quickly looked away, blushing at the thought that they might be talking about me.

Everything had felt perfect. The gallery was humming with life, and my heart was light and full of joy. But that sense of peace shattered the moment I saw Emily walk through the door. She wore a stunning red dress that accentuated every curve, her blonde hair cascading down her back in soft waves. There was an effortless confidence in the way she moved, and for a brief moment, I couldn't help but feel that familiar pang of insecurity. I glanced down at my simple blue dress, modest and soft, far from the striking image Emily presented. I wished I'd had more time that morning to do something with my hair, or pick out something that made me feel more . . . powerful.

Emily's gaze zeroed in on Ethan, her intentions clear as day, and my stomach tightened with dread. I'd hoped that after our run-in at quiz night, she would have backed off. I'd managed to avoid her since then, thinking maybe she'd gotten the hint. But clearly, that hadn't lasted long. Here she was again, making her presence known, her moves bolder and more calculated than ever.

As she made her way toward us, I saw her flash a smile—one that was all too practiced, and dripping with a saccharine sweetness that didn't fool me for a second. Just as I braced myself for whatever she was about to pull, Ethan found his way back to my side, his presence instantly grounding me.

"Ethan, there you are!" Emily reached us, her voice laced with false cheer. Her eyes sparkled with a determination that made my skin crawl. "I've been looking for you. I wanted to talk about the upcoming volunteer program at the library. I figured you might want to lend me a hand with the reading sessions for kids."

Ethan's grip on my waist tightened, a subtle but clear signal of his discomfort. "Emily, this isn't the time," he said, his voice polite but firm.

"Oh, come on," she persisted, completely ignoring the tension in the air. She stepped closer, her attention focused solely on Ethan. "It'll only take a minute."

I felt a wave of irritation rising, my chest tightening with the effort to keep calm. Emily's blatant disregard for my presence, and the way she so easily dismissed me, was infuriating. But before I could say anything, Ivy smoothly intervened, her tone sharp beneath the veneer of politeness.

"Emily, why don't you grab a drink and enjoy the event? There's plenty of time to discuss that later," Ivy suggested, her eyes narrowing as she stepped.

Emily's smile faltered, a flicker of annoyance flashing in her eyes before she quickly masked it, and she shot Ivy a pointed look but forced her lips back into a smile. "Of course. I wouldn't want to interrupt the *big day*," she said, her voice dripping with insincerity. She turned on her heel, her movements graceful as she sauntered off into the crowd, but not before casting one last lingering look over her shoulder at Ethan.

I let out a sigh, my heart still racing from the tension, and Ivy met my gaze, her eyes full of understanding. "Don't let her get to you," she said softly. "Emily's just trying to stir things up."

Ethan turned to me, concern etched on his face. "Are you okay?" he asked, his voice gentle.

I nodded, though the knot in my stomach hadn't completely unwound. "I'm fine," I replied, forcing a smile. "Thanks for stepping in, Ivy."

She waved it off, but her expression remained serious. "Anytime. And remember, Vinnie, you're the one here with Ethan, not her."

As I nodded, grateful for her timely intervention, my relief was short-lived. Out of the corner of my eye, I saw Emily returning, a glass of wine in her hand, and a renewed sense of determination in her stride. The smile she wore was as fake as the sincerity in her voice.

"Oh, Vinnie, I didn't see you earlier," she cooed, her tone dripping with false pleasantness. "You must be so busy with everything."

Before I could respond, Emily's foot seemed to *accidentally* catch on the rug, and, in a dramatic flail, the contents of her glass went flying—straight onto my pastel blue dress. The red wine splattered across the fabric, spreading like a stain on my mood.

"Oh my gosh, I'm so sorry!" Emily exclaimed, her voice full of faux concern, but the gleam in her eyes betrayed her delight at the damage she'd caused.

It's fine," I managed through gritted teeth, my gaze flicking to Ethan, who was now standing beside me, his brow furrowed with concern.

"Let me help you clean it up," he offered, but I shook my head, forcing a tight smile.

"I'll be right back," I said, excusing myself as I made a beeline for the bathroom in the back of the gallery.

Once inside, I grabbed some paper towels and started blotting the stain, but the more I tried, the worse it seemed to get. My reflection in the mirror stared back at me, seething with frustration. "She did that on purpose," I muttered, scrubbing harder. It wasn't just the dress. It was everything. The way Emily moved, the way she smiled, the way she *clearly* had no boundaries when it came to Ethan.

Taking a deep breath, I tried to calm myself. "Don't let her ruin this for you," I whispered fiercely. "Today is too important."

After doing what I could to salvage the dress, I straightened up, taking one last steadying breath before heading back out but, as I neared the gallery floor, the sight that greeted me stopped me in my tracks. There was Emily, standing way too close to Ethan, her hand lingering on his arm as she leaned in, speaking in low, hushed tones. Ethan's eyes darted around, clearly uncomfortable, but Emily wasn't giving him any space.

"And you know, Vinnie had quite the wild side back in Cresden," Emily was saying, her voice dripping with false sweetness. "I heard some pretty interesting stories about her and that ex of hers—Sebastian."

Her words made my blood run cold at the way she spoke, and the implication behind her words. *How did she know about Sebastian?* That wasn't something I'd shared publicly, especially not here in Hallow's End. My gut twisted with a sense of dread.

"That's enough, Emily," I said sharply, striding forward. My voice cut through the air like a knife, drawing both their attention. "This is neither the time nor the place for your gossip."

Emily turned to me, her expression one of feigned innocence. "Oh, Vinnie, I was just making conversation," she said, her tone as sugary as ever, but I could see the satisfaction gleaming in her eyes.

"Well, make it somewhere else," I snapped, finally having enough with her petty games and drama. "And keep your hands off my boyfriend."

Ethan's arm instinctively wrapped around my waist, pulling me closer, the firmness of his grip reassuring. But this time, he didn't just stand by. He turned to Emily, his expression hardening with a seriousness I hadn't seen before.

"Emily, this has to stop," he said, his voice firm and steady. "I've tried to be polite, but you need to understand something. I'm not interested, and I never will be. I'm with Vinnie, and she's the one who matters to me. Nothing you say or do will change that."

His words hung in the air, heavy with finality, and Emily's face paled, her confident facade slipping just for a moment before she forced a tight smile.

"Of course," she said, her tone brittle. "I was just . . . trying to catch up. No harm meant."

Ethan didn't let go of me, his gaze unwavering. "You've said enough, Emily. It's time to move on."

Her eyes darted between us, her expression unreadable, before she nodded and turned to leave, her steps quicker than before.

Once she was gone, Ethan turned back to me, his gaze softening. "I'm sorry you had to deal with that," he said, his voice full of sincerity.

"Thank you," I whispered, my voice thick with emotion. "I needed to hear that."

He smiled, leaning down to press a soft kiss to my forehead. "You deserve nothing less."

"Well," I said, trying to lighten the mood, "I guess I just declared you my boyfriend in front of the whole town."

Ethan's serious expression broke into a laugh, the sound rich. "I noticed," he said, his eyes twinkling with amusement. "And you know what?

I was actually going to ask you to be my girlfriend later tonight. But it looks like you beat me to it."

I grinned, a blush creeping up my cheeks. "Guess I couldn't wait."

He chuckled, his arm tightening around my waist. "Honestly, Vinnie, I'm glad you did. It's about time we made it official. I've been wanting to call you my girlfriend for a while now."

As the late afternoon sun began to dip low in the sky, the opening event started to wind down. Guests milled about, finishing their drinks and snacks, admiring the last few pieces of art. The energy in the room was still buzzing, but there was a sense of contentment now, a feeling of a day well spent.

Ivy caught my eye from across the room, gesturing for me to come over. "Hey, Vinnie," she said with a smile, "I think it's time you thanked everyone and did the raffle draw. Also, we need to pick the winner for the GoFundMe page. I've got the laptop ready."

I nodded, taking a deep breath to steady myself. "You're right. Let's do it."

She handed me a small microphone, and I tapped it lightly to get everyone's attention. The chatter in the room gradually died down as people turned to face me, their expressions expectant and supportive.

"Hi, everyone," I began, my voice a little shaky at first, but gaining strength as I continued. "I just want to thank you all for being here today. This gallery has been a dream of mine for so long, and seeing it come to life with all of your support means the world to me. I couldn't have done it without each and every one of you."

The crowd responded with warm applause, and a surge of gratitude washed over me. "Now," I said, smiling, "we're going to do the raffle draw. Good luck to everyone who entered!"

Ivy held up the bowl filled with raffle tickets, giving it a good shake before holding it out to me. I reached in, my fingers brushing against the crinkled paper before pulling out a ticket. I unfolded it and smiled as I read the name aloud.

"And the winner is . . . Laura Stevens! Congratulations!"

Laura, the friend of Caroline's whom I'd met several times, stepped forward with a broad smile, her eyes lighting up with excitement. She was a familiar face in the community, always warm and welcoming, and it felt fitting that she'd win. The crowd clapped and cheered as she made her way up to claim her prize.

"Thank you so much, Vinnie!" she said, beaming as she accepted the prize.

"I'm so glad you won, Laura." The crowd applauded again as she thanked me, clearly thrilled.

I stood before the laptop. "And now," I said, my voice carrying over the soft hum of conversation, "we're going to select the winner of our online fundraiser. Thank you so much to everyone who donated."

I glanced at the laptop screen, where hundreds of names of the donors were ready for the draw. Although the crowd couldn't see the screen, Amelia was live-streaming the event for those who couldn't make it, her phone pointed at me as I prepared to announce the winner. I took a deep breath and clicked the button to start the random selection.

The digital wheel spun, the names flashing by in a blur, and my heart raced along with it, the anticipation filling the air. As the wheel began to slow, the names flickering one by one, I found myself holding my breath. Finally, the wheel stopped, and the winning name appeared on the screen as my heart dropped into my stomach.

Sebastian Sterling.

My hand froze on the mouse, the smile faltering on my face, and I quickly cleared my throat, trying to mask the shock that was threatening to overwhelm me. "Looks like we have a little technical difficulty," I said, forcing a lightness into my tone. "Let's try that again."

I clicked the button once more, and the wheel spun again. But, as it slowed, the name on the screen was the same.

Sebastian Sterling.

My pulse quickened as my mind raced, and a low murmur ran through the room as I stared at the screen in disbelief, my heart pounding in my chest. It felt like the universe was playing a sick joke on me. I clicked the button one last time, hoping desperately for a different result, but when the wheel stopped, it was the same name again.

Sebastian Sterling.

My mind raced, struggling to comprehend what was happening, but Ivy quickly stepped in, her voice smooth and confident. "And the winner is . . . Danny Clark!" she announced, effortlessly faking the name as if it had been on the screen all along.

The crowd cheered, none the wiser, as Danny, beaming with excitement, stepped forward to claim his prize. Ivy handed it over with a smile, skilfully diverting attention away from the unsettling situation.

I forced a smile, trying to keep my composure while glancing at the screen one last time before shutting the laptop. My mind was spinning, and the shadow of Sebastian's name lingered in the back of my thoughts. But I knew I couldn't let it ruin this day, not with so many people here to support me.

As Danny waved to the crowd, the cheerful atmosphere began to settle back in, and I did my best to shake off the unease. Ethan, standing nearby, met my gaze with concern, but before I could get too lost in my thoughts, the pops of confetti from everyone around me brought me back to the present.

This day was about celebrating everything I'd worked so hard to achieve. And I wasn't going to let anything take that away from me.

Chapter 24

THE WARMTH OF THE BONFIRE flickered against my skin, a welcome contrast to the crisp October breeze that had begun to settle in. Dinner at Ethan's parents' house had been just what I needed—full of laughter, delicious food, and filled with easy conversation that made me feel like I truly belonged with his family. Now, we were all gathered outside around the fire, the flames crackling and dancing in the night air.

Ethan's aunt and uncle had joined us, along with their kids, who were now chasing each other around the yard, their laughter echoing through the cool night. I was wrapped up in a fluffy jacket, with Ethan's arm draped comfortably over my shoulders, his warmth seeping into me and grounding me in the moment.

The weirdness from the gallery opening a few days ago had started to fade, but it still lingered in the back of my mind, like a shadow that refused to fully disappear. I had told Ethan about Sebastian's name popping up during the raffle draw, expecting him to laugh it off as a bizarre coincidence. And he had, at least on the surface, brushing it aside with a casual remark about how the universe worked in strange ways sometimes. But I could sense a flicker of uncertainty in his eyes, a hint of something unspoken that had settled between us.

That night, after the gallery had closed and the guests had gone home, we'd talked about it. Ethan had asked more about Sebastian, wanting to know the full story, and I'd told him everything. How my relationship with Sebastian had started out passionate, but had spiralled into something unhealthy and painful. How leaving Cresden had been the hardest thing I'd ever done, but also the most necessary. Ethan had listened quietly, his hand never leaving mine and, when I'd finished, he'd pulled me close, kissing my forehead with a tenderness that made my heart ache.

As I gazed into the fire, my mind drifted back to that conversation with him. I could still see the flicker of doubt in his eyes, and the way he'd hesitated before telling me he trusted me. I knew he did, but I also knew how hard it was for him to push past that lingering fear—that what we had could somehow be overshadowed by someone from my past.

Ethan hadn't outright said it, but I could sense the unease that had settled between us since that day. It wasn't just the strange coincidence of Sebastian's name appearing in the draw. It was more than that. Our relationship had blossomed so quickly, moving from a tentative beginning to something deep and intense in what felt like no time at all. For me, it felt right—like everything had fallen into place exactly as it should. But I could tell that for Ethan, the speed of it all left him with a sense of uncertainty.

He was worried that maybe I had rushed into this with him, and the way I spoke about Sebastian during our late-night conversation had only added to his unease. I hadn't meant to, but maybe I'd been too careful, too measured in my words, trying to downplay how deeply Sebastian had once been woven into my life. Ethan had picked up on that, and it had made his confidence waver.

He'd confided in me that he'd never felt this way about anyone before—that he hadn't even *dated* much, because he'd been waiting for the right person. Someone who made him feel like this was where he was meant to be. And now, with everything moving so quickly between us, he couldn't help but worry that maybe I hadn't had enough time to process my break up, and my quick move from Cresden. That maybe I wasn't as sure as he was. The thought that it all might be too much, too soon, seemed to linger at the edges of his mind, and I wanted so desperately to make him believe that Sebastian didn't matter anymore, that the only person who had any power over my heart was him. The fire crackled, and a log splitting open with a loud pop pulled me out of my thoughts. I blinked, focusing on the present moment, where the world felt simple and good.

Caroline was chatting with her sister-in-law, Susana, their voices low and warm. Across the fire, Lily was chasing after one of her cousins, their giggles floating through the air, while Robert kept a close eye on the kids, occasionally waving them back when they got too close to the fire. The scene was idyllic, a perfect snapshot of family and togetherness, and it was exactly what I needed to pull myself back from the edge of those darker thoughts.

When I shifted in Ethan's arms, he must have caught the lingering tension in my expression because his hand squeezed my shoulder gently, and I looked up to find his gaze fixed on me, concern etched in his features.

"You okay?" he asked, his voice low.

"Yeah," I whispered back, the word feeling truer now than it had a few moments ago. "Just thinking."

He nodded, but I could see the question in his eyes. "About what?" he asked.

I hesitated, not wanting to risk dampening the moment. But before I could answer, one of Ethan's cousins, Derik, called out to him from across the fire. "Hey, Ethan! You still owe me that hiking trip you promised this summer! Remember? The one that got cancelled because you broke your leg?"

Ethan chuckled, the sound light and easy as he glanced over at Derik. "I haven't forgotten, man. We'll make it happen before the first snow, I promise."

As he looked back at me, something in my expression must have given away where my thoughts had drifted.

"Are you thinking about him?" he asked quietly, careful not to let the conversation carry past us, though the fire's crackling would drown out anything we said.

I sighed. "Maybe a little," I admitted, turning my gaze back to the flames. "It's just . . . everything's been a lot lately. I thought I'd put him behind me, but then his name popped up, and it's like . . ."

"Like he's still here, even though he shouldn't be," Ethan finished for me, his voice calm, but tinged with something deeper.

I nodded, appreciating his understanding. "Yeah, exactly. It's like there's this tiny gap between us that he's still managing to wedge himself into."

Ethan's fingers traced slow circles on my arm, his touch grounding me. "Vinnie," he said softly, "we don't have to let him have any more space in our lives than he already has. He's your past, and I get that, but I'm your present. And hopefully . . . your future, too."

The sincerity in his voice made my chest tighten, and I looked up at him, my heart swelling with affection for this man who had become so important to me. "You are," I said, the words carrying a weight of truth. He smiled, his eyes softening as he leaned down to press a tender kiss to my lips.

But a part of me couldn't shake the feeling that Sebastian's appearance in my life again, even in this distant, shadowy form, was a desperate attempt to get my attention. He had always been possessive, never able to let things go easily. I had blocked him on everything, cutting off all communication, so how could he reach me now?

Even if he had somehow managed to find out about the gallery, and donated to get my attention, the act of drawing his name—three times in a row—was something beyond even Sebastian's control. It felt too coincidental, too strange, and the thought gnawed at the edges of my mind. I wanted to let it go, to believe that it was just some bizarre fluke, but the uncertainty lingered, a stubborn whisper in the back of my mind.

Just then, Lily's voice broke through my thoughts as she came bounding over, her eyes bright with excitement. "Ethan, can we roast marshmallows now, please?" she begged, tugging at his hand.

"Sure thing, Lil. Let's get those marshmallows roasting." He turned to me, a question in his eyes. "You coming?"

I managed a smile, needing a moment to collect myself. "I'll join you in a bit," I said, giving his hand a reassuring squeeze. "Just need to use the bathroom first."

Ethan nodded, giving me one last look before Lily tugged him back to the fire, her voice bubbling with excitement about the perfect way to toast a marshmallow. I watched them for a moment, and something deep inside me shifted, like a lock clicking into place. As I saw him kneel down to her level, showing her exactly how to hold the marshmallow without burning it, the realization hit me with a quiet but undeniable force.

I was in love with him.

The word *love* lingered in my mind, taking shape in a way that felt both new and inevitable. It wasn't just about the way he was with Lily, though that played a part. It was everything about him. The way he made me feel seen and valued, the gentle way he touched me, like he was always careful with my heart. The way he could make me laugh, even when I didn't feel like it, and how he was there for me, steady and reliable, no matter what.

Watching him now, with the firelight dancing in his eyes and that easy smile on his face, I realized that Ethan had become my safe place, the person I wanted to share my life with in every way that mattered. The love I felt wasn't just about passion or excitement. It was something deeper, something that had been growing quietly, day by day, until it was undeniable.

I'd always worn my heart on my sleeve, diving headfirst into love with an intensity that often left me breathless. But after everything with Sebastian, I'd found myself hesitating, afraid of losing myself in love again. That kind of consuming, all-encompassing love had taken so much from me before, leaving me shattered in ways I never wanted to experience again.

But with Ethan, it was different. Loving him didn't feel like losing myself. It felt like finding something I didn't even know I was missing. It wasn't a risk. It was a return to something true and steady. The thought filled me with a warmth that spread through my chest, leaving me breathless and a little overwhelmed, but in the best possible way. It was love, but it was safe and secure—a love that let me be myself, without fear of losing who I was. With Ethan, love felt like home.

I stepped inside the house, the warmth of the fire fading as the cool air wrapped around me. My thoughts were a jumble, swirling with everything I'd just realized about Ethan and how much he meant to me. I wanted to show him, to let him know just how deep my feelings ran, and how much I wanted to push past the doubts and uncertainties that Sebastian's sudden reappearance had stirred up. Ethan had done so much to make me feel safe and loved, and I wanted to do the same for him.

As I walked down the hallway, lost in my thoughts, I didn't notice Caroline until I nearly bumped into her.

"Oh, I'm so sorry!" I exclaimed, jolting back to reality as I stepped aside. Caroline smiled warmly, her eyes crinkling at the corners in that familiar, motherly way.

"No need to apologize, dear," she said, her voice soft and understanding. "You looked a little lost in thought. Everything okay?"

I hesitated for a moment, then nodded. "Yeah, just . . . a lot on my mind, I guess. But nothing bad," I added quickly, not wanting her to worry.

Caroline studied me for a moment, then reached out to gently touch my arm. "I'm glad you came tonight, Vinnie. It's been wonderful getting to know you. You've been such a positive influence on Ethan."

Her words caught me off guard, and I felt a sudden rush of emotion. "Thank you," I said, my voice thick with gratitude. "That means a lot."

She smiled, a touch of sentimentality in her expression. "I was worried about him for a while. Ethan's always been a bit shy and reserved, especially when it comes to relationships. But in the past few weeks, I've seen him come out of his shell in ways I haven't seen before, and I think that's thanks to you."

My heart swelled at her words. "He means a lot to me," I said quietly, my voice barely above a whisper. "I just want to make him happy."

"You already have," Caroline assured me, her tone full of warmth. "And that's all a mother could hope for."

Just as I was about to respond, Robert walked into the kitchen, his presence breaking the tender moment. "Caroline, you're not stealing Vinnie away, are you?" he teased, his eyes twinkling with good-natured humor.

She laughed, giving my arm a gentle squeeze before letting go. "Not at all. We were just having a little chat."

I smiled at them both, feeling a renewed sense of determination. Whatever doubts had lingered, whatever shadows had crept in, I knew one thing for certain—I was all in with Ethan. And I was going to make sure he knew that, too.

Chapter 25

E THAN HAD DROPPED ME off last night after the bonfire, but he couldn't stay over. He had an early start at work and was a bit behind on grading papers. As we stood by my front door, his arms wrapped around me in a tight hug, and I felt a twinge of disappointment, but I understood. Life had its demands, and we both had responsibilities.

"You know, I'm blaming you for this," he said with a playful glint in his eyes, his lips brushing against mine in a lingering kiss.

I frowned, confused. "Blaming me for what?"

"For falling behind," he teased, grinning. "You've been distracting me."

A wave of guilt washed over me but, before I could apologize, he chuckled and shook his head. "Not really. I'm just teasing, Vinnie. I wouldn't trade our time together for anything."

Relief washed over me, and I smiled, leaning into him. "Good. Because I'm not done distracting you."

He laughed, his warm, rich laughter echoing in the night. "I can't wait," he murmured, kissing me again before reluctantly pulling away. "But for now, I need to catch up. I'll see you tomorrow, okay?"

"Okay," I agreed, standing on my tiptoes to give him one last kiss. "Good luck with the papers."

As he drove off into the night, I felt a strange mix of emotions. Happiness, contentment, and a growing determination that had kept me up late into the night, planning.

This morning, I woke up with a sense of purpose. Last night, I had made a decision—I was going to tell Ethan I loved him. The realization had hit me like a ton of bricks by the bonfire, and I couldn't shake the overwhelming need to tell him. But how? I wanted it to be special, something he'd remember. And with Halloween coming up this weekend, the town's festival seemed like the perfect opportunity. Now I just had to figure out the small details.

While heading to the gallery, I shot a quick text to the girls' group chat, my fingers flying over the screen.

> **Vinnie:** Hey, are you guys free for lunch today? I need some girl time.

It didn't take long for the replies to come in.

> **Amelia:** Of course! I'm down. Where and when?

> **Ivy:** Yes! How about Harvest Moon Coffee at 12?

I smiled at their quick responses, my heart swelling with affection for my friends. They always had my back, and I knew they'd help me figure out the perfect way to tell Ethan how I felt.

As I was typing out a reply, lost in thought, I didn't notice the sleek black car parked just outside the gallery, or the man standing beside it, until I collided with him.

The impact jolted me out of my thoughts, and I stumbled back, looking up to apologize. But the words died on my lips as I took in the man standing before me. He was tall, with a commanding presence that made my stomach drop. His sharp features, neatly combed blonde hair, and the familiar intensity in his emerald eyes made my heart skip a beat.

It couldn't be.

But there he was, standing right in front of me.

Sebastian.

His smile was a mix of charm, and something darker. It was a look that had once made me feel safe but now sent a chill down my spine. As always, he was dressed impeccably, in black trousers, and a beige, relaxed-fit Oxford shirt, with a blazer draped over one arm, and I caught a whiff of his cologne—a clean scent with notes of cedarwood, musk, and pepper. The sight and scent of him brought back a flood of memories, both good and bad, leaving me unsettled.

"Hey, V," he said, his voice smooth and familiar. The way he used that nickname, one I hadn't heard since Cresden, sent a ripple of tension through me.

For a moment, I couldn't speak. My heart pounded in my chest, and the breath caught in my throat. It felt like the world had shifted beneath my feet, the solid ground I'd found with Ethan suddenly feeling precarious and uncertain.

"What are you doing here, Sebastian?" I finally managed to ask, my voice coming out steadier than I felt.

He flashed a smile that was too smooth, too practiced. "I'm here on business," he replied, his tone casual, as if we were merely old friends catching up. "You might've heard—I've been promoted to Vice President of Operations. I'm overseeing some of the projects at my father's company, and with the merger, I'm also working closely with your father's team. Merging operations, expanding . . . you know how it goes."

My stomach twisted at his words. The idea of Sebastian being tied even closer to my life here, through our families' businesses no less, was almost too much to bear. Hallow's End had been my refuge, the place where I found myself again, where I built something new away from the chaos and heartbreak of my past. This town had become mine in a way that Cresden never was, and now, with Sebastian standing here, it felt like he was tainting it, bringing with him the very shadows I had tried so hard to escape. The fact that he was standing in front of me now felt like a cruel twist of fate.

"But more importantly," he continued, his gaze sharpening as it locked onto mine, "I'm here for you. You're a hard girl to reach these days." His tone took on a subtle edge as he added, "You haven't responded to any of my texts or calls. And your mother? She's been shutting me down every time I ask about you. It's like you've dropped off the face of the earth."

"I'm not that hard to reach, Sebastian," I shot back, feeling a surge of defiance rise within me. "I just didn't want to be reached *by you*."

He looked momentarily taken aback, then recovered quickly, a small, almost pained smile tugging at the corner of his mouth. "I miss you, V," he said, softer now. "I thought after I made that large donation to your gallery, maybe you'd reach out. But when I heard nothing, I had to come here."

"So you just thought you'd show up out of nowhere?" I asked, incredulous. "And what, Sebastian? What's your plan?"

He hesitated and, for a moment, the confident facade slipped, revealing a flicker of uncertainty. "I don't know, V!" he admitted, his voice rising slightly. "But everything that happened between us—the way we broke up—it's bullshit. We owe it to ourselves to at least talk this out when emotions aren't running high."

I stared at him, my mind swirling with a storm of conflicting emotions. The man in front of me was both familiar and a stranger, and I couldn't forget the last texts he had sent me—drunken, raw messages filled with emotions that were hard to untangle. Anger, regret, desperation. They had been a window into his heart, one that I had slammed shut when I blocked his number, but the echoes of those words still lingered.

Part of me wanted nothing more than to walk away. To leave Sebastian, and everything he represented, in the past where it belonged. But another part of me, the part that remembered the good times, the laughter, and the love we once shared, hesitated. Despite everything, I knew Sebastian had loved me, in his own twisted, possessive way. And the thought of hurting him more than I already had gnawed at me, tugging at the guilt I had buried deep within.

But that didn't change the fact that I was terrified of letting him back into my life, even for a conversation. I had built something beautiful here, something that felt safe and real. And the idea of letting Sebastian's presence—his *chaos*—disrupt that, made me feel like I was standing on the edge of a precipice, with the ground crumbling beneath me.

"And what, Sebastian? You think talking it out is going to change anything?" I asked, my voice hardening. "What's done is done."

His jaw clenched and, for a brief moment, I saw the Sebastian I remembered. The one who couldn't stand not being in control. "Maybe it won't change anything," he said, his voice low and intense. "But we can't just pretend that everything between us is gone. *I* can't."

A silence fell between us, heavy with unspoken words and unresolved tension, and I glanced at the gallery door, wishing I could disappear inside.

"I'm happy here, Sebastian," I said finally, my voice firm. "I've moved on. You should, too."

His expression shifted, a flash of desperation breaking through his usual controlled demeanor as his eyes searched mine, pleading for something I wasn't sure I could give. "Vinnie, please," he said, his voice rough with emotion. "I just need to see you—*talk* to you—before I leave. We don't have to end things like this."

He reached into his pocket and pulled out a card, holding it out to me. My eyes flicked to it, relief flooding me when I saw the address in Brookside. It was a small comfort, knowing he wasn't staying right here, in the place I had claimed as my own sanctuary. But the fact that he was still so close sent a shiver of unease through me.

I hesitated before taking the card, my fingers brushing against his. I wasn't sure why I accepted it—maybe to appease him, maybe because I didn't want to argue anymore, or maybe because a part of me was too tired to resist. I just wanted this confrontation to be over.

As I slipped the card into my pocket, Sebastian's gaze shifted over my shoulder, and before I could react, he stepped forward and pulled me into a hug. The suddenness of it made me freeze, his arms wrapping around me in a way that felt all too familiar, yet completely unwelcome. His body dwarfed mine, his scent overwhelming my senses.

My first instinct was to pull away, but something—maybe shock, maybe old habits—made me hesitate. His breath was warm against my ear as he leaned in, his voice a low, intimate whisper. "You've built something beautiful here, and I respect that. But I can't stand the thought of you with someone else. We belong together, Vinnie. I know you still feel it, too."

The words sent a jolt through me, the intensity in his tone making it clear he wasn't just talking about the past. A chill ran down my spine as his lips brushed the shell of my ear, a move that once would have made me melt, but now only made me stiffen with unease. The chemistry between us, the magnetic pull that had once been so strong, now felt like a dangerous current I had to fight against.

He stepped back, his hand lingering on my arm for a moment longer than necessary, a smile playing on his lips. It wasn't the warm, genuine smile I had fallen for years ago. It was something darker, more calculated. And then, with a wink that made my stomach twist, he turned and walked to his car, sliding into the driver's seat with an ease that belied the tension in the air.

I was rooted to the spot as I watched him drive away, a swirl of emotions churning inside me. Relief that the encounter was over, anger at his audacity, and a gnawing sense of dread that I couldn't quite shake. As much as I wanted to believe that I had put Sebastian behind me, his presence—his words—had reopened a wound I thought had healed.

With a heavy sigh, I turned to head back into the gallery, needing the familiarity of the space to ground me. But as soon as I took a step, I froze.

Ethan.

Ethan was standing just a few feet away, his expression unreadable, his body tense. My heart dropped, dread pooling in my stomach. How long had he been there? How much had he seen or heard?

His eyes met mine, and the hurt in them was unmistakable. The easy warmth that usually colored his gaze was gone, replaced by something far more unsettling, and I swallowed hard, the taste of panic rising in my throat. I could almost see the wheels turning in his mind, the questions forming, the doubt seeping in. Sebastian had seen him, and had taken full advantage of the moment to create exactly the kind of distance he'd wanted between us. And, judging by the look on Ethan's face, it had worked.

"Ethan . . ." I started, but my voice cracked, the words faltering on my tongue. What could I even say to make this right? To explain what had just happened without making it sound like I was still tangled up in something I desperately wanted to leave behind?

Ethan just looked at me, with those eyes that had once made me feel so safe, but were now filled with uncertainty. His jaw was clenched, and I could see the internal struggle written all over his face. He was trying to keep it together, to not let the doubt that Sebastian had sown take root, but I could tell it was taking everything he had.

"How long have you been standing there?" I managed to ask, my voice barely above a whisper. The silence between us was suffocating, thick with tension and unspoken fears.

"Long enough," he replied, his voice low and strained. There was a tightness to his tone that I hadn't heard before, and it made my heart ache.

I winced, guilt gnawing at me. "Ethan, whatever you saw, it wasn't what you think," I rushed to explain, taking a step closer to him, but he didn't move. "Sebastian . . . he's just trying to get under your skin. He knows how much you mean to me, and he's doing everything he can to ruin that."

Ethan looked away, his gaze shifting to the ground as he ran a hand through his hair in frustration. "And it's working, Vinnie. Damn it, it's working."

The raw honesty in his voice cut through me like a knife. This was exactly what I had feared—that Sebastian would find a way to wedge himself between us, to poison the trust and the connection that Ethan and I had built together. And here we were, with that wedge firmly in place.

I reached out, my hand hovering just inches from his arm, desperate to bridge the gap that was growing between us. The thought of having this conversation out in the open, where anyone could walk by and see us, made my stomach twist with anxiety. I needed to get him inside, to make sure he wouldn't just turn around and leave.

"Ethan," I said softly, my voice trembling slightly, "can we go inside the gallery? I don't want to do this out here."

He hesitated, his eyes searching mine as if he was trying to decide whether to stay or walk away. For a moment, I feared that he might choose the latter, that he might let Sebastian's shadow linger between us. But, after a long pause, he nodded, and I led him into the gallery, closing the door behind us.

The familiar scent of paint and wood filled the air, the dim lighting casting long shadows across the room. It felt safer here, more intimate, but also more vulnerable, and when I turned to face him, the distance between us was like a chasm.

"Ethan, please," I began, my voice carrying the weight of the emotions I'd been holding back. "You know how much I care about you. Sebastian . . . he's just a part of my past, a past that I left behind. *You're* my present. *You're* the one I want to be with."

He let out a shaky breath, finally meeting my gaze again, and his eyes were filled with so much emotion—hurt, confusion, and something else I couldn't quite place. "I want to believe that, Vinnie. I really do. But seeing him with you, hearing the way he talked to you . . ."

"Don't doubt us," I pleaded, my voice breaking. "Please, don't let him get between us! What we have, it's *real*, Ethan. It's the *only* thing that feels real to me!"

His eyes softened at my words, and I could see the struggle playing out in his mind. There was so much unsaid between us, so many fears that neither of us had fully voiced, and I could sense the weight of his insecurities, the doubt creeping in despite the love that had been growing between us.

As we stood in the quiet of the gallery, I wanted him to understand how much he meant to me, how desperately I wanted to make this work. But instead of easing his mind, my words seemed to stir something darker within him. He looked down, his brow furrowing as if he was trying to piece together his own thoughts.

"Do you . . . do you still love him, Vinnie?" His question hung in the air between us, thick with vulnerability. He didn't look at me when he asked it, his voice barely more than a whisper.

The question caught me off guard and, for a split second, I hesitated. Not because I still loved Sebastian, but because I was trying to find the right words to say that would make Ethan believe that. But that hesitation, that tiny moment of silence, was all it took for his doubt to harden into something more.

His gaze lifted to meet mine, and the pain in his eyes was unmistakable. "I feel like I'm losing you before I even really had a chance," he said, his voice cracking with emotion. "When I saw him out there, I knew this would happen. I can't compete with Sebastian. He's got the charm, the history with you . . . everything. And here I am, just the guy who stepped in when he messed up."

"Ethan, no—" I started, but he cut me off, the words spilling out of him in a rush, as if he'd been holding them back for too long.

"I saw the way he looked at you, Vinnie," he continued, his voice trembling with frustration and fear. "And I saw the way you reacted when he hugged you. It's clear that there's still something there. I just . . . I adore you, Vinnie, and I've put everything I have into us. But I can't keep hoping to be enough for you if your heart isn't fully here with me. If it still belongs to Sebastian."

The raw honesty of his words cut deep. He wasn't just lashing out. He was genuinely afraid, and that fear was pushing him to the brink. I opened my mouth to speak, to reassure him, but nothing came out. The truth was, I had no idea how to untangle the mess of emotions that Sebastian had stirred up by showing up here. I wanted to tell Ethan that he was the one I wanted, the one who mattered most, but the heaviness in the room made it feel like anything I said would fall flat.

Ethan mistook my silence for confirmation of his worst fears. His shoulders slumped, the fight seeming to drain out of him. "Vinnie," he said, his voice soft and trembling, "I love you. And I've never said that to anyone before, but I mean it with everything I am. You've become such an important part of my life, and I need you to know how much you mean to me. But please, don't say it back unless you're absolutely sure. I need to know that, when you say it, you're all in, with no doubts and no hesitations."

My heart broke at the raw vulnerability in his voice, and I wanted so desperately to tell him I loved him, too. But the moment felt wrong, tainted by the tension between us, and the ghost of Sebastian still lingering in the air. If I said it now, I knew he wouldn't believe I truly meant it. The words would feel hollow, a desperate attempt to soothe the pain rather than a genuine confession.

"I can't," I whispered, my voice cracking under the weight of the emotion. "Not like this, Ethan. Not when everything feels so . . . complicated."

His expression faltered, and the hope drained from his eyes as he nodded slowly, his face a mixture of heartbreak and resignation. "I just want you to be happy, Vinnie," he murmured, leaning in to press a soft kiss to my forehead. "No matter what. Do what you feel is right."

Before I could say anything more, Ethan turned and walked out of the gallery, leaving me standing there alone, the echoes of his confession hanging heavy in the air, and I watched him go, my heart splintering at the sight of the pain in his eyes. The realization that I was losing him—maybe even pushing him away—was a sharp, aching pain that I hadn't been prepared for. I wanted to chase after him, to tell him that I was ready to love him with everything I had. But instead, I stood there, frozen, as the weight of the situation bore down on me.

Chapter 26

I CURLED UP ON THE COUCH, wrapped in a thick blanket, the soft crackling of the fire the only sound in the room. The warmth from the flames should've been comforting, but it barely touched the cold knot in my chest. I had cancelled my lunch with Amelia and Ivy, unable to face their concerned questions, unable to put into words the tangled mess of emotions I was still trying to sort through. Even my mom's text, which would normally have made my day, couldn't lighten the heartache that weighed me down.

> **Mom:** Lavinia, I saw the fundraiser online. Despite your father's disapproval, I want you to know I'm proud of you. You're following your heart, and that takes courage. Love, Mom.

The words had been enough to bring tears to my eyes, not just because they were so unexpected, but because they made me realize how far I'd come on my own. Yet, they also reminded me of how much I still had to figure out.

Where exactly had Ethan's insecurity come from? Was it really just about Sebastian? Or was there something deeper, something from his past that he hadn't shared with me? The thought nagged at me, making me feel even more adrift, and I couldn't shake the feeling that there was more to his reaction. That something had triggered this deep-seated fear in him. But without knowing what it was, I felt powerless to fix it.

My thoughts drifted back to that first sleepover at Ivy's, when we'd performed that silly ritual to let go of Sebastian. I'd been so sure that I'd put him behind me that night, that I was finally free of his shadow. But now, with everything that had happened, I was beginning to doubt that I'd ever truly let him go.

A sudden gust of wind rattled the windows, making me jump. The weather had taken a turn, with dark clouds gathering outside, thick and ominous. A storm was coming, the kind that seemed to roll in out of nowhere, and I watched as the first flash of lightning lit up the sky, followed by the low rumble of thunder that reverberated through the cottage. The air felt heavy, charged with an almost tangible energy and, for a moment, I could have sworn the flames in the fireplace flickered higher, as if reacting to the storm outside.

I pulled the blanket tighter around me, unease creeping into my bones. Hallow's End had always felt different, but tonight, it felt almost *alive* with something I couldn't quite name. The legends about the ley lines, and the strange energy they amplified, echoed in my mind. The storm seemed to be feeding off that energy, making the air in the room feel thick, almost oppressive.

Another flash of lightning illuminated the room and, in that brief instant, I thought I saw something—a shadow that didn't belong—flickering in the corner of my eye. My heart skipped a beat, and I quickly turned to look, but there was nothing there. Just the fire, burning steadily, and the wind howling outside.

I shook my head, trying to dismiss the unease that was gnawing at me. But the storm, the shadows, the strange feeling in the air—it was all too much, too coincidental. I couldn't shake the sense that something was pushing me, urging me to take action, to rid myself of the past that still haunted me.

The fire crackled again, louder this time, sending a shower of sparks up the chimney. It was as if the flames were trying to tell me something. I could almost hear the whispers in the air, soft and insistent, urging me to do something—*anything*—to sever the lingering thread with Sebastian.

The storm outside raged on, the wind whipping against the windows as the rain began to pour down in sheets, and the atmosphere in the room shifted, the air growing colder despite the fire's warmth.

Without fully understanding why, I found myself getting up, my movements almost automatic, the small box tucked away in the back of my closet calling to me. My heart pounded as I retrieved it. Inside was the photograph of Sebastian and me from years ago, the memento I hadn't been able to throw away.

I pulled out the photo as the storm outside grew fiercer and the wind howled louder. The temperature in the room seemed to drop; a cold draft brushing against my skin. With trembling hands, I flipped the photo over and grabbed a pen, scrawling on the back: I WANT TO MOVE ON AND LEAVE SEBASTIAN BEHIND. ONCE AND FOR ALL. The words felt heavy, as though they carried more than just ink on paper.

Returning to the living room, I knelt by the fire, the flames now eerily still, as if they were waiting. I hesitated for a moment before tossing the photo into the hearth, watching as the flames consumed it almost instantly, crackling louder, the fire flaring up as if in triumph.

But then, the flames turned a deep shade of blue, and the fire crackled in an unnatural rhythm. Twisting and swirling, the shadows in the room created strange shapes that danced in the air as the smoke from the burning photo spiralled upward.

I watched in wide-eyed disbelief as the flames grew higher and the photo's ashes rose from the hearth, swirling in the air before disappearing up the chimney, carried away by the storm.

For a moment, everything was eerily still. Then, without warning, the fire that had been crackling moments before suddenly extinguished, as if smothered by an unseen hand, the lights in the entire house flickered out simultaneously, leaving me in utter darkness, except for occasional bursts of lightning that cast quick, fleeting shadows on the walls.

The hairs on the back of my neck stood on end, and I felt a deep sense of foreboding settle over me. Just as I was about to step away from the hearth, a loud, insistent knock echoed through the cottage, cutting through the thick silence like a knife, and sending a jolt of fear through me. My breath caught in my throat as I turned toward the door, dread coiling in the pit of my stomach. The knock came again, more forceful this time, shaking the door on its hinges.

I hesitated, every instinct screaming at me to stay away, to ignore the pounding on the door. But the knocks grew louder, more insistent, as if whoever—or *whatever*—was outside knew I was alone and vulnerable. My breath hitched as fear twisted in my gut, the sensation cold and heavy like a stone.

I glanced around the room, my eyes landing on the heavy iron poker by the fireplace. With trembling hands, I grabbed it, the cold metal grounding me as I held it close to my chest. The weight of it was reassuring, but not enough to quell the rising panic.

Taking a deep breath to steady myself, I slowly approached the door, the poker gripped tightly in my hand. My heart pounded in my ears, each beat echoing louder than the last as I neared the threshold. Every step felt like a journey into the unknown, the darkened room behind me offering no comfort, only the creeping sensation that I was walking straight into danger.

The knocking came again, hard and furious, rattling the door on its hinges as if whatever was on the other side was desperate to get in. I paused, my hand hovering inches from the doorknob, the icy metal sending a shiver through me even without contact.

I shook my head, chastising myself for letting my imagination run amok. *Get a grip, Vinnie*, I thought. It was just a storm. A particularly fierce one, and perhaps the darkness was amplifying my paranoia. The power outage, the extinguished fire, the eerie atmosphere—it was all just a series of unfortunate coincidences. Nothing more.

Surely, the knock at the door was just a neighbor seeking shelter from the storm, or maybe someone needing assistance. The logical explanations were plentiful, and I needed to focus on those rather than succumbing to irrational fears.

With a final deep breath, I turned my attention back to the door and forced myself to reach for the knob, my hand shaking as I wrapped my fingers around it. With a final, shaky breath, I turned the knob.

Chapter 27

A S THE DOOR SWUNG OPEN, I was struck by the sight before me, my breath catching in my throat. Sebastian stood there, a figure pulled straight from the depths of a storm, his once-pristine clothes now drenched and clinging to his sculpted body, outlining every hard line of muscle beneath the soaked fabric. His dark blonde hair, usually impeccably styled, was plastered to his forehead, rainwater dripping down in slow, deliberate streams that traced the sharp angles of his face. His chiselled jaw was clenched, the droplets pooling at his chin before cascading down his neck, where they disappeared beneath the collar of his shirt.

The storm behind him was relentless, forming a ferocious backdrop to his unexpected appearance. Lightning streaked across the sky, its blinding flash briefly illuminating the scene, casting Sebastian in a stark, almost otherworldly light, and the thunder that followed rumbled deep and low, as if the very heavens were protesting his arrival. Shadows danced across his face, highlighting the intense expression that darkened his features—something between determination and desperation.

His chest rose and fell with each breath, the soaked fabric of his shirt clinging to him, nearly translucent from the rain. Those emerald eyes, vivid and striking even in the dim light, locked onto mine with a gaze that seemed to hold the storm itself within them.

"Vinnie," he said, his voice low and almost drowned out by the howling wind. There was something unsettling in the way he looked at me.

Shock and confusion battled within me. "Sebastian?" I finally managed to ask, the words coming out as more of a breathless whisper. "What are you doing here? How did you even find me?"

He shrugged, his expression somewhere between a smirk and something more serious. "It wasn't hard. Everyone's so friendly in this town. Like we're all old friends. They're more than willing to give away information, especially when they think they're helping someone."

I didn't know what to say to that, my mind racing to process his sudden appearance. I remained rooted to the spot, still standing in the doorway, blocking his entrance as the rain continued to pour down.

"What do you want, Sebastian?" I asked, my voice stronger now, but my hand still gripping the door, not letting him in. I glanced around awkwardly, trying to gather my thoughts, but everything felt off-kilter with him standing there, soaking wet and out of place in this small town.

He sighed, the tension in his shoulders easing slightly. The vulnerability in his eyes was stark, and a sharp contrast to the confident, composed man I once knew. "Vinnie, I just wanted to talk," he said, his voice rough around the edges, like he was holding back more than he was willing to let on.

He stepped closer, "I was at the hotel, sitting there in that empty room, and I couldn't stop thinking about you. About us. After today . . . after seeing you again, hearing your voice—it stirred up everything I thought

I'd buried. I know I don't have the right to just show up like this, but I couldn't sit there with all these thoughts running through my head. I had to see you. I had to try to make sense of it all."

His gaze dropped to the ground for a moment, a flash of uncertainty crossing his features. When he looked back up, those emerald eyes were filled with a desperate, almost pleading intensity. "I keep replaying everything in my mind—the way things ended, how it all went so wrong. And being here, in this town, knowing you've built this whole new life without me . . . I can't help but feel like I need to at least *try* to make things right. Even if it's just for a moment, I need to know if there's any part of you that still feels what I feel."

Another flash of lightning illuminated the sky, casting his face in a harsh light that made the raw emotion in his expression even more pronounced. "I know you've moved on, and maybe I'm a fool for thinking we can talk this out, but I couldn't just leave it like this. Not without trying."

Another flash of lightning split the sky, followed by a thunderclap so loud it made me jump. Sebastian flinched, too, and when his eyes met mine, he looked almost desperate. "Can I come in? Just for a bit?"

I stood there, torn between the urge to protect myself, and the nagging sense of responsibility that came from years of knowing him. Every instinct screamed at me to keep the door shut, to send him back out into the storm where he belonged—far from me, far from the life I was trying so hard to build without him.

I glanced past him into the darkness, half expecting to see his car, but there was nothing—just the pitch-black night and the unforgiving weather. He'd have to wait for a taxi, probably for a long time in this downpour, and the thought of him standing out there, soaked to the bone, gnawed at my conscience.

My grip on the door tightened and, for a moment, I truly considered sending him away. But as much as I wanted to, I couldn't bring myself to do it. Not with the way he looked at me, like he was searching for some kind of redemption, some chance to make things right. Despite everything, there was still a flicker of compassion in me. A whisper that reminded me of the good times, the history we shared, and the fact that, once upon a time, I'd loved this man.

Reluctantly, I took a step back, my heart heavy with the decision I was making. The door creaked as I opened it wider, the warmth from the house spilling out into the cold night. "Come in," I said softly, the words tasting bitter on my tongue.

As he crossed the threshold, I caught the unmistakable scent of alcohol on him, the sharp, bitter smell mingling with the rain and my heart sank, a heavy weight settling in my chest. I knew then that I was going to regret this—letting him in, letting him close again, even if just for a moment.

He glanced around the room, taking in the space that had become my sanctuary, his presence a stark contrast to the warmth I usually felt here. "It's nice," he said. "Very . . . you."

I closed the door behind him, my grip tightening on the doorknob as I fought the urge to tell him to leave, to undo this mistake before it could escalate. But the storm outside roared on, and here I was, caught between the echoes of a past I thought I'd left behind, and the fragile reality of my present. The line between then and now blurred, leaving me standing in the middle, uncertain of which way to turn, uncertain of what came next.

I forced a smile as I gestured toward the hallway. "The bathroom's just down there," I said, trying to keep my tone neutral. "I don't have any dry clothes for you, but I can dig up your old shirt and maybe some gym shorts. They're probably still around somewhere."

As soon as the words left my mouth, I winced. I hadn't thought it through—mentioning that I still had some of his clothes lying around. It could be taken the wrong way, like I'd been holding on to them for sentimental reasons, which couldn't be further from the truth. I just hadn't bothered to toss them out yet.

Sebastian turned back to me, a small, knowing smile playing on his lips. "Thanks, V," he said, his voice warm, almost teasing. The way he looked at me sent a shiver down my spine, but not in the way it once might have. I nodded stiffly, turning away before he could see the conflict in my eyes.

With the power still out, the cottage was plunged into near darkness, save for the occasional flash of lightning that illuminated the room in sharp, fleeting bursts. I flicked on my phone's torch, the narrow beam of light cutting through the gloom. The fire was still out, and a chill was starting to seep into the room, so I made a mental note to get it going as soon as possible, maybe light a few candles to bring some warmth and comfort back into the space.

But first, I needed to find something for Sebastian to wear. I made my way to the bedroom, the torchlight casting long, eerie shadows on the walls, and busied myself rummaging through the back of my closet. I found his old dress shirt, shoved behind a stack of forgotten clothes, now more of a paint-splattered relic than anything worth keeping, and the gym shorts were stuffed even further back, still soft from countless washes, but now devoid of any meaning.

Clutching the clothes, I approached the bathroom door, expecting him to crack it open just enough to take them. But instead, when I knocked lightly and called out, "I've got your clothes," the door swung open wide.

Sebastian stood there, completely unabashed, his body on full display. The hours he spent in the gym were evident in his sculpted abs, with each muscle defined and glistening under the bathroom light. His chest was broad and firm, tapering down to a lean waist that showcased the perfect V of his hips. As he reached for the clothes, his biceps, thick and powerful, flexed slightly.

Every inch of him was chiselled and perfect, like a sculpture crafted with the utmost precision. His skin, slightly tanned, glistened with droplets of water that trailed down his body, accentuating the contours of his muscles.

But, as I took in the sight of him, there was no reaction within me as there once was. No stirring of desire or longing. Where once the sight of his body might have left me breathless, now, it left me cold. It was as though I was looking at a stranger. Someone that once made my heart race now instead filled me with a hollow emptiness.

There was no spark. No heat. Just a profound realization that the connection we once had was truly gone. Sebastian's perfect exterior meant nothing to me now. It was just a hollow shell that no longer had any hold on me.

His emerald eyes glinted with something that bordered on mischief, and I realized too late that he was testing me, pushing boundaries like he always did. "Thanks for this," he said, his voice dropping into that familiar, seductive tone he'd used so many times before. He stepped closer, his hand brushing against mine as he reached for the clothes. "You know, we could—"

"Don't," I cut him off, the word coming out sharper than I intended. I dropped the clothes into his outstretched hand and slammed the door shut before he could say anything else. My heart pounded, not with desire, but with frustration—at him, at myself, at the whole situation.

I stormed back into the living room, my footsteps echoing in the quiet space. I couldn't believe I had let this happen, that I had allowed Sebastian to unsettle the peace I had fought so hard to achieve.

Determined to regain control, I knelt down in front of the hearth and began to rebuild the fire. My hands shook slightly as I placed fresh logs on the embers, but my resolve was stronger. As I reached for a match, something caught my eye—a small piece of paper, half-buried in the ashes. It was charred around the edges, but the words were still visible, standing out in bold letters: MOVE ON.

I froze, staring at the words. It was a fragment of the picture I had burned earlier. The one I thought had been completely consumed by the flames. The message was so simple, so clear, yet it felt like a revelation. If Ivy were here, she'd be making some grand speech about the magic of Hallow's End, about how the town had a way of guiding people toward the paths they were meant to take. For a moment, I just sat there, the words echoing in my mind.

MOVE ON.

A small laugh escaped my lips, but the amusement quickly gave way to a feeling of acceptance. Maybe there was some truth to the legend of this town. Maybe it *really did* have its own kind of magic. Or maybe it was just a coincidence. Either way, it didn't matter.

With a steady hand, I struck the match, and watched as the flames took hold, licking at the edges of the paper, letting the fire consume it until nothing was left but ash. The fire roared to life, casting a warm, comforting glow across the room and, for the first time that night, I felt a sense of clarity. I was ready to let go of the lingering doubts, and the fears that had been holding me back. It was time to move on.

As the fire crackled and roared to life, I felt a newfound determination settle over me. The warmth from the flames chased away the cold that had seeped into my bones. I was in control. The past belonged in the ashes, and that's where I intended to leave it.

Chapter 28

J UST AS I WAS BEGINNING to feel more centered, the bathroom
door creaked open, and Sebastian emerged, now dressed in the clothes
I'd given him. The shirt was tight across his broad chest, the sleeves pushed
up to his elbows, and his damp hair was tousled, giving him a rugged,
almost boyish look. The soft light from the fire cast sharp shadows on his
face, highlighting the intensity in his eyes.

"Thanks for the clothes," he said with a casual grin, but there was
something unsettling about the way he looked at me—something that set
off alarm bells in my head.

I stood my ground. "Sebastian, you need to leave. I'll call a taxi for you."

He ignored my words, taking a step closer, his grin widening as if he
hadn't heard me at all. "You know, V, seeing you tonight . . . it's brought
back so many memories. I couldn't stop thinking about you after today.
And being here, in this cozy little cottage with you . . ."

His voice was smooth, and dripping with the charm that used to draw me in so easily. He let his gaze trail over me, a predatory glint in his emerald eyes. "You look incredible, by the way. Even better than I remember." His tone darkened as he took another step closer, his eyes locking onto mine. "I've missed seeing you like this, V. The way you move, the way you look at me . . . it always drove me crazy. And I know it still does something to you, too."

The way his words wrapped around me, laced with that old, familiar temptation, made my skin crawl. He was leaning in now, his voice a low murmur. "Come on, V. You can't tell me you don't feel it—the tension between us, the way your body reacts when I'm this close. I've been dreaming about this. About you. And I can see in your eyes that you've been thinking about me, too."

I shifted uncomfortably, a wave of nausea rolling through me. I was suddenly grateful I hadn't changed out of my work clothes when I got home—thankful for the extra layers between us, the fabric a small barrier against the way his presence made my skin prickle. His gaze felt like it was burning through me, and the air around us grew heavy with an uncomfortable tension that I wanted nothing more than to escape from.

I crossed my arms over my chest, putting up a barrier between us. "You need to leave. Whatever you're trying to do here, it's not going to work."

He chuckled, the sound low and dismissive. "Come on, V. We were good together. You can't tell me you've forgotten that. And this . . . art gallery *thing*, it's nice, but you and I both know it's not going to sustain you. Not in the long run."

Sebastian's words hit me like a slap, stinging more than I expected, and my hands clenched into fists at my sides, the anger bubbling up inside me. "That's not true," I shot back, my voice rising with fury. "I've worked hard for everything I have here. This isn't just some *art gallery thing*, Sebastian.

It's my *dream*. And I don't need you—or anyone else—telling me what I can or can't do!"

As I watched him take that final step closer, his eyes darkened, brimming with a desperate, predatory intensity that made my skin prickle with unease.

"You need me, Vinnie," he said, his voice a low, insistent murmur that grated against my nerves. "You always have. This small-town life, this hobby of yours? It's not *you*. You're meant for something bigger, something more. And you know it."

His words should have stung, but instead, they only ignited a fiery resolve within me. I looked at him then, *really* looked at him, and saw the man who had once been the center of my world. A man who had always been so sure of himself, and so sure that I'd always be there, hanging onto his every word. But now, standing in the dim light of the cottage, with the storm raging outside, he seemed smaller somehow—diminished by the weight of his own arrogance.

"You really don't get it, do you?" I said, my voice steady and filled with a calm fury. "You never saw me for who I was. You were too busy trying to fit me into your perfect little life. This gallery, this town—it's *mine*. It's everything I've worked for, everything I've wanted. And it's enough for me, even if it isn't for you."

As his hand reached up to touch my face, I slapped it away, the sharp sound of the impact echoing through the room. The movement was instinctive, a reflex born from the anger and frustration that had been building inside me for far too long. Sebastian stared at me, eyes wide with surprise, as if he couldn't believe I'd actually dared to push him away.

I stood my ground, my gaze locked on his, refusing to back down. "You don't get to touch me, Sebastian. Not anymore."

For a brief moment, his expression flickered, revealing a crack in his carefully constructed mask of confidence. Then, with a swift and deliberate movement, he stepped forward, backing me against the wall, his presence and weight overwhelming. The space between us disappeared, and I the cold, hard surface of the wall pressed against my back as he leaned in, trapping me.

His smirk deepened, as if my resistance was nothing more than an amusing challenge to him. "You're making a mistake, Vinnie," he murmured, his voice dripping with disdain. "You really think this little fantasy you've built is going to last? Playing house in some backwater town with that small-time guy? He's not even in your league, V. You deserve better, and deep down, you know it."

He leaned in even closer, his presence suffocating. "What's he ever going to give you? A dull, predictable, *ordinary* life? You need excitement, and passion—someone who actually knows how to keep you on your toes. He's just a placeholder, Vinnie. He'll never be enough for someone like you."

My heart pounded with anger and disgust as his words sliced through me. The way he dismissed Ethan, the way he dismissed everything we'd built together, as if it were meaningless, made my skin crawl. Sebastian's arrogance was suffocating, and his belief that he was the only one who could offer me anything of value was infuriating.

I forced myself to stay calm, refusing to let him see how his words affected me. "You don't know anything about me, Sebastian. Not anymore. And you sure as hell don't know what I need."

He leaned in closer, his breath hot against my ear. "You need someone strong, someone who can take care of you. That guy? He's nothing. You can do so much better, V. You need someone like me."

His breath was hot and heavy against my ear and, before I could react, his hand slid up my arm, his fingers grazing the sensitive skin of my neck. The smell of whiskey on his breath made my stomach churn, and I recoiled in disgust.

"Knock it off, Sebastian," I snapped, pushing him away with more force than I realized I had. His smirk faltered, replaced by a flash of irritation as he steadied himself.

I was hit with a wave of nausea, not just from the alcohol on his breath, but from the realization of how far removed this man was from the person I had once loved. Was he always like this? Had I been blind to his true nature, too caught up in the love I thought we had to see him clearly? The rose-colored glasses I once wore had been shattered, leaving me to see him for what he really was—a man desperate to cling to control, even as it slipped through his fingers.

And now, as he stood before me, trying to twist my life back into his narrative, he tainted the good memories we had shared. All the moments that had once felt so significant, so full of meaning, were now tarnished by his arrogance, and his refusal to let go. He was erasing the man I had once loved, replacing him with this bitter, desperate version that I wanted nothing to do with.

"The only fantasy here, Sebastian, is you thinking that I need you. I don't. I never did. You were a chapter in my life, but I'm done with that story now. I'm writing a new one, and you're not in it."

His eyes darkened, the facade of control slipping just enough for a shadow of desperation to emerge. He leaned in, his breath hot against my skin, his voice dripping with a twisted mix of bitterness and longing. "You know, V," he murmured, "I've got women lining up, who are more than happy to take what you threw away. But none of them are you. Jessica?

Sure, she's eager, but she's not you. She doesn't know how to love me the way you did. How to make me feel like I was the only one that mattered."

The mention of Jessica made my stomach twist, and I remembered the picture I'd seen on Instagram not long after our breakup—her perched on Sebastian's lap, smiling like she'd won a prize. At the time, I'd convinced myself it didn't mean anything, that it was just another one of her games. But now, hearing him talk about her so casually, it all fell into place. They'd been a thing, even back then, and I couldn't help but wonder if he had sent me those desperate, drunken texts while she was right there with him.

The realization hit me like a punch to the gut. While he was pretending to be heartbroken, he was already moving on with someone who had always been circling, waiting for a chance to take what I had. And now, he was standing here, trying to manipulate me into believing that none of it mattered, that he still wanted me. Needed me.

"You're right," I said, my voice cold and unyielding. "Jessica isn't me. And she never will be. But maybe that's exactly what you deserve, Sebastian. Someone who doesn't know the real you, who can't see through your bullshit. Someone who's content with the scraps you throw her way. But that's not me. Not anymore."

Sebastian's expression hardened. The mention of Jessica had clearly been an afterthought, a slip that revealed more than he intended. The truth was, no matter how many women he surrounded himself with, he knew they would never measure up to what we had—and that was his real fear. That the only woman who truly saw him, who loved him despite his flaws, was the one who walked away.

"Shit, Vinnie, I didn't mean to say that. The whole thing with Jessica . . ." His voice dropped, almost as if he was trying to convince himself as much as me. "We're together, but not really. You know how it is. I'm with her, but it's not serious. It's nothing compared to what *we* had."

Bile rose in my throat at his casual dismissal of Jessica. At the way he tried to downplay it. Something inside me snapped, and I pushed against his chest, using his surprise to create distance between us.

Sebastian stumbled back, a flash of confusion crossing his face, and I seized the opportunity to step away from him, my heart pounding in my chest. The space between us felt like a lifeline. A necessary barrier that I desperately needed to keep intact.

I laughed, a bitter, humorless sound that echoed through the room. "So let me get this straight. You're with Jessica, but you're *here*, in *my* cottage, begging *me* for another chance? You're insane, Sebastian. Truly, you are."

He opened his mouth to respond, but I held up a hand to stop him, the anger and disbelief burning in my chest. "You can't stand the idea that I've moved on! That I'm happy without you! That's what this is really about, isn't it? It's not love, Sebastian. It's control. You're here because you can't handle the fact that I don't need you anymore."

His face twisted in frustration, the cracks in his carefully maintained facade growing deeper. "Vinnie, it's not like that. You don't understand—"

"No," I cut him off, my voice firm and unwavering. "I understand perfectly. You can't manipulate me anymore, Sebastian. You don't get to come here and disrupt my life just because you can't deal with your own insecurities. I'm done."

The words hung in the air between us, heavy with finality, and Sebastian stared at me, his jaw clenched, the reality of the situation finally sinking in.

He flinched, but quickly masked it with a sigh, his expression turning almost pleading. "It's not like that, V. I do love Jessica, but she's not you. I just need one night—one night with you for closure, so I can finally move on."

The sheer audacity of his request made my blood boil. "Closure?" I spat the word at him, my voice filled with disbelief. "You think sleeping with me will give you *closure*? You think I'm just going to let you back into my life, into my bed, because you need to feel better about your own choices?"

Sebastian's eyes flashed with anger and desperation as he stepped forward, closing the distance between us in an instant. Before I could react, his hands were on me, one gripping my arm while the other cupped my face. His touch was rough, fuelled by the alcohol, and his growing frustration, and he backed me against the wall with a force that sent a jolt of fear through me. The heat of his body pressed against mine, trapping me there as his thumb traced the line of my jaw, his words dripping with a twisted mix of longing and resentment.

"You ruined everything, Vinnie," he hissed, his voice thick with the effects of the whiskey on his breath. "We had a plan! A future! You were supposed to be with me, by my side, building a life together. But you threw it all away! You destroyed everything we were working toward, everything I had planned!"

As he spoke, he leaned in closer, his breath hot against my skin, the desperation in his eyes a stark contrast to the confidence he tried to project. His hand slid down to my waist, pulling me even tighter against him, his body pressing me into the wall. I felt sick, both from the smell of the alcohol, and the realization of just how far he was willing to go to reclaim what he thought was his.

"I had it all planned out, V. We were going to get married, start a family, build an empire together," he growled, his voice low and menacing. "You were supposed to help me take charge of your father's company, and we would've made it unstoppable. And then you just *walked away*. You think you can just erase everything we had, everything I had mapped out for us?"

Before I could respond, his lips were on my neck, kissing me with a roughness that sent a surge of panic through my veins. His hand tightened on my waist, holding me in place as if trying to rekindle a fire that had long since gone out. I felt trapped, suffocated by the weight of his body and the twisted passion behind his actions.

That was the final straw. I snapped. With all the strength I could muster, I shoved him hard and forced him to stumble back. "*Get out!*" I screamed, my voice trembling with anger and fear. "Get out of my house, Sebastian! We're done! Do you hear me? We're done!"

Sebastian was stunned, his expression full of shock and fury, but I didn't care. I was done playing his game.

"And don't you dare contact me again," I added, my voice firm and unyielding. "Don't come near me, don't try to talk to me, and don't even *think* about sending me another text or call. If you do, I'll get a restraining order. This is the last time you'll ever see me or talk to me, Sebastian. We're finished. And if you think you can keep haunting me, I'll make sure you regret it."

His face twisted into a snarl, but he didn't say anything. He simply turned and stormed out of the cottage, slamming the door behind him with a force that rattled the windows.

Breathing hard, my heart pounded as I tried to calm the storm of emotions inside me. The fire crackled in the background, a stark contrast to the silence that now filled the room. But even as I stood there, shaken and exhausted, I knew one thing for certain. This was the last time Sebastian would ever have power over me. The man who had once held so much sway in my life was finally out of it for good.

I turned back to the fire, letting its warmth slowly seep into my skin, and the adrenaline that had been coursing through me ebbed away, leaving behind a bone-deep exhaustion. Yet, there was also a profound sense of relief, of clarity—a feeling that I had finally closed a chapter that I had been rereading for far too long.

Just as that realization settled in, the lights in the house suddenly flickered back on, casting the room in a familiar glow. It was as if the universe itself was signalling the end of this tumultuous night, ushering in a sense of normalcy, and a return to the life I had built for myself—a life free from Sebastian.

I basked in the newfound light, before the need to cleanse myself of the evening's events overwhelmed me, and I headed to the bathroom, stripping off my clothes and stepping into the shower. As the hot water cascaded over me, I scrubbed at my skin, as if washing away the remnants of his touch, his words, and the emotional hold he had once had over me.

I hadn't realized how much I was still holding on to the past, allowing it to define who I was and how I saw myself. Tonight, with Sebastian's unexpected appearance, I understood that there were still parts of me that had been clinging to the hurt, the disappointment, and the unresolved tension of what we once had.

And now, as I rinsed away the soap and shampoo, I felt an unexpected sense of gratitude. Tonight had forced me to confront those lingering doubts and finally let go. The drama, the tension, even the raw emotions, were all part of the process, part of the closure I didn't know I'd still needed.

I wasn't that girl anymore. I was stronger now. The invisible string that had tied us together for so long was finally breaking, fraying bit by bit, until it dissolved completely, setting me free. And, as I stood in the shower, my eyes closed, and my heart open, the water washed away the last remnants of my old life, cleansing me of all traces of Sebastian.

Chapter 29

I TOSSED AND TURNED, my bed feeling too big, too empty. The clock on my nightstand blinked 12:00 A.M. The red numbers piercing through the darkness. It was officially Halloween, a night when the strange and unexpected could happen—if the legends about Hallow's End were true. But instead of feeling the thrill of the holiday, all I could think about was Ethan, and the way we'd left things unresolved, and the gnawing ache that came from the uncertainty hanging between us.

Frustration bubbled up inside me, mixing with regret. The image of Ethan's face before he walked out of the gallery kept replaying in my mind, his eyes clouded with hurt and insecurity that I hadn't been able to chase away. I could still see the doubt etched into his features, and the way he'd looked at me as if he was questioning everything we'd built together so far. And now, hours later, the memory of that look made my chest tighten painfully.

Why had I let him walk out? Why hadn't I said something, *done* something to stop him? I hated myself for standing there frozen as he left. It was stupid—so *incredibly stupid*—of me to just let him go like that. And now, all I wanted was to make it right. To tell him everything I should have said then. But the clock was ticking and, with each passing minute, it felt like the distance between us was growing into an insurmountable chasm that I couldn't bear to face.

I wanted to go to him. To knock on his door and pour out everything that was in my heart, but it was so late. He was probably asleep by now, and what if he didn't even *want* to see me after everything that had happened today? The thought of him turning me away made my stomach twist with anxiety. But, at the same time, the idea of waiting until morning was unbearable. I couldn't stand the thought of another sleepless night, tossing and turning, knowing that we'd left things in such a mess.

With a frustrated sigh, I tossed the covers aside. Sleep was a lost cause. My mind was tangled with thoughts, each one pulling me further away from any hope of rest. In a half-hearted attempt to distract myself, I reached for the remote and flicked on the TV, hoping that something—anything—might take my mind off the mess I was in.

The screen lit up, and the familiar strains of *Hocus Pocus* filled the room, the Sanderson sisters cackling as they plotted their mischief. I was pulled back to a simpler, happier time, just a few weeks ago, when Ethan, Lily, and I, had curled up in the fort to watch this very movie. I could still feel the warmth of that night. The way Lily's giggles had filled the room, and how Ethan's arm had draped over my shoulders, pulling me close. The memory sharpened the ache in my chest, and every scene of the movie felt like a cruel reminder of what could slip through my fingers if I didn't do something.

I couldn't just lie there, tormented by what-ifs and regrets and, before I even realized what I was doing, I threw back the covers and swung my legs over the side of the bed, my movements fuelled by determination and desperation. The cold floor bit into my feet, grounding me, and giving me the push I needed to act. I wasn't going to let this fester, to let the night stretch on with all these unresolved feelings tearing me apart.

I pulled on my shoes and shrugged into my coat, the weight of the decision settling over me like a heavy mantle. It was late—far too late to be showing up at someone's door—but I couldn't wait until morning. The idea of lying in bed, staring at the ceiling while the tension between us grew, was unbearable. I needed to see Ethan. To talk to him. To fix this before it spiralled beyond repair.

As I grabbed my keys and made my way to the door, the pull inside me grew stronger. It was more than just a need to talk; it was a force I couldn't resist, something that wouldn't let me rest until I saw him.

I reached for the doorknob and pulled the door open, my breath catching in my throat when I found Ethan standing there, his hand halfway raised as if he'd been about to knock. His eyes widened in surprise when he saw me, mirroring the shock I felt at finding him on my doorstep.

The cool night air carried the fresh, earthy scent that comes after a heavy rain, and the sky above was clear, the moon shining brightly, casting a soft glow. Ethan looked just as dishevelled as I felt. His brown hair was a tousled mess, even more unruly than usual, as if he'd been running his fingers through it repeatedly. He wore a pair of faded jeans and a dark jumper, the fabric slightly rumpled, like he'd thrown it on in a hurry.

It was clear he hadn't slept either. There were faint shadows under his eyes, a testament to the restless night we'd both endured, and the sight of him—vulnerable and unguarded—tugged at something deep inside me. It made my heart ache to know that he'd been just as consumed by this as I had. That he'd been up thinking about everything, just like me.

The absurdity of the moment hit me all at once, and I couldn't help the laugh that bubbled up inside me. It started as a small chuckle, but quickly grew into something uncontrollable. The kind of laughter that comes from sheer relief. Here we were, both too stubborn, yet too anxious to sleep, showing up at each other's doors in the middle of the night.

Ethan's lips curved into a tired smile, and soon he was laughing, too. For just a second, it was as if everything was okay again, as if the tension from earlier had dissolved into the night air. When the laughter finally subsided, I wiped a tear from the corner of my eye and smiled at him.

"I was just coming to see you," I admitted, shaking my head at how ridiculous it all seemed.

Ethan raised an eyebrow, his smile turning a little sheepish. "Guess I saved you the trip," he said, his voice warm despite the exhaustion that tinged it. But there was something in his eyes—a flicker of doubt, and vulnerability.

The air grew thicker with the unresolved tension creeping back in, and my smile faltered as I stepped aside, opening the door wider to let him in. Ethan walked past me, the warmth of his presence filling the small space and, as he entered, I caught the familiar scent of him. The faint aroma of soap, mixed with something earthy and distinctly *him*.

I closed the door behind him, the sound echoing in the silent house, and turned to face him. We stood there for a moment, looking at each other, the weight of our emotions hanging in the air between us. The pull that had brought me to the door was still there, stronger than ever, urging me to reach out, to close the distance.

"Vinnie," he began, his voice soft but heavy with the weight of everything he needed to say. "I shouldn't have just left like that."

I opened my mouth to respond, but he continued, his words rushing out as if he'd been holding them back for too long. "I was scared, okay. I've never felt this way about anyone before, and I let that fear get the best of me. I let it convince me that I wasn't enough, that maybe you were still tied to your past with Sebastian, and that maybe I was just a . . . placeholder."

His confession hit me hard, the vulnerability in his voice cracking something open inside me that I hadn't realized was still closed off. I took a small step closer, closing the distance between us, my heart pounding in my chest. My hand reached out instinctively, fingers trembling as they brushed against his arm, stopping him before he could say more. "Ethan, no. You don't need to say sorry," I said, my voice shaking with the weight of my emotions. "I'm the one who should be apologizing."

His eyes searched mine with an uncertainty that made my chest ache. It was the same doubt I had seen in him earlier, the one that had cut me so deeply when he'd walked out of the gallery.

"I'm sorry I didn't stop you when you walked out," I continued, my voice trembling as I forced myself to speak the truth. "I didn't know what to say. I was scared, and confused, and I let that fear hold me back. But I should have tried. I should have fought harder to make you understand how much you mean to me."

He remained silent, his gaze never leaving mine. It was as if he was holding his breath, waiting for me to say the one thing that would make everything okay again.

"Sebastian . . . he's not important to me," I said, my voice steadying as the words finally spilled out. "He's my past. A chapter that's closed, and one I never want to revisit. *You're* the one I care about. The one I want to be with. And I should have made that more clear."

His eyes softened at my words, emotions swirling within them as I stepped even closer, closing the distance between us until I could feel the warmth of his body, and the steady rhythm of his breath. My hand slid down his arm, finding his hand and intertwining our fingers.

Ethan's shoulders relaxed. "I should have been more understanding," he admitted, his voice laced with regret. "I shouldn't have asked if you still loved him. It doesn't matter if you did, because you're with me now. I just … I've always had this insecurity, this fear, that I'm not enough. The only girl I ever dated seriously in college ended up cheating on me with her ex, and I guess that's something I've never really let go of."

My heart ached for him, and for the pain he carried that I hadn't even known about until now. "I'm sorry, Ethan," I whispered.

He let out a shaky breath, his hand tightening around mine as if he was afraid to let go. "I want to be your future, Vinnie," he murmured, his voice rough with emotion. "But I need to know that you're all in. That you're not holding onto anything from your past. I need to know that I'm enough for you."

I could see the fear in his eyes. "Vinnie, I need to know you're okay with the life I can give you. I'm not Sebastian. I can't offer you the luxury he could, and I'm not leaving Hallow's End. This is my home. My family's here, and I need to know that you're here because you want this life, not just because you're trying to get away from something else."

His words hit me like a wave, the raw honesty of his fears breaking my heart all over again. I took a deep breath, wanting to find the right words to reassure him this time, to make him understand how much he meant to me.

"You're everything to me, Ethan," I whispered, my voice thick. "You make me feel alive, and like I can believe in love again. I don't want the life Sebastian could have given me—I want the life we're building. Together. I want this town, this home, and I want *you*. You are more than enough, Ethan. More than I could ever ask for. You're the only one I want, and the only one I need."

His gaze softened, the tension easing from his shoulders as my words sank in. "Are you sure, Vinnie?" he asked, his voice quieter now, almost afraid to believe it. "Are you sure this is the life you want? Here, with me?"

I nodded, my heart swelling with love for this man who had become the center of my world. "I'm sure, Ethan. I'm all in. This is where I want to be—with you, in Hallow's End. I don't need anything else. You are my home."

Ethan's eyes softened, searching mine as if trying to understand the depth of my words, and I could feel the weight of what I was about to say next, the words I'd been holding onto for so long, finally pushing to the surface.

"There's something I've wanted to tell you," I began, my voice trembling slightly. "I wanted it to be perfect, to say it at the right moment, but the truth is, I should have said it at the gallery. It felt wrong then, but now . . . it feels like it can't wait any longer."

Ethan's gaze never left mine, his eyes filled with anticipation and a hint of nervousness. "Vinnie, what are you trying to say?"

I took a deep breath, feeling my heart race as I prepared to let the words out. "I love you, Ethan. I love you. For the way you make me laugh. For the way you believe in my dreams. For the way you see me—*really* see me. You make me feel safe, and you make me feel like I'm enough, just as I am."

His expression softened, a flicker of hope in his eyes. "Do you really mean it?" he asked, his voice barely above a whisper.

I nodded, tears brimming in my eyes as I looked at him. "Yes, I mean it. I love you, Ethan. I've never been more sure of anything in my life."

His hand came up to cup my face gently, his thumb brushing away the tears that had started to spill down my cheeks. "I love you too, Vinnie," he said, his voice thick with emotion. "I've wanted to say it since that day at the lake, but I didn't want to scare you away. I thought it might be too soon, that you weren't ready, but I've loved you for a while now."

A tear slipped down my cheek. A tear of happiness, and relief, and the overwhelming feeling of finally being on the same page. Ethan tilted his head, his eyes locking onto mine with an intensity that made my breath catch as his lips brushed against mine.

The kiss started out tender and gentle, a soft connection that conveyed everything we had just confessed. But as it deepened, it grew more urgent, more hungry. It was as if all the emotions we had been holding back were pouring out as Ethan's hands slid into my hair, pulling me closer, while my arms wrapped around his neck, needing to be as close to him as possible.

When we finally broke apart, both of us were breathless, our foreheads resting together as we tried to steady ourselves. His hands cradled my face, his thumbs tracing my cheekbones as he gazed into my eyes with a look of pure adoration.

"We're going to be okay," he murmured, his voice carrying a quiet but unwavering determination. "I never want to lose you, Vinnie."

I nodded, the weight of his words settling in my heart, anchoring me in this moment. "We're going to be okay," I echoed softly, the words a promise to him. To us. "And I'm not going anywhere."

Chapter 30

THE CHILL IN THE LATE October air sent a shiver down my spine as I adjusted the wide-brimmed hat perched on my head and smoothed the front of my witch's dress, which clung to my curves before flaring out to just above my knees. The fabric shimmered under the streetlights, with the slits on either side revealing glimpses of my thigh-high stockings as I moved, and my lace-up boots clicked against the cobblestones. The streets of Hallow's End were alive with the vibrant energy of the Halloween festival—children darting between candy stands, couples in matching costumes, and groups of friends laughing as they meandered through the festivities.

The air was thick with the sweet scent of caramel apples and pumpkin spice, mingling with the sound of eerie music that played from hidden speakers, and every corner was decked out with cobwebs, jack-o'-lanterns, and flickering candles.

Beside me, Ivy and Amelia were adjusting their own costumes. Ivy's dress was a deep, velvety purple, cinched tight at the waist with a corset that accentuated her figure. The hemline was asymmetrical, revealing long, fishnet-clad legs that ended in knee-high boots. Amelia's outfit was a short black skirt paired with a lace-up bodice, her purple pixie cut adding a pop of color against the dark fabric.

We all had matching black cloaks that billowed dramatically as we walked, adding an extra layer of mystique to our witchy ensembles. The hoods were pulled up just enough to cast our faces in shadow, making us look like something out of an old storybook.

"We look like a twisted version of the Sanderson sisters," Ivy joked, flipping the edge of her cloak with a flourish. "Only hotter."

"So, we're officially a coven now?" Ivy asked, her blue eyes glinting

"If we're going to be witches, we might as well look the part," Amelia said with a grin, twirling her broomstick like a baton. "Besides, how else will we strike fear into the hearts of mortals?"

I laughed, the infectious energy of the night seeping into my bones. "Ready to face the undead?" I asked, nodding toward the entrance of the haunted house looming before us. The building had been transformed into a decaying ruin, complete with shattered windows, creeping vines, and the unsettling sound of groaning zombies coming from within.

"I was born ready," Amelia said, her voice full of bravado as she linked arms with Ivy and me. "But if I scream, just know it's all part of the act."

Ivy gave a mock-serious nod. "Of course, Amelia. We all know you never get scared."

Stepping toward the entrance, the three of us exchanged grins. With our matching costumes and confident strides, we felt invincible as we entered the haunted house, which was themed around a zombie apocalypse and had drawn quite the crowd.

The three of us moved through the haunted house in a chaotic mix of laughter and screams, dodging zombies and jumping at every eerie sound. Each room felt darker and more twisted than the last, but the thrill of being scared out of our minds only made us cling to each other more. Ivy shrieked every few minutes, Amelia's bravery wavered with every new surprise, and my heart pounded as adrenaline surged through us all. By the time we stumbled out of the final room, gasping for air and laughing uncontrollably, we felt both exhausted and exhilarated.

Emerging onto the street, we were met with the cool night air, the sounds of the haunted house still echoing faintly behind us.

"Okay, that was intense," I said, wiping a hand across my sweaty forehead.

Ivy grinned. "I can't remember the last time I screamed like that. It was kind of therapeutic." At that, we all laughed, and continued on our tour of the town's festivities.

As we strolled through the heart of the festival, I spotted Ethan moving through the crowd, with Lily fluttering around him like an excited little sprite. She wore a fairy princess costume, complete with glittering wings, a sparkling tiara, and a wand that trailed behind her in her whirlwind of energy. Her giggles were infectious, drawing smiles from everyone who passed by.

Ethan, however, looked like he'd been reluctantly drafted into a costume, and the result was both hilarious and endearing. He was clad in a wizard's robe that was clearly too long for him, and it nearly tripped him up with every step. The pointed hat on his head kept slipping down over his eyes, and he carried a crooked stick that looked like he had found it in the backyard.

"Nice costume, Gandalf," Amelia teased as we joined them.

Ethan gave her a mock glare, adjusting the hat for the umpteenth time. "I had no choice," he said with a resigned grin. "When a fairy princess demands you dress up, you don't really have much of a say."

Lily twirled around us, her wings catching the light. "Vinnie! Look at me!" she squealed, her eyes shining with excitement.

I crouched down to her level, taking in her outfit with an approving nod. The glitter on her wings sparkled under the festival lights. "You look absolutely magical, Lily. The prettiest fairy princess in all of Hallow's End."

She beamed, her cheeks flushed with happiness, and then she turned back to Ethan, tugging on his hand. "Can we go apple bobbing now? Please?"

Ethan glanced at me, his eyes softening as he searched my face for an answer. I smiled and nodded. "Let's go bob for some apples," he said. Before Lily tugged Ethan and me away, I turned to Ivy and Amelia. They were still giggling about Ethan's ridiculous costume, their faces flushed with amusement.

"Hey, you guys go on ahead," I said, giving them a quick smile. "I'll catch up with you later, okay?"

Ivy raised an eyebrow, a knowing smirk tugging at her lips. "Sure thing, Vin. We'll be over by the pumpkin-carving contest if you need us."

Amelia winked. "Don't have too much fun without us."

I laughed, waving them off as they disappeared into the crowd, leaving me to focus on the two most important people in my life.

Chapter31

T HE AIR WAS ALIVE with laughter and excitement as we made our way to the apple-bobbing station. Kids crowded around the large barrel, filled with water and floating apples, their faces lighting up with the soft glow of orange and purple lights strung overhead. The scent of caramel apples and cinnamon wafted through the air.

Lily's turn came up and, just as she was about to lean over the barrel, Ethan's parents appeared, their faces lighting up at the sight of us. Caroline was wearing a pumpkin-themed sweater that was delightfully over-the-top, her smile as warm as the autumn breeze. Robert, in his flannel shirt and wide-brimmed hat, looked every bit the picture of a small-town dad enjoying a night out with his family.

"Well, don't you all look fantastic!" Caroline exclaimed, her eyes sparkling as she took in our costumes. "Especially you, Ethan," she added with a laugh. "That wizard hat is definitely a keeper."

Ethan groaned, running a hand through his hair as the hat slipped down over his forehead again. "A few of my students have already spotted me. I won't be living this down anytime soon."

Caroline chuckled, pulling out her phone. "Well, you might as well give them something to remember. Smile for the camera, you two!"

Ethan sighed dramatically but couldn't hide the fond smile as he slipped his arm around my waist. "Mom, you don't need to take pictures of everything."

"Yes, I do," she insisted. "I need these pictures for memories and, one day, you'll be glad I took them."

We both laughed, knowing there was no arguing with Caroline when she was in picture-taking mode. As she snapped the photo, Ethan's grip on my waist tightened; a small but reassuring gesture that made me feel completely at home.

Lily leaned over the barrel, her small hands clasped tightly behind her back as she focused on catching an apple with her teeth. After a few determined attempts, she finally managed to grab one, lifting her head with a triumphant grin as she held it between her teeth. Her laughter rang out, pure and infectious, and we all clapped and cheered for her success.

"That's my girl!" Ethan said proudly, his voice full of warmth as he knelt down to help her dry off with a towel. Watching him with Lily, and seeing how deeply he cared for her, made me fall even more in love with him every day.

Caroline leaned in closer, her voice soft but filled with a playful warmth. "You know, I could tell how much you cared about Ethan from the very first time I saw you two together. The way you looked at him . . . it was like you were already in love."

I laughed softly, a hint of surprise coloring my tone. "I didn't even know I was in love with him then."

Caroline's smile deepened, her eyes twinkling with that maternal wisdom only years of life experience could bring. "Love has a funny way of sneaking up on us when we least expect it. Sometimes, our hearts know before our minds can catch up. But when it's real, it's undeniable."

I turned my gaze back to Ethan, a smile tugging at my lips as I watched him carefully adjust Lily's tiara. Something caught my eye in the crowd behind him, and my breath hitched as I noticed a woman standing a little apart from the throngs of people, her posture straight and composed, her clothes immaculate and out of place amid the casual, festive atmosphere.

My mother.

She looked almost like a mirage, standing there with her perfectly tailored coat and well-coiffed hair, her expression unreadable as she scanned the crowd. I stood frozen in place, unsure of what to do or say. My world felt like it had just tilted on its axis, the festival noise fading into the background as I tried to process the fact that my mother was here, in Hallow's End, at the Halloween festival.

"Mom?" I murmured, more to myself than anyone else.

My mother's gaze locked onto mine, and the look in her eyes was enough to tell me why she was here. I turned back to Ethan, who had noticed the shift in my demeanor. His brow furrowed in concern but, before he could say anything, I gave his hand a reassuring squeeze. "I need to take care of something," I said, offering a small, strained smile. "I'll be right back."

Ethan's eyes flicked from me to the woman standing in the distance. Understanding dawned on his face and he nodded, giving my hand one last squeeze before letting me go. "Take your time," he said softly.

I began to weave through the crowd, my heart pounding with anxiety and anticipation. As I approached my mother, I could see the tension in her posture, the way her hands clenched the strap of her purse. She was out of her element here, but she had come anyway.

When I finally reached her, we stood in silence, the distance between us feeling both vast and fragile. She gave me a hesitant smile. The kind that showed she wasn't entirely sure if she was welcome.

"Mom," I said. "What are you doing here?"

She looked around, taking in the sights and sounds of the festival. "I wanted to see you," she replied softly. "I'm sorry I didn't come sooner, to the gallery opening. I should have been there."

Her vulnerability took me by surprise. "It's okay," I said, though I wasn't sure if I entirely believed it.

"I've seen pictures of your gallery online, Vinnie. It's absolutely amazing—so full of life and character, just like you. Even from the photos, I can tell how much heart you've put into it. Your artwork . . . it's so beautiful and raw. I'd love to see it in person." My mother's gaze softened as she spoke.

Her words caught me off guard, filling me with a warmth I hadn't expected. The thought that she had taken the time to look at my work, to really see it, meant more than I could express. "Thank you," I managed, my voice thick with emotion. "That means a lot."

She sighed, glancing down at her hands before meeting my eyes again. "I've been thinking a lot lately. About the distance between us, and how much of it was because I wasn't there for you when you needed me most. I was so focused on trying to keep everything together—your father's work, my own duties—that I closed myself off. And in doing so, I shut you out, too."

Her honesty, and her willingness to admit where she had gone wrong, touched a deep part of me that had been waiting years to hear these words. "It hurt, Mom," I said, my voice trembling. "But hearing you say this now . . . it means everything to me."

She nodded, a tear slipping down her cheek. "I'm so sorry, Vinnie. I should have been more present, more supportive. I should have been there for you. And I regret every day that I wasn't."

A tear slipped down my own cheek as I listened to her words, the sincerity and regret in her voice touching a deep part of me. "But I'm here now," she continued, reaching out to take my hand. "And I want to be a part of your life, if you'll have me."

I squeezed her hand, a wave of relief and happiness washing over me. "Of course, I want you in my life, Mom. I've always wanted that."

She smiled. "I've always been so proud of you, even if I didn't show it. You've made a life for yourself here, something I didn't understand before. But now, seeing it, seeing *you* . . . I'm so proud of the woman you've become."

"I'm glad you're here," I said softly, my voice filled with emotion. "It means a lot to me."

We stood in silence again, the years of distance and misunderstanding slowly dissolving. I could see the pain in her eyes, the regret for the times she had been so blind to my desires. But more importantly, I saw love, and hope.

"What about Dad?" I asked cautiously.

She sighed, a hint of sadness in her eyes. "He's still coming to terms with it. He has a hard time letting go of his expectations, but I believe, in time, he'll come around. For now, it's important that we take this step, you and I."

I nodded. "I hope so. I want him to see that this is where I belong, that I'm happy here."

"We'll work on it together, Vinnie," my mother said, radiating genuine tenderness. "We'll mend what's been broken, and build the relationship we should have had years ago."

As we stood there, surrounded by the festive lights and laughter of the Halloween festival, I felt an overwhelming sense of peace. The bond between us was beginning to heal, and while the road ahead might be long, it felt like we were on the right path.

My mother stepped closer, hesitating for a moment before wrapping her arms around me. At first, the hug was stiff and awkward, as if we were both unsure how to navigate this unfamiliar territory. But then, as if by mutual agreement, we both relaxed into the embrace. The scent of her perfume—a blend of jasmine, vanilla, and sandalwood—enveloped me. It was the kind of fragrance that spoke of elegance and sophistication.

There was a warmth to her scent. It brought with it a sense of peace, a hope that maybe, just maybe, we could find our way back to each other.

When we parted, I noticed Ethan watching us from a distance, and I turned back to my mother, giving her hand one last squeeze before letting go. "Come on, I'll introduce you to Ethan," I said, my voice steady. "He's been a big part of my life here."

She nodded, a small smile playing on her lips. "I'd like that, Vinnie. I'd like to get to know the man who's made you so happy."

As we walked back toward the apple-bobbing station, my heart raced. Introducing my mother to Ethan felt like a significant moment, one that bridged two very different parts of my life.

"Ethan," I began, trying to keep my voice steady, "I'd like you to meet my mom, Victoria. Mom, this is Ethan."

He extended his hand with a warm smile. "It's nice to meet you, Mrs Carlisle."

My mother hesitated for just a moment before taking his hand, her smile polite but reserved. "Please, call me Victoria," she said, her tone friendly but still holding a touch of formality.

His smile widened, though I could sense a hint of nerves behind it. "I'm glad to finally meet you, Victoria. I'm really happy you could be here tonight."

The conversation paused, a bit of awkwardness settling between them as they both sized each other up. My mother's critical eye evaluated Ethan, but he stood tall, in his wizard cloak and hat.

Before the silence could stretch too long, Lily came bouncing over, her face glowing with excitement, holding up a glistening apple between her small hands. "Vinnie! Did you see me? I got the biggest apple!" she exclaimed, her voice full of pride. She twirled in place, her fairy wings fluttering in the crisp evening air as she showed off her prize.

Before I could respond, Lily's attention shifted, and her wide, curious eyes landed on my mother. With the innocent curiosity only a child could muster, she pointed at her and asked, "Are you Vinnie's mommy?" Lily's bright gaze moved between the two of us, as if trying to piece together this new connection as my mother offered Lily a warm smile.

"Yes, I am," she said gently. "And who might you be, little fairy?"

"I'm Lily! And Ethan is my brother," she announced proudly. "If Vinnie and Ethan get married, does that make you my grandma?" My mom blinked in surprise, taken aback by the question. Before she could respond, Caroline and Robert approached.

"Lily!" Caroline laughed softly, placing a hand on her shoulder. "Sweetheart, you don't just ask things like that."

Lily blinked, her brow furrowing slightly. "Oh . . . why not?" she asked, looking genuinely confused but not upset. After a brief pause, she shrugged it off. "Okay, never mind! Can we still get hot chocolate?"

"Of course we can," Caroline nodded.

Ethan smiled. "Mom, Dad, this is Vinnie's mom, Victoria."

Caroline stepped forward with her usual warmth. "Victoria, it's so nice to finally meet you." Robert nodded in agreement, his smile kind and welcoming

"Likewise," Victoria replied, her voice soft but sincere. "I'm glad to be here."

The conversation flowed easily, and it was a relief to see, especially after everything that had happened between us. They laughed together, sharing stories about the town and the festival.

"Your mom seems really nice," Ethan whispered, his voice full of encouragement.

I nodded, a warm glow spreading through my chest. "She is. And it means everything to me that she's here, trying to be a part of my life."

After a few minutes, Robert turned to Ethan smiling. "Why don't you two go enjoy the festival for a bit? We'll keep Victoria company and make sure she gets the full Hallow's End experience."

Mom nodded, smiling at me. "Go on, Vinnie. I'm here for a few days, so we'll have plenty of time to catch up. Enjoy yourselves."

I hesitated, but Ethan's hand in mine was all the encouragement I needed. "Thank you," I said, my voice filled with gratitude as I looked between them all. "I really appreciate it."

"Let's try some of the games," Ethan suggested, nodding toward the rows of brightly lit stalls lined up along the square.

I grinned, feeling a thrill of excitement. "Sure, but fair warning—I'm terrible at these."

We moved from game to game, with me missing almost every target—beanbags slipping past cans, rings falling short of the bottles, and darts flying wildly off course. Each time, Ethan hovered close behind me, his teasing touches and whispered encouragement making it impossible to concentrate. My aim was hopeless, and his playful distractions didn't help, though his laughter made it hard to stay frustrated. By the end, I threw up my hands in defeat. "I'm terrible at everything!" I groaned, half-laughing, half-pouting as I looked over at him.

He chuckled, his lips brushing against my skin as he whispered, "Maybe you just have to try a bit harder." His hands slid down to my waist, pulling me even closer. His breath on my neck was warm and tantalizing, and it took everything in me to keep from moaning out loud, aware of the crowd around us.

"Ethan," I whispered, my voice shaky as I tried to compose myself. But he was relentless, his kisses growing bolder, more insistent, making my knees weak. His hands slid around my waist, hidden beneath the flowing cloak I wore, and his fingers gripped me firmly, possessively, the pressure sending a jolt of heat through my body. The cloak shielded us from view, allowing his hands to roam more freely, gripping my hips, trailing up my sides, his touch electrifying even through the fabric.

Ethan's hands slid lower, his fingers trailing down my hips and around to grip my ass firmly. I could feel the heat of his hand through the thin fabric of my costume, the short hemline leaving little to the imagination as his hand slid even lower, teasing the edge of my thigh. His touch was bold, sending waves of electricity through my body, each movement making it harder to focus on anything but him.

"You're impossible," I murmured, trying to keep my voice steady despite the way he was making me feel. The crowd was just feet away, blissfully unaware of the fire he was stoking within me.

"And you love it," he whispered, his hand slipping up my thigh, fingers brushing the sensitive skin just beneath the hem of my costume. The thrill of it—the secrecy, the heat between us—made my heart race, my body arching into his touch as I struggled to keep my composure.

"Ethan," I whispered again, the word a soft plea.

His grip tightened, his fingers digging into my thigh, and he leaned in closer, his voice a low murmur in my ear. "I can't get enough of you, Vinnie. Not now, not ever."

His hand slowly slipped away, leaving me aching for more, the sudden loss of his touch making me bite back a frustrated groan as he stepped back, his lips curling into a mischievous grin.

"That's not fair," I muttered, crossing my arms in mock annoyance, though the flush in my cheeks betrayed how much his teasing affected me.

He laughed softly, the sound warm and full of promise. "I'll make it up to you later," he whispered.

As the night deepened, we drifted away from the crowd, finding a secluded clearing bathed in the soft glow of lanterns and twinkling fairy lights. The air was cool, and crisp with the scent of autumn leaves, and the stars above seemed to shimmer just a little brighter. It was as if the world had slowed down, allowing this moment to stretch out, perfect and unending.

Ethan pulled me into his arms, and we began to sway to the gentle rhythm of the music that drifted over from the festival. His hands settled on my hips, his touch firm yet tender, grounding me in the here and now. As I rested my head against his chest, the steady, comforting beat of his heart echoed through me, and a deep sense of contentment washed over me.

I caught sight of my mother laughing with Caroline and Robert in the square, their faces illuminated by the soft glow of the lights, their joy evident in every shared smile and easy laugh. It was a sight that filled me with warmth. A picture of acceptance, of families blending together, of love expanding and growing in ways I hadn't imagined. Everything felt right, like the final pieces of a puzzle falling into place.

"This is where I'm meant to be," I whispered, looking up at Ethan, my voice soft but filled with conviction.

Ethan's gaze met mine, his eyes reflecting the love and promise I felt in my heart. "This is just the beginning, Vinnie," he murmured, his lips brushing against my forehead in a tender kiss. "We have so much ahead of us, and I can't wait to see where life takes us."

As the night wore on, the stars continued to shimmer above us, and the music played softly in the background as I settled into the peace of my new reality. The ghosts of my past had finally been laid to rest, and the life I had built here, in Hallow's End, was more than I had ever dreamed of. Surrounded by love, laughter, and the promise of a bright future, I knew, without a doubt, that I had found my true home in Ethan's arms.

Epilogue

T HE COZY CANVAS WAS a haven of festive cheer as Christmas approached. Twinkling fairy lights adorned the gallery, casting a soft glow over the artwork and decorations. Garlands of holly and mistletoe hung from the rafters, and a beautifully decorated Christmas tree stood proudly in the corner, its branches heavy with ornaments.

I stood in the middle of the gallery, admiring the festive atmosphere in a cozy, oversized sweater and a Santa hat, my cheeks flushed from the cold outside. Ethan was by my side, his arm draped casually around my shoulders. Our relationship had grown even stronger over the past months, and the love between us was tangible.

The gallery buzzed with activity and laughter, the walls full with the colourful expressions of my students' work. Seeing them pour their hearts into their art, and watching their confidence grow with each brushstroke, brought me an indescribable happiness. The Cozy Canvas had become more than just a gallery—it was a sanctuary where people could express their emotions, and work through their experiences in a creative and healing way.

Ethan's support had been unwavering. He'd encouraged me, helped set up classes, and even took part in a few, much to everyone's delight. Together, we watched as the gallery transformed into a community hub, a place where dreams were nurtured and spirits lifted. With the generous donations from the gallery opening, I was able to fund art supplies, start a series of workshops, and even offer day classes for school trips.

"Everything looks amazing," Ethan said, his eyes shining with pride.

"Thank you," I replied, leaning into him.

As the evening progressed, friends and family gathered in the gallery, filling it with laughter and joy. Ivy and Amelia were there, effortlessly moving through the crowd and spreading their cheer, and my mom mingled easily with the guests, our bond growing stronger with each day.

However, the absence of my father was a lingering thought in my mind. He hadn't been able to come, as he still grappled with the changes in my life and our relationship. Yet, earlier in the day, he had called to wish me a Merry Christmas. It was a small step, but it filled me with hope. His voice had been softer than it usually was, and it gave me a glimmer of belief that he might eventually come around.

Ethan noticed the wistfulness in my eyes as I recounted the phone call to him. "It's a start," he said, squeezing my hand. "Maybe we could visit Cresden for New Year's, spend some time with both your parents? It might help bridge the gap."

I nodded, a smile touching my lips at the thought. "I'd like that. It's been too long since I've seen him, and maybe seeing us together, and happy, will make a difference."

Ethan pulled me into a comforting embrace. "We'll make it happen. Together."

The brisk night air cooled my flushed cheeks as we locked up the gallery, the excitement of the evening lingering between us. The walk to Ethan's place was short, but the anticipation stretched every step into a tantalizing journey. By the time we crossed the threshold of his house, my pulse was racing, my body humming with anticipation.

Ethan closed the door behind us, the room embracing us in its warm comfort. The scent of pine and cinnamon lingered in the air, and I could barely contain my excitement for what I had planned.

"Wait here," I whispered, casting him a playful smile before disappearing into the bedroom. His curiosity was piqued, and when I reemerged, the look on his face was worth every second of preparation.

I stood in the doorway, wearing a daring red lingerie set that left little to the imagination. The lace hugged my curves perfectly, the garter belt attached to sheer stockings, and a pair of delicate heels completed the ensemble. My hair cascaded in loose waves around my shoulders, and I relished in the way Ethan's breath caught, his eyes darkening with lust.

"Merry Christmas," I purred.

Ethan crossed the room in two strides, his gaze locked on me, every inch of his body radiating need. "You look . . . *incredible*," he murmured, his voice hot with desire, as if he could hardly believe what he was seeing.

I took a step closer, my fingers trailing down the front of his shirt, feeling the hard muscle beneath. "I'm your present," I whispered, my voice sultry. "Now it's time to unwrap me."

His hands shook slightly as he began to undress me, peeling away the delicate layers of lace with an almost reverent touch. With each piece of fabric falling to the floor, his kisses became more urgent and possessive, filling the room with the sound of our heavy breathing, mingling with the rustle of clothing.

Just as his lips trailed down my neck, leaving a burning path in their wake, he suddenly scooped me up, his arms wrapping around me with a strength that made my breath catch. My legs instinctively wrapped around his waist, and I could feel the hardness of his desire pressing against me through his jeans. His lips never left mine as he carried me toward the bedroom, each step deliberate, his pace slow enough to keep the tension between us sizzling.

When we reached the bedroom, Ethan paused just long enough to push the door open with his foot before crossing the threshold. The room was dimly lit, the soft glow of the Christmas lights casting a warm hue over the bed.

He set me down with a gentleness that contrasted with the heat in his eyes. As he hovered over me, his body a tantalizing weight against mine, raw desire burned in his gaze. His hands caressed my body, exploring every inch as if he was committing it to memory, his fingers trailing down my sides, over my hips, and back up to cup my breasts, his thumbs brushing over my sensitive nipples.

"Vinnie," he groaned, his hands roaming over my now-bare skin. "You have no idea how much I want you right now."

I pulled back just enough to lock eyes with him, my breath catching at the intensity of his gaze. "Show me," I whispered, my voice trembling with anticipation.

A slow, wicked grin spread across his face, a spark of mischief dancing in his eyes. He reached for a ribbon he had tied around one of my Christmas gifts, gently unwinding it before wrapping the soft fabric around my wrists. He secured them with a loose bow, the delicate restraint sending a thrill of excitement through me and heightening every nerve in my body.

The ribbon binding my wrists filled me with a heady mix of vulnerability and desire, and Ethan's eyes darkened with something primal as he took in the sight of me, bound and ready for him. I smiled, my body responding to the hunger in his gaze, my skin tingling with anticipation.

Slowly and deliberately, his hands began to explore, starting at my wrists and trailing down my arms, leaving a path of fire in their wake. When his fingers reached the curve of my hips, he squeezed lightly; a touch that made me gasp. The sensation was electric, sending jolts of pleasure through me as he gripped me firmly, his hands hot against my skin.

His lips followed the path his hands had taken, kissing and nibbling along my collarbone before moving lower. When he reached my breasts, he paused, his breath warm against my skin as he took one nipple into his mouth, his tongue flicking against the sensitive peak, making me arch into him.

I moaned softly, my fingers tangling in his hair as he lavished attention on my breasts, switching from one to the other, his hand teasing the nipple he wasn't sucking. The sensation was overwhelming, the pleasure building in waves that left me gasping. Sensing my desire to take control, Ethan reached up, gently but firmly pushing my tied hands back down against the bed, his fingers wrapping around my wrists to hold them in place.

"Let me," he murmured, his voice a husky command that sent a thrill through me. The restraint made every sensation sharper, more intense, and the fact that he was in complete control only heightened my need. His lips resumed their journey, his mouth hot and demanding as he continued to lavish attention on my breasts, each flick of his tongue and teasing nips making my body arch toward him, desperate for more. Ethan's grip on my wrists tightened just slightly, a reminder that he was the one setting the pace, guiding the pleasure that was quickly becoming all-consuming.

As his mouth travelled lower, anticipation built like a coiled spring inside me. Even though I was already bare beneath him, Ethan didn't rush. His kisses were slow and deliberate, leaving a burning trail down my stomach. Each press of his lips sent a shiver of longing through me, and the ache between my legs grew almost unbearable.

He paused just above my hips, his warm breath ghosting over my skin, making me quiver with anticipation. His hands, still holding my wrists in place, slid down to grip my thighs, spreading them apart with a gentle but insistent pressure. The cool air against my heated skin made me gasp, my body arching involuntarily toward him, desperate for more.

Ethan hovered there, his breath hot against my most sensitive spot, teasing me until I was trembling with need. When he finally pressed his mouth against me, his tongue moving in slow strokes, the pleasure was so intense it was almost painful. I cried out, my hands instinctively tugging against the soft restraints, but he held me firmly in place, his grip grounding me even as he pushed me toward the edge.

The way his tongue moved, flicking and swirling with expert precision, made my body tremble uncontrollably. He alternated between soft teasing licks, and deep focused strokes that had me gasping for breath, my entire world narrowing down to the incredible sensations he was creating.

"Ethan, please," I begged, my voice a breathless plea. "I need you."

He looked up at me, a wicked grin tugging at his lips. "Patience, darling," he murmured, his breath hot against my most sensitive skin. "I want to savor this." His hands tightened on my thighs, holding me open as he continued his torturous, exquisite assault.

Finally, just when I thought I couldn't take it anymore, Ethan's mouth moved with purpose, his tongue finding a rhythm that drove me straight to the brink. The waves of pleasure crashed over me, my body shaking with the intensity of my climax.

"Ethan," I gasped, my body arching off the bed as I finally teetered on the edge.

The release was so powerful it left me breathless, my body trembling with aftershocks as he slowly, gently, eased me back down from the high.

His hands roamed over my body as he kissed me deeply, and the taste of myself on his lips only fuelled the fire burning within me. The heat of his own arousal pressed against my thigh through his clothes and, in one swift motion, he reached for the hem of his shirt, tugging it over his head and tossing it aside. He leaned back in, capturing my lips in another searing kiss, his hands already working on the buttons of his jeans.

He shed the last of his clothes, the rustle of fabric the only sound in the room besides our ragged breaths and when he returned to me, the heat of his bare skin against mine was electrifying.

He positioned himself at my entrance, his eyes locking onto mine, filled with a promise of what was to come. Slowly, almost torturously, he pushed inside me, the sensation of him filling me completely overwhelming. I moaned into his mouth as I wrapped my legs around his waist, pulling him deeper. The feeling of being so completely connected to him left me breathless, every movement pushing me closer to the edge.

Ethan began to move, each thrust deep and deliberate, his pace un-hurried as if he wanted to make this moment last forever. The pressure and my pleasure built with each movement, the ribbon around my wrists tightening slightly as I gripped the sheets, the restraint adding a delicious edge to the sensation.

"Vinnie," he groaned, his breath hot against my ear, the sound of my name on his lips sending another wave of desire through me. "You feel so good. So perfect."

I could barely form words, my mind lost in the overwhelming pleasure he was giving me. "Ethan, I love you," I managed to gasp, my voice trembling.

He quickened his pace, his movements becoming more urgent, more desperate. "I love you too, Vinnie," he whispered, his voice raw with emotion. "Always."

Our bodies moved together in a perfect rhythm of need and love, the connection between us deepening with every thrust, every touch. The tension coiled tighter in my core as he drove me closer and closer to another climax.

When it finally hit, it was like an explosive burst of pure ecstasy that left me breathless and shaking beneath him. Ethan followed me over the edge, his own release powerful, his body trembling as he collapsed beside me.

As the waves of pleasure slowly subsided, leaving us both breathless and trembling, he gently untied the ribbon that had bound my wrists, his fingers moving tenderly as he worked the knot loose, and his touch soothing against the slight indents left on my skin. Once my hands were free, he brought them to his lips, kissing each wrist softly, his eyes filled with warmth and affection.

"I'm sorry," he murmured, his voice a gentle caress. "Did I hurt you?"

I shook my head, a playful smile tugging at my lips. "I loved every second of it."

His lips curled into a teasing grin as he raised an eyebrow. "Good to know," he said, his voice laced with mischief. "Because I'm definitely going to enjoy exploring that interest of yours a lot more in the future."

A thrill ran through me at his promise. "I'm looking forward to it." I sighed contentedly, snuggling up against him. "I love you," I murmured, the words slipping out naturally once more.

He kissed the top of my head, pulling me closer and draping a blanket over us. "I love you too, Vinnie," he whispered, his voice soft. "More than you know."

As I nestled into his side, the steady rhythm of his heartbeat lulling me into a peaceful haze, and I sunk into a profound sense of contentment. I might not have believed in magic, but there was something in the very fabric of this town that seemed to know exactly what I needed, even when I didn't. It had brought me a happiness I never expected, weaving together the threads of my life in ways I never could've have imagined. As my eyelids grew heavy, I drifted off to sleep with a smile, wrapped in the warmth of Ethan's embrace, and certain that whatever magic lived in Hallow's End, it had brought me exactly where I was meant to be.

Acknowledgements

This book holds such a special place in my heart. Like Vinnie, I'm embracing a new chapter in my life—one where I get to follow my dream of writing. It's been a wild, thrilling ride, and I truly hope that as you dive into this story, you find pieces that resonate with you. Whether it's the charm of Hallow's End, the friendships, or those moments of self-discovery, I hope you fall in love with these characters as much as I did while writing them.

Now, I have *so* many people to thank for joining me on this crazy journey and for supporting me every step of the way. Without you, this dream wouldn't have become a reality.

To my readers—first and foremost, thank you for being here and giving this book a chance. Seriously, your support means the world to me! For those of you who have been cheering me on since the very beginning, I see you, I appreciate you, and I've been absolutely loving all your reactions to the teasers and posts. (No, really, I've been stalking every comment, and yes, I've cried happy tears a few times.)

A *special* shout-out goes to Katie and Brooke—you two have been next-level with your insane support. Between sharing, interacting, and all the encouraging DMs, I feel like I've found some lifelong book besties! (Remember when our parents warned us about talking to strangers online? Guess we're proving them wrong, because look at us now!)

And to everyone who's taken a chance on me by picking up this book today—thank you from the bottom of my heart. You have no idea how much it means to me. I'm beyond excited to share this journey with you!

To Jack (my real-life Ethan)—your endless belief in me is basically the fuel that's kept this whole writing thing going. Thank you for picking up all the slack around the house, making sure I actually *eat* and drink water while I'm cocooned in my gremlin cave, surviving solely on caffeine and writing like a madwoman for twelve hours straight. And for surviving my mood swings when I lose sleep because I stayed up way too late obsessing over plot twists and my fictional people—you're a saint.

Honestly, I'm so damn lucky to be married to my best friend. Without you, none of this writing would even exist. (Or I'd have starved, whichever came first.) You're the real MVP here, and I love you more than words on a page could ever say.

To Mikala—the absolute best personal assistant and content wizard I could've asked for. Thank you for helping me connect Hallow's End with so many amazing readers, and for somehow making me look like I actually know what I'm doing on social media. Honestly, without you, I'd still be sitting here, staring blankly at Instagram wondering if I'm supposed to post a selfie or a cat meme. You're a lifesaver, and I'm beyond grateful for all your creativity, dedication, and for making my life so much easier. (Also, if I haven't said it enough—Dramione forever.)

To Lauren—the best editor I could've ever asked for. I'm *still* blown away that I found you on my first try, especially in a sea full of editors! Somehow, I managed to reel in the absolute perfect one for me and my book babies. You've been nothing short of incredible, guiding me from a messy draft (that I can't even *look* at now) to an actual, *real* book. Honestly, I don't think words can describe just how grateful I am for the magic you've worked. You've loved my characters as much as I do, and as a thank you, I officially grant you the rights to have Ethan as your book boyfriend.

To Amy—my very first reader and absolute ride or die. You've been cheering me on from the very start, back when Hallow's End was barely a flicker of an idea. You've listened to all my ramblings, my writing melt-downs, and every struggle in between. I'm so lucky to have shared this wild journey with someone who actually *gets* the whole self-publishing chaos (because let's be real, it's a whole *thing*). Also, total pinch-me mo-ment—we're both *published authors* now! I couldn't have asked for a better buddy to freak out with, and honestly, without you, I'd have had way more breakdowns and no one to rant to. Plus, how crazy is it that we're not only publishing in the same month but also getting married in the same month? Who knew we'd be syncing up our life milestones, too?

And to my fellow authors and friends in the book communi-ty—I'm honestly so honored to be navigating this wild publishing journey with you all. The way we've shared ups, downs, and every plot twist in between—it's been incredible. Thank you for always being here, cheering me on, and validating my caffeine addiction. Seriously, I couldn't have asked for a better crew to fangirl with and rant to about all things writing. Here's to more books, less imposter syndrome, and maybe one day actually finishing our TBRs (a girl can dream, right?).

About the author

Patricia Prior is a romance author who believes in the magic of small towns, second chances, and swoon-worthy love stories. When she's not buried in her latest manuscript, you can find her sipping pumpkin-spiced lattes, getting lost in fan fiction, or plotting her next romantasy adventure. Much like her characters, she's on her own journey of embracing new chapters and chasing dreams. She currently lives in England with her husband, where she's always on the hunt for the perfect playlist to match her latest story. Her debut novel, **Between Then and Now**, is the first in the Hallow's End series, with more to follow. Follow her writing journey and love for all things bookish on Instagram @authorpatriciaprior

Connect with Patricia

GOODREADS: Patricia Prior
INSTAGRAM: authorpatriciaprior
EMAIL: authorpatriciaprior@gmail.com

Milton Keynes UK
Ingram Content Group UK Ltd.
UKHW022354251024
450161UK00004B/147